STRIKE
THE DRAGON

STRIKE
THE DRAGON

A NOVEL BY
CHARLES DYER
AND
MARK TOBEY

If
Dyer

© 2007 by
CHARLES DYER AND MARK TOBEY

ISBN-10: 0-8024-3908-X
ISBN-13: 978-0-8024-3908-6

Cover Design: studiogearbox.com
Cover Images: iStock and Photos.com
Interior Design: Smartt Guys design
Editor: Elizabeth Newenhuyse

We hope you enjoy this book from Moody Publishers. Our goal is to provide high-quality, thought-provoking books and products that connect truth to your real needs and challenges. For more information on other books and products written and produced from a biblical perspective, go to www.moodypublishers.com or write to:

Moody Publishers
820 N. LaSalle Boulevard
Chicago, IL 60610

Library of Congress Cataloging-in-Publication Data

Dyer, Charles H., 1952-
  Strike the dragon : a novel / by Charles Dyer and Mark Tobey.
    p. cm.
  ISBN 978-0-8024-3908-6
  1. Terrorism--Fiction. I. Tobey, Mark (Mark T.) II. Title.
PS3604.Y45S77 2007
813'.6--dc22

                                   2007025640

1 3 5 7 9 10 8 6 4 2

Printed in the United States of America

CONTENTS

PROLOGUE

BALATA, WEST BANK The shrill ring of the cell phone startled her from a fitful sleep. She moved slightly in response. The early morning sun filtered through the thin curtain on the window, doing little to pierce the fog that wrapped her brain like a shroud. Her eyes blinked to focus, scanning the ceiling, while dark demons from the night retreated into her subconscious—the place of shadowed, haunting scenes in which she alternated between being the hunter and the hunted, troubling images that left her soaked in sweat.

The phone chirped again. This time she reached across the table by the bed, fumbling toward the wooden box to pick it up.

"Allo," she whispered, so as not to wake her young son, lying in absolute tranquility next to her.

"It's time," a man's voice mumbled before the phone went silent. The stark words jolted her awake and brought the room into view. She pulled herself out of bed, rubbing her face so as to rub away the sleep. *It is time*. . . . She remembered the instructions and sat back down on the bed.

As she did she looked intently again at her two-year-old son, Yousef. *The sleep of the innocent,* she thought.

She consciously tried to slow her rate of breathing to match the child's, her lungs inhaling and exhaling, rising and falling with his. She had to regain a sense of calm, of peace, of surrender. She focused intently on the boy's face—his long dark eyelashes, his thick eyebrows, his coiled jet-black hair beaded with moisture from the hot night. The sweat tightened his curls and made them glisten like crystal in the sunlight. He looked like his father. Everyone said so. Most did anyway. And that thought gave her both peace and purpose.

She dressed slowly, first changing into clean undergarments and then reaching for a shirt and trousers folded neatly on the stool in the corner of the room, a square, cramped place with walls pale and peeling from neglect. The shirt and pants was the exact outfit her husband wore the day they had been married. She wrestled with the tiny buttons, the fabric still stiff from a fresh starch the day before. She cursed the number of them. *Why must there be so many buttons?* The silly frustration brought yet another rush of emotion. The tears filling her eyes made it even more difficult to finish dressing. She couldn't cry. Not now. Not today.

She looked back at her son. In a few hours his life would be forever altered. And while it was part of God's great arrangement, she knew how he would feel, for she had experienced the same heartache and profound sense of loss less than six months ago. That was when she learned her husband—Yousef's father—died a martyr's death fighting the Israeli occupation of the land of Palestine. She mourned, yes; but her grief was eased by her pride in her husband's martyrdom—pride, and a seething hatred of the Israelis who cut short his life.

Gently she picked up his prayer rug, the soft, handwoven cloth that had once belonged to his father, and his father before him. It was worn and tattered from years of prayerful handling. She placed it beside her sleeping son, who had turned unconsciously away from the bleeding rays of sun. Perhaps one day he'd understand the spiritual legacy now being passed along to him by those whom he had given such joy during their short time together. She paused one last time to look at his tiny bronze face, one not yet hardened by anger or fear. She resisted the urge to lean down and kiss him on the head, fearing she might wake him. Then, as she watched one of his arms stretch before returning to his side, she committed the day—and her destiny—to God.

As she closed the door to the room, she turned to see her mother seated on a small chair.

"You startled me, Mama," she whispered. Her mother sat staring blankly at her but quickly shifted her gaze to avoid eye contact. Seeing her daughter dressed in her son-in-law's clothes told her more than she wanted to know. Seventy and showing little sign of decline, she had learned her best defense against the harshness of life was to maintain a conscious ignorance of the future. If fate has already decreed what lies around the corner, then foreknowledge brings only a prolonged dread of that which cannot be changed. Better not to know what the day would bring, than to know and not be able to alter it.

The fleeting look of anguish on her mother's face brought her back to the reality—and the danger—she now faced. She quickly reached for her *abaya*, the flowing robe once worn by most of her people before the ways of the West had crept into their very closets. Stretching to her ankles, the hooded garment would veil her secret from those who might not understand and be offended, and from those who might very well understand and seek to stop her. Trying to sound as cheerful and upbeat as possible, she broke the silence.

"Yousef will be hungry when he wakes. He likes some milk and sweet bread. And he knows not to play around the gate." Her mother sat staring at a small lamp and the idiot moth still flopping blindly against the bulb that had stayed lit through the night. The futility of it struck the old woman as she watched her only daughter wrap her *hijab* around her head and flee out the door, perhaps sparing her the pain of trying to respond.

Closing the front door of the five-room, cement-block home in which her parents had raised eleven children, she slipped through the narrow alleyway barely wide enough for a small car. The maze of streets and alleys was named Balata, which in Arabic means "rock." She knew that the town, created in 1948, had begun as a temporary refugee camp housing Arabs who fled the war that led to the formation of the State of Israel. As she walked through the narrow alleys she glanced at those she was passing and saw the look of hopelessness and desperation on their faces. She wanted to stop and tell them, to give them hope. *Soon enough,* she thought, *they will know that the strength of rock still resides in Balata.*

When she reached the mosque, she instinctively looked back to see if she had been followed. The alley felt strangely quiet. Nothing moved save a mangy street dog, molesting a downed garbage container in search of breakfast. Looking again to make certain no one had seen her, she stepped through the open doorway leading into the outer courtyard of the mosque, moving instantly from sunlight to shadows. The coolness calmed her slightly. She paused to let her eyes adjust. As she did, she heard the voice from the wake-up call. "Are you alone? Were you followed?"

"I wasn't followed. I'm alone, and I'm ready."

"Good. Follow me."

An older, bearded man in a pale blue abaya led her to another doorway. Pausing at the entrance, her guide turned and fixed his eyes on her. "Do you remember the instructions?"

"Of course I remember. As I said, I am ready."

The door offered passage into a side room that served as an annex to the mosque, and it appeared to be used primarily for storage. A pile of handwoven carpets stacked on an old kitchen table stood watch over the clutter of boxes, broken oil lamps, and crowded corners filled with religious-looking junk. A pale light hung from the ceiling and cast shadows across the uneven dirt floor. Just above was a small window to the street, allowing a thin shaft of light to illuminate the tiny specks of dust rising continually from the old carpets. On the far wall, another doorway appeared to lead outside. Just to the right of the doorway cardboard boxes were stacked from the floor nearly to the ceiling.

She was so busy looking at the boxes and carpets that she almost failed to notice the two men seated just to her left near the center of the room. The scent of coffee spiced with cardamom alerted her to their presence. For a fleeting moment, a scene from her childhood flashed across her consciousness. She remembered walking into the kitchen of her home, smelling the aroma of the coffee, and seeing her father and uncles seated at the table playing backgammon. But just as quickly the past faded from view, vanishing back into her secret vault of memories.

The men were seated at a wooden table, holding small cups of coffee. Steam rose from the frothy brown liquid. On the near side of the table sat a brass coffeemaker with its well-worn wooden handle. When the two men recognized the bearded man, they placed their cups on the table and rose to their feet.

"This is the package you must deliver," said the bearded one. "She knows what to do." The two men nodded in agreement. The bearded man turned and slipped back out the same doorway he had entered.

The taller of the two men pointed toward the pile of rugs. "The vest is over there, under the rugs. You'll need to move quickly."

She found the vest under the top layer of rugs. At first she was surprised by its heaviness. She only weighed fifty kilos, about a hundred and ten pounds, and the vest seemed to weigh almost as much as she did. "It seems so heavy," she said, turning toward the men.

"Of course it is," the taller of the two replied, annoyed. "It's packed with twenty kilos of explosives, plus an additional ten kilos of ball bearings. Are you not sure you can handle the task? There are others willing and ready."

"No worries. *Inch' Allah*, I'm ready," she shot back. "But how will it fit under my shirt?"

"It is designed to go over your shirt. You will then wear *this* over the vest," replied the shorter of the two men. As he spoke he handed her a white serving jacket with a name tag attached just above the pocket. The tag was from the Eshel Hashomron Hotel, and the Hebrew name on the tag read *Yael*.

"Bring the vest and jacket and come with us. Our car is parked just outside. We will give you the remaining details as we drive. It will take us awhile to work our way around the checkpoints on the highways. But, *inch' Allah*, we will get you there in time. You can remove your abaya and put on the vest and jacket once we are near the target. This will indeed be a day of celebration, and of mourning!"

CHAPTER 1

MOSHE AND ESTHER

ISRAEL The groan of the car engine magnified the silence of its occupants. Moshe and Esther Zachar were on their way to the wedding of Esther's favorite cousin, Rachel. Rachel Anna Levin, the vivacious thirty-four-year-old daughter of Esther's aunt Talia, would soon finish a surgery fellowship at Hadassah Hospital, nearly the last step in an arduous path toward becoming a board-certified pediatric surgeon.

For Moshe and Esther, the wedding should have been a time of great celebration. Rachel, the absolute delight of her father and mother, shone with joy and promise like a Galilean sunrise. The wedding would be a festive, magnificent occasion for most family and friends, but for Moshe and Esther it only dredged up tensions they had spent years of their marriage trying to defuse.

Moshe glanced over at Esther in time to catch her gaze.

"I know you hate the thought of this day," she whispered, almost to herself.

"I can't understand you when you mumble like that, Esther," he shot back. He was a large, handsome man, with thick dark hair that curled over the nape of his neck. Broad shoulders and muscular arms bespoke a youth slinging fish crates in the summer alongside his father on the docks at Haifa. Esther had loved this man from the moment they met, but the prickly family relations had rubbed their young romance raw.

She'd seen this reaction a thousand times before. He'd begin contemplating the obligatory niceties of conversing with her mother, or worse, her mother's mother. With each imagined word the inner corners of his dark, thick eyebrows pulled down together, twisting his face into a scowl.

Esther interrupted his thoughts and blurted, "Moshe, just admit it once: You loathe these family gatherings. Say it! Still, you don't have to make *me* share your misery!" Esther swallowed hard, her voice nearly breaking as a lump grew in her throat.

"Rachel will be beautiful," she said, trying to smile. "I can't wait to see her—I've longed for this day. I won't let you spoil it because you despise my family and their politics."

He groaned, pretending to ignore Esther's rebuke. His conscience confronted him. *She's right, of course. This is not the time to settle a family squabble. Bury it deeper still,* he thought. *How bad could this be? Tables and tables of food, limitless wine—ah, . . . "You prepare a table before me in the presence of my enemies."* Moshe chuckled to himself at the poetic allusion.

Both Moshe and Esther were Sabras—native-born Israelis—but their family backgrounds were vastly different. Moshe came from a line of Ashkenazi Jews whose lineage stretched back to czarist Russia. His family had been forced to flee during one of the many pogroms and had eventually made their way to Ottoman-controlled Palestine. Settling on a *kibbutz* in the broad Jezreel Valley, Moshe's family had helped turn the once malaria-infested wetlands into the now-blooming breadbasket of Israel. Moshe's parents inherited the can-do spirit of their ancestors, but they felt confined by the socialist principles governing the tiny kibbutz.

Eventually his family moved to Haifa where Moshe grew up in a mixed Jewish/Arabic neighborhood.

Moshe felt proud of his roots. Though his father had been a dockworker at the port of Haifa, Moshe's family had never lacked the basic necessities of life. He grew to know, and appreciate, the rich cultural mosaic within his neighborhood. It seemed natural to be able to speak Hebrew, Arabic, and Russian—three languages Moshe mastered as a child. He learned English in high school.

After serving in the Israel Defense Force—the *Tzva Haganah Leyisrael*, often abbreviated to the single word *tzahal* from its three Hebrew letters—he attended Tel Aviv University where he majored in international business with a minor in linguistics. His goal in life was to land a job in a corporation that would allow him to leave Israel and see the world. And then he met Esther in a class on classical Arabic, and life became much more complicated.

Esther came from a line of Sephardic Jews who had immigrated to Israel from Iraq in 1950, two years after the formation of the Jewish state. Both sets of Esther's grandparents, all newlyweds at the time, were spirited from Baghdad with only the meager possessions they could carry. Everything else—*everything*—was confiscated by the government of Iraq as the price these Jewish refugees had to pay for their freedom. Operation Ezra and Nehemiah brought them, along with over a hundred thousand others, back to Eretz Israel.

Eventually settling near Tel Aviv, these two families from Iraq formed a strong bond of friendship, providing a sense of normalcy in an otherwise changing world. It just seemed natural that the son of the one family should marry the daughter of the other. Their first child, Esther, was born the summer following the Yom Kippur War. Both her father and one of his brothers fought in that war. Her father returned, but his brother—Talia's father—was killed when his tank took a direct hit from a

Syrian artillery shell on the Golan Heights, at a place known as the Valley of Tears. While still a young child, Esther heard about this solemn place, which her family visited on many occasions. For them, and for many others, the ground was sacred, sanctified by the blood of the Israeli soldiers who fought to the death to hold back the advance of six hundred Syrian tanks. These brave men had helped keep Galilee from falling to the Arab enemy.

Esther was proud of the uncle she'd never met, and she understood the anger and contempt her family held toward Arabs. Her family's tiny apartment outside Tel Aviv couldn't compare to the homes her grandparents had been forced to abandon in Baghdad. Yet even here they could not live in peace. Her uncle died keeping the Syrians from overrunning their tiny country. If the Jews could not live in peace in their own land, then where else could they go? Likely these events were what had driven Esther's family to become so passionately Zionist that they were among the first to move into the Jewish settlements that had sprouted up in the West Bank—ancient Judea and Samaria. At least that was how it appeared to Moshe.

"I promise, no complaining," he spoke softly to Esther, forcing a smile, and reaching his hand to touch her knee.

Moshe pressed his foot against the bare metal accelerator of the red '89 Toyota Corolla and sped away from the security checkpoint on Highway 5. The road that snaked eastward from the Mediterranean connected the bustling, affluent suburbs of Israel's sparkling Tel Aviv with the Arab towns and scattered Jewish settlements on the West Bank. Now the Toyota pushed past the Subaru wagons that were seemingly the automobile of choice for West Bank settlers. Moshe grimaced as he corrected himself out loud—"settlers in Judea and Samaria." *This is going to be a difficult day,* he mused a second later, while grinding into fourth.

"Moshe, what's wrong? Do you see something?" Esther asked. Drivers in the West Bank constantly watched for signs of trouble, and Moshe seemed to be searching for something on the horizon.

"There," he said simply and pushed his chin off toward the right. She turned to look where Moshe had motioned. And in the distance she could see the city of Ariel, framed in white high-rise apartments rising from the deep green slopes of the surrounding hills. Begun as a settlement in 1977, the community bustled as a town of over twenty thousand people.

Pausing for a moment at a red light, Moshe whipped the Corolla off the main highway onto the narrower street leading toward Ariel. Another sharp right turn brought them to the tree-lined entrance of the Eshel Hashomron Hotel. He parked the car at the far end of the parking lot, already filled with cars that had spilled countless well-dressed passengers onto the hotel grounds.

As Moshe came around the back of the car to take Esther's arm, he stopped and held his breath. There she stood—the bride of his youth, still stunning and elegant in a long black gown. He loved the way she pulled her black hair tight away from her face and gathered each strand neatly and simply in the back. *She glistens in the sun,* he thought, as a smile eclipsed his frown. He loved her deeply and that was all that mattered.

Noticing her husband's gaze, Esther smiled and took his hand. He flashed a wide grin that said he had returned from his journey to the dark, contemplative side of his mind. The friendly, more charming Moshe emerged just in time to accompany Esther into the wedding celebration.

* * * * * * * * * *

"Mazel tov!" boomed Moshe, as he shook the groom's hand. He was always the loudest at family gatherings. He swooped to the bride and planted a mandatory kiss on the cheek, holding her shoulders firmly. "Rachel, you look splendid. You are a delight to us all, my dear cousin." Esther took hold of Rachel's arm and squeezed it gently.

"Mazel tov, Rachel. This is your special day, yes?" she whispered in the young bride's ear. Rachel smiled and nodded. As more guests gathered around the giddy couple, Moshe ducked into the courtyard to smoke a cigarette and escape the onslaught of relatives.

Though Moshe found little to like about West Bank settlers, he couldn't help but be impressed by the Eshel Hashomron's open inner courtyard. The hotel's rooms flanked the two long sides of a sparkling swimming pool, while the lobby and dining room boxed off the third side. The upper side was open, offering a breathtaking view of the mountains of Samaria—rugged olive- and oak-covered hillsides.

The true focal point remained the inner court, which had as its centerpiece a waterfall extending the width of the garden, cascading endlessly into the pool. The water poured from above over large rough-cut blocks of hard limestone—the rock native to much of Israel. The pool formed by the cascading water was separated from the swimming pool by a deep green carpet of grass. On either side, majestic date palms reached high into the sky, providing thin patches of shade from the afternoon sun. *Perhaps ancient Eden looked like this,* Moshe thought as he strolled through the crowd—though he didn't really believe the myths contained in the Torah.

His cell phone vibrated and broke his peaceful thoughts. He pulled it from his belt and flipped up the front. The name on the display read Nissim Cohen. That name made him smile. This would be the third time Nissim's number appeared on his caller ID this week. *What could that old scoundrel want?* Moshe wondered.

Mashing the Talk button, he put the phone to his ear. "Nissim! *Ma nishma?*"

"Moshe, my old friend! How's life been treating you?"

"It's been good. I'm well; so is Esther."

"Splendid. Ah, Esther! What a prize. What did she ever see in an old camel like you?"

Moshe roared at the insult. He and Nissim had spent four years together studying at the University of Tel Aviv, and though it had been years since they'd spent any time together, the chemistry between them remained strong.

"Tell me, Nissim, what's so urgent? Don't tell me *you're* getting married after all these years!"

"Don't be foolish! Seriously, I heard through a mutual friend you might be looking to change careers. That's why I'm calling. Is that true?" Nissim's tone grew surprisingly serious and made Moshe pause a moment before he answered.

Moshe decided to keep it light. "Nissim, you clever spy! As a matter of fact, I am considering a change. I've been with this company for ten years, and the challenge is gone. I'm bored. I'm really looking for a place where I can use my language skills and a situation that would allow Esther and me to do some extended traveling. Between you and me, I'd like Esther to be a little farther away from her extremist family."

"Ah, still playing diplomat, eh, ol' friend," Nissim responded, but with little emotion.

Moshe laughed. "You sound too serious. What's really going on? How did you know I was looking for a new job?" The phone crackled.

Nissim broke in. "I would love to answer your questions, but now is not the proper time. I *can* tell you I work for an institution that values the skills you possess. We are looking for individuals with your . . . talents . . . your abilities . . . your *politics*. That's all I can say for now. I'm starting to lose the connection."

The phone went dead, and Moshe stood on the lawn, bewildered.

He rehearsed the conversation in his mind. Nissim's cryptic responses raised a torrent of questions. *What company would be concerned about even mentioning its name on a cell phone? Perhaps a governmental agency?*

But what government agency would be so concerned about guarding its privacy? Just as significantly, what agency would be interested in Moshe's special skills? Only two names came to Moshe's mind. *Shin Bet*, Israel's counterintelligence and internal security agency, or *Mossad*, the Israeli national spy agency responsible for intelligence gathering and counterterrorist activities outside Israel. It was all very curious. What could be so confidential? Why him? Why now?

Moshe closed the phone and clipped it back on his belt. He hadn't realized that while talking with Nissim he had wandered away from the wedding party to the far side of the pool. He stood in the gap between the one wing of the hotel and the building housing the lobby. Moshe dropped his half-smoked cigarette and stomped it out on the sidewalk. He kept thinking about Nissim and his "secret" employer. Could he work for the government? For Mossad? Both were certainly possible. But *possible* was not the same as *probable*.

As he turned back toward the wedding party, a slight movement off to the right caught his eye. At the far end of the courtyard he saw a waitress making her way down from the area above the waterfall to the lower level carrying an empty serving tray. Moshe turned back toward the crowd, but something again made him stop. He looked back at the woman dressed in a white food-service smock and black trousers. *That's strange*, Moshe thought. *None of the wedding party is up there, and the kitchen is the opposite way.*

Moshe looked more closely at the woman now awkwardly trotting toward the crowd, and a sense of uneasiness swept over him. Something about her appearance wasn't right. Her face and legs were very thin, but her chest appeared way out of proportion. Bulging almost. Like a rotund woman on stilts with a head two sizes too small for her body. All this took mere seconds to process.

Suddenly a horrific thought burst into his consciousness. Like a flash from the future, from somewhere beyond the next few seconds, that awful realization would forever be imprinted in his mind. Everything seemed to slow to a haunting crawl. He hadn't even noticed his racing heart and heavy breathing as every beat pumped adrenaline into his bloodstream.

The woman increased her pace, perhaps startled by Moshe's intense gaze. Then he knew. This was no waitress! Moshe pointed toward the woman and shouted to the crowd, "Bomb! Bomb! . . . Esther, where are you? Esther!" He heard himself screaming, but the din of the music swallowed his words. At Moshe's alarm the waitress broke into a sprint, heading straight for the knot of people gathered near the bride and groom.

Moshe bolted toward the guests, flailing his arms and screaming. Slipping on a wet patch of sidewalk that skirted the pool, he tripped and rolled headlong into a rubble of stones, twisting his ankle and scraping the palms of his hands. He pulled himself to his feet and tried to run, but the pain forced him to alternate between hopping and limping.

He was still twenty meters from the main reception patio when the woman reached the wedding table and pushed the small plastic plunger clutched in her hand. The horror unleashed in a blast of flame, smoke, and searing heat. The roar of the bomb popped his eardrums, and all went silent. A plume of black smoke covered the entire courtyard as the suicide bomber was ripped in half, sending her body parts like projectiles into the crowd. In that same split second, a thousand fiery ball bearings shot like cannon fire across the courtyard, ripping through bodies and ricocheting off furniture as they flew. The shards of metal scattered like shrapnel, dicing the wedding party into fragments of muscle and bone.

Moshe's hearing slowly returned. An occasional hellish scream rose above the whimpering coming from the courtyard. People lay dying in front of him and there was nothing he could do. A sharp pain pierced his side as if a hot knife had ripped through his abdomen. A spot of red emerged on his shirt, a bloodred dye staining the white wedding garment around a hole the diameter of a pencil. He had been hit by something from the explosive belt, perhaps a nail, a screw, or a ball bearing. He was bleeding, but the rush of adrenaline masked the pain.

Trying to focus, Moshe blinked back toward where the wedding party had been seated. The bride and groom lay on top of each other, smoldering and shredded beyond recognition. The force of the explosives had sent the young couple flying straight up in the air, killing them both before they hit the ground. None of the wedding party could be alive. No one within a few meters could have escaped the fiery blast. Everywhere, wedding guests and hotel employees lay dead or seriously injured and covered in pools of blood—some of the dead bodies were intact, others were missing arms or legs or other body parts—all lay mutilated and twisted.

Esther had been standing off to the side of Rachel, talking with Rachel's mother, her aunt Talia. She was just far enough away to have escaped the blunt force of the detonation. Still, a barrage of ball bearings had torpedoed her body, one piercing her left lung and another tearing a hole in the main artery near the left side of her heart. She had been thrown against Rachel's mother, and the two of them lay sprawled facedown on the ground, motionless. Talia was dead.

Moshe stumbled toward Esther and fell beside her. He felt the sting of death. He wiped the blood and sweat from his face and gently rolled his sweet Esther onto her back. Her once-dancing eyes now stared at him, wide and hollow. A rush of panic overwhelmed him. "Esther, say something. Can you hear me, Esther? Please, say something!"

The faint yelp of sirens echoed across the hills while hotel security guards barked unintelligible orders to the increasing number of people now entering the horrific scene.

Esther squinted, then groaned. She gasped for air and choked on the fluid now draining into her airway. Moshe drew a soiled hanky from his trouser pocket and wiped her mouth. He wept uncontrollably, hardly able to speak. Esther struggled to formulate words. "Moshe, what happened?" she asked, her voice gurgling.

"It was a terrorist, Esther. She blew herself up. Everyone's dead. But, Esther, you're going to be fine. You're okay, Esther. Don't worry; I'm here. Right here. Esther, dear . . . please . . . please don't . . . oh, Esther. God help me! You're going to be fine." Moshe smelled death on her fleeting breath. She gasped hard for a scrap of air.

The image of the bride engulfed in the blinding explosion replayed itself in Moshe's mind. He blinked as if to erase the image from his consciousness.

"Esther, just stay with me till help arrives. God—someone—please, help us! My Esther's dying. Please, God, no!" His words came now with a mounting sense of desperation. He watched, sobbing, as the color drained from Esther's marred face and her eyes rolled back in their sockets. "Esther! Please don't go! Stay with me! Esther! God of heaven, have mercy! No, no, no, no, no!"

Esther's eyes closed; her labored breathing stopped. He felt her spirit slip from his grasp. She was gone.

The cries of those writhing in pain, the screams of the survivors, and the approaching wail of ambulances went eerily silent. The universe collapsed—reduced to the lifeless, bleeding face he held in his hands.

"Oh, God, no!" he screamed. "No! Please don't let her die! Esther, please come back!"

Moshe gently laid Esther's head on the ground and stumbled back to his feet. The scene around him spun wildly as he sought to steady his legs beneath him. Someone walked up to him and asked him his name, but it was as if the person was speaking in another language. Moshe could see that he was talking, but he couldn't understand what the man was trying to say. Then everything went black. Moshe's last conscious thought was of falling forward and a pair of arms reaching out to grab him.

* * * * * * * * * *

The sun shone brightly in Balata at that very hour, and the market streets buzzed with commerce. Faint sounds of sirens blaring could be heard in the distant west by a little black-headed Arab boy who jumped and played happily around the alley gate.

CHAPTER 2

IBRAHIM

SAMARRA, IRAQ Ibrahim al-Samarri answered the knock and opened the door of his third-floor apartment to face three armed men. They each clutched a Kalashnikov rifle. Two of the men had large duffel bags slung over their shoulders.

"May we come in?" the first man spoke, moving forward, not waiting for a response. Each gunman held two ammunition clips taped together—the preferred way to prepare clips so they could be changed rapidly in a firefight.

"What do you want here? We have nothing," Ibrahim said as the two other men pushed past him. "We don't even have enough food to fill our own stomachs." Calm was not something he could muster under duress.

"We are not here to steal your belongings, or to eat your food, or to molest your wife," the leader of the group replied, motioning for the others to inspect the room.

"We only need to commandeer your apartment for the next few hours. Follow our instructions and no harm will come to you."

The man sounded unsure of the latter. Ibrahim wanted to believe him.

"We will do all we can to make you feel welcome until, *inch' Allah*, it is safe for you to continue your journey," Ibrahim nervously replied, thinking only of his family. He wanted to believe these men were only here to hide from the Americans, but the guilt of the murder made him afraid.

The three men made their way through the small kitchen and headed straight into the living room that overlooked the street outside. They pulled back the curtains and peered up and down the deserted street. The apartment had an unobstructed view from the third floor in both directions. Satisfying themselves with what they saw—or, Ibrahim hoped, what they didn't see—they seemed to relax. They laid down their duffel bags, leaned their rifles against the wall, and sat down on the couch and chair.

"Do you have some *qahwah*?" asked the leader, not surprisingly a head taller than the other two men, both smaller and less imposing, except for their weapons.

"Of course! I will prepare it myself!" Ibrahim answered, darting back into the kitchen. He reached for a bag of recently roasted beans and threw a handful of them into a small wooden mortar. He then took a long wooden pestle and pounded the beans into a fine powder. The more he thought about the men in the next room, the harder he pounded. His nerves felt raw and jumpy. He threw a pinch of cardamom into the crushed beans and pounded more. Later, as the coffee boiled, Ibrahim turned to offer a reassuring look at his wife watching him from the table. Ibrahim said, loud enough for the three men in the other room to hear, "Why don't you go put Ali to bed?" Then he whispered, "Go to the back bedroom and stay there. I'll come for you when the men are gone."

"What do they want? Why are these men in our home? Ibrahim, they are killing people they believe to be sympathizers with the Americans," she said, wiping tears from her cheeks.

"Shhh, Minu. They'll hear you. I don't know what they want. Just to use our place for a few hours, that's all," he whispered. "Everything will be fine. Go now. Take the baby and wait in the back room." Ibrahim saw the fear in Minu's eyes as she left quickly.

Ibrahim watched the coffee boil on the stove. He also kept a close eye on the men as they took turns glancing out the window surveying the street. They were waiting for someone—or something. He wasn't sure. Hussein was long gone now, but Iraq was no better off. The initial lull in fighting after the American invasion had ended up being short-lived as the country raced toward all-out civil conflict.

The Sunni triangle was full of groups who agreed on only two things—a vehement opposition to the American occupation of Iraq and an equally vehement resistance to Shiite control. Their goal was nothing short of driving out the Crusaders from the land and reestablishing Sunni control. Some hoped to form an Islamic state, while others dreamed and fought to restore the Baath party. Ibrahim shuddered at the thought of it—both from knowledge and from fear. And the events of his last night serving in Hussein's army came back as vividly as the nightmares he had suffered through the now-countless nights since.

* * * * * * * * *

Ibrahim was serving in the Iraqi army at the time of the American invasion of Iraq. His unit was deployed in al-Hilla to help repel the expected invasion. The progress of the American forces could be traced by the steady stream of deserters walking in silence up the highway ahead of the American advance. One of the politically connected commanders in Ibrahim's unit tried to halt the rout by making an example of some deserters. He ordered Ibrahim and the other soldiers under his control to stop everyone in military uniform and demand their papers. They were to arrest anyone who didn't have valid orders authorizing travel to Baghdad.

By midday Ibrahim's company had captured 153 Iraqi soldiers who had fled the battlefield—all of them without proper orders. The men begged for their lives. They described the scenes of carnage and chaos from which they had fled. They had been poorly trained, poorly equipped, poorly led—in their words "like twigs gathered and thrown into a fire."

"My friend, have mercy," cried one soldier to Ibrahim. Still standing but shaking, nursing a severely mangled right arm in a sling, he pleaded, "Have mercy on my wife and child. If I'm killed, they'll die. Saddam is not a devout Muslim. He's not worth dying for. Please, let me go! I beg—"

A burst of gunfire from just behind Ibrahim sent the pleading man flying into the air. Ibrahim's surprise turned to horror and fear as the man who only seconds before stood pleading for his life dropped straight back onto the ground like a rag doll—his body riddled with smoking holes. Ibrahim's head spun around in time to see his captain lower his AK-47, freshly discharged and glimmering in the sun.

"Anyone else wish to join this stupid man in criticizing our great leader?" shouted the grinning gunman to the huddled prisoners now shaking visibly in the dust.

Almost instinctively, Ibrahim raised his rifle and fired a long burst into his captain, killing him instantly. He dropped to the ground without even a *thud*.

There was silence for a couple of long minutes. A dog barked in the distance. No one spoke.

"He was a dog," Ibrahim snorted, holding back tears. "He deserved to die like a dog." He immediately thought of Minu, his young wife, and also of his child. He'd just signed his death warrant. Everyone knew it.

Under Hussein's rule, anyone caught actively opposing the government was tortured to the point where he or she longed for death as a blessed escape from the unrelenting pain. And knowing the viciousness of the secret police, Ibrahim knew he would likely be forced to watch his

IBRAHIM

own wife and son die before he was killed. The thought of what he had just done—and what would soon be done to him—made him sick to his stomach.

But a strange calm and sense of relief came over the group. Somehow, a measure of justice had been accomplished. Ibrahim's fellow soldiers stared at him in silence, their arms hanging limply at their sides. Then one soldier simply threw down his rifle and started walking north toward Baghdad. Another shouted, "Why should we give our lives for Saddam and his excrement?" and threw his rifle on the corpse of the man who had been his captain. One by one, they laid down their arms and walked away.

Ibrahim threw his rifle onto the growing pile and joined the procession walking north toward Baghdad. He was still fearful that someone would challenge him for what he had done, but no one did. They all just wanted to go home. Yet he remained troubled. He had taken the life of his commander, but it was done to protect the lives of other Iraqi soldiers.

After walking for about an hour, the group crossed a small branch of the Euphrates just north of al-Hilla. Off to the left were the ruins of ancient Babylon. Three artificial hills, constructed in 1988 by Saddam Hussein as part of his plan to wrap himself in the splendor of ancient King Nebuchadnezzar, bracketed the city. The two hills nearest the roadway were nothing more than empty mounds of dirt, but on the hill off to the northwest Ibrahim could see the outline of a glittering palace. It was one of Hussein's many mansions, this one built overlooking the rebuilt palace of Nebuchadnezzar. Ibrahim kept turning to look at the palace, imagining that Hussein might just be there, watching him.

As the soldiers passed the rebuilt Greek theater, Ibrahim finally made up his mind. Turning to the left, he started walking down the road leading toward Hussein's palace on the hill.

"Where are you going, my friend?" shouted one of his fellow soldiers.

33

"*This* is the road to Baghdad, not that one."

"I know, but I must go explain to President Hussein why I had to shoot our captain," said Ibrahim. "I know he will understand."

"He is not there. He is hiding in Baghdad. But even if he were, you would just be wasting your breath—and your life. Stay with us. Your secret is safe. You are a noble man, Ibrahim."

He kept walking. A few soldiers watched momentarily to see if he would change his mind. But after a few minutes even they gave up on him and continued toward Baghdad.

As he walked toward the palace, he tried to think of what he was going to say to Saddam if he should actually meet him. He had grown up knowing nothing but the rule of Hussein and the Baath party. Raised in the center of the "Sunni triangle"—the region from which Hussein received his greatest support—Ibrahim had been taught to believe that Hussein was a wise and powerful leader, a man who cared for all Iraqis. This was the man he sought. A man of reason and justice.

He was so absorbed in his thoughts that he scarcely noticed the restored ruins of another despot from an earlier age. But he stopped daydreaming when he found himself standing in front of a massive blue brick gate. On the gate were bulls and grotesque dragons, painted yellow and white. He shielded his eyes to see the gate now being backlit by the setting sun.

Walking around the side of the gate, he again saw the hill on which Hussein's palace stood. And its closeness now stopped him in his tracks. Pausing to mumble a prayer for protection, Ibrahim started walking up the road that circled around the hill, winding its way to the top.

He reached the top as the sun was about to set. The Euphrates River shimmered with a golden hue; the palm trees on the far side stood like black silhouettes against the reddish-orange sky he had come to appreciate as a young boy. To the south, he could see the lights of al-Hilla begin to twinkle in the twilight.

The palace looked even larger and more imposing up close than it had looked from a distance. Carved onto the lintels over the windows were intricate portraits of Saddam Hussein intermingled with symbols of dragons and palm trees. A magnificent swimming pool, imposing even when empty, spoke of the grandeur of this site. Yet Ibrahim was suddenly aware of how quiet and empty it was.

"Hello!" Ibrahim's voice echoed out across the courtyard. "I am here to speak to President Hussein! May I come in?" Suddenly he felt foolish. He was a madman—the heat had caused him to hallucinate, perhaps. There he stood in a deserted city, on an empty hill, shouting into a vacant building. Like so much of Saddam Hussein's rule, everything was done for show, but there was little of substance behind it. Why did a country with such oil wealth have such poverty? His wife and son barely had enough to eat in Samarra, and he and his friends scavenged for food in the southern part of the country while serving in a military that killed its own soldiers for daring to care enough about their families to give up on a hopeless cause. What kind of wise and benevolent ruler would allow such things? And then he looked up and saw the palace with a different set of eyes. What kind of ruler? One who would build himself many luxurious palaces while his people lived in ever-deepening poverty and despair. One who cared for himself, not for those over whom he ruled.

The realization of his—and the nation's—folly in following Hussein overwhelmed Ibrahim. In anger he reached down and grabbed part of a clay brick lying on the ground. "Here is what I think of you, you thief and liar!" shouted Ibrahim as he hurled the brick at the palace. The sudden shattering of glass brought him back to his senses. The brick crashed through an intricate latticework of stained glass, and the glass shards and brick clattered on the marble floor inside the palace itself. *What if there is a security detail in the palace?* Realizing the foolishness of what he had just done, he crouched in the low bushes beside the palace for several minutes, waiting to see if someone would come out, or if a truckload of soldiers would come bounding up the road from a nearby barracks. But all remained quiet.

The growing darkness gave Ibrahim a renewed sense of hope and purpose. It was time to get away from this palace—away from any hope that Saddam Hussein ever cared about him. It was time to head back to Samarra, back to his wife and child, back to a new life in a new Iraq. And so Ibrahim retraced his steps back to the highway. As he started walking north, he looked back to see the single light of a car coming up the highway. One headlamp was completely gone, and the other was taped over, except for a small slit that allowed only enough light to help the driver see the highway. The orange fenders on the otherwise white car identified it as a taxi. *So, even the war doesn't slow down the desire of some to make a living!* And he began waving his arms to get the driver to stop. An hour later Ibrahim was in Baghdad, and by morning he had found a ride to Samarra. For him the war was over.

Ever since that time he had lived with the secret of what happened in al-Hilla and in Babylon. He was a murderer, a deserter, and someone who had dared to stand against the authority of Saddam Hussein and the Baath government. He always expected a knock on the door from those still loyal to the Baath party seeking revenge, and now these men were in his house.

* * * * * * * * * *

Ibrahim didn't notice the man at the window turn and signal to the others.

One of the armed men in the other room shouted to him, "Turn off all the lights and get down on the floor."

Ibrahim reached for the light switch behind him and turned off the overhead light. He then dropped to the floor and slid behind the kitchen counter.

The curtains were pushed back, and the windows themselves had been pushed open. The night air that blew in through the open windows made Ibrahim shiver. He knew now that they had not come to arrest him. But that was little comfort because it meant they had decided to use his home to set up an ambush against someone else. And the likely target would be an American patrol.

He watched through the gap in the kitchen door as one of the men pulled three RPG-7 rocket-propelled grenades from the duffel bag and laid them on the floor next to the window. The second man pulled two launchers from another bag and leaned them against the wall. They each took a launcher and inserted a rocket/grenade into the front. As they did so, the leader of the group took a flashlight and pointed it out the window to an apartment building across the street. He pushed the button and a single beam of light flashed across the dark street. In a few seconds three other dots of light flashed back at him.

"They're ready," said the leader. "And just in time." The road where Ibrahim's apartment was situated was lined with three- to five-story apartment buildings on both sides, creating a canyonlike pass through the center of town. About a kilometer before the ambush site, the road took a sharp turn to the left. A lookout positioned in a building on that corner watched intently for the patrol's approach. As the American vehicles made the turn, he ran to the back of the apartment and flashed a signal up the street to the men waiting in Ibrahim's apartment. Once the patrol went by, those in that building were prepared to launch an attack from the rear while the group at the other end of the street would try to disable the lead vehicle with a roadside bomb—or IED. The canyon would become the perfect killing zone.

Ibrahim heard the low rumble of the engines grow louder as the convoy worked its way down the street. The men watched as the faint outline of the lead vehicle came into view.

"They're coming; get ready. Wait! They have a tank," the lead gun-man announced, sounding surprised. It was an M1A1 Abrams tank. A bit more firepower than he had been expecting, but they could still disable it with the IED. Two rocket-propelled grenades fired from this apartment would be aimed at the tank's thermal sights to try to "blind" the driver. Other groups would then attack the rest of the convoy. *Inch' Allah* they would be able to completely disable the first vehicle, trap-ping all the others behind it. The trap was set, and the foolish Americans were falling for it.

Suddenly the lead tank stopped only two hundred yards from Ibra-him's apartment, and fifty yards short of the IED.

"What's he doing?" the leader whispered, half to himself. "I'm not sure we'll reach him from here. He must come farther." The other men started to fidget, knowing they could be fired on in seconds if the Ameri-cans had spotted them. "Don't fire. Be patient and let the viper crawl into the trap," the man said with a sneer.

The calm night burst into day as red fire exploded from the muzzle of the Abrams tank, lighting the street like fireworks. The building on the other side of the street imploded in a heap of rubble. Tons of brick and wood rained down, killing everyone in the building.

A second explosion lit the sky, sending a red-hot RPG from its launcher to its target, a Bradley fighting vehicle at the back of the patrol. The pro-jectile struck the pavement just behind the Bradley, which hopped and teetered from the pieces of asphalt blown from the roadway. A miss.

Sustained bursts of light rained down from the sky—from an airplane the Americans called "Spectre," an AC-130 gunship. The flashes of light were followed several seconds later by the rapid-fire sound of a Gatling gun, the whizzing of bullets, and the shattering of glass and marble. Smoke and dust rose from the building at the end of the street as a hail of bullets tore through it. Then the large cannon on the gunship fired, hitting the building square on. It collapsed in smoke and dust.

The Americans had set a reverse trap.

"Fire your RPGs, you idiots, then run like mad or they'll kill us all!" shouted the leader to the two men watching out the window in shock. They fired wildly at the lead tank and unloaded all their rounds. One missed wide to the left, hitting a car parked along the road. The car exploded into flames. The other RPG hit the tank but ricocheted off into the alley.

"Grab your rifle and get out!" the lead gunman shouted to the others as he sprinted toward the door. Ibrahim stood up, blocking their path. The leader grabbed his arm. "Come on! Get going! This apartment will be a pile of rubble in seconds!" Ibrahim tried to pull away. "My wife and son! I need to get them!"

"Get going!" said the leader. He shoved Ibrahim through the door and onto the steps. Ibrahim almost fell over the wrought-iron railing, but he caught himself just in time. The three men behind were pushing so hard that Ibrahim had to keep going down the steps or risk being pushed down and trampled on by them. At the bottom of the steps he jumped to the side, hitting his shoulder against the wall.

"Come on; get out before you are killed!" they shouted back to him. "Don't be a fool."

"No!" he shouted back. "I must get my wife and child." He darted back up the stairs, breathing hard, his mouth dry from swallowing dust and smoke.

The other three men ran down the hallway toward the back of the building, pushed open the rear entrance, and fled into the darkness, finding safety in the twisting maze of alleys.

"Minu! Ali! Come—now!" Ibrahim shouted, bounding up the stairs, now nearly out of breath. But the noise of explosions and rockets drowned out his voice. A deafening roar swallowed his words. The Abrams tank had trained its barrel on the twin trails of smoke from the rocket-propelled grenades that pointed back to the apartment from which they had been launched. The round exploded against the back wall of Ibrahim's living room, blowing it back into the bedroom, instantly killing his wife and son.

The building shook, causing Ibrahim to lose his balance. As he stumbled back to his feet, he knew his wife and child were dead. The walls around him creaked and groaned as they buckled under the pressure. Bricks, chunks of cement, and pieces of wood fell like hail. He had to escape, or risk being buried in the rubble.

Ibrahim wept and wailed for his wife and son as he ran back down the steps, through the lower hallway, and out the back door. The door bounced open as he heard the churning of the plane's Gatling gun. A loud explosion threw him off his feet as a round from Spectre's cannon ripped through his building, bringing it to the ground in a twisted pile of dust and brick. Minu and his son were gone. Buried by the Americans.

He knew the Americans had the ability to track him in the dark. He ran down an alley, and in a panic dropped through an unlocked door into a private residence. An older man, his wife, and their two grandchildren sat huddled and shaking in the corner, staring at this man who had just burst in from the alley.

"Don't be afraid! I'm an Iraqi, and I'm not a soldier. I'm running from the Americans' bullets!" Ibrahim whispered, catching his breath.

They all sat in silence through the night, strangers bound together by their fear. No one slept. Ibrahim sobbed, thinking of his family.

In a morning light and quiet, Ibrahim left his temporary place of refuge to retrace his steps back to his apartment building. He turned the final corner and saw the spot where he used to live. Hope drained from his soul at the sight of the pile of rubble that was his home. The Americans were gone, but in their wake they had left complete devastation. Three different buildings on his block—the three chosen by the fighters for their ambush—no longer existed.

O most merciful Allah, why? He prayed as he climbed the mountain of brick and concrete to a spot that looked like his apartment. He began pulling pieces of brick and marble and wood from the pile and throwing them off to the side.

He dug for three hours before he finally found the broken, bloodied remains of Minu and Ali, still clutching each other on the cracked floor. Scores of others had come to help him dig—seemingly from out of nowhere, people who knew and who had seen this too many times before. Ibrahim gently laid the bodies on the street and covered them each with a sheet he had pulled out from under a mattress. Iraqi ambulances had arrived, but much too late to do anyone any good. The firefighters and security personnel pretended to bring some direction to the chaotic scene. Ibrahim sat watching others look for their loved ones. He found a cool place under a canopy on the far side of the street. He could only sob and pray as he watched the workers look for still more bodies in the rubble.

As he prayed, a bearded, middle-aged man, dressed in abaya and turban, sat down next to him. "Ibrahim," the man said, "I want you to know that my heart sorrows with yours in this time of great pain."

Ibrahim turned to look at the man. He recognized him at once as one of the new *mullahs*, the religious leaders who had slipped back into Iraq after the fall of the Baath government. Hussein had opposed many of these leaders because they threatened to replace his secular form of government with an Islamic republic. Though a Muslim, Ibrahim had never been overtly religious. But perhaps religion was what he needed now. "Why did this happen? Why did my wife and son have to die?" he asked the man, still looking across the street.

The mullah's answer surprised him. "Allah the merciful and compassionate truly understands your sorrow. And though this is part of his great plan, it was caused by those who oppose his will."

"But I don't understand," said Ibrahim.

"Saddam Hussein was not a true follower of Allah, though he did pay lip service when it so suited his political ends. He put to death many who followed Allah because he saw them as a threat to his political ambitions. Those who planned last night's attack were part of a group seeking to restore that type of government once again in Iraq. Such a government is not Allah's will, and your family suffered at their wicked hands."

Ibrahim listened but was confused. He didn't understand how Iraqis could be responsible for his family's death.

The mullah continued. "In the same way, the Americans who are now here are not here with the blessing of Allah. They are the Christian crusaders from the West who have been tricked into coming here by the Jews who secretly control much of the world. Their goal is to destroy Islam and all those who worship Allah. And your family has suffered because of their presence in our land, as have many others throughout the Middle East."

"But if that is so, what can we do? I'm just a poor man who has lost everything he loves in this life because of forces beyond my control," Ibrahim asked, wiping some tears from his now-swollen eyes.

"My son, there is *much* you can do," the man answered with a gentleness Ibrahim had never experienced. "Or, should I say, there is much that Allah can do through you . . . if you are willing to be his obedient servant. Would you like to learn how to defeat wicked men like Saddam Hussein, and the crusading Christians, and the manipulative Jews? Perhaps Allah has allowed all this to happen so that you would be prepared to do his bidding."

Ibrahim looked directly at the mullah. The man's piercing eyes startled him and made him blink. This man somehow understood his pain and saw a purpose for his life that transcended his own existence.

"What must I do?"

"Come with me," answered the mullah. "You need some rest. Then you shall see."

CHAPTER 3

JILLIAN

FBI HEADQUARTERS, J. EDGAR HOOVER BUILDING, WASHINGTON DC "Come on, Frank! I might have the lowest grade and rank, but I didn't just ride into town on a turnip truck! This assignment's a one-way ticket to obscurity, and you know it!"

Jillian Foster liked Frank O'Banion and she liked the FBI, but she wasn't about to let either one pigeonhole her because of some stereotype. She was a woman on a mission, and God help *anyone* who tried to side-track her from that mission.

"Jillian, calm down. I assure you it *isn't* a one-way ticket to obscurity. And you weren't selected because you're a female. You're smart, ambitious, and you graduated tops at the Academy. Don't be so paranoid."

She sensed a frustration in Frank's voice. Her journey to the FBI actually began on September 11, 2001, the day her older brother died in the fiery collapse of the South Tower of the World Trade Center. At the time Jillian had just started her final year of law school at Southern Methodist University in Dallas. Until that day her general goals in life had been to have a good time, get her law degree, and eventually find a job in a firm specializing in corporate real estate.

It's not that Jillian was lazy or shallow. She worked hard in school and got good grades. And she kept herself informed about events in the rest of the world, but in a detached, intellectual way. She read the *Dallas Morning News*, as well as *Time* and *Newsweek*, but also *People* magazine just to keep it real. She thought about events in the rest of the world the way an atheist might ponder the details of theology—being fully satisfied with a cursory understanding because the information had such little impact on, or relevance to, one's day-to-day existence.

All that changed when a group of Islamic fundamentalists commandeered an airplane and crashed it into the building where her brother, Tom, worked. His body was never recovered. She remembered exactly where she was when she first heard the strange report of a plane hitting the World Trade Center. It was 8:15 a.m. in Dallas, and she was just finishing her breakfast and was getting ready to head to a lecture on tort reform. Her phone rang, but she didn't want to take the time to pick it up, so she let it go to her answering machine. The panic-stricken words of her mother, calling from home, would haunt her forever. "Jillian, this is your mom! When you get this message turn on your television. Something terrible has happened at the World Trade Center. Pray for your brother. He's . . . I—I . . . please pray." And then she heard her mother sob as she hung up the phone.

Jillian's first impulse was to hit Redial and talk to her mom. But then she thought about what her mom had just said. Maybe she should flip on the television to see what was happening before she called her mom back. Jillian even remembered the words going through her mind as she hit the On button on the remote. *I wonder what channel Mom was watching? I wonder if it was a national or a local program? I hope I can find whatever it was she had seen.*

Five hours later Jillian was still sitting in her tiny kitchen apartment watching. She flipped through the channels searching for any additional scrap of information, hoping somehow to see Tom running by one of the cameras or being interviewed by a reporter. But the hours turned into days, and the days into weeks. Calls to his cell phone, his apartment, local hospitals, the Red Cross, and all his friends turned up nothing. Three weeks after that tragic day, the family couldn't take the suspense of not knowing whether Tom was dead or alive. Her father flew to New York to see if he could find out something for himself. A week later he came home, finally accepting the grim reality. Tom was dead. One of the several thousand lost in the fiery crush of the collapsed towers. He was gone forever.

All through the spring semester Jillian waited in vain for a call from her mom or dad saying the coroner's office had identified Tom's remains. Real estate law seemed pointless now. Too hedonistic. What had it done to protect those who were practicing it in the World Trade Center? The collapse of those twin towers was an epiphany of sorts for Jillian. It showed her how quickly the things she had always valued could vanish.

She had to do something: for her brother, for the other victims, for herself. And from that time of reflection Jillian developed a new sense of focus and direction. She would pursue criminal law and use her skills to help put the "bad guys" behind bars.

But where could she use her abilities most effectively? She thought initially about pursuing a career in the Dallas County district attorney's office. But as satisfying as it might be to get bank robbers, car thieves, and rapists off the street, Jillian had a much more personal agenda. She wanted to go after terrorists, like the followers of Osama bin Laden who had killed her brother. Terrorists were usually prosecuted at the federal—not the local or state—level. So where could she best use her skills on that level?

On the Friday before spring break, Jillian walked into the Blanton Student Services Building to pick up information on cap and gown rental for graduation. A small poster just to the right of the door caught her attention. The poster announced a Job Placement Fair to be held on campus the following Monday. The poster listed some of the employers who would be participating, and one particular name seemed to jump off the list—the FBI.

Three days later she cut her final class of the day to visit the Job Placement Fair. She wandered through the aisles looking at the different booths until she saw the display for the FBI. The booth was occupied by a man in his midforties who was wearing a name tag that identified him as Jim Casper. He was standing toward the front of the booth, which was little more than a folding table with a sign supplied by the Career Center. Several different brochures were arranged in rows on the table.

Jillian approached the recruiter and introduced herself. Casper, she found, was a knowledgeable—and friendly—insider. He was more than happy to talk with her and answer any questions she might have about careers with the FBI.

She tried to maintain a professional demeanor as she talked to Jim about her educational background and professional goals. But when Jim asked her why she would consider the FBI, Jillian felt tears well up in her eyes. She told him about her brother's death in the World Trade Center and about her desire to make a difference in the future.

Jim's response caught Jillian off guard. "Well, that just goes to show how wrong you can be."

"Excuse me?"

"Oh, I'm sorry. I was referring to myself being wrong, not you! You see, when the office asked me to come here, I wasn't that excited. My impression of Southern Methodist University is that it's not a school that produces a large number of graduates anxious to serve their country.

When you walked up I had already put you into the category of 'friendly but uninterested.' It just goes to show how wrong first impressions can be; that's all." The man looked embarrassed by it all, and then turned more serious. "Please accept my apology, and my condolences for your brother."

"Apology accepted. But what I want most is an answer to this question: Is the FBI interested in law school graduates?"

Jim smiled broadly. "In a single word, yes! We have a critical need for special agents with law degrees. Having the degree doesn't mean you are automatically qualified, though. There's a great deal of testing, plus you would also need to attend the FBI's academy for specialized training. I can't make any promises, but you just might possess the mettle needed to make FBI agent."

The Academy had been rough, but in a different sort of way from law school. The technical information wasn't that difficult to learn, and she had always kept herself in good physical shape. But she had to work hard to master the other skills needed to be a special agent.

After a series of brief postings in different cities, Jillian had finally been transferred to the FBI's headquarters in DC. And now, her first major assignment looked to be nothing more than a glorified desk job that would move her away from the center of the action.

* * * * * * * * * *

"Jillian! Have you even heard a single word I've said?"

Jillian blinked and tried to refocus. "Sorry, Frank, my brain took a short detour. Tell me again why I should be excited about this assignment." She walked across the room to look out the window. DC looked gray to her most days.

Frank took a single deep breath, and then got up from the table to join Jillian at the window.

"You should take this assignment because it has everything—

everything—to do with trying to fix what went wrong on September 11. We had all the information we needed to stop those freaks before they ever boarded those airplanes. We knew most of their names. We had information that Al Qaeda was planning something with airplanes. We had communication chatter preceding the event. We even had some general tips that something was about to go down. But those tiny bits of important information got buried in oceans of data, and each of those oceans was supervised by a different government agency. After the attack we could backtrack and discover all the pieces. But we failed to prevent the attack because we weren't able to connect the dots."

Frank walked over to a map of the United States hanging just to the side of the conference table.

"What did we know? An agent in Phoenix received a tip about terrorists taking flight training. But nothing came of it because most of the training was taking place in Florida." To emphasize his point Frank grabbed a box of pushpins and dumped them in his hand. He pushed a red pin into the map at Phoenix and a yellow pin in Tampa.

Sticking another red pin into Los Angeles, he continued. "We had information here that a known Al Qaeda operative was living in the U.S. and receiving support from a foreign diplomat. Meanwhile in Chicago, we had a Muslim 'charity' funneling funds to a number of terrorist groups, including Al Qaeda. It's likely that some of the funding for those terrorists, and for their training, came from unsuspecting U.S. citizens."

Frank took one last pin between his thumb and first finger and held it up in front of his face. "The only reason there wasn't a fifth hijacker on the plane that went down in Shanksville, Pennsylvania, on its way to DC is that an immigration inspector in Orlando didn't allow him to enter the country.

"I could go on, but I'll run out of pins before I run out of key pieces of data that we overlooked. And I haven't even begun to talk about the

NSA telephone intercepts, the CIA reports on worldwide Al Qaeda activities, including those in Germany, the information from the first Al Qaeda attempt to bomb the World Trade Center, or the billions we've spent on sophisticated computer programs to do social-network analysis and data mining. We had *all* the information we needed to stop the attacks, but we didn't know we had it because it was buried among so much other information that we couldn't connect the dots."

Frank had to pause to regain his composure. He didn't want to tell her, but one of those who also lost his life on September 11 was Frank's best friend, Danny Keil. They had gone through the Academy together, and each had been best man at the other's wedding. The failure of intelligence had cost Frank his closest friend. Frank walked back and sat down at the table.

"One of our country's main goals now is to look for ways to identify and share relevant data among the different governmental agencies. It's a mandate that came from the 9/11 Commission report, and it is being implemented by the national intelligence director. The FBI, the CIA, the NSA, and the Department of Homeland Security are looking for ways to work together—and to work with state and local law enforcement agencies—to identify any threats to America or Americans. The name of the game is cooperation, not competition. And that's what makes your assignment so important, Jillian. Most governmental snafus come up because the way things are supposed to work—that is, the way they are drawn up on paper here in Washington—is seldom the way they actually unfold out in the field. We're convinced we need to start at the grass-roots data collection level to see if we can develop a system that will allow us to sort out the wheat of good information from the chaff of inaccurate, incomplete, or false information."

"How can I make a difference in all that? I mean, let's be real. I'm just a rookie," she said with a mounting sense of inadequacy.

"That's just the beauty of it. You're new. You're uninhibited and ambitious enough to think out of the box," Frank said, smiling. "I want you to spend the next year 'on assignment.' This is *not* because I want to move you from the heart of the action here in DC. Rather, I want your fresh set of eyes to evaluate the places where most of the data is actually collected—before it is refined, collated, summarized, and sent to us. Your assignment is profoundly simple, and infinitely complex: I want you to help us determine what we must do to identify, collect, and distribute on a timely basis the information that most directly impacts the security of the United States. Mostly, I want you to question everything. Use your imagination. Doubt the facts and analyze the hunches. We lacked imagination the first time, Jillian; now we need it in spades!"

Jillian flashed a smile and threw up her hands in a sign of mock surrender. "Okay, boss, I give up! Seriously, I didn't realize the importance of the assignment. I know I just made a typical rookie mistake, but I promise I'll give this my full attention and focus. By the way, where do I go?"

Frank allowed himself to relax, and a smile crept across his face. "No problem. If I had been in your shoes, I'd have probably been complaining too, not knowing what was involved. I'm posting you to Chicago to work with our office there. It's a major city with some potentially significant terrorist targets. And it has prime entry points terrorists could use to enter the U.S. You'll begin next Monday. They'll help you find temporary housing, and they'll also introduce you to the other local, state, and federal agencies."

Chicago, thought Jillian. "I hate the cold," she mumbled.

CHAPTER 4

WHAT WAS IN THE TRAVEL PHOTOS

CHICAGO, ILLINOIS Greg Hanson was frustrated.

"Here I am on a Saturday night," he muttered to no one in particular, "surfing the Net like some pathetic nerd, and I can't even find a stupid picture of one of the most photographed buildings in the world! And now I'm talking to myself! Lord, I need to get out more!"

Greg pushed his chair back from the desk and poured himself some more coffee in the kitchen. At the last minute he had been asked to lead the high school class he and a friend taught at church. Greg was a professor at a small Christian college in the Hyde Park neighborhood of Chicago, a stone's throw from the Gothic spires of the University of Chicago. His expertise lay in historical geography and archeology, and he had traveled to the Holy Land a number of times. His specialty was connecting events and people in the Book—the Bible—with places in the Land—Israel. So now he was searching for a photo of the Dome of the Rock in Jerusalem, located on the Temple Mount where it was thought the Temple had stood in ancient times.

He loved the work and loved teaching, but his dating life was another story. As a single, not bad looking, and totally available, young professional guy, it seemed as though it shouldn't be too hard to meet eligible women in a city as large as Chicago. But his teaching schedule conspired against him, especially this semester. The church he had joined had an excellent class for young, single professionals; but he couldn't attend because of the class he and John were coteaching.

So here he was on a Saturday night searching the Internet for additional pictures to illustrate his message on Jesus at the Temple in Jerusalem. He had some digital pictures from his time in Israel, and he quickly pulled them from his file.

The pictures from the large model of Second Temple Jerusalem were a great place to start. The model, which had recently been moved to the Israel Museum, visualized Jerusalem as it would have looked just prior to the Jewish revolt against Rome in AD 66. Greg's pictures of the Temple in that model could help bring to life events from the time of Christ. He also opened a Bible software program he kept on his computer. The program had a section that provided a 3-D tour of the Temple. He snapped some screen shots to drop into the presentation. They would help the students understand what it might have looked like to actually walk through the Temple at that time.

Everything was going like clockwork until he searched for a current picture of the Temple Mount area. He found that inserting current pictures helped make the lesson seem more relevant to his students. It gave them a sense of perspective and realism for events that otherwise seemed so distant. But all his pictures of the Dome of the Rock—which now sits on the spot where the Temple once stood—were inadequate. Some were shot from too far away; others were from the wrong angle. Greg wanted a shot that would show the Dome of the Rock sitting on the platform so the students could see the relationship between the ancient Temple and its more modern usurper.

This is why they invented Google! Greg thought as he opened his Web browser. He typed in "Dome of the Rock" and "photographs" and hit the Search button. In 0.19 seconds Google responded with nearly twenty-eight-hundred potential sites that he could examine. *So far, so good.* But forty-five minutes later his enthusiasm had diminished greatly.

After searching through almost eighty of the sites, Greg had found no pictures that seemed to be usable. Some were too small, others were from the wrong angle, and still others did not have sufficient pixel density to give good clarity. He decided to change tactics. He went to Flickr, the photo-sharing Web site, and typed "Haram es-Sharif," the Arabic name for the area on which the Dome of the Rock sits. At first he was disappointed that his search only returned twenty-seven pictures. *This might be another wild-goose chase.* But as he looked through small pictures, one seemed especially promising. It was labeled "Haram es-Sharif" and was posted by "Smith Family Vacation."

Greg clicked on the picture to view a larger version. He thought it just a bit odd that the picture referred to the Holy Land as Palestine since most people refer to it as the land of Israel. He clicked on the link to the other Smith family pictures and watched as five photographs from the Jerusalem area loaded onto the screen: the Dome of the Rock, the Al-Aksa Mosque, a crowded street scene in the Old City, the Damascus Gate, and the Citadel of David.

The picture of the Dome of the Rock—or Haram es-Sharif, as it was labeled—looked as if someone with little artistic experience had shot it. It was *not* the kind of picture that would win any photography contests. But it was exactly what he had been looking for. It must have been taken from somewhere on the Mount of Olives, because it showed both the Dome of the Rock and the surrounding courtyard. Even more significantly, the picture seemed to be uncompressed. The file size was 3.3 megabytes, which would certainly discourage anyone with a dial-up modem from downloading it. But it also meant that the picture would have sufficient detail to use in his PowerPoint presentation on Sunday.

Greg copied the file to his hard drive and then logged off the Internet. He had the photograph he needed. Now all he had to do was prepare it for his presentation. And for that he would use Adobe Photoshop, his software of choice for enhancing digital photographs. He fancied himself something of an amateur photographer, but he didn't have the time tonight to give the picture a complete digital makeover. No, tonight he needed to use his patented five-minute-enhancement process.

The fact that the image had not been compressed meant that he didn't need to make any changes in size or resolution. And since he only planned to use the picture for his Sunday school class presentation, Greg decided to use just a few image adjustment features to quickly enhance the quality of the photo. In less than five minutes, he had a picture that was good enough for what he needed for class.

Now there was only one step left in the process. Greg's time in higher education had made him a stickler for rules and regulations, so even though the picture was posted on a public site for unrestricted use, he decided to check the picture's copyright status. Since he was still in Photoshop, he selected File Info to see if it was copyrighted.

"Whoa! What have we here?" he mumbled as the File Info box popped up on the screen. The Copyright Status was set to Unmarked, which meant there was no copyright assigned to the picture. He was free to use it. But in the Caption box was a rather cryptic message: "Dad thought you should pay particular attention to this photo."

Now what does that mean? he wondered. His first thought was to go back to the picture to see if an obscene word or pornographic image might be embedded in it. *That is not the kind of thing I want to have pop up on the overhead in church!* But then he paused. Before looking at the picture, perhaps he should check the rest of the data in File Info. He searched through the Origin and EXIF sections of the box . . . and let out a low whistle.

Greg went over to his apartment window. He seemed to think better standing on his feet, and he needed to think about this. The lights of the Sears Tower twinkled in the distance, but he barely noticed. Instead, he focused all his attention on trying to solve a puzzle that seemed so obvious, and yet made no sense. After nearly an hour he gave up. His head throbbed, and he could barely keep his eyes open. He felt like he was lost in the woods during a heavy fog. The swirling gray mist blocked his view of those distant landmarks he needed to gain his bearings. Instead, all he saw were a myriad of trees that all looked alike. He knew there was an answer, but he also knew it would elude him as long as he remained in this fog.

He wearily completed the lesson and shut down his computer. He knew tomorrow's lesson would not go down in history as one of his finest. But, under the circumstances, it was the best he could do. And that just had to be good enough.

He turned off the lights and crawled into bed. The silky smoothness of the sheets wrapped around his body as his head sank into the inviting softness of his pillow. In less than a minute his breathing turned soft and rhythmic as his mind entered that unexplored region called sleep.

"Wait a minute!" he shouted as he sat upright in bed. He looked around, but the room was still cloaked in darkness. The clock read 2:30 a.m. Awakening suddenly from sleep can be disorienting, and he had to pause a moment to remember what had just jolted him awake. And then it came back to him with all the stark clarity he had experienced only moments before. While he lay sleeping, his mind had continued to ponder the puzzle, searching for an answer. Like discovering the right set of numbers on a combination lock, the tumblers aligned and the locking mechanism clicked open.

Greg jumped from bed and pushed the On button to start his computer. But when it had booted, he didn't open to the picture of Haram es-Sharif. Instead, he opened his Web browser and did another Google search—this time looking for the phone number of the local office of the FBI.

* * * * * * * * * *

As Greg was printing out the phone number for the FBI, a cryptic e-mail was being sent from a suspected Islamic extremist in the United States to a nondescript Yahoo Web mail account. The text of the message was intercepted by the National Security Agency computers, along with tens of thousands of other messages that originated from—or were sent to—individuals in the Middle East. But the algorithm designed to search for key words or phrases that would identify communication between terrorists deemed the message *unimportant*. The message simply read, "We inspected the house. The plumbing seems to be working just fine. No leaks can be detected. We are ready to turn on the water."

The head of the secret cell group finished reading the e-mail on his computer and smiled. "Good, the message has arrived. Not even the fancy American computers can see it," he murmured. "They will see it soon enough."

CHAPTER 5

ON A STREET CALLED STRAIGHT

The cool desert breeze dried the beads of sweat trying to form on Moshe's forehead. He shivered. "Nerves! It's only nerves," he kept telling himself. "Just remain calm and nobody will notice your fear."

Moshe walked slowly through the *suq*, the market area of old Damascus. This was his first undercover assignment for Mossad. In spite of the secret peace talks that had just been restarted, Syria remained one of Israel's most implacable enemies. As a young schoolboy he had read *Our Man in Damascus*, the story of Israel's great spy Elie Cohn, who had infiltrated the highest echelons of Syria's government in the 1960s. *But Cohn was eventually caught, tried, and hanged, and the Syrians were so upset over the affair that they still won't return his body to Israel.*

Moshe tried not to dwell on the possibility of his being caught as a spy, but the thought never left his mind. Mossad had given him specific training on what to expect—and what to do—if captured. But the bottom line was simple: Avoid capture at all cost. The short, brutal life of a captured spy would begin with weeks of torture in a dark, fetid prison cell somewhere in the bowels of the headquarters of *Mukhabarat*, Syria's secret police. Once the Mukhabarat felt they had extracted all the information one possessed, there would be a public trial and execution, followed by an anonymous burial in an unmarked grave.

Moshe had been sent to Damascus to contact an informant whom he knew only by the code name Nevi—"prophet." He was to meet with Nevi because the agent had sent word to Mossad through his normal contact in Damascus that he possessed vital information too sensitive to send through normal channels. Sharing the information could even expose Nevi's identity to the Syrians, so he had been sent to hand-deliver instructions on how Mossad would extricate Nevi from Syria, if necessary.

Nevi's identity was such a closely guarded secret that Mossad would not even share it with Moshe. "But how can I contact Nevi if I don't even know what he looks like or where he lives?" he argued.

"Don't worry," responded his director. "Proceed to the designated place at the right time, and Nevi will contact you."

Mossad carefully crafted Moshe's cover. He flew from Israel to Italy, where Mossad provided him with a forged Egyptian passport. Using his new identity, he then flew to Cyprus and on to Syria. He arrived in Damascus posing as Ziyad Abu Ali, an Egyptian businessman looking for "back-channel" suppliers who could deliver goods and supplies from Iraq via Syria that could be sold in other Middle Eastern or European countries. From handwoven rugs to oil to military surplus weapons—if there was a supply, Ziyad/Moshe claimed he could find a market. With a generous supply of euros to use as *bak sheesh*, he found the appropriate government offices more than willing to provide necessary transport documents and export permits. More important, in a matter of two weeks these same corrupt officials had helped him establish contacts and even broker some small deals.

It was Wednesday of his third week in Damascus, and Moshe had spent most of the day talking with a group of businessmen who claimed they could provide him with a continuing source of handwoven wool carpets from Iraq. As payment, they had hinted that they would much prefer night-vision goggles, American military uniforms, and radioactive medical waste rather than euros. But if Ziyad/Moshe couldn't provide the equipment, they would accept the cash. Moshe left them with vague promises that he would check his sources in other countries to see if a deal could be arranged. In reality, he would present the idea to his supervisors to see if this was an opportunity Mossad could exploit to help track down the flow of arms from Syria to the different terrorist organizations inside and outside Iraq—and Lebanon.

If anyone had been following him, that person would have seen nothing more than an Egyptian businessman spending his day in an extended meeting with a group of rug dealers. Now, with the sun starting to drift lower on the western horizon, this businessman was walking back through the suq toward his hotel. A sudden stop might have momentarily raised some suspicion, but only until the tail—if there even was one—noticed where he had stopped. Moshe's digital watch flipped to 17:45, as he turned and entered Bekdach's, one of Damascus's most popular ice cream parlors. Throughout the day, the store produced fresh vanilla ice cream by pounding the cream with large wooden mallets in cold metal containers. The vanilla ice cream was excellent by itself, but Bekdach's then hand-rolled the ice cream in pistachios and scooped it into glass cups. How natural for someone from Egypt to want to sample one of Damascus's wonderful treats.

Moshe found a small table in the corner. When the waiter came by in his starched white coat, he ordered ice cream and qahwah. His Arabic was flawless, but it was clear to the waiter from his accent that he was not from Damascus. The waiter returned with his order and asked nonchalantly, "What brings you to our great city?"

"Ah, my friend, I came all the way from Cairo because I wanted to taste some *real* ice cream!" Moshe replied, laughing loudly. Being from Cairo was sufficient to explain to the waiter why he spoke with a slight accent. For the first time in over two weeks he felt almost relaxed.

"Excuse me; did you say you were from Egypt?" came a voice from just off his left shoulder. Moshe was startled.

"Yes, I did," said Moshe, turning slightly to notice a middle-aged woman carrying two flimsy yellow bags filled with groceries—fresh pita bread in one and grape leaves in the other. She appeared to be stopping off on her way home from shopping to indulge in a little ice cream.

"I'm sorry to interrupt, but I have a sister who lives in Cairo near the Muhammad Ali Mosque. You don't happen to live in that area, do you?"

Moshe's eyes widened, but only for a moment. He had just heard the first part of the pass code, the phrase by which he was told he would recognize Nevi. *Could this woman be Nevi?* His mind raced back through the conversations he had had with his contacts at Mossad. He hadn't thought of a woman.

"I'm sorry; I don't live in that area, though I do visit the mosque often. I find it almost as magnificent as the Great Mosque of Damascus. Tell me; have you ever been to Cairo?" he countersigned. A long silence followed that made Moshe nervous.

"I've not been to Cairo, but I have visited Alexandria," the woman answered. *It's Nevi, indeed. Why didn't they tell me to expect a woman?*

"The place certainly seems busy today. Could I just set my grocery bags on this empty seat while I go over to the counter to order? Would you be willing to watch them for me?" Nevi asked calmly. She stacked her bags on the chair without waiting for his answer.

"Of course. By the time you have purchased your ice cream, I'll have eaten mine, and I'll be ready to leave. When you come back you can have the table."

As Nevi walked over to the counter, Moshe continued to eat his ice cream. Grabbing a flimsy napkin from the metal dispenser on the table, he took his pen and scrawled out in flowing Arabic the words *Madhanat Issa*, a reference to the Tower of Jesus at the Great Mosque. He knew this tower was named for Jesus, whom the Muslims revered as a prophet, because local Muslim tradition believed that this minaret is where Jesus will appear on the Day of Judgment. Nevi would also know this local tradition, and he hoped she would realize he was asking to meet her there. Reaching into his billfold, he pulled out a Syrian £50 note, worth just under one euro. Glancing around to make sure no one was watching, he folded the napkin and placed it just under the £50 note.

When Nevi returned from the counter, he stood and gave her his chair. He also said, loud enough so that the waiter would hear, "Madame, you can have my table as long as you are also kind enough to hand this £50 note to the waiter. It should be more than sufficient."

Moshe handed the money and napkin to her, and she deftly folded them into the palm of her hand. As he turned to leave, he noticed the waiter watching from the corner of the room. He motioned toward the woman and signaled to the waiter that he had given her the money. The waiter nodded to let Moshe know he had heard—and seen—the transaction. As Moshe walked out the door he glanced back to see the waiter stop at the table. Nevi had the £50 bill in her hand ready to hand to him. She also opened her purse and reached in to get her own money to pay for her ice cream. The waiter didn't notice the folded napkin she dropped into her purse as she fumbled for her money.

Rather than walk directly to the mosque, Moshe took a more roundabout trip. He first walked down *Madhat Pasha* street, a road the relatively few Christian pilgrims to Damascus know as Straight Street from the reference to it in the New Testament book of Acts. Someone at Mossad had thought it was a tidbit worth sharing when Moshe was briefed on the history and culture of Damascus.

Madhat Pasha street, with the last word pronounced *Basha* because Arabic has no *p* sound, was originally the major east/west road of Roman Damascus. The Romans adapted their city planning directly from the *castrum*, or military camp, with its rigid, gridlike framework. Roman cities were organized around a major north/south road, called the *cardus maximus*, and a major east/west road, called the *decumanus maximus*. Two roads, the *cardo* and the *decumanus*, intersected at right angles in the center of the city and divided it into four quadrants. Even the present Old City of Jerusalem was divided into four quarters because the Roman emperor Hadrian tried to remake Jewish Jerusalem into a Roman city he renamed Aelia Capitolina. Moshe wondered how many other cities throughout Europe and the Middle East owed their basic design to the Romans. More than most people realized, he was sure.

He found it oddly amusing that the most famous street in Muslim Damascus was designed by Romans from the West and made popular by a Jew who later became a leader in the early Christian church. Saul of Tarsus met Jesus on this road and spent three sightless days in Damascus on the street called Straight. Later another God-fearing Jew, Ananias, came to restore his sight. *Jews, Christians, and Muslims! So much in common, including our shared animosity toward each other,* Moshe marveled.

"*Allah u Akbar*, Allah is great!" The voice of the *muezzin* blared from the loudspeakers attached in the minaret towers of the Great Mosque. The high-pitched prayer cry brought Moshe back to reality. The minaret on the southeastern corner of the Great Mosque was the *Madhanat Issa*, the Tower of Jesus. He prayed Nevi would come as agreed. The mosque sat just a few blocks north of Madhat Pasha street, and he sauntered off in the direction of the loudspeakers. Nevi would take her time leaving the ice cream parlor, so as not to raise suspicion.

He couldn't help but wonder about his newfound colleague. He knew

Nevi was Israel's highest-ranking spy in the Syrian government since Elie Cohn. She didn't appear to be Jewish, but he had already learned that appearances can be deceiving. His first, and most important, assignment was to retrieve the information that Nevi felt was so important. At the same time he was to share with her Mossad's instructions for smuggling her out of Syria.

The other purpose for the operation, secondary in importance though still significant, was to see if he could develop contacts into the large smuggling operations in Syria. Syria seemed to be the main transit point for people and supplies entering or leaving Iraq and Iran. Mossad hoped to uncover the sophisticated smuggling networks that supplied terrorists worldwide, including Hezbollah in Lebanon—the menacing Arab faction that continued to threaten Israel's northern border.

With secret peace negotiations again taking place—between Israel and the Palestinians, Syrians, and Saudis sponsored jointly by the United States and the Europeans—Mossad expected Iran and other Islamic fundamentalist nations and groups to step up their opposition. And that usually meant an increase in terrorist activities. Israel wanted to know about any threats before, not after, they came to fruition.

Moshe walked up the narrow street running along the southern side of the mosque. The bases of the densely packed buildings were already in shadow, but the setting sun reflected bright pink and yellow hues off the white stone of Madhanat Issa. Moshe was focused so intently on the sheer beauty of the golden stone against the deepening azure sky that he didn't notice the woman step from the shadows.

"The ice cream was good, yes?" the woman asked directly.

Startled, Moshe turned to face Nevi. The woman appeared to be in her fifties, but in a faint, surprising sort of way she reminded him of Esther. She looked to be little more than five feet tall. Her face and hands were plain, no lipstick or fingernail polish, but she had pretty and innocent eyes. Nevi certainly did not look like Moshe's idea of a spy. The plastic bags of pita bread and grape leaves still swung loosely in her hands.

"Let's walk together to a nearby park. There are some nice benches there where we can sit and talk," she suggested confidently, her eyes narrowing slightly against the sun.

Moshe nodded and followed in silence as the woman led him through the maze of streets and alleys. Eventually they came to an open space the Syrians would call a park. A few scraggly olive trees stood guard at one end of the lot, which was largely a hard-packed dirt field with soccer goals at either end, net-less and listing. Half a dozen shoeless children stood at the far goal taking turns trying to kick the ball past the goalie. At the other end of the lot, near the olive trees, were several benches, all vacant. She led Moshe toward the last of the benches, one that seemed to be set a little apart from the others. Carefully setting her plastic bags in the middle of the bench, she sat on the right side and motioned for him to sit on her left.

"I'm not exactly the person you envisioned meeting, am I?" she said in a kind but direct way, purposely breaking the awkward silence.

"I must admit, I'm surprised. But your reputation speaks for itself, Nevi," Moshe answered, almost stumbling on his words.

"I'm a woman, not a man; and I'm an Arab, not a Jew. You expected neither, did you?"

"My superiors likely assumed this was information I didn't need to know, and it doesn't matter anyway," he replied, feeling more relaxed.

"That might be true, but now you must know that—and much more. It is vital for the State of Israel and for the United States, so please listen carefully. I don't look like a spy, and that's because I'm not one. At least I didn't start out to be one."

Nevi paused. *Lord, give me wisdom,* she prayed silently. Then, turning to look directly into his face, she said, "To understand the importance of what I'm about to share with you, you must also know my background. I'm originally from the village of As Suwayda, about a hundred kilometers south of Damascus. We are Arabs, but my family is Christian, not Muslim. For generations our village has been predominantly Greek Orthodox. Do you know much about Christianity?"

Moshe turned to face her more directly. "I know a little, I suppose. It's one of the three monotheistic religions to originate in the Middle East. It believes that Jesus is a God. And it claims to have supplanted the Jews as God's chosen people. Beyond that I'm afraid all I know is that, from the early church fathers through the Crusades—and from czarist Russia to Hitler and Mussolini—Christians believe one of their divine assignments is to purge the world of the 'Christ-killers.'"

The look of pain on her face made Moshe uncomfortable. "I hope I didn't offend you. But, from the Jewish perspective, that is all we have ever known of Christianity. And now Islam seems determined to pick up where Christianity left off."

"It pains me to confess that growing up I was taught just what you described," Nevi confessed, smiling. "But then, almost ten years ago, I met some people—evangelicals, they are called here in Syria—who taught me what the Bible really says about who killed Jesus. And I found out, from the Jewish prophet Isaiah, that Jesus was pierced for *our* sins and bruised for *our* iniquities. I discovered He died to pay the eternal price for *my* sin."

Moshe had grown increasingly uneasy with the conversation, so he tried to get her to return to the purpose for the meeting. "This seems very important to you, but I'm not sure what this has to do with us today. Since our time is short, could we get back to the message I'm to take home?"

"I'm sorry—I'll try to be as brief as possible. When I became a follower of Jesus, it created a major division in my family. My parents, and many of my other relatives, felt I was abandoning Christianity—at least

71

the Christianity they held to. Some relatives even threatened my life. My mother and father asked me to leave home, and I left my village for the city of Damascus. There I joined a small group of followers who were studying the New Testament. I took a job as a household domestic. Cooking, cleaning, laundry, that sort of thing."

Moshe sat wondering what all this had to do with him, with Mossad. He decided to be patient.

Nevi continued. "Two events happened over the next year that I believe were part of God's plan for my life. First, I studied the Bible and came to realize that the Jews are God's chosen people. Both the church I grew up in and the Muslims around me said that the Jews were accursed and rejected by God. But then I read the words of the apostle Paul—the Jew who came to know Jesus on the road to Damascus—and I learned that—how does he say it in his letter to the Romans—the Jews are loved because of the patriarchs, for God's gifts and call cannot be revoked. God made a promise to Abraham, and the Jews have a future because God will never break that promise."

Moshe's face stayed blank, carefully hiding whatever he was thinking. So Nevi pressed on. "The second event was that I found a job as a domestic for the family of an officer in the Syrian Army. He is a godless and brutish man with intensely selfish ambitions. He is a longtime member of the Baath Party and recently became a brigadier general and minor member of the Baath Party Central Committee. I was hired because he felt housework was an unworthy task for the wife of a member of the Central Committee. This man loves to come home and brag to his wife and friends about how important he is.

"One day I overheard him brag at a dinner party for some of his friends about the chemical weapons Syria was developing to—and I'll never forget his words—'finish what Hitler started.' That's when I knew that God had put me in his house, like an Esther, to thwart his evil plans."

On hearing where she worked, Moshe suddenly became very interested. "What is this man's name?"

"His name is Habib. Ahmed Habib. I wanted to stop him from doing evil, but I didn't know how to do it. So I prayed and asked God for guidance. Then one day I saw a group of American Christian tourists getting off their bus to visit the Great Mosque."

"How did you know they were Americans?" asked Moshe.

"Their clothes, and the way they talked, showed they were Americans. And they didn't seem too interested in visiting the Great Mosque, so I assumed they were not Muslim. Anyway, I asked God to have them next visit Madhat Pasha street if they were indeed Christians, and then I took a piece of paper and wrote on it my name, address, telephone number, and the words 'I know about Syria's chemical weapons.'"

Moshe sat dumbfounded. He could hardly speak. "You wrote down your personal contact information! Do you know English?" he asked, owning his confusion.

"No, I only know Arabic. I realized that if the paper fell into the wrong hands I would lose my life, but I felt certain God wanted me to do something, and this was the only thing I knew to do. I walked to Madhat Pasha street and waited to see if the group would come there. They came. God had heard my prayer.

"I asked God to lead me to the one person who could be His messenger. One older man appeared to be the leader of the group, and I just sensed he was the one I should approach. At one point the guide let the people take a few minutes to look at the shops along the street. When she did, I carefully made my way up to that man and tugged on his sleeve."

Moshe could not believe his ears. This woman, now serving as the most prized operative for Mossad, is speaking of Jesus and praying and asking God to guide her. It was all too much to believe.

"Are you listening?" she asked, sensing his break in concentration.

"Yes; please go on."

"I only had a few seconds to try to explain to him what I wanted, but I had thought about what to do for several weeks. Looking directly into his eyes, I said, 'Issa,' and then I used my two index fingers to make the sign of the cross. Again I said 'Issa,' and pointed first to heaven and then to my heart. I then reached into my purse and pulled out the piece of paper with my name and address on it. I had folded the paper so nothing could be seen from the outside. I motioned to his hand, and then I took his hand and slipped the paper into it. I folded his fingers over so that the paper was hidden. Then, still holding his hand, I looked straight into his eyes and whispered in Arabic, 'For the Jews! For Israel!' By the look on his face I could tell that he didn't really understand. He stared intently at the paper, as if trying to decipher it, before finally slipping it into his pocket. I nodded in thanksgiving and whispered one last time, 'For the Jews! For Israel!' And then I slipped away into the crowd."

"Weren't you afraid of being turned in to the Syrian guide?" asked Moshe.

"I knew that was a possibility, and I was prepared to die for what I believed God had asked of me."

"Nevi, what happened?" he asked, adjusting his right leg to regain some blood supply.

"One evening, several weeks later, I received a phone call from someone who said that a friend from America had passed along a piece of paper with my name on it. He asked if we could meet, and I agreed. I assumed that if it were the Mukhabarat they would not have contacted me in such a polite way. I found out that the man to whom I had given the piece of paper was indeed a true follower of Jesus who was the spiritual leader of the group. He had returned to America and showed the note to a professor who knew Arabic. The professor gave him a rough translation, and they both realized my message might be important. The pastor then visited the Israeli consulate in a nearby city. He gave them the note, saying that it had been handed to him by a stranger in Damascus who had asked him to pass it along.

"My meeting with the man—I never really learned his name, but he works for the State of Israel—went well. I shared with him, in slightly more detail, what I have just shared with you. He helped set up a system for me to contact him if I had any information to pass along. In the morning I would hang a "Hand of Fatima" amulet in my apartment window." She quickly added, "I don't believe in the *hamsa*, or Hand of Fatima, as a way to ward off the evil eye. But the man felt it was something very distinctive that could be put in the window as a sign and that would not be highly unusual. I have never felt comfortable using it, but God knows that in my heart I don't believe it possesses any magical powers. He is greater than all the spiritual forces of darkness."

Moshe smiled to himself as he reflected on something he hadn't really thought about since his childhood days in Haifa. The good luck charm Nevi described—called the hand of Fatima by the Arabs, after Mohammad's daughter, and the hand of Miriam by the Jews—looked like a stylized hand with the fingers pointing straight down. The amulet was also known as the *hamsa* hand in Arabic or *hamesh* hand in Hebrew, using the respective Arabic and Hebrew names for the number five. The sign was designed to look like the five fingers of a hand and was seen as a good-luck charm to ward off the evil eye.

Nevi continued explaining how she passed information on to her handler. "Then on my way to work I would pause at one specific olive tree and lean against it to fix my shoe. As I did, I would slip a piece of paper with the information into a hollow crack just below one of the large branches. I never went back to check, but I assume the man came by later in the day and retrieved the piece of paper. We never met or talked after that first meeting. The last time I left a piece of paper, it was to let him know that I had just learned something very important that I needed to share in person. That must have frightened him, because instead of arranging to meet me, I came home one day to find a note under my door telling me to go to Bekdach's Parlor today at precisely 17:45 to meet a man who would come personally to hear my story. You are that man, Ziyad; praise the God of heaven."

Moshe let out a soft whistle as he ran his right hand through his coarse, dark hair. One of Israel's greatest assets in Syria was an older Arab-Christian woman who "took up spying" the way someone else might have taken up knitting. This was too good. She had just described the classic dead drop used to pass information without detection, yet she probably had no idea why she was passing along information in that fashion. Surely there had to be more behind this woman's service other than simply a love for God and the Jewish people.

"Has our government compensated you?" he inquired, trying to sound official.

"Nothing. The man offered financial help for me during that first meeting, but I told him I wasn't motivated by money. As I said before, God has already done so much for me; I want to do this as my one way to say thank You to Him. After all, He is the One who arranged to have me working where I am, is He not?"

Moshe's mind raced. What in the world was he to do with such a bizarre twist of fate? He personally doubted the very existence of a divine being, but here was a woman absolutely convinced that God was directing her life—and because of that trust she feared nothing and no one.

"Thank you for sharing your history," he said, hoping to change the subject from the religious to the more mundane matters at hand. "As you said, it does indeed help me understand what you have been doing. But that brings us to today. What is the information you have that you feel so important that you were afraid even to write it down?"

Nevi paused and glanced around. Though they were thirty meters from the nearest other person, she instinctively lowered her voice to speak.

"About a month ago my employer had a dinner meeting with a number of important government officials. After dinner he announced to them that a new day was about to dawn on the Middle East. Plans were almost in place to 'humble the Americans'—those were his exact words—and to force them to send their soldiers back home across the Atlantic Ocean."

"How could this individual hope to accomplish that?" asked Moshe.

"Several of the guests asked almost the same question, though they were more guarded in expressing their doubts. But then General Habib told them a new group was completing its training in Pakistan that would soon unsheathe the sword of Allah once again on America's shores. The team—and their weapons—would pass through Syria on their way to America, and General Habib was in charge of arranging for their safe passage from Syria."

"How would they be traveling; how many would there be?" he asked, still convinced she was telling the truth.

"Those details were not divulged, though he did say that the group had trained eight or nine teams and would be ready to deploy within two months—that was a month ago. Oh, there was also one last item. He said—let me see if I can say it just as he did—he said, 'The attack would be in the soft underbelly of the Great Satan's power.' That's what he said."

Moshe thought for a moment. *The soft underbelly.* "Since that party, has General Habib kept to his regular schedule, or has there been any change in his daily routine?"

"Well, up until three days ago I would have said that it was very routine," she responded. "But then last Sunday when I showed up for work I found the general's wife and children preparing to leave for Aleppo. It seems that the general was going to be very busy for the next five days, so he thought it would be a good time for his wife and children to visit her family. Whatever came up to occupy the general's time must have happened *after* I left work on that previous Friday evening. That indeed was a very unusual change."

"Nevi, there's something else. I've come with a plan from Mossad for your safe passage out of Syria. You may be in great danger."

Nevi hesitated only a moment.

"No, I must stay. If God allows me to be caught, I only pray I will remain faithful to Him, even to death. And, as I said before, it is possible that God has more for me to do as His Esther, for such a time as this, to thwart these evil plans."

Moshe shuddered. His mind could not help but conjure images of his own sweet Esther, lying cold and pale in a bloody pool in Ariel. It was still too tender to bear.

Then, after exchanging brief good-byes, the grieving Mossad agent and the unlikely Syrian spy parted as inconspicuously as they had met.

* * * * * * * * * *

Moshe settled back into seat 4B on EgyptAir flight 723 from Damascus to Cairo. As the plane's nose tilted skyward he felt his body relax. Though he still had to travel from Cairo to Larnaca, Cyprus, before he could make the full transformation back to his true identify, he knew that the greatest danger had passed—for now.

Still his mind kept rehearsing the words of Nevi's cryptic warning. *An imminent attack on America by a new—and as yet unknown—Islamic extremist group. An obscure reference to America's soft underbelly.* So strange. Was the team still in Pakistan? Or had they already made it to the United States? Were the Americans tracking this? Could Israel share the information without compromising its own spy network?

The whine of the Boeing 767 muted slightly as the plane rose to its cruising altitude of thirty-four-thousand feet. Moshe drifted off to sleep still thinking of Esther, that beloved name gently invoked by his mysterious new acquaintance in Damascus.

CHAPTER 6

"I THINK I MAY HAVE FOUND SOMETHING"

Jillian Foster struggled up the stairs of the Jackson Street subway station. At the street a gust of wind sliced through her jacket. *That's what I get for buying a winter coat in Washington DC,* she thought, reaching to pull the top of the coat closed. Her other hand—also gloveless—gripped the handle of her briefcase filled with office memos—her "homework"—and a government-issued laptop.

Wind funneled down Chicago's high-rise canyons, blowing at a brisk twenty miles per hour with gusts at double that. The rushing air brought back another memory from that first cold Chicago day two months prior—and made her smile.

It was her third day in the office, and the wind howled furiously as she fought her way down the block from the subway station to the federal building. She walked into the office that morning with windblown hair and windburned cheeks and loudly announced to no one in particular, "Now I know why Chicago is called the 'Windy City.'"

"Well, actually, that expression has nothing to do with the weather."

Jillian turned to see Special Agent Bill Johnson emerging from his cubicle. Johnson had already struck Jillian as something of a nerd. Office folks considered him the resident expert on Internet-related matters, which to Jillian made him all the more quirky.

"So then, why *is* Chicago called the windy city?" she asked, instantly regretting engaging Johnson.

"Well, there is still some debate on the subject, but the most common explanation is that it was coined by a reporter with the *New York Sun* to describe the hot air generated by Chicago's politicians and promoters when they competed with New York to host the Columbian Exposition and World's Fair. They were always talking up Chicago, and the reporter decided that with all the self-promotion and bragging going on, it must be the windiest city in the world." Agent Johnson took some satisfaction in delivering to Jillian a bit of info she hadn't already known herself.

"Thanks, Johnson, that's really . . . interesting." She disappeared into the tiny cubicle that served as her supposedly temporary office. So far she'd gathered two critical pieces of intelligence: The term "Windy City" had nothing to do with Chicago's blustery weather—and any form of social interaction with Special Agent Johnson was not advisable. This could be a long assignment.

* * * * * * * * * *

Now Jillian finally managed to shoulder her way through the pedestrians traveling the other way on Dearborn. At the entrance to the Dirksen Federal Office Building, she leaned against the large revolving doors to get them moving and was almost pushed into the lobby. She joined the queue of office workers waiting to pass through the security station. The X-ray machine and walk-through metal detector seemed out of place in the marbled lobby, designed decades before the threat of terrorism made such machines a necessary part of the décor. *Another layer of protection, and expense, caused by terrorism.* But the machines hadn't helped her brother or the other 2,751 men and women who had died in the attack on the World Trade Center. Plug up one hole, and the rats simply scurry around looking for another way to enter.

Jillian's eyes filled with tears. She and Tom had been close. They were made closer than ever after their parents' divorce. Every thought of Tom prompted an overwhelming sense of anger and sadness.

She blinked her moist eyes and tried to focus on the dedicatory plaque on the wall. The building was named in memory of Illinois' late Senator Everett McKinley Dirksen, a Republican leader who had reached "across the aisle" and worked with his Democratic counterparts to pass landmark civil-rights legislation. Reading this, she thought of what she had learned at school in Texas about Lyndon Johnson. Suddenly she felt a stab of homesickness.

Jillian joked with her "Yankee" friends about her Texas heritage, but deep down she was proud of the state she called home. She loved the azure-colored bluebonnets that carpeted the hills and plains in the spring. And she loved the Dallas Cowboys, Willie Nelson, fajitas, and Dr. Pepper. It even bothered her that the one steakhouse chain in the North claiming an association with Texas didn't even know enough to properly match the colors on their logo with the colors on the Texas flag.

Today was definitely not a day when she looked forward to spending a lot of time with people at work. The weather matched her mood—cold and blustery. She hadn't been able to make any friends in the short time she had been posted to this regional office. She saw her time in Chicago as a temporary assignment and therefore resisted the need to develop close ties with anyone.

At least the leaves were beginning to come out here in Chicago, although months after the Texas spring. But the wind still served as a reminder that this had been a long, cold winter.

* * * * * * * * * *

When she reached her office Jillian noticed the pink call slip on her desk. *Great; someone already needed to cover for me.* The call was from a Dr. Greg Hanson, and the time said that he had called at 8:45. The message read: "Will call back after 10:00. Claims to have information on terrorist communication." *Wonder what kind of doctor he is?* Jillian was skeptical about people calling themselves doctors. Her daddy really was one and had worked hard to become one. *The only real doctor*, she thought, *was the kind that could open you up and remove your spleen.*

Jillian spent the next fifty minutes scanning a report from Washington. It was actually a summary of the boatload of information collected by the FBI, CIA, and NSA over the past forty-eight hours on potential terrorist threats. In reality, the report read like a Cliffs Notes summary of the original documents. It contained a potpourri of hard data along with reports, tips, speculation, and leads—much of which turned out to be incorrect or unintelligible. *Someone in a bar overheard someone speaking with a foreign accent who implied that he knew someone who knew Osama bin Laden!* That stuff was pretty routine.

Frank O'Banion's words were coming back to haunt her. He had sent her on this assignment to "sort out the wheat of good information from the chaff of inaccurate, incomplete, or false information." She was being given access to all the data but no means to separate fact from fiction. Working after the fact, commissions could take two years to analyze intelligence failures and determine how the FBI and CIA missed connecting all the dots. *But it's infinitely easier to separate the few true leads from the mountain of false ones once the events have unfolded. How do we sort fact from fiction on the fly, in real time, when the number of potential leads exceeds the number of people available to track them down?* Time never sides with those seeking to prevent a crime from taking place.

The phone on her desk rang. Taking just a second to compose herself, she picked it up in the middle of the second ring and said, "Chicago FBI, Agent Foster speaking."

"Hi, I'm Dr. Greg Hanson, and I called earlier. When I told the person what I had discovered, they told me to call back and speak to you."

"I got your earlier message. Now what's this about information on some terrorist link? I've got only a few minutes here. Please be brief." Jillian always tried to appear abrupt and direct.

Greg cleared his throat, seeming to sense an already doubtful recipient on the other end of the line. "Well, I'm not sure how to say this in a way that doesn't sound utterly insane, but I think I might have stumbled across something on the Internet that may be important. It could be some sort of code or secret message or something. I'm not sure."

Great, Jillian thought. *Someone else playing spy.* She tried to sound both reassuring and clinically detached. "Just tell me what you saw. Start at the beginning and describe what you were looking at." She had heard hundreds of reports of such calls coming from people with way too much time on their hands, hoping to play some small part in saving America from another terrorist plot. *I should have been a private practice attorney. At least I could bill people for their time on the phone.*

"Okay. Here's the short version. I was preparing a Sunday school lesson—"

"Did you say 'Sunday school'?" Jillian interrupted.

"Yes, late Saturday night. Sunday school is a time when we meet at church to study the Bible—"

"I know what Sunday school is," Jillian said. "I just didn't hear you clearly. Go ahead." This was not the first encounter she'd had with one of these Jesus people who see Bible prophecy and secret Bible codes in everything from taco salads to phone book ads. *Why me?*

Greg continued, "I needed a picture of the Temple Mount in Jerusalem to insert into a PowerPoint presentation. During my search I stumbled onto a Web site that said it contained photos of this family's trip to Palestine. Actually, I thought it was odd that they mentioned 'Palestine' instead of Israel. Anyway, I found a great picture. But before using it, I wanted to make sure the picture wasn't copyright protected, so I checked its EXIF data and—"

"You just lost me," she interrupted again.

"Oh, sorry. Well, most people aren't aware of it, but when they shoot a digital picture the camera converts the image into a digital file. The file actually contains more than the image itself. Other information—like the date, time, and shutter speed—is also embedded with the picture. This is called EXIF, Exchangeable Image File, data."

"Okay, I'm tracking with that," she said. "Go ahead."

"Virtually all digital photo enhancement software have ways for you to view this data and to insert other information about the picture . . ."

Greg's "geek speak" was starting to push Jillian past the limits of her attention span, so she interrupted again. "But what does camera data have to do with secret messages? Are you saying you have discovered secret messages in pictures on the Internet?"

"Well, yes, but there's more to it than that. There is a photo-storing technique that allows you to hide data attached to pictures that is clearly accessible to individuals who have the specially designed software. What I came across is what appears to be one of those secret messages hidden *inside* the EXIF data of this photo of the Temple Mount."

"I see." She looked up to see Bill Johnson walking by. Waving her hand for him to stop, she said to Greg, "Excuse me for interrupting, but we're shorthanded this morning, and I have another line flashing on my phone. Can I put you on hold? Thanks."

Jillian pushed the Hold button, looked up at Bill, and rolled her eyes. "I think I have a religious nut who claims he's found a secret message in some photo on the Internet."

"Another John the Baptist, huh? Welcome to the holy land, Agent Foster! What's on his mind?"

"He says he thinks he found some code embedded in an EXIF file in a picture of the Temple Mount! Is that wild, or what?"

Bill's response startled her. "You're saying that this guy claims to have found evidence of someone hiding information in the EXIF data of digital pictures? That's interesting. I would never have thought to do that, but it certainly *is* possible. This might be worth looking into. Are you going to meet with this guy? Only way to really check it out."

"Well, I guess so, and I suppose you probably want to come along, right, Johnson?"

"Affirmative, Agent Foster . . . and the sooner the better. I've got poker tonight!"

* * * * * * * * * *

They agreed to meet at a Hyde Park Starbucks after Greg's last class. As soon as Greg pushed through the door he spotted them, two "suits," one male, one female, looking official yet friendly enough. They waved him over to their table.

"I hope you haven't been waiting too long," he said. "I had a few students stay after class with some questions."

Jillian smiled. "Don't worry about us. We weren't sure about traffic, so we left a few minutes early. I'm Special Agent Jillian Foster, and this is Special Agent Bill Johnson. And you must be . . ."

"Hanson. Dr. Greg Hanson. But please call me Greg. I see you've already ordered your coffee. Excuse me a moment while I go get something."

Jillian's eyes followed him as he went to place his order. He looked to be about her age, just a little over six feet tall, with short blond hair that framed his angular chin. The first thing she had noticed about him were his clear blue eyes peering out at her through his glasses. He looked trim and athletic. *Perhaps one of the many bikers who takes advantage of the trail along the lake.* As he sat down with his cappuccino grande, Jillian felt her face flush slightly. *I really need a life,* she thought.

Reaching into his bag, Greg pulled out his PowerBook. He glanced up in time to see Agent Johnson trying to hide his look of incredulity. "I take it you're not a Mac user," Greg said, knowing what the answer would probably be.

"No, I like to work on *real* computers." Bill snorted again, meaning to be condescending.

"Ignore him. He's just the driver," Jillian said, turning her attention fully to Greg's computer.

"That's fine," Greg said. "My parents bought me a Mac when they first came out in 1984. I learned how to use a PC in high school, but then in college I switched back to a Mac. It's just far more intuitive for me, and I want the computer to work for me—rather than having it the other way around. Anyway, I know we're not here to debate the merits of the different operating systems!"

He turned on his computer and connected to the Internet. "Do you want me to take you through the process by which I discovered the message, or would you rather start with the message that I found?"

"Let's start with the message first," Jillian suggested, in her most convincing-sounding FBI voice. If the discovery turned out to be bogus, she didn't want to waste a lot of time learning how he discovered it. *Cut to the chase, Bible Man. I've got a pile of paperwork still waiting for me back at the office—and all I want to do is go home, take a hot bath, and watch some news. Boy, that sounds nice right now.*

He opened Adobe Photoshop and then selected the picture he had downloaded from the site. "I have several different applications for opening images, but Photoshop is the most complete. After finding the message, I decided not to make any changes to the picture. Sometimes the EXIF data can be lost as a picture is being modified."

Jillian and Bill watched from either side. A picture of the Dome of the Rock appeared on Greg's computer. It was a nice, though not spectacular, photo. Neither Jillian nor Bill was particularly religious, but each recognized the image from the many times it had appeared in the backdrop to a news story coming out of Jerusalem.

"What's that building called?" asked Bill.

"That's the Dome of the Rock. The name on the picture, Haram es-Sharif, is actually the Arabic name that refers to the entire platform on which the building is located. Literally, it means 'noble sanctuary.' The Jewish people, and most Christians, know the site as the Temple Mount because it's where the Jewish temple was located.

"The picture was unusual for two reasons. First, using the Muslim name for the platform, and for the land of Israel, seemed a strange way to label vacation pictures for a family named Smith. Second, most people compress pictures they post to the Internet. In other words, they send photos as an e-mail attachment because the larger files slow everything down. But these pictures were totally uncompressed. They were taken by a three-megapixel camera, and that makes for rather large files. Virtually no one downloads these size pictures because they would take too long. But since I was looking for a high-quality photo of the Temple Mount, the larger image was perfect."

"Could you tell me again why you were searching for this particular image?" Jillian asked, her interest rising.

"I teach at Hyde Park Christian College. I've also been volunteering this quarter to coteach a high school Sunday school class at the church I attend. My topic has been 'lessons from the land.' I prepare a PowerPoint presentation to help the kids really experience a particular event in the Bible in its historical setting. Anyway, I was trying to find a picture of the Temple Mount to prepare my lesson on being with Jesus in the Temple. And I came across this."

The answer satisfied her for the time being. He seemed a strange fellow, this Dr. Greg Hanson. Pretty articulate, not bad looking at all, and with a quirky interest in Bible lands. The odd combination intrigued her.

He slid the cursor to the menu bar and clicked on File. The menu opened, and he deftly ran the cursor down the column to the File Info command. He clicked a second time, and a pop-up menu appeared on the screen. In a box labeled Caption was a cryptic sentence:

Dad thought you should pay particular attention to this photo.

Agent Johnson leaned forward to read the words.

"I had really come to this spot," Greg continued, "just to check and see if the picture had a copyright notice. You can see right here there is a box for Copyright Status. A photographer can mark this box to let others know if the picture is a copyrighted work or if it is in the public domain. But when I saw that strange statement just above, I got a little curious. So I checked the other Section topics. And when I clicked on Origin I found the following."

Greg clicked on the Section box and slid the cursor down to Origin. When the new box appeared on the screen, both Jillian and Bill read the words and blinked in unison.

"That's exactly how I felt when I read the message. Who takes time to write under Instructions: 'As soon as you see this, report back to Dad'?"

"But it's so out in the open . . . how . . ." she started to ask, but Greg interrupted.

"Yes, I know, but as I said on the phone, it just looked to me like someone was trying to attach this message to the picture in a way that could be found by those who knew where to look . . . but in a format virtually invisible to anyone else."

"Were there any other messages?" asked Jillian, now sitting more upright in her chair.

"No, I checked all the other pictures posted from the 'Smith family.' There were no other messages. In fact, the odds of my coming across that one picture on this particular Web site are nearly impossible," he answered.

Johnson sat silent, staring at the screen. But then he spoke up.

"Our government is constantly intercepting telephone calls and e-mails, trying to uncover the communication links between terrorist operatives and those who control them. But we would never consciously think to look for a message like this. It's almost too simple. It's too embedded, and it's too passive. We are looking for messages being sent *to*, or *from*, certain accounts—millions every day. This is nothing more than a non-descript public Web site that would likely never catch the general eye of the NSA. Only those who know about the site would know to log on to it for instructions. It's elegant, simple, and effective. I like it. Jillian, I think this merits follow-up."

She didn't know if she fully comprehended the implications of the discovery, but she had a feeling about it, and apparently so did Johnson. Jillian looked straight at the professor, but directed her question to Bill.

"So you are saying that by embedding notes in a picture's file information, these people can hide information in plain sight without any fear of being detected?"

"Well, yes, and no," offered Bill. "Yes, it is highly secure in the sense that we would not have been able to detect this communication using our current sweep. But by hiding the information in plain sight, as you called it, they leave themselves vulnerable to someone else stumbling onto it. Someone like Hanson here getting ready for Sunday school."

"So how do we confirm this is actually a secret message from some terrorist group and not a little thing going on between some harmless tourists?" Jillian asked.

"It's going to take some deeper analysis, I think. But let's think hypothetically for a minute. Let's say this is what Greg thinks: An embedded message was sent from a terrorist cell to someone who needs the secret information. Let's also assume the person is smart enough to use the site's recent activity counter to keep track of how many times it is accessed. If it is accessed too often, the game will be up. Fearing they've been discovered, they would simply switch to a new site or use a new name, and we are back in the dark. Assuming they would have a number of agents in the U.S., and assuming those agents have been instructed to go to the site periodically to check for instructions, they have a rough idea about how many 'hits' or visits the site should receive. So Greg's few visits probably did not cause any alarm. But we will definitely need to be careful about how closely we monitor this thing."

Greg raised his hand slightly to interrupt Bill and Jillian. "Sorry to interrupt, but can I say something?"

"Sure," said Bill.

"Well, I think you are right about being careful in how you monitor the site. I'm the one who stumbled on it, and I would be happy to continue to monitor it for you. But one thing you said is troubling. They might continue to use this site, or they could switch sites on a regular basis. If they stay with this site, it is relatively easy for me to monitor. But how will you track them if they randomly set up other sites?"

"I think I have an idea on that," said Bill. "It won't be easy, but we might be able to use our team in DC to write some type of program to search all the photo-sharing sites for high-quality pictures. We might even be able to eliminate a lot of pictures before we start. Many of the high-resolution pictures on the Net are on porn pages—which I assume you aren't using to prepare your Sunday school lessons. But those *are* sites with high traffic. If I'm a terrorist trying to send a message in a picture, I don't want to embed it in a picture at a site that receives a lot of visitors.

So we can start by eliminating those kind of high-traffic sites."

Jillian smiled. "I should have known, Johnson, you'd have the info on porn sites! Oh, brother. Do you think you can get those guys in DC to take a closer look?"

"I think we might be able to set some other parameters. For example, there are commercial sites that sell high-resolution digital pictures. But to access those sites you need to establish an account—credit card information and the like. That leaves a paper trail, and I would assume our friends don't want to be giving out credit card information with their home address."

"Couldn't they use a stolen credit card or false information?" Greg asked.

"They could, if it was a one-time access. But remember, they probably need to access the site multiple times. It would be too risky to try to steal a new credit card each time you need to check for messages. No, I think a good working assumption is that we can also eliminate commercial sites selling stock photos."

"So does that mean the search might not be that difficult after all?" asked Jillian, a bit more hopeful.

"Not exactly!" said Bill. "If we put those parameters in place and then ask to find only those sites containing pictures with a file size greater than two megapixels, we could still have hundreds of millions of pictures. And someone will need to open and check the EXIF data of each one. And thousands of new pictures are added every day. No, it will *still* be like searching for the digital needle in the Internet haystack!"

Jillian pondered where to go from here. "Bill, you and I need to meet with a few others in the office to share what we have learned. In the meantime, I think it probably is a good idea for Greg to monitor the site, but without drawing too much attention. Frankly, a site with religious pictures on it is probably one I don't feel comfortable navigating my way through. I will need to check with my boss but, assuming he is even interested, would you be willing to meet with a small group to explain to them what you found? And assuming they also give us permission to ask, would you be willing to monitor this site for us to let us know if any new messages appear?"

Greg grinned and stuck out his hand. "I'd be happy to help. As a kid I wanted to be a junior G-man! I hope it turns out to be nothing more than a harmless prank. But if it's not, I'd give just about anything to know who they are and what they are planning."

"Whoa there, ace, let's take it one step at a time," Jillian said, smiling at Dr. Greg Hanson from Hyde Park. "We'll be in touch. Here's my card."

His hand touched hers slightly when he grabbed the small white business card. They both looked at each other and traded smiles.

"Nice to meet you, Ms. Foster," Greg said quietly. He then looked down at the card in his hand: Jillian Foster, FBI. *Impressive.*

He looked up in time to see both agents push through the door onto the sidewalk and disappear.

CHAPTER 7

THE TEACHER

Ibrahim sat in silence, wondering why he had been summoned. The waiting area was small and cramped. A dark patch of mold, nourished by the winter rains that seeped through the roof, clung to one wall while flecks of green plaster dotted the concrete floor. The entire room had a faint, musty smell that reminded Ibrahim of his father's prayer rug—the only possession he had salvaged from his destroyed apartment.

A door to his left led to an area known as the forbidden part of the compound. He and the other fighters had been given strict orders prohibiting them from going there. Only *Dabir*—the Teacher—and his inner circle were allowed access. And whatever they said or did there was hidden from those in "training."

Now Ibrahim and one other, Suleiman, had been brought to the forbidden area.

"This is nonsense for us to sit in ignorance," Suleiman grunted, wanting to spit on the soiled floor beneath him.

"Shut up, you fool! Don't you know someone could be listening?

You would have us both killed for your stupid temper? Don't be an idiot," Ibrahim snapped hard, not wanting to draw any more suspicion. All he knew was that he was told to come here and wait.

For what reason they did not know. Ibrahim sat on a plain wooden bench along the wall facing the outer door. To his left was the doorway leading into the rest of the forbidden area, but he could see nothing because the door was closed. Suleiman sat sulking next to him on the floor, still stinging from Ibrahim's rebuke.

Ibrahim glanced around the room, looking for clues as to the reason for his summons. He did not want to appear too curious, or too afraid. He had heard stories of secret viewing rooms, where individuals were left to themselves, only to be watched and studied through a peering hole in a wall or corner of a ceiling. The idea was that anyone harboring a secret would betray himself under the pressure of the "room." The verses he quoted in his mind from the Quran helped little to calm him.

The creaking of the door on its hinges startled both men. Ibrahim snapped his head to the left, toward the source of the sound. The Teacher pushed open the door, and Ibrahim immediately jumped to his feet. Suleiman scrambled off the floor. Both turned to face the Teacher, lowering their chins and nodding their heads in respect.

"*As-salaam-alaikum*—peace be upon you—Ibrahim al-Samarri!" the Teacher said. He slowly walked toward Ibrahim and stopped in front of him. He reached out both hands to grasp Ibrahim's shoulders and spoke in whispering tones. "You are such a young man, Ibrahim."

He then leaned forward to kiss Ibrahim on each cheek. Ibrahim returned the gesture and stepped back from the formal greeting.

"*Wa-alaikum as-salaam, abdullah barakatu*—Peace be upon you also, blessed servant of God." Ibrahim's insides gurgled, and he fought to keep from coughing nervously.

The Teacher repeated the highly formalized greeting with Suleiman.

Then he said to both men, "Please come into my office. We have much to discuss. Your journey is upon you—your mission for Allah must begin."

As Ibrahim walked through the doorway, his eyes scanned the room. To his left was another open doorway that led into a small bedroom. He could see a simple cot, a plain wooden chair, and a small table with a tiny lamp. Someone had left a worn copy of the Quran on the table in the corner. The rest of the area was windowless, purposely preventing the breaking of light into the room.

Turning to look back at the room he had just entered, Ibrahim saw a computer sitting on a desk to his right. The large flat screen monitor and stylish case seemed strangely out of place against the mud-brick exterior coated with plaster and pale green paint. A dark black cord stretched from the single wall socket to a power strip lying conspicuously upside down on the floor. Plugs from the power strip led to the computer, a printer, and some other box with which he was not at all familiar. Learning to use a computer had been part of their training, but the two older computers the mujahideen shared looked nothing like this sleek machine.

"I see you admire my computer, Ibrahim," said the Teacher. "One will be yours soon enough. Your mission as mujahideen is unique. America's fat, lawless land awaits your terror, young ones. You both will earn for yourselves a place of honor and distinction as you bring the Great Satan to its knees."

Ibrahim wondered if Dabir spoke of martyrdom. Perhaps, but he had not said so directly. Certainly he was about to participate in some type of military action against Americans. He felt the sweat bead across the top of his forehead. His heart pounded and he could feel his throat begin to go dry. He swallowed hard and wiped the moisture from his chin.

His training told him he could be going onto American soil for this mission. The thought made him want to shout and curse at the same time.

"You are emotional, Ibrahim, I see. Good; I like passion in my fighters.

Suleiman here would do well to learn from your zeal."

"I too desire nothing but to serve Allah, Teacher," Suleiman chimed in unconvincingly.

"We shall see soon enough if your resolve equals your words, Suleiman. Character lives in actions, not words. . . ."

Ibrahim shot a glance of disbelief at his counterpart. *How could he be so foolish?*

The Teacher continued: "I summoned you here because you will be partners on this mission. I cannot share with you right now where the other teams will be going. And I must insist that you not talk about this with anyone. Simply understand that it is best for the entire operation that you only know the part you will play. Is this clear?"

Ibrahim and Suleiman nodded.

"Good—then sit down beside the computer. Listen carefully to my instructions."

As the two men walked to the chairs just to the right of the computer table, the Teacher walked back into his bedroom. In just a few seconds he returned holding a cardboard box.

"These are your assignments." He placed the box on the table and pulled out two large brown envelopes from the box: one marked, "Ibrahim" and the other, "Suleiman."

"You will be going to a place called Chicago. Your packet contains information about the city as well as a small book on rules for driving in Illinois. You must study these materials carefully over the next two weeks. Commit everything to memory, and then burn these documents before you leave for your journey to America.

"You will also find in your envelope a credit card. You know what these are from your training. It is a valid card, though it is made out in the name of a new identity you will soon assume. You will be receiving new passports in these names before you depart for the United States.

"Our contact in Chicago will meet you at the airport and assist you when you arrive. He has secured a room for you with an older couple from Jordan. They own and manage a small restaurant in the city. They know nothing about your mission, so never talk with them about it. We also have contact with someone who works in an office where drivers' licenses are obtained, and she will issue you a license."

Suleiman was growing visibly restless. "How long will we live in Chicago before we make our move against Satan's land?"

"You must learn patience, Suleiman," counseled the Teacher. "It is critical that you be patient. It will not be long, and you must use every available moment to travel around the city together, planning for the attack. You will be told exactly when to strike."

"How will we stay in contact with you and the others, Teacher?" Ibrahim asked, wiping his beard of the moisture that had dripped from his hairline down his cheeks.

"One of the first things you will do is purchase a computer," the Teacher answered. "Our local contact has already determined the best place to buy it. He will help you install the software and secure an Internet account. He will also teach you how to check the Web site where we will post messages. He does not know the code, so pay close attention to my instructions. When you go to the site, look for 'Smith Family Vacation' pictures. Watch for any new pictures posted to that site. Now let me show you how to find the message."

Learning how to operate a computer still seemed strange to both men, though Ibrahim knew this was important and had worked hard to master it. His destiny now lay in the hands and purposes of the man he called Teacher and the mission he was accepting.

"There are $9,500 U.S. dollars in each envelope. When you get to America, you must both set up bank accounts and deposit most of this money."

"This seems like a great deal of money," blurted Suleiman. "Why do we need to carry so much, and why put it into a bank account? Will that not draw attention to us?"

"Those are good questions, Suleiman, but let me explain why this is necessary. First, the United States government seems to be obsessed only with amounts that are larger than $10,000, so your deposit will go unnoticed."

"Second, America does not operate using paper money as we do here. While small purchases are indeed made with paper money, most Americans pay their monthly apartment rent using checks. And most major purchases at stores and gasoline stations are done with a credit card. The credit card will help you blend in nicely—no one will even notice."

Ibrahim and Suleiman nodded their heads in agreement, though the only personal experience they had with credit cards and bank accounts was what they had been taught in their classes.

"In two weeks all of us will leave for Islamabad. We will depart in four groups, at four specific times. It will take us all day to make the journey because we will be taking several different routes. On the following day you will board a Gulf Air flight to Abu Dhabi. The tickets are in your envelopes. It is a three-hour flight from Islamabad to Abu Dhabi. After a three-hour layover at the airport there, you will board another Gulf Air flight from Abu Dhabi to Damascus. During your time in the airports, and on the airplanes, I want each of you to have no contact with each other—or, for that matter, with any of the fighters. Travel as individuals so as not to draw attention to yourselves.

"The first part of this journey is very simple, but it is also very dangerous. You will journey to Damascus using your current passports. The tickets are issued in these names as well. And yet, you will be carrying credit cards issued in another name, as well as a large amount of American currency. This will not be a problem unless you are taken aside for questioning. Hide the money and the credit card in a safe, inconspicuous place. Inside your socks or underwear will be fine.

"When you land in Damascus, someone will meet you in the baggage claim area. Look for a man holding a sign saying, "Delegates for Conference on Agriculture." Introduce yourself to the man holding the sign, and he will take you to your contact in Damascus. Remember, you are to watch for the man holding that sign. Is that clear?"

Again, Ibrahim and Suleiman both agreed, though the volume of instructions was beginning to overwhelm them.

"Good. In Damascus you will receive some final documents along with specific instructions. The individual there will help get you to America. Pay close attention to his directions. This will be most valuable to you. . . . Do you have any questions?"

Both men shook their heads from side to side, and the Teacher was about to dismiss them when he paused, as if remembering one more detail. He stroked his graying beard and looked deeply into both men's eyes. "Remember that the United States is the Great Satan, the stronghold of the Christian crusaders who now occupy our lands and kill our wives and children"—here he glanced at Ibrahim. "When trying to kill a dragon, it is never wise to attack directly. The dragon's greatest weapons of destruction—his eyes, his teeth, his claws, and his fire-breathing mouth—are all in front. In the same way, when trying to kill the Great Satan—the crusading dragon of the United States—it is never wise to attack head-on. The cowardly U.S. watches our every move from space and launches missiles from miles away, far beyond our reach."

The Teacher then walked over to the corner where the boxes of SA-7 training missiles were stacked and placed his hands on them, almost as if bestowing a blessing. "No, to kill a dragon you must creep up on it from behind and grab it by its tail. Carefully look for the soft underbelly, and then thrust your sword deep into its vital organs, before it has the chance to turn and strike. How appropriate that Allah has given us an opportunity to grab the Great Satan's tail! I only pray that Allah permits him to turn his head just in time to see the fatal blow struck. Too late to do anything to stop it but soon enough so that he has time to feel the fear of Allah before he is struck down!"

As they walked out of the Teacher's office, Ibrahim noticed two of the other fighters sitting on the wooden bench, fidgeting—the next to receive their assignment, he assumed. He hurriedly said good-bye to Suleiman with a "don't do anything foolish until we get to Damascus" and hurried back to his room to study the packet of material.

* * * * * * * * * *

Everything has gone well so far, thought the Teacher as he handed the eighth pair of mujahideen their specific assignments. Unfortunately, the most difficult task still remained. The Teacher opened the office door to let the two men out, and as he did he saw Jamil the Pakistani sitting alone on the wooden bench in the waiting area. Jamil had passion and zeal, but he did not possess the aptitude to be one of the mujahideen. He was just too dull-witted, and he was controlled too much by his emotions. This made him unstable and unpredictable, a liability to the team and the operation. He could not allow Jamil to participate, but how best to break the news to him? *Inch' Allah,* this would also go well.

"Ah, Jamil! So good to see you!" And after the appropriate greeting, "Please step into my office.

"Jamil, your zeal and passion have been a great encouragement to us all. And perhaps, someday, Allah will be pleased to have you serve on the front lines as one of his leading warriors. But, my son, today is not that day. You tried hard, but you are not yet ready to assume a role that demands so much."

Jamil sat on the chair, staring directly at the Teacher. His face was impassive, but his eyes remained riveted on the Teacher, trying to discover the real reason for this rejection . . . this humiliation.

Not choose me? Why? I am the most skilled, the most cunning, and the most resourceful of all the students. Is it because I'm a Pakistani and all the rest are Arab? Yes, that must be it! This was not true, of course. Of those completing their training, six were Saudis, three were Syrians, two were Pakistani, and the rest were each from different countries: Iraq, Yemen, Egypt, Lebanon, and Palestine. But Jamil searched to find a reason for his rejection that excluded personal responsibility for his own failure. To accept the Teacher's explanation was to admit he was not competent, something he was unwilling to accept. To blame his failure on the prejudice of another was more comforting. That eliminated his personal responsibility. But it did little to diminish his anger.

"Jamil, are you listening to what I have just said?" the Teacher interjected.

Jamil realized he had not been paying attention. He rubbed his hands over his face, mentally trying to wipe away any trace of anger and incredulity.

"Yes, I believe I heard you say that I was not chosen to take part in the attack. Is this decision final?"

"*Habeebi,*" the older man said, using the Arabic expression of endearment, "do not view this as a personal rejection. You are not yet ready. But this will not be the last mission. Time is your friend—anger your enemy."

"Yes, Teacher," said Jamil, even more insulted by this last patronizing remark. Inside, his stomach twisted in resentment. "I accept your decision, though I am displeased."

"Jamil, in two weeks the other instructors and I will leave for Islamabad. We will be taking the other sixteen men with us. The journey will be long and hazardous. I believe it will take us three days to travel to Islamabad, deliver the men to those who will help them on their journey, and then return. I would like you to remain here to guard the compound, and all the families. Those who stay behind and guard also play a vital role in the overall plan, do they not? You will free up the men's minds from concerns about their families, so they can focus on doing all that Allah asks of them."

"I understand. I will do my part for Allah. I will stay here to guard the compound, especially the women and children," Jamil answered. He would have to act quickly once they were gone.

* * * * * * * * * *

Jamil watched as the last of the four Toyota Helix trucks disappeared over the hill to the east. Each truck had driven off with two men sitting inside and three others squatting on bags of wheat and pistachios in the truck bed. To a guard at a Pakistani roadblock—or an American spy satellite—the caravan would look like a group of farmers taking crops to market. The Teacher had been careful to make sure the men were unarmed, or at least as unarmed as one would expect a Pakistani to be in an area that had its share of roadside robberies.

He waited for two hours before putting his plan into motion. If he could not be part of their attack against the Americans, then he would undertake his own. Only he would launch his attack in Pakistan.

He walked over to the tool shed and grabbed a crowbar and canvas tarp. Just outside the tool shed, parked to the side, was one of the remaining Helix trucks. He peered into the driver's side window to make sure the keys were sitting on the front seat. They were. He opened the door, and threw the tarp and crowbar onto the passenger's seat. Sliding the key into the ignition, he started the truck and jerked it into gear. He had been given some driving lessons during his training, but it had been on an old, imported American-made car. That car had an automatic transmission, and the steering wheel had been on the left. But the Helix, jointly produced by Toyota and Pakistan's Indus Motor Company, had a manual transmission and a diesel engine, and—thanks to the British influence on

Pakistan—the steering wheel was on the right.

Jamil spent several panicky minutes trying to get the truck moving forward without stalling. Each time he released the clutch, the truck lurched, sputtered, shook, and died. After nearly fifteen minutes of desperate practice, he was able to put the truck in gear and get it moving by easing his foot off the clutch while mashing down on the accelerator. Once the truck bounced forward, he changed gears without too much difficulty.

He drove past the main building and parked by the large storage building off to the right. Inside the building, he spent several minutes moving sacks of grain and pistachios. He then used the crowbar to pry four of the boards from the floor, revealing a hidden underground room piled high with boxes. He knew exactly what he was looking for. Pushing one of the large boxes up the crude wooden ladder, he balanced it over his head until it was out of the hiding place on the floor. He then went back down into the room to find an AK-47 and several clips of ammunition. This was all he would need to strike a blow against the Americans and vindicate his name!

He climbed back out of the hiding place and carried the rifle and ammunition clips out to the truck. Throwing them on the passenger's seat, he returned to the building and dragged the box out the door.

Jamil cursed as he wrestled the box into the bed of the truck. "He will know my courage and I will have my honor. That fool *Dabir*. That pig will regret rejecting me!"

He grabbed the tarp and threw it over the box to hide it from view and began to climb back into the truck.

"What are you doing there?" said a voice from the shadows. Jamil cursed and fell back out of the truck, landing on his backside in the dust. "Who is there? Where did you come from?" Jamil demanded.

He stood quickly and wiped the dust from his arms and hands. Once up he turned to see the Teacher's teenage daughter, Lallo, standing at the corner of the storage building. She was clothed from head to foot in the *burqa*, the traditional covering of the women. In his anger and haste he had forgotten about the women and children who had remained behind. Stupidly, he hadn't thought to dampen the sounds of his escape, and he had been found out.

"Go inside, woman! How dare you even speak to me! I will tell your father, and he will beat you to within an inch of your life for your sinful insolence." Jamil's voice betrayed his fear.

"Your name is Jamil," answered the girl, undaunted. "And I know why you are not part of the group. I overheard my father talking with the other instructors. You failed the training, so they left you behind. And now you are trying to steal weapons and a truck. When my father comes home, I will tell him. And it is *you* who will suffer his hand."

"You dare speak to a man so boastfully? You act more like a harlot than a daughter of Islam. And perhaps that is what you really are! I think I shall find out for myself!"

Reaching into the truck and grabbing the crowbar, Jamil started walking toward the young woman. In that one instant his anger toward her father was transferred to her. Sensing danger, she turned to run toward the house, but her foot got tangled in the burqa, and she tumbled to the ground. Before she could get up, Jamil's strong hands grabbed her around the waist, squeezing the air from her chest.

"Remove your filthy hands from me!" she managed to wheeze before nearly passing out for lack of air.

"Shut up, woman!" he growled, placing his hand over her mouth to stifle any screams. He tightened his grip so he could lift her off the ground. He carried her inside the storage building and threw her down into the hiding place. Her head smashed into the side of one of the boxes, and her world went black. She felt the pain in her eyes, but she couldn't see anything.

Jamil started climbing down the ladder. *The Teacher humiliated me before all the others, and now his daughter mocks me in the same way. Well, I'll teach you both a lesson! I will humble you both!* Jamil kicked her side and pulled off her burqa.

* * * * * * * * * *

Jamil climbed from the cellar. The young girl's screams had diminished to a faint whimper, barely audible outside the building. He pulled the ladder from the hole and threw it into the corner. The anger and passion drained from his body, and he instantly felt regret. *What have I done? I've dishonored the daughter of the Teacher. I've brought shame on myself and on my family. I'll be despised, hunted down, tortured, and killed.*

He fell to his knees and pulled hard against the hair of his beard, ripping pieces of skin from his face. Blood flowed onto his arm as he cried to heaven, "Merciful and compassionate Allah, I have done a great dishonor. Please tell me what I can do to correct this injustice. Do not let me be shamed. I have done this evil thing. Oh, have mercy on me!" Jamil dropped his face to the ground and pounded his fists against the dust.

The remorse lasted only moments as a new plan entered his mind, a plan that would blot out the shame and dishonor he had brought on himself. And it could still guarantee his destiny in paradise. But he would need to hurry, before others discovered what he had done.

* * * * * * * * * *

Ibrahim hit a wall of stifling heat exiting the plane onto the jet bridge. The Damascus terminal was modern and open, but the press of people trying to push their way into the line for customs made him choke. Ibrahim's time in the mountains of western Pakistan had instilled in him a passion for solitude. Spending time alone, staring off into the sparkling night sky had provided him time to think, to meditate, to contemplate.

Now those days were past, probably forever. A three-hour Gulf Air flight from Islamabad to Abu Dhabi, followed by a three-hour layover and a three-hour flight from Abu Dhabi to Damascus, had brought him to the heart of this cosmopolitan Syrian metropolis. He had shared the flight with the other fifteen fighters, but he had taken special care not to talk with them, as he had been instructed. This had been more difficult than he had imagined since they had all been assigned seats in the same section of the airplane.

Ibrahim glanced around the room, waiting for his luggage. His eyes widened as he spotted the man holding the "Delegates for Conference on Agriculture" sign. He looked to be in his late thirties, with typical Middle Eastern features—dark wavy hair; dark eyes; and a neatly trimmed moustache. He was dressed in a light suit with a silk tie. He seemed too young to be the one in charge of the operation but too well dressed to be a go-between. *Who are you?* thought Ibrahim. *Well, it does not matter who you are. I will find out shortly, if it is something I even need to know.*

Ibrahim reached down to pick up his suitcase as it rolled by on the conveyor belt. Each man had purchased a black, McKlein twenty-six-inch wheeled duffel bag that served as his suitcase. The bags were made from nylon and were very durable. They were more than adequate to carry the men's few meager belongings, also purchased in Islamabad just prior to the flight. He walked slowly over to introduce himself to the man.

"Hello, I am Ibrahim."

"Welcome to Damascus, friend," he replied. The two shook hands and walked out of the terminal together.

The bus ride from the airport to the villa was comfortable, though a little long. The bus appeared to be one of those normally used to transport foreign tourists. It was air conditioned, and the seats were soft and comfortable. The bus could hold fifty passengers, so the sixteen men— seventeen counting the host—each could spread out over two seats.

Ibrahim stared through the smudged glass, wondering about Suleiman as the bus crawled through the heavy traffic. *Let's hope he can man-*

age to keep quiet. The motion of the bus finally lulled him almost into a trance.

The buildings reminded him of Samarra, his hometown in Iraq. And the vivid memory of events that had happened more than two years ago forced their way into his consciousness as if they had taken place just yesterday. The battered, lifeless bodies of his wife and child. The smell of the gunpowder mixed with the dust of crushed cement. Here, the women and children walking the streets could have been his—had he been born in Syria rather than Iraq.

Was he to blame for his condition? Was it Allah's punishment for his past deeds, an immutable scale of justice that demanded the death of his wife and child to balance out the life he had taken? Perhaps, but had he not killed the officer to save the lives of others? And wouldn't a compassionate God understand this? Convinced of his own innocence, and of Allah's mercy and compassion, Ibrahim couldn't reconcile his personal loss with his understanding of God—like countless others before him stretching back to Job.

His attempt to reconcile the impossible caused his head to ache. He felt as if he was trying to catch the wind as it whistled by. He wasn't even sure if he could adequately explain the problem, let alone try to solve it. Did he believe God was sovereign? Yes, he did. God was sovereign over all. Then could God not have spared his family? Ibrahim paused for a moment to make sure his thoughts were not leading him toward blasphemy. He decided that what he was asking was not improper, so he allowed himself to continue. If God is almighty, then yes, he could have spared his wife and child. But if God could have spared them, why did he allow them to die?! If he is both great and good, then wouldn't he want to spare Ibrahim's family?

Either Allah must have brought this calamity to punish me, or else He permitted the evil to accomplish a greater good. Even though he nursed nagging feelings of guilt about his killing of an Iraqi officer, Ibrahim could not bring himself to admit guilt or to accept the death of his wife and child as punishment for his actions. No, there had to be a better explanation. What could it be?

Over the past two years, the Teacher had planted a thought in Ibrahim's mind that now shined with the brightness of an Iraqi sunrise. It had to be related to Islam's struggles with the Jews and Christians! God wasn't responsible for the death of his family; it was the Christians who destroyed his apartment building and killed them. Allah must have permitted it as part of his divine will. This was now his destiny—to fight for Allah, to carry out his divine will.

"Ibrahim! We are here!" The voice startled him. He looked up to see a nicely dressed man standing over him with his hand nudging Ibrahim's shoulder. The man's hand was large, covered in gold rings, one on each finger except for his thumb.

The bus had stopped in front of a large villa, and all the other fighters were already walking toward the front door.

"You have had a long journey, my friend. Please come into my house and share a meal with me. We have much to discuss."

* * * * * * * * * *

"Friends and fellow fighters for Islam, welcome to my home!" The man who had been their host since meeting them at the airport bowed slightly, his arm sweeping toward the right, as he both welcomed his guests and directed them toward the lavish dining room. "I am sorry that I could not properly greet you at the airport. I am General Ahmed Habib, but who I am and what I do is not important. However, what you are about to do is most important, and I am grateful to Allah for the small part he is allowing me to play in this glorious plan. Now come in, and we will talk over dinner."

The men entered the dining room as an older, almost matronly servant placed the last tray of rice on the table. Seeing the men coming into the dining room, she bowed and scurried toward the kitchen door. The men scarcely noticed her as they focused on the host and on the feast spread out before them.

"Take your seats and fill your plates! This is a time of feasting and celebration in preparation for what will, *inch' Allah*, be a great victory for Islam—and a great blow to America and its Zionist-controlled masters. Come, we have hummus, tehinah, tabbouleh, and other fresh salads, freshly baked pita, mushroom soup, lamb and rice, grilled chicken, kabobs, along with kenafeh and watermelon for dessert!"

As the men sat and ate, General Habib shared with them additional information they would need for their journey. Again the servant woman entered the room unnoticed, placing plates of more grapes, fresh olives, and sugar cookies around the room, as the proud general excitedly went about delivering the information these men needed for the next leg of the trip.

"The next phase of your journey will take you from Damascus to Mexico City. You will be traveling on South African passports. Don't worry; they are completely valid. A 'friend' in the South African embassy arranged for their purchase. From Mexico City you will travel to Matamoras on the American border, where you will cross into Brownsville, Texas. The man who will meet your flight in Mexico City will explain the details for the last part of your journey at that time. My role has been to secure passports and transportation as far as Mexico City. I do not concern myself with how that part of the operation will unfold. But I can assure you that the part I'm in charge of will work without failure.

"Tomorrow we will take your photographs and complete your passports. You will need to shave off your beards tonight before you sleep. You are permitted to have a moustache as long as it is short and neatly trimmed. You will find a toiletries kit on your bed that contains shaving cream and a razor. Leave the razor here, but put everything else back in the kit to take with you on your trip. *Inch' Allah*, within the next three or four days you should arrive in the United States."

Nevi, the house servant, continued to shuffle unnoticed between the kitchen and the dining room, hiding her astonishment and fear behind a mask of indifference. "Lord," she prayed, "give me the strength to make it through tonight. Keep me safe from harm, precious Lord. And give me the ability to remember everything I'm hearing." Nevi also wondered how long it would take to make contact with Mossad.

The plan had unfolded more quickly than she had anticipated.

CHAPTER 8

THE ALLIANCE

The gentle *thump* followed by a jolting reverse thrust told Moshe the plane had touched down. Finally. But the trip, he thought, had not been all that strenuous. The flight left Tel Aviv just after midnight Sunday evening. The longest leg—nearly twelve hours—was from Israel to Newark, New Jersey. But leaving at night and flying west kept the airplane in darkness almost all the way across the Atlantic. Moshe had slept for over half the trip.

The passengers filed like cattle through American customs in Newark. Most disembarked there, but the rest reboarded the plane bound for the final destination, Chicago. During the flight to Chicago, Moshe started feeling restless. Part of his struggle was physical. He had been sitting far too long. But part was emotional. He was being sent to Chicago to share important—but incomplete—information with a special task force on terrorism. The news he had was not good, but that wasn't what made him feel ill at ease. Rather, it was the fact that the information wasn't all that helpful.

"We have received a report that a terrorist group is planning an attack in the United States. But we don't know where, how, or by whom. And we can't compromise our sources by even sharing how we obtained the information," the emotionless director giving him the assignment had said.

The terse nature of the report gave Moshe an uneasy feeling about the trip.

Such limited information could have easily been delivered via a phone call. But the head of Mossad believed it was very important that the agency take the time to have the agent who gathered the information share it directly with the Americans. Could this be his country's attempt to go the extra mile after a spate of recent news reports had suggested there might be growing friction between Israel's prime minister and America's new president? Moshe didn't know. But he felt responsible to share whatever scraps of information he had gathered that could help prevent a terrorist attack. He knew all too well the wreckage left by terrorists. The thought brought a faint memory of Esther, lying in his arms.

"Selicha, mah shimcha?" The flight attendant's question startled Moshe. He looked up to see her standing beside him, holding what appeared to be a computer printout.

"I'm Moshe Zachar," he responded back in English.

"Mr. Zachar, could I see your passport, please?" she asked. He leaned forward and grabbed for the travel-worn satchel he had slipped under the seat in front of him. He pulled out his passport and handed it to the flight attendant. She scanned it slowly, pausing several times and alternating her gaze between Moshe's face and the passport.

"Thank you, Mr. Zachar. I was instructed to check your passport before handing you this message. I appreciate your patience."

"Thank you." He smiled and nodded as he reached for the piece of paper. Moshe unfolded the paper to read the message.

TO: MOSHE ZACHAR

        EL AL FLIGHT 027

        SEAT 27C

FROM: SPECIAL AGENT JILLIAN FOSTER

PLEASE WATCH FOR MAN AT THE TOP OF THE JET BRIDGE HOLDING A SIGN WITH YOUR NAME. SHOW HIM YOUR PASSPORT, AND HE WILL EXPEDITE YOU THROUGH BAGGAGE CLAIM. WE HAVE ARRANGED TRANSPORT FOR YOU TO OUR OFFICES IN DOWNTOWN CHICAGO. SEE YOU ABOUT 11.

* * * * * * * * * *

Jillian arrived at the office feeling wired from "breakfast," the double espresso she had gulped down on the way in the building. Her mind had churned all night like a Texas hurricane brewing off Galveston.

For some strange reason, Jillian remembered her fascination with such a storm when she was a young girl. Their family had gone on vacation to Galveston, but they had to cut short their time because of an approaching tropical storm. As her mom prepared breakfast on the morning they were to leave, her father had taken her by the hand, and they both walked down to the beach for one last look at the water. The sun was just beginning to rise to the east as dark clouds gathered against the horizon. A strong wind had replaced the gentle breeze of the night before.

As they walked along the shore, they watched the waves pushing ever higher onto the beach, retreating only to launch another attack— the crashing roar, the taste of the salt spray picked up and driven on by the wind, the whitecaps dancing in their wild madness. She wanted so much to run into the waves one last time, but her father cautioned her about playing in the surf during an approaching storm. "The waves might look beautiful at a distance, but the undertow will pull you out to sea. I remember my dad telling me this kind of sea is like the Devil. He offers something that looks wild, exciting, fun, but in the end he brings only death and destruction." At the time it was a strange comment from her father—talking of storms and devils, but today the connection between the two had the ring of truth.

So why had she not been able to sleep? It had to be today's meeting. Weeks of meetings, interviews, and leads had gone nowhere. Then two calls out of the blue had propelled her task force into high gear. The first had been Greg Hanson's about mysterious messages embedded in online pictures. Greg, serving as a consultant to her committee, would be at today's meeting. The second call had come from FBI headquarters. Israel's Mossad had stumbled across a planned terrorist plot against the United States. One of their agents was flying to Chicago to meet with Jillian and the team and share information that Mossad judged too sensitive to send through other channels.

Jillian knew that the primary reason she hadn't slept well last night was the sense of anticipation she felt about today's meeting. Though fairly routine at this stage of the process, it all felt like a brewing storm. Knowing Mossad's reputation, she certainly hoped the purpose for sending the agent was to share the identities of those behind the threatened attack.

That was the official reason she was wired for today's meeting, but she had to admit to herself that there was another reason she felt so excited. And it was probably the same reason she had also taken time to press her suit, shine her shoes, and take just a little longer putting on her makeup. As she thought about it, she actually felt herself blushing.

Jillian had been so focused on her career that dating had always taken a backseat. It had never been a priority, and she really didn't regret her decision. That is, until she met Greg Hanson. She really didn't know what it was about Greg that she found so attractive, but she found herself drawn to him. He was cute, but not Brad Pitt handsome. He was smart, but so were many others. No, the thing that seemed to set him apart from everyone else was the fact that he just seemed so at peace with himself.

Greg hadn't tried to impress her in that first meeting. He just seemed to be himself. And she found that refreshingly attractive.

But today is not the day to get rainbows in your eyes. Concentrate on the task at hand! Jillian finished arranging the chairs in the conference room and took a final look around. Everything was ready for the meeting—and with thirty minutes to spare.

As she emerged into the reception area, Special Agent Walter Duffy walked through the main doors with a dark-haired stranger in tow. Walter was carrying a garment bag while the stranger held a small suitcase in one hand and a briefcase in the other.

"This must be our friend from Israel," Jillian said.

Walter set the garment bag on a nearby chair and said, "Jillian, I would like you to meet Mr. Moshe Zachar. Mr. Zachar, this is Special Agent Jillian Foster." Jillian and Moshe shook hands, and Jillian noticed the growth of stubble on his face. He looked weary. "Mr. Zachar, our meeting is scheduled to begin in thirty minutes. I know you spent a good part of the last day on a plane. Would you like to freshen up and change before we begin?"

"I would like that very much, thank you," Moshe answered.

"Great! We have a small supply of washcloths and towels here for just such occasions, and the men's room is just down the hall. Can I also get you a cup of coffee or something to eat?"

"No, thank you; I'm not really hungry. Some cool water on my face will do just fine."

"Excellent! As I said, the meeting will begin right here in about thirty minutes." She pointed toward the open conference room door.

* * * * * * * * * *

After all the pleasantries and introductions, Jillian took her place at the head of the table. "Let's get started," she spoke over the conversations. "Mr. Zachar, on behalf of the FBI Task Force on Domestic Terrorism, it is my pleasure to welcome you to the United States. I've been told that you have a matter of some importance to share with us, and we are very anxious to hear what you have to say. Please begin."

Moshe cleared his throat as he walked to the front of the table. He turned to face the other people in the room and said, "As the old saying goes, 'I've got good news and I've got bad news.' Unfortunately, most of the news I have is bad."

Moshe had spent some time on the flight from Newark to Chicago trying to decide how best to deliver the message. Looking at the faces around the table staring at him, he decided the best approach was to be bold and direct. "Mossad has a highly placed contact in Damascus. I have met with him personally, and I can vouch for his access to people in high places and for his truthfulness."

He smiled, hoping to put the others and himself at ease. The fact that the contact, Nevi, was a woman had to remain one of Mossad's closely guarded secrets. He could share information from Nevi with the Americans, but he had to do everything possible to guard Nevi's identity. He knew the Americans would do the same.

"Can you tell us any more about this contact? Is he a government official? Is he a member of the Baath Party? Is he in the military?" The question had come from a deputy agent eager to get at the details, and who appeared to Moshe, based on his body language, somewhat suspect of his motives.

"Alas, my friends, I cannot share that degree of detail; I'm sorry. All I can say is that my government has come to rely on the information supplied by this individual, and that the information we have recently received is important enough for me to fly here to be with you."

Jillian understood why Moshe's words were guarded. Such compartmentalization made perfect sense. The larger the circle of individuals who knew a person's identity, the more likely it was for the information to leak out. Secrets were best kept when they were known only to a few.

"Moshe, I speak for us all when I say that we understand your need to protect the identity of your source. For the record, let's acknowledge that the source's identify is off limits to inquiry. What information can you share with us?"

He turned slightly to face her directly. "Our source has discovered that a new Islamic fundamentalist group in Pakistan has trained as many as eight or nine teams of terrorists to enter the United States. We don't know exactly when, but it sounds as if they could be entering your country at any time. Both the terrorists and their weapons will be traveling through Syria. We believe they have been trained to target commercial aircraft. Unfortunately, our source did not have any other specific information, though he is trying to find out more details. You know how difficult it is to inquire about such specifics without drawing unnecessary attention to yourself."

Several hands shot up at once around the table. "You said there are as many as eight or nine teams, but how many people are on each team?" "Do these individuals have Pakistani passports, or are they a mixture of foreign nationals?" "Are they planning to hijack airplanes, like September 11, or is this a different kind of attack?" "Do you think the terrorists are already here in the United States, or are they still overseas?" "Do we have even a general idea of where—or when—they are planning to attack?"

Moshe closed his eyes and shook his head as the different individuals around the table asked their questions. "Those are all good questions, and I wish I had good answers. But the truth is that we don't have answers to *any* of them. We are working with our contacts to see if we can find answers. And if we do, I assure you that the information will be shared immediately with your government. But the bottom line right now is that there is a specific terrorist threat being planned against the United States. We don't know the specific target or targets, and we don't know if the terrorists are yet in the country. But we do know that something big is being planned."

Jillian stood and faced him. "Thank you, Mr. Zachar, for sharing this with us. And please extend our deepest thanks to Mossad. Okay, people, we have credible, though not specific, information about a potential terrorist attack. What other information do we have, and what are our options? Greg, do you want to share with everyone what you discovered? By the way, Greg is a professor at a local school who is serving as a temporary consultant to the FBI for this specific task force."

Greg Hanson opened the lid of his portable computer and slid it to the end of the table. He then stood up and walked over to it. "I'm sorry the screen is so small, but the information I'm about to share is significant. I believe I have stumbled on a system developed by a possible Islamic group for disseminating information to its various cells throughout the world. Simply put, the data is hidden in plain sight inside a picture's EXIF file. Relatively few know these files exist. Even fewer bother to check them. The fact that the test file was done using one of Islam's holiest sites could indicate that the group using this system is motivated by Islamic fundamentalism."

He walked the group through the first message he had uncovered.

"I think this first message might have been intended as a test. Whoever sent it wanted to make sure the system would indeed work as planned. I've been watching the site since that time, and I've not discovered any additional messages. In fact, the initial picture has since been removed from the Web site. That would tell me that the intended recipients saw the information and sent some type of confirming message acknowledging that to the source. Once the source had heard from everyone, he—or she—pulled the picture off the Internet, further lessening the possibility that someone might stumble onto the information."

Greg quickly scanned the room to gauge the initial reaction. There was a strange silence that made him uncomfortable. After all, why in the world would a group of trained intelligence and law enforcement agents give any real credence to a college professor with a weird fascination for digital images?

One agent raised a crucial question. "If this is what you believe it to be, how do we know the group will keep using this site or that they won't change locations?"

"Truthfully, we have no way of knowing if they will continue to use the same site or if they will switch to an alternative site. Agent Foster has asked me to continue to monitor this site, and I think there might be some people searching for others, but I can't speak to that."

"NSA has it too," Jillian said. "They've initiated a special trace to try to locate specifically any additional cryptic messages or postings. That base is covered for now."

"Any evidence that we're talking about the same group Mossad has intercepted?" asked another agent.

She stood up to answer. "I'll take that one. Right now we don't know of any connection. At the same time, we don't know of anything that would eliminate such a connection. It's best simply not to make *any* assumptions. Follow the facts and let them lead you to conclusions."

Moshe's pager vibrated once, signaling a text message had arrived. He reached down to unclip it from his belt. CALL OFFICE IMMEDIATELY, URGENT blinked twice on the display.

"Excuse me, Jillian, but can I make a phone call?" Moshe asked in a muted voice, motioning toward the hallway.

"Sure, Moshe. Do you want us to take a break until you come back, or should we continue?"

"Why don't you keep going? This should only take a few minutes. Is there a secure room where I can make a call?"

She pointed down the hall toward her office. "Use my office. It's the second door on your right. We have it swept for listening devices on a regular basis. You can use my phone if you want."

"Thanks, but I'll use my cell phone. I really just need a quiet place to talk. But thanks for the offer!" Moshe was kind, but firm, in his refusal of Jillian's offer to use her telephone. It might not be tapped by outsiders, but that didn't guarantee that his conversation wouldn't be monitored.

He closed the door to Jillian's office and dialed the local number to a Jewish import/export business. After a few clicks—which guaranteed that this local call made it all the way to the preferred destination in Jerusalem—he heard the familiar ring of an Israeli phone.

"Shipping and receiving. How may I help you?" said the voice on the other line.

"I'm calling for Mr. Herbert Greenfeldt. Is he available today?" asked Moshe, using the fictitious name assigned for when he had to make unsecured calls.

"One moment, please." A minute later the voice on the other end responded. "Mr. Greenfeldt will be available in just a few minutes. Please hold."

Moshe listened to the Israeli version of elevator music for nearly a minute before it was replaced by a human voice. "Moshe Zachar, where are you and what are you doing?"

"Good evening"—as Moshe mentally added the eight-hour time difference between Chicago and Israel—"I'm calling for Mr. Greenfeldt. Is he in?"

"This is he. What can I do for you?"

Moshe breathed just a little easier. "I'm calling because I just received a pager message telling me to do so. Is there a message for me?"

"Yes, you are instructed to fly to London as soon as possible. You will receive additional instructions on arrival. How soon can you be going?"

"I don't know. I can leave here immediately, but I'm not sure when the next flight to London will take off."

"We've already checked on that. There's an American Airlines flight to London that leaves at 5:10 from O'Hare. We've already made reservations for you on that flight. Someone will meet you in baggage claim at Heathrow."

"One last question. Is there anything I need to do to prepare for the meeting?"

"Well, there is just one thing. Try to get some sleep on the journey because you will have some additional traveling once you reach London. You have been summoned by 'the Prophet' for an important meeting."

The prophet—Nevi! So my journey will end in Damascus, not London. But what is so important that I must cut short this meeting less than an hour after it began?

Moshe returned to the meeting and apologized for the sudden interruption, and explained his need to leave immediately. Jillian spoke for the group. "That's okay, Moshe. We've all had emergencies come up. And we realize you can't share the nature of this emergency with us. We look forward to working with you in the coming days. And, remember, you always have a home with the FBI in Chicago!"

"Thank you, my friends! I'm not sure what the future holds, but I feel certain that I will be back again . . . perhaps very soon!"

The group stood to shake Moshe's hand, and most followed him out into the hall to head back to their offices. Greg shut down his portable computer and started to disconnect the power cord and other cables when an almost imperceptible shadow caused him to look up. There was Jillian standing in the doorway, silhouetted against the light from the hallway. He smiled and stopped his work.

"Jillian, thanks for letting me be at the meeting. How'd I do?"

"You did well. I had hoped the meeting would go longer and that we would be receiving more information from the Israelis, but all in all I think it was very profitable."

"Can I ask you one question?"

"Sure; what is it?"

"During the meeting, someone asked if there was any connection between the information we've uncovered and the terrorist plot presented by Moshe. Your response was very equivocal—you said there was no evidence either way. But what does your gut tell you? If you had to make a guess, do you think they might be connected?"

"I do think that's a good possibility. But I framed my answer the way I did because we can't afford to become so focused on one possible lead that we ignore others."

Greg smiled. "So Solomon was right. 'It is good to grasp the one and not let go of the other'!"

Jillian looked quizzical. "You just lost me!"

"Oh, sorry. It's from Ecclesiastes in the Bible. Solomon made the same observation you just made. There are times when the wisest course of action is to keep two items in tension—to hold on to one without letting go of the other."

Jillian stared thoughtfully at him. *What a strange, charming fellow, this Dr. Greg Hanson.* She decided not to respond, but smiled and turned toward the door. Then she paused and turned back to face him.

"I have a few questions I really need to ask you, but this is not the right time or place. Is there any chance we could get together for dinner some evening?" As soon as she asked, she felt her face growing warm.

"How about tonight? I've got some grading to do this afternoon, but I could be free any time after five," he answered, hoping not to sound too eager.

"Tonight would be great! Let's meet at seven at the Grand Lux Cafe on Ontario off of Michigan. You know the place?"

"Sure. I'll see you there at seven."

Jillian turned and walked out the door as Greg resumed packing up his computer. *I wonder what's on her mind. Don't overanalyze this, Hanson!* he warned himself. *You'll know soon enough.*

CHAPTER 9

THE EMERGENCY VISIT

Moshe's unexpected flight to London was short and fitful—punctuated by an all-too-real nightmare in which an airplane was falling from the sky. Moshe sat in the pilot's seat desperately pulling back on the yoke, trying to ease the plane out of a steep dive. The plane shook violently, and the roar of the groaning engines was deafening. Next to him sat a dark-haired woman in an oversized waiter's jacket, pushing against the yoke with all her might. The cockpit door flew open, and Moshe looked back to see Esther, terrified and screaming in the first row. Her eyes widened and she recoiled in shock and horror, her hand stretching forward as if pointing at something beyond Moshe. He turned in the direction she was pointing and saw the ground rushing toward the plane even as he tried helplessly to wrestle control from the female terrorist. He awakened with a gasp, trying to tear away the remnants of the nightmare.

"Are you all right, sir?" asked the flight attendant standing beside his seat. Moshe must have cried out in his sleep.

"Yes, I'm okay," he answered, half-embarrassed. "I guess I was just having a bad dream. Would it be possible to get a cup of coffee?" he asked. He felt a migraine coming on.

* * * * * * * * * *

Greg joined the crowd pushing its way through the revolving door into the lobby of the Grand Lux Cafe on Chicago's sparkling Michigan Avenue. He had arrived five minutes early. He caught the express bus from Hyde Park that dropped him off at the corner of Ohio and Michigan at 6:45 p.m. The walk down Michigan Avenue—the Magnificent Mile— to the restaurant only took ten minutes and reminded him again that he lived in a rich man's city. *No wonder these extremists hate us so,* he thought. *They see our gluttony and despise our freedom.*

As he got in line to place his name on the call list he heard someone shout, "Greg! Greg Hanson! Over here!" He turned to see Jillian standing by the escalators, waving her arms and smiling. "We're already on the list! I took care of it!" He waved at her and then snaked his way through the crowd to get to her.

"Sorry I'm late," he said, feeling sheepish for making her wait.

"You're not late. I just got here five minutes ago myself. But I pulled rank and called ahead to let them know we were coming," she said, immediately regretting the pretense.

He looked dumbfounded. "I called too, and they told me they didn't accept reservations."

Jillian smiled. "They don't," she said, taking his arm and moving him across the lobby to a less crowded corner. "But Chicago is a town that has always been friendly to those carrying a badge."

"Foster, party of two, please proceed to the escalators where someone will meet you and direct you to your table." A tall, well-dressed hostess had appeared from around a corner and announced that their table was ready.

* * * * * * * * * *

After taking their order the waitperson slipped away to get their drinks and a basket of bread. Greg's mind was whirling. Here he was sitting with a woman who was the link to discovering the key to opening this mysterious world he had entered without knowing it. He knew little about her, but he felt oddly safe in her presence. He liked the feeling but tried not to make too much of it in his mind.

Jilian, too, was feeling relaxed. So much so that she decided to broach something that had been bothering her. "Greg, I have to bring this up. You're a very intelligent, knowledgeable man. Obviously you've done well, and you have a wide breadth of experience in everything from computers to teaching to obscure Bible quotations."

Greg blushed slightly. "Thanks—I think!"

"No, I'm being serious. You seem, well, normal. And yet you are a Christian who sincerely believes the Bible—and all that . . . well, stuff about Jesus, right?" She took a deep breath as she pulled her thoughts together. She hoped she wasn't embarrassing him. "I don't want to offend you, but I really struggle with religion—especially religion that motivates blind obedience, even to the point of violent behavior and extremist views. How can you believe so deeply and still be so intelligent?"

He broke into a broad grin. "So your purpose in asking me to dinner wasn't to thank me on behalf of the FBI for volunteering to help save our nation, or to spend a quiet evening with a quirky Bible professor from Hyde Park! You want to know how anyone with any degree of intelligence can believe the Bible. And for this I put on a clean shirt!"

Jillian smiled. "Look, I grew up in what I would call a Christian family, but a few years ago my mom had some kind of religious experience that, frankly, scares me. She's really gone off the deep end. She's almost fanatical, really. I don't question her sincerity. And it's not like she's shaved her head, or signed over her life savings to some kook preacher, or anything like that. But she's changed—she's different, somehow more serene and contemplative. She prays daily, she's constantly reading the Bible, and she goes to church every week. You seem to believe a lot like she does, and yet you seem to be so normal. I guess I'm just looking for some type of assurance that my mom hasn't jumped into the deep end of the pool, religiously speaking."

Greg thought for a moment, and as he did so his expression turned more serious. "Jillian, I respect and admire you very much, and I would never want to respond in a way that doesn't take your concerns seriously. It sounds like your mother's experience is very real. I don't think you need to fear what she's embraced. Sounds like she's found Jesus—and He's made her life worth living again."

She appreciated his openness and sincerity. For some reason, she trusted him. And for the first time she tried to put into words the real issues that bothered her about her mom's faith. "I guess I have two—no, actually three—major struggles. First, I have trouble believing the Bible the way you do. To me it seems like an incomprehensible book, a mixture of profound thoughts, antiquated beliefs, errors, even contradictions. And how can it be the only way to God when other religions make the same claim? It just doesn't make sense to me, I guess."

"Actually, that's a very good question!" Greg said. "If what we know about God comes from the Bible, then the reliability of the Bible is a foundational issue. So let me ask you a question. Have you ever read through the Bible for yourself, or is your statement about the Bible containing errors only secondhand information?"

"Okay, I admit that I've not read the Bible myself—at least not most of it. My mom gave me a Bible, but it's just sitting on my shelf. I remember as a kid struggling with all the *thee*'s and *thou*'s. I don't think I could read through it and understand it."

"Jillian, do me a favor and whack me on the head if I start sounding like a teacher lecturing a student. But I'm sure you realize that the Bible wasn't written in Elizabethan English. There are at least a half dozen excellent modern translations of the Bible that went back to the original languages and then translated the text into modern-day English. Do you know what Bible translation you mom gave you?"

"I don't. It's big . . . and black. That's about all I know."

"Well, do me a favor. When you get home, look and see. If it is the old King James Version, let me know and I'll personally buy you one of the new versions. But if it is some other translation, read part of it and see if it's more understandable than you remember from your childhood."

"That's a fair request. I'll do it. But even if it's easier to read, how do you explain away the errors and contradictions. What do the new translations do with these?"

"You might find this hard to believe, but I'm convinced the Bible doesn't contain errors and contradictions. I have yet to discover an absolute, verifiable error in the Bible. Some things people have called errors are mistakes that crept into the Bible as it was copied from generation to generation." He went on to share examples he used with his students.

Jillian, watching him, noticed how animated he became when speaking of long-gone historical figures like King David. *This is so real to him,* she thought. She didn't quite understand everything he was saying, but she did sense his love for the topic at hand.

Still, she had questions: "But since some errors crept in, how can we be sure that the majority of the Bible we have today is still accurate?"

"That's a good question—and one that until about sixty years ago had no definitive answer, at least as far as the Hebrew Bible is concerned. But then some manuscripts were discovered in the Judean wilderness by the Dead Sea. Do you know much about the Dead Sea Scrolls?"

Jillian shook her head. "I know the name, and I know they are old manuscripts. But that's about all."

"The Dead Sea Scrolls are important for many reasons, and their discovery is rather miraculous. But they are vital for the topic we're discussing because they give us copies of the Bible that were about a thousand years older than the most ancient copies then available. In other words, we had the rare opportunity to get into a time machine and go back to around the time of Jesus to check on the accuracy of the biblical text. And what did we learn? We discovered that the text we have been using is very accurate. The Jewish people had done a remarkable job of preserving the biblical text."

The server arrived with the drinks and bread, so Greg and Jillian broke off their animated discussion. They ordered their entrées, and the server left. Greg started to butter a section of sourdough bread but paused and looked at Jillian. "You said you had three concerns about Christianity, but we've only discussed one. Do you want to talk about the other two?"

"The second problem I have is with all the hypocrisy in the church. I've read too many reports on so-called Christian leaders who have been involved in everything from theft and fraud to adultery and child molestation. Believe me; I'm no saint! But I think I'm a better person than some of these charlatans who claim they have the inside track to God but end up living like devils. Sometimes you're your own worst enemy, don't you agree?"

"Honestly, yes," Greg said. "The truth is that some of these people who do these things might very well be otherwise sincere Christians. Christians are just as capable of doing evil as anyone else. They're not perfect. Even Peter, one of Jesus' original followers, went through a period when he failed to be a consistent follower of Christ. Christians do blow it on occasion. And you know, hypocrisy isn't just limited to Christianity. What about that FBI agent who was selling secrets to the Russians?"

"His name was Robert Hanssen, and his treachery cost the lives of two American agents in Russia," she said. "It happened a few years before I came on board with the FBI. But I know his actions shook the agency to its core because he had served for twenty-five years in counterintelligence. And I also believe blowback from his actions was a distraction to the FBI just seven months before the attack on September 11. I can't help but feel that the turmoil following his exposure was at least partially responsible for the FBI's failure to focus on domestic terrorism. And for that he shares at least some of the blame for my brother's death at the World Trade Center."

"I'm so sorry about your brother," Greg said, reaching to touch her hand, then withdrawing it a second later. "But my point is that no one can condemn all the FBI just because of the evil actions of one agent. Nor can someone condemn an entire police force because of the actions of a few bad cops. Every profession that is based on trust—medicine, the legal profession, law enforcement, finance, and ministry—are harmed when a few bad apples brazenly abuse the trust granted to them by others. But don't throw out the baby with the bathwater."

"Okay, point well taken. And here comes our meal. Let's push pause on the discussion and focus instead on enjoying our food. No more God-talk till after dinner! So, Greg, tell me about you."

* * * * * * * * * *

The rest of the dinner was delightful. The restaurant had given Jillian and Greg a booth next to the large glass windows fronting Michigan Avenue, still bustling with Chicago shoppers and late commuters heading home for the night. The entire street was ablaze with lights. From where he was seated, Greg could look north all the way to the Hancock Center with its signature pattern of lights forming a series of X's on its dark black exterior.

Jillian surprised him when she asked the waiter for the check. "Hey, wait, I'm supposed to get that," Greg protested.

"Since when?" replied Jillian. "I invited you, and I made the reservation. In fact, I'm planning on having us walk down Michigan Avenue to

Starbucks. After all, I still have one more question!"

Greg found it difficult to find any fault with the evening. In fact, he had discovered that he and Jillian shared much in common. They were both from small families. Their fathers had both been veterans. And Greg and Jillian were both baseball fans.

As they rode the escalator back down to the entrance, he was surprised to see that the crowd had grown even larger. They threaded their way through the mass of people and out onto the street. A few minutes later they were at the Starbucks. After ordering their coffee, they found a small table in the corner of the seating area and settled in.

He took a sip and then looked at Jillian. "This has been a great evening so far, but I think you said you still have one other concern about Christianity. What is it?"

Jillian stirred her coffee. She ran her index finger around the top of the lid and stared off to the side, as if searching for the words to her question in one of the pictures hanging on the wall. "I'm not even sure I can express this clearly. I guess I would say that I have trouble with a God who causes such horrible suffering. I heard someone say it this way once. If He is a great God who can control everything, then He can't be very good because He allows so much pain. I can't believe in a God, certainly not a good, loving God, who would let my brother die so horribly in a senseless attack. *My brother* was good and loving. Why did he have to die?"

Greg saw that she was close to tears. He also knew that she would not stand for a simplistic answer. "If I could, I would offer you some profound explanation that would ease *your* suffering and make sense of it all," he said quietly. "But . . . I can't." *Lord, help me answer Jillian in a way that honors You and will help her see You, not me.*

"I know, and I understand. I guess it's a question with no answer."

"Well, the best answer we have is found in the Bible." He proceeded to tell Jilliam—who, he noticed, was listening attentively—about the righteous man Job and the ancient battle between good and evil. While he felt himself on sure ground with Scripture, he also sensed her pain and wanted to respond with compassion and not a lecture.

"To sum up, here is what I think the book of Job is saying that helps me put the problem of suffering in a larger perspective. First, there are times when human suffering is caused by a cosmic conflict that extends beyond our normal universe. Second, God is not the source of evil. He is not a cosmic sadist. Rather, evil comes from the Evil One, who opposes God and His plans. Third, even though God may permit suffering for reasons that are beyond our ability to comprehend, He is still in sovereign control. He imposed limits beyond which the Evil One could not go. Fourth, God does not always owe us an explanation. When He finally confronted Job at the end of the book, it was to help Job realize that he didn't understand how the universe really works. Since we don't fully understand, we must learn to trust in a God who does."

"I'm not sure if I can accept that explanation, but I appreciate your honesty," said Jillian. "If I hear you correctly, you are saying that God is both great and good. And yet for some reason not completely known to us, He has allowed evil to exist in this world. We don't fully know why, but we are to accept the fact that God does." Jillian's ability to quickly analyze and summarize information would serve her well here.

Greg knew she was starting to wrestle with God's nature. "Yes, that's a fair explanation. The only other part I would add is that God makes it absolutely clear that there will come a day when He will right all wrongs, judge all evil, and reward those who have chosen to trust Him. That is the time when He will demonstrate—for all eternity—that He is indeed both great and good. You see, the fact that reality extends beyond this current life into eternity is God's ultimate trump card. The final chapter has not yet been written. But someday it will be."

Jillian stared deeply into Greg's eyes, to the point where he began feeling uncomfortable. But instead of breaking eye contact he stared back, trying somehow to beam his concern and compassion directly into her soul—hoping she could understand how much he believed the truth he had been sharing. And praying that this truth could become part of her very life. Finally, she blinked and looked away.

"Greg, thanks for a truly thought-provoking evening. You have given me much to think about. I can't say that I accept all you've said, but I will think about it. And maybe someday we can continue this conversation."

After they parted, she paused at the corner, searching for a cab and feeling a yearning in her soul. *Can what he said be true? I just don't know, but it does seem to make sense. Oh, God, if You do even exist, please reveal Yourself to me and show me what to believe.*

* * * * * * * * * *

RAWALPINDI, PAKISTAN Over the first few hours, Jamil gained sufficient experience driving the truck to be able to start, stop, and change gears without stalling the engine or causing the truck to lurch. But he still had trouble judging distances and keeping the truck on the road. Several times he had drifted off the worn dirt road into the ditch. But each time he had forced the steering wheel to the right and pulled the truck back from the edge.

At first he was afraid he would encounter the Teacher or the other mujahideen. What if something went wrong and he came across them parked alongside the road? What if they forgot some equipment and had turned around to retrieve it? What if someone discovered the Teacher's daughter and contacted them?

But as the hours drifted by, Jamil's fear of encountering the Teacher was replaced by a fear of the unknown. He had never driven before, let alone traveled by himself to Islamabad. He really didn't know the route to the capital, and every unmarked fork in the road was another opportunity to make a wrong turn. He had thought to load several tins of petrol in the truck bed, and the gas gauge said the tank was still half full. But he had no money to buy additional fuel, nor did he have any money for food or lodging. In reality, he had *no* plan apart from a burning desire to inflict harm on America—and in so doing to atone for the great shame he had brought on himself. He knew this was a one-way journey, and he only hoped it would lead to martyrdom rather than to another tragic failure.

As he drove along, he developed a simple, though sound, process for choosing which roadway to take. He knew Islamabad lay to the east, so anytime he had a choice he'd choose a road leading toward the sunrise. If two roads led in the same direction, he chose the one that was larger, or that seemed to have more traffic. And these choices eventually brought him to the southern edges of Islamabad, near Rawalpindi.

Unfortunately, the roads near the capital were also crowded with more cars, trucks, and lorries. And there were far more exits from which to choose. But Jamil was having so much difficulty just driving in the increased traffic that he couldn't even think about choosing a different road. Gripping the steering wheel as one might hold on to a lifeline, he found himself staring intently at the cars and trucks directly in front of him. He kept drifting into the opposite lanes of traffic only to be forced back by the blaring horn of an oncoming car. He would quickly pull the steering wheel to the left, only to hear the car or truck on that side honk its horn as he crossed the line into its lane.

"Merciful Allah, please help me!" Jamil cried. "Get me off of this highway, and show me where you want me to use the weapon you have supplied."

Almost as if in answer to his prayer, he looked above the truck he was now following and saw an airplane gliding over the highway on final approach to the Islamabad International Airport. "Thank you, most merciful one!" he shouted as he gauged the distance to where the plane had passed over the highway. When he reached the spot, he took the first exit and found himself in an area dominated by factories and warehouses.

I need a place where I can see the airplanes taking off and landing—a place with good visibility but where I will not draw attention to myself. Then he spotted a large open field. It appeared to be some sort of park with four football fields. The end of each field was marked off by a set of portable goals, the metal tubing looking forlorn with no netting attached. The fields were empty, probably because it was a school day. In reality, the school day had ended several hours earlier, but the children had stayed for a special program.

The truck screeched to a halt, sputtered, then went silent. Jamil turned off the ignition and looked around. For nearly a minute he sat, scarcely breathing, waiting to see if anything would happen. A few cars and trucks drove by, but otherwise the park was deserted. He stepped from the truck and pulled the tarp off the box inside the truck bed. Then he gently unfastened the straps and pulled the box over the side of the truck. Setting it on the ground—on the side of the truck bordering the playing field—he carefully opened the lid and stared at the rocket launcher. It looked beautiful, and deadly—and he prayed that he would remember all his instructions.

Five minutes later Jamil stood ready. All he needed now was an approaching plane. He had been taught to fire at aircraft during takeoff, but that had never seemed important. *Any airplane a thousand meters off the ground with fuel in its wings is a good target. It will crash, and everyone on board will die. Who cares whether it is taking off or landing?*

He didn't want to appear too suspicious, so he set the launcher on top of the box and covered it with the tarp. *It will be easy enough to retrieve when the time comes.* He lit a cigarette and leaned against his truck, all the while scanning the sky for a target.

Twenty minutes after arriving at the athletic field—which seemed like an eternity to Jamil—he spotted a dot in the sky. He had no way of knowing that it was Gulf Air flight 772 arriving in Islamabad from Abu Dhabi.

The Airbus 332 was on final approach, with an expected arrival time of 5:50 p.m., ten minutes ahead of schedule.

The plane approached rapidly, though Jamil could not yet hear it. In his excitement he threw the tarp to the side, grabbed the SA-7, and pointed the sight at the approaching plane. Though instructed to wait until he heard a chirping noise, which told him the infrared sensor had locked onto a heat source, he felt vulnerable and exposed holding the SA-7 on his shoulder in an open field in broad daylight. *Come on, come on! Lock onto the engine, you fool weapon!*

The sound of an approaching truck startled him, and Jamil turned his head and upper body to see what it was. A package delivery truck had just turned off the highway and drove directly toward him. His heart was beating loudly, and his hands felt cold and clammy. He quickly turned back toward the plane, which was almost directly overhead, aimed the missile in its general direction, and pulled the trigger.

Jamil's failure to follow instructions, and his panic over the approaching truck, doomed his attempt to bring down the plane. The engine on a descending jetliner produces less of a heat signature than an engine at full thrust on takeoff. The SA-7 had not locked onto the heat source prior to launch, nor was it able to acquire it in flight. The rocket flew harmlessly toward the location where the airliner was when the rocket fired. However, by then the airplane was a kilometer closer to the airport, and two hundred meters closer to the ground. The SA-7 exploded harmlessly in the air behind it.

The launch flash, spiraling trail of smoke from the ascending rocket, and subsequent explosion startled the driver of the DHL delivery truck. "That's . . . that's a rocket!" He leaned forward to watch it explode behind the airliner, which continued its descent toward the airport. By now the delivery truck was almost at the spot where the rocket had been launched. The driver looked at the truck and saw a young man standing on the other side still holding the launcher. Then he watched in his rearview mirror as the man threw down the launcher and reached into the cab of his truck to pull out a rifle—and point it in his direction.

The DHL driver stomped on the gas pedal and reached for his radio. "Base, this is truck twenty-three. I just witnessed a man trying to bring down an airplane with some type of missile. And now he is firing a rifle at me!" The driver saw flashes coming from the barrel of the rifle, and almost simultaneously he heard the thumping of the bullets tearing into the back of the truck. Stacks of packages absorbed the barrage of bullets. "Please call the authorities and give them my current position. Fool—he's trying to kill me! I need to get out of here!"

The DHL truck was equipped with GPS technology that allowed the company to track its every move. This could help the company evaluate the speed and effectiveness of its drivers. But it also allowed them to identify a driver's location in the event of an emergency. And an attempted terrorist event certainly qualified as an emergency. The dispatcher placed a call to the local police that was quickly relayed to the army. Several vehicles started converging on the scene.

Jamil began shaking. The excitement, fear, and anger caused a rush of adrenaline through his body. What should he do? His first impulse was to jump in the truck and flee. His second was to pursue the driver of the truck and silence him before he could file a report. If they didn't know what he looked like—or what he was driving—he had a better chance of escape. He decided to go after the other driver.

He twisted the key to start the engine. In his haste he released the clutch too quickly, and the truck lurched forward and died. He tried again, pushed hard on the accelerator, and heard the tires squeal as the truck shot forward. Off in the distance he saw the DHL truck driving up a ramp to get back on the main highway. *He might try to escape, but he will not succeed!*

"Base, truck twenty-three! Please tell the police I'm back on the highway and that the driver appears to be following me. I think he is trying to catch up with me. Tell them where I am, and tell them to hurry!" the young driver pleaded.

The DHL van was still accelerating, but Jamil was gaining on it. Its distinctive yellow and red markings made it easy to spot, and he was getting ever closer. He reached across the seat for his rifle and thrust it against the passenger's side window, trying to break the glass. But he didn't have the strength in his left hand, or the leverage, to apply sufficient force. In frustration he pulled the trigger and watched as the window exploded and shattered into hundreds of small pieces. He had almost reached the truck.

The DHL driver saw a muzzle blast, and then glass exploded in his rear window. A shard hit him in the right side of his neck and felt like a bee sting. He started to bleed, and he cursed loudly at his pursuer. Now it *was* life or death. It was obvious what this lunatic intended to do. "Well, I'll make this as hard for him as possible," vowed the driver, and he steeled himself to use his truck as a weapon.

Jamil first heard the faint wail of the siren. Then he looked in his rearview mirror to see the flashing lights in the distance. Someone must have seen him and phoned in a warning. Time was running out, and he needed to get away. But first he had to eliminate the one man who could still identify him. He moved to the far right passing lane and pulled even with the back of the truck. He rested the muzzle of the gun on the passenger-side door so he could fire a long burst into the cab.

The DHL driver saw what the man was about to do. He waited until the small truck was beside his larger one—though not yet even with the cab—and then he turned his wheel to the right and made a sudden lane change—the yellow van smashed directly into Jamil's pickup truck, sending him careening off to the right.

The impact buckled the fender and bent it down almost to the tire. Jamil instinctively dropped the rifle and turned the steering wheel to the left to avoid driving completely off the highway. As he did, the DHL driver again smashed into his truck. This time the crumpled fender knifed into the tire, causing it to puncture. At almost the same moment his two right tires dropped off the shoulder onto the soft dirt beside the road where they dug in.

The DHL driver watched in his side mirror as the truck began rolling to its right, flipping over three times before coming to rest on its flattened tires. During the first or second roll—he wasn't exactly sure which—the driver was ejected from the cab. The truck appeared to roll over him before truck and driver disentangled and landed about ten meters apart. The DHL driver skidded his truck to a halt and jumped out to await the arrival of the police. As he stepped from the truck his legs were so weak he nearly collapsed. He sat down in the doorway of his truck, gasping for air, as the emergency vehicles drew ever closer.

CHAPTER 10

GOOD COP, BAD COP

Moshe chuckled as he went through customs at London Heathrow. This time there was no special arrangement to expedite his arrival. Britain, though a close ally with the United States, had a far different relationship with Israel. Britain had historic ties to the various Arab countries in the Middle East—a legacy born in equal parts by the British/Arab alliance against the Ottoman Empire in World War I, and by the Sykes-Picot Agreement between Britain and France that carved out spheres of influence in the Middle East for both nations following that war.

Though the British had issued the Balfour Declaration, pledging to work for "the establishment in Palestine of a national home for the Jewish people," they had also promised postwar independence for all former Ottoman Arab provinces, including the land of Palestine. Following World War I, Britain tried to administer the League of Nations Mandate over the area. In effect, they tried to administer land they had promised to both the Jewish and Arab residents.

Moshe remembered the history of that period from his classes at university. Some in the British army had great sympathy for the Jewish people. Perhaps best known was Orde Wingate, the Christian Zionist who helped train Jewish fighters. He was given the nickname *hayedid*—the friend—for his invaluable contribution to Jewish independence. But many other British soldiers, officers, and politicians favored the Arabs in their struggles with the Jews. Britain helped train the Arab Legion, the premier fighting force among the surrounding Arab nations at the time of Israel's independence.

Britain's relationship with the Jewish nation remained strained. Neither the purpose for Moshe's trip nor his connection with Mossad was shared with the British Foreign Office. He was simply an Israeli citizen traveling to Britain from America. Mossad had already supplied Moshe with an appropriate cover. His company stationery—embossed with his name and title—and his business card identified him as a midlevel manager for a small electronics firm based in Israel.

He carried his luggage through customs, choosing the Green Line since he had nothing to declare. As he walked through the doors into the waiting area, he heard someone shout his name. "Moshe! Moshe! Welcome to London!" Moshe scanned the crowd, finally spotting someone about his own age waving at him—someone Moshe remembered from his time in training at Mossad.

"Yitzhak. So good to see you. What brings you to London?" Moshe still felt a bit fuzzy from the whirlwind of travel.

"I'm here to see you. We only have about four hours before our meeting, so we must talk quickly," Yitzhak said, falling in step beside him.

Moshe knew this was no chance encounter. Whatever he was being sent to do, it must have arisen at lightning speed. Yitzhak had been flown in from Tel Aviv—most likely to brief him on the assignment and to provide him with whatever documentation necessary.

"So, my friend, where shall we meet?" Moshe asked with a deep breath.

"You will see. Just follow me." They walked in silence to the parking garage. Once in the car, Yitzhak lifted his hand to silence Moshe even before he could speak. He then turned on the radio and located a station playing what sounded like American-style rap music. Speaking almost in a whisper, Yitzhak turned toward Moshe and said, "Wait until we get to the restaurant."

Rather than turning onto the M4, Yitzhak drove east along Bath Road, skirting the edge of Heathrow. Just east of the airport, in the town of Cranford, he pulled the car into the Ramada Hotel. "I've already called in registrations for both of us. We'll be in adjoining rooms. We'll eat first, and then you can clean up."

The restaurant remained open all night but now was virtually empty. Moshe wasn't really sure what time it was—at least for his body clock. "I'm not sure if I should be eating breakfast, lunch, or dinner," he said to no one in particular.

The two men ordered strong black coffee to begin. Moshe turned to his companion. "Yitzhak, why was I summoned from Chicago so suddenly? And why are you here?"

"You will know very soon, my friend. But here comes our server with our coffee. Let's order first and talk afterward."

Yitzhak smiled at the young man. "Hello, my friend! You are just in time to satisfy the ravenous appetites of two hungry travelers. Tell me, what would you recommend?"

Once the waiter had left the table, Yitzhak glanced around the room, then turned and nearly whispered, "Moshe, you have been summoned because we need to send you to Nevi."

"Why?"

"Two days ago Nevi arranged for a drop. Our contact went to the drop point and found a note urgently asking Mossad to send you. According to the note, you are to meet Nevi at the 'same place, same time.' We hope that makes sense to you."

Moshe frowned. "It does. That's why the one-way passage to London, and you meeting me. Sounds like I'm headed to Damascus, not Tel Aviv." Moshe's mind raced back to his conversation with Nevi. He wondered what had happened to have her summon him on such short notice.

"I've brought along all the appropriate documents as well as your clothes and suitcase," Yitzhak said, pulling a cache of papers from his coat. "By the way, thanks for leaving everything in a place where we could retrieve it quickly," he said as he handed Moshe the papers.

"All done according to the manual!" responded Moshe, grinning. "I take it my cover remains essentially the same?"

"Yes," said Yitzhak. "You're an Egyptian businessman in a hurry to make a connection and leave. Based on the urgency of Nevi's message, we probably need you to get in, get the information, and get out. In fact, you are scheduled to return from Damascus to London the following day, but that ticket can be changed too, if needed."

"What is so important?" Moshe asked, picking through the salad that had arrived mysteriously without his even noticing.

"I'm not sure. Mossad's best guess is that it has something to do with the suspects traveling through Syria. Perhaps Nevi knows their names or itineraries. But whatever it is, Nevi believes it is vital we make contact now, if possible. What worries me is the two-day delay in Damascus. But that can't be helped." Moshe watched his dinner companion almost leave the restaurant in his mind and go to another place. There was much more behind this man than was on display, to be sure.

"So when do I fly out?" he asked, drawing Yitzhak back into the room.

Yitzhak glanced down at his watch. "In about five hours. So you need to be back at the airport in about two. That gives you an hour to eat and an hour to clean up and go through your suitcase to make sure you have everything you need."

The server appeared with the rest of their order, so Moshe and Yitzhak stopped talking and turned their attention to the food. Moshe wondered if he really had all he needed to do this right.

* * * * * * * * * * *

Jamil awoke to the sound of muffled voices. He opened his eyes, but shut them quickly because of a bright light shining directly onto his face. A throbbing in the back of his head made him feel as if his brain was being squeezed in a vise. He tried to lift his arms to shade his face from the bright light, but nothing happened. He couldn't feel his arms or his legs.

He forced his eyes open and tried to talk. His speech was slurred, and his throat felt hoarse and husky. "Where am I? What is going on?"

Someone twisted the flexible stem of the lamp so the light was not shining directly on his face. As his eyes adjusted, he saw faint images of two men standing on either side of him. A bank of blinking monitors lined his bed, and a stand with a bag of clear liquid hung just over his head. He heard a soft beeping that sounded like an intensive care unit he visited years ago when his grandfather was recovering from a stroke. A tube snaked from the bag down toward his left arm. He tried to lift his head to look around, but it would not move.

The man to his right broke the silence. "So this failure of a man can speak! Well, it's about the only thing he can still do. Listen, you contemptible dog. We should have left you to die along the highway. You failed in your mission to shoot down the airplane. It landed safely. And you failed in your attempt to kill the driver of the delivery truck. Instead, he forced you to crash, and you are now paralyzed from the neck down. Your arms and legs are useless. You will never walk again; nor will you ever hold a woman. You will go from this bed directly to your grave in utter disgrace!"

Jamil groaned and tried again to speak, but the second man interrupted. "Nazir, why do you dishonor this young man? I don't see a dog; I see a mujahideen warrior who risked his life to serve our God. It's all in Allah's hands, no? Many who serve Allah die without seeing the final victory, but Allah rewards them all."

"Shaheed, you would defend this son of a prostitute?" the man almost shouted back. "He is not worth the price of the rope that will be used to hang him. I say let's just finish him off here and now and save our country the cost of a trial and execution!"

Nazir reached down toward Jamil's neck, his powerful fingers ready to clamp around his throat. But Shaheed grabbed his hands and pulled them away. "No! You cannot do this; I won't allow it. Get out of here. Get out now, or I will have *you* arrested!"

Jamil stared in wide-eyed terror at the struggle taking place just inches from his face. His head still pounded, and it felt like a bad dream.

Nazir hesitated, and then finally drew back his hands. "I'm not remaining here to guard and nurse this worthless pile of dung. You can choose to do so if you like, but I've got better things to do." He turned and left the room quickly, cursing under his breath.

Jamil stared at the remaining guard as tears welled up in his eyes. To be so close to death, and so helpless, was truly frightening. And this man had risked his own life to save him. "Thank you for your kindness," he said, managing to eke out some words. "You are indeed blessed of Allah."

"How could I let someone like that worthless policeman raise his hand to harm one of Allah's brave servants? I'm sorry for your injuries, but I salute you for your service to Allah."

Jamil felt calmed by the man's words, though he still did not know what or who he was. *He must be a police officer, but he has never said so. Well, whoever he is, it's obvious he shares my passion and conviction on jihad.*

And that makes him a brother. "Thank you. I am grateful for your kindness and your courage. But who are you?"

"I think it best if you only know me as Shaheed. I'm sure you learned in your training, as did I in mine, that it is not wise to share too much information with those we don't know," the man answered, walking to look out the small window at the corner of the room.

He is a fellow mujahideen! What good fortune to be guarded by a brother in the struggle!

Almost as if he could read Jamil's mind, the man leaned down and spoke softly to him. "Yes, I am a fellow soldier. But you took me by surprise, because I thought I was to be told about all operations taking place in my region. Did your leader not pass along that information to you?"

Jamil was surprised and a little ashamed. His had been a rogue operation, an unauthorized attempt to strike a blow for Allah. But surely this fellow warrior would understand if he knew the circumstances, or if he knew at least part of the circumstances that had propelled Jamil forward on his one-man jihad.

"I'm sorry for the trouble I have caused, but I did not pass along the information because I was not told to do so. You see, all the other members of the team with whom I trained were sent on for their assignment. Unfortunately, I was left behind. But I knew in my heart that God had called me to serve as his instrument of jihad, so I took this assignment on myself." Jamil felt his throat starting to swell from talking.

"Another team? I have heard of the actions of no other team, only of your brave deed. Could it be that they have suddenly become women, afraid to follow through on their service?"

"Oh, no, they are all brave men. They were trained for an attack not here but elsewhere—a thrust deep into the belly of the Great Satan. You will hear of their attack soon, very soon. And when it comes, you will know how brave my fellow mujahideen really were."

"My brave young lad, please don't think that I doubt you, or the men with whom you trained. But since the attack will happen soon, what should I be watching for so I can know to give thanks to Allah when it takes place?"

"Watch for many airliners in America to go down in flames! Watch for their economy to experience a shock greater than the one caused by the airplanes that hit the Twin Towers and the Pentagon. Watch for America to have a new date that, *inch' Allah*, will even eclipse that of September 11."

"Indeed. But if I may be so bold as to question the wisdom of your plan. What will they do to make sure they don't miss their target, as you did? As you yourself know, it's not always easy to hit a moving target."

"They will succeed for two reasons! First, they will operate in teams. I had to operate alone, but they will not. Second, they will be told what targets to hit, targets that are taking off, not landing."

"A wise plan! But how many teams are there? How many explosions should I look forward to rejoicing over?"

Jamil had a sudden realization that he was sharing far too much information with his newfound friend. Was he indeed a fellow mujahideen, or was this a trick to get information from him? He didn't know, but he sensed that he had said too much. "I'm sorry, but I can't share that information. You will know soon enough."

"Ah, yes, you are indeed wise. That is information I do not need to know, and you are right to withhold it from me. Before I leave, is there anything I can bring for you? Or anyone you would want me to contact to let them know where you are?" The man moved back across the room and stood beside Jamil's bed.

"No, I'm fine. But thank you for asking. You will visit me again, will you not?"

"Of course I will. We share much in common, and we have much to discuss. Perhaps we can talk again when you have begun recovering from your injuries."

Shaheed walked from the room and closed the door behind him. Standing out in the hall was his partner, Nazir. Nazir was about to speak when Shaheed put his index finger on his lips to signal him to be quiet. They walked in silence down the hall and out of the hospital. Once they were outside, Shaheed turned to Nazir. "You were marvelous. Even I started to hate you! But more significantly, he hated you. And he did see me as his friend and protector."

"Good. But did he share anything of significance with you? Did he tell you where he got that missile? Or if he is connected with a specific group?"

"I got some information, but I'm convinced he still possesses more. Our country is safe, but an unknown number of teams have been sent to America to shoot down multiple airplanes. Evidently the group was trained here and just sent out recently. But he started becoming suspicious and would not tell me how many teams were sent. I didn't get the opportunity to ask him where he had trained, or who the leader was, but we have much more time to extract information from him."

"Let's head back to headquarters. I'm sure there are people in our country, and in the United States, who will want to know what you just heard."

As they drove toward their office, the story of the attempted attack—and of the capture of the attacker—made the evening news. The terrorist's name was not mentioned, but images of the truck did appear in the broadcast. And one of those watching with more than a little interest was the Teacher. "Pack everything we can carry into the trucks and be prepared to leave within the hour! I suspect that very soon there will be troops searching this compound."

"But how do you know they can trace Jamil to us?" asked his second-in-command. "Do you believe he will confess?"

"He doesn't need to. The license plates on the truck are all the evidence they need to tie him to us. Now get moving. We have little time."

* * * * * * * * * *

Moshe, exhausted, arrived at his Damascus hotel late in the evening. The message from Nevi had told him to go back to the same bench where they had first met, at exactly the same time. Tomorrow afternoon he would retrace his steps from the ice cream shop to the park, trying to arrive at each location at the same time as before. The morning would be used to make some business contacts.

The next afternoon he went to Bekdach's and ordered qahwah and ice cream. He sat at a table for almost twenty minutes, but Nevi failed to appear. He glanced around to see if he could spot any members of the Mukhabarat. If they had somehow captured Nevi and gotten her to talk, they would likely stake out the meeting places to watch for her contact. But no one in the shop appeared suspicious. Time to revisit Madhanat Issa, the Tower of Jesus, at the Great Mosque.

Moshe made his way slowly toward the Great Mosque. His head felt still in a daze from all the traveling. His body protested every step. He felt tired and sluggish. He just wanted to sleep—he wanted to sleep next to Esther and wake to her warm smile. To sip coffee with her and talk. Instead he was wandering through Damascus, always watchful, looking for a secret contact in a very dangerous place.

In spite of mounting anxiety, he took great care not to appear nervous or in a hurry. Pausing as if to look at items on display in the shop windows, Moshe checked several times to see if he was being followed. He finally found himself on the south side of the mosque in the same dark shadows that enveloped the area before. This time no one stepped from those shadows.

There was only one option left—to go to the park. He walked to the bench where he and Nevi had first talked. The sun had almost set when Moshe sat down. He gathered his topcoat around him, tucking it between his legs. The zipper on the old thing had broken two years ago and he'd never bothered to replace it. Small groups of people walked past, but the number of strollers decreased as the night shadows lengthened. There was no sign of Nevi. Moshe didn't notice the man come up behind him.

"Don't make a sound. Get up very slowly and turn around." Moshe's heart raced, and he debated whether to put up a struggle or try to run away. But the voice behind interrupted his thoughts. "Please do as I say, and you will not be harmed. And don't think about fleeing. You are surrounded. Just do as I have asked, and you will be safe."

Moshe rose to his feet and turned to face the man who was speaking. His hands were in his coat pockets, but he was clearly holding something in his right hand. Moshe assumed it was a gun and started to raise his hands, but the man stopped him. "Please keep your hands down. We don't want to draw unnecessary attention to ourselves. Just walk slowly toward the car parked over there." And with that the man gestured with his head toward a white Peugeot parked on the street. A man was sitting in the front seat looking at them. "Walk toward the back of the car and get in. There is someone who wants to meet with you."

Moshe did as he was told, but he felt like a steer being led to slaughter.

CHAPTER 11

AT THE POTTERY SHOP

The Peugeot twisted its way through the streets of Damascus. Moshe sat in silence in the backseat, next to the man from the park. He looked to be in his midthirties, just under two meters in height, with jet-black hair and dark eyes. He wore civilian clothes and was clean-shaven except for a neatly trimmed moustache. He didn't look particularly threatening, though Moshe had learned that horrifying day at the wedding that looks can be tragically deceiving. For a moment he flashed back to the scene of the server, carrying an empty tray, with an oddly stuffed shirt, headed for the wedding party. He felt nauseated. If only he'd recognized the threat a second or two earlier. Perhaps none of this would have transpired. . . .

The driver of the white Peugeot was much younger, probably early to midtwenties. Moshe could see only his head and shoulders, so he couldn't tell whether or not the man was armed. He assumed that he was. The driver kept glancing at him though his rearview mirror, but his expression remained neutral.

Did these men know Moshe was with Mossad? Or had he simply done something that made him appear suspicious? If they knew he was with Mossad, then Moshe had nothing to lose by trying to escape. If he was to be imprisoned, he could expect only weeks of torture and interrogation followed by a swift public trial, and certain death by execution. But if they didn't know he was with Mossad, then he still had a chance. If he could convince them he was indeed an Egyptian businessman, perhaps he would be allowed to go free, after several hours—or days—of unpleasant confinement.

Moshe decided to test his captors to see what they knew.

"My friends, there must be some mistake. Why are you taking me against my will? I'm a businessman who arrived in Damascus only yesterday. I'm not rich, but you can have all my money. Can you at least tell me where you are taking me?"

"I'm sorry, but your questions will be answered shortly," answered the one who had spoken to him in the park. "In the meantime, please sit quietly—and don't make any sudden moves."

Moshe frowned and settled back in the seat. He wondered again about Nevi. *Perhaps they have gotten to her too.*

The buildings along the highway started thinning out. Short blocks of apartments and stores soon gave way to scattered apartment buildings and single-family villas, stacked intermittently along the road. Eventually, even the streetlights disappeared. The streets fell dark except for the lights from the Peugeot speeding on through the night. After what to Moshe seemed like half an hour, the car turned from the road onto a dirt driveway, bouncing through the rutted entrance.

He peered out. On the right side of the road, about thirty meters in front of them, rose a white, three-story building now lighted by the dim headlights from the car. The structure was typical of the region, built of concrete and stone. The first floor had a storelike appearance, though Moshe couldn't be sure because the lights were off. He could see shelving through the glass windows, and he also noticed a sign above the windows on the far side, but he couldn't make out what it said. It was an odd place for a store to be so far off the main highway.

He noticed light shining through closed curtains on the second floor of the building. The third floor was completely dark. Across the top of the building, at regular intervals, he could just make out rods of rebar silhouetted against the night sky, extending from the concrete pillars. Like so many houses in the area, this one was built one story at a time. When the owners saved enough money—or had a male child reach marriageable age and needed a home for his new bride—then an additional floor would be constructed.

A deserted, out-of-the-way location—the perfect place to torture someone since nobody is nearby to hear the screams. Moshe remembered his training at Mossad and began mentally to prepare himself for the physical pain that would inevitably follow.

The car stopped, and the driver flicked his high beams on and off three times in rapid succession. From behind the house, and just to the left, someone holding a flashlight answered with three quick flashes. The man in the backseat turned to Moshe and said, "We are here. Now you will have your questions answered. Please, exit the car from my side, and do so very slowly."

Moshe obeyed.

The door to the "store" opened, and someone stood in the entrance, silhouetted against the light from inside. Moshe squinted into the light, trying to see who it was. The darkened outline said in a female voice, "I'm sorry for the trouble we have put you through. Please come in." *Nevi,* Moshe thought. He wondered who she really was.

* * * * * * * * * *

Jamil awoke to the rhythmic hum of the electrical equipment in his hospital room, the only illumination coming from a small light plugged into the wall. By Western standards the room was sparsely furnished, but the equipment itself was as modern as that in most American hospitals. The bed had bars along the side, raised to prevent him from rolling out. Not that they were really necessary. He was completely paralyzed from the neck down. He could breathe on his own, but he was incapable of any movement except for his head and face muscles.

To his left was a movable cart filled with an array of boxes, cables, and monitors. But all of the equipment seemed to be turned off. The monitor was dark. A chrome stand was fastened to the side of the bed near his head. He could move his eyes to the left just enough to see that a bag of clear liquid still hung from the stand with a plastic tube that ran from the bag down toward his left arm. He assumed the bag was somehow connected to his arm, but he didn't feel anything, and he couldn't raise his head far enough to see.

He was just about to drift back to sleep when he heard a soft, but distinct, scrape and *click*—the sound made by a door latch sliding across a strike plate and then snapping shut. Perhaps it was time for one of the nurses to check on him. Certainly it was too early for one of the investigators to be returning. And it wasn't a policeman or soldier because the staff hadn't bothered to post a guard when it became clear that he wasn't a threat to escape. "Hello? Is someone there?"

No one answered. Perhaps the sound came from a room down the hall. Or perhaps he had imagined it. But then he heard the quiet shuffle of sandals on linoleum. "I know you are here! Who are you? Show yourself!" Jamil raised his voice slightly, wanting the visitor to know he was awake and aware of his presence, but not wanting to disturb anyone else lest he bring some type of punishment for causing a commotion. He knew he was already in a great deal of trouble.

"Don't be afraid, Jamil, and don't cry out. It is I," said the quiet yet familiar voice.

Jamil strained to see who it was, but it was several seconds before the man who spoke moved over to the right side of his bed and peered down at him. It was the Teacher.

"I'm . . . I'm sorry to have caused you so much trouble!" said Jamil. "I apologize for taking the missile and crashing the truck. But I wanted to do my part for Allah. Please forgive me, but I acted as one of your loyal followers." Jamil didn't mention the rape of the Teacher's daughter. Perhaps she had been too embarrassed or ashamed to tell others. And if there was even a small chance that the Teacher didn't know, Jamil didn't want to be the one to tell him now.

"Everything in its time," the Teacher answered. "I'm here to take you from this place. But before I do, I must ask you some questions. And it's *very* important for you to answer truthfully and completely. Will you do that?"

"Yes, of course. What do you wish to know?"

"It is most important to know what you told these people about our plans with the mujahideen. How much did you share with them?" Somehow the Teacher had learned of his conversation with the two police guards.

"How did you know I spoke with those men? I told them nothing specific about our plans, though the man I talked to is one of us. I did tell them that I was but a small part of a larger army being sent to unleash Allah's wrath on the Great Satan. But I assured him that all the teams had been dispatched to America. I had been left behind and acted alone to avenge my honor. I am sure he believed me that I acted alone and that there were no other attacks planned in Pakistan. And I know he will not share the information with others because he is a fellow mujahideen."

The Teacher's hands were at his side, just below the edge of the bed. Jamil could not see him curl his fingers together until they formed two tight fists. When he had returned to the compound, he had found his daughter in hysterics. His wife shared with him the sordid details of Jamil's brutal attack on his daughter's—and his—honor. She also told him about Jamil's theft of a missile and his threat to launch his own attack.

Then came the reports of the attack on an airliner in Pakistan and the pictures of the wrecked truck—his truck—with his license plates still attached! In those first few hours at home, the Teacher had been forced to make several hard choices. He had to abandon his compound. Quickly. It would not take the authorities long to break Jamil or to trace the license plate on the truck he had stolen. An operation had just been launched, and now he had to find a new location from which to monitor his mujahideen.

More important, he now realized the operation was no longer a secret. The fool Jamil had told the authorities that multiple teams had been sent to America, and his use of a missile made it relatively easy for them to guess what type of attacks would be launched.

Everyone in the compound worked frantically packing up and loading the computer equipment and files. They burned all the other records, anything that could identify the operation or those involved. They also tried to hide any remaining weapons and equipment that could not fit into the trucks. It seemed futile since the Teacher was certain the soldiers would find it. *No doubt they will disassemble the entire compound brick by brick.*

Thankfully, he had prepared for such an eventuality and had purchased another farm several hours away. The buildings were in need of repair, and it was far less suitable as a training camp. But it would allow him to resume operations. He still had one loose thread that remained to be tied up—Jamil. And that was why he had driven all the way back to Islamabad and searched for the hospital where he had been taken. Once he had discovered the hospital, it was very easy to enter posing as one of the janitors cleaning the building during the night. He had spent almost an hour searching for his prey in the halls of this smelly building. And now it was time to reward this one who had caused so much trouble.

"Teacher, how will you take me from here? I'm not able to move my arms or my legs; they were crushed when the truck rolled over. Will it not cause a disturbance if you try to push my bed out past the nurses?" Jamil felt stabs of fear but knew he could only trust this man whom he had so violently betrayed.

"Don't worry, my son; I have the perfect plan." As he said those words the Teacher reached behind Jamil's head and pulled on his pillow, forcing Jamil's head to fall backward onto the mattress.

"What . . . what are you doing?" gasped Jamil.

But before he could say anything else, the Teacher took the pillow and jammed it over his face. Crawling onto the bed, the Teacher leaned forward and put all his weight on the pillow, using both hands to hold it in place.

"What am I doing? I'm sending you to hell, you stupid fool!" he hissed into the pillow as Jamil thrashed his head from side to side. "You humiliated my daughter and dishonored me. And you have done much to destroy the plan for which I have worked so long. I only wish I could make you suffer to the extent you deserve!"

The Teacher pushed harder still on the pillow until the thrashing ceased. When he lifted up the pillow he saw that the fool lay still. He climbed off the bed, careful not to knock over any of the equipment. He paused a few seconds to allow his own breathing to return to normal.

Finally, the Teacher turned back to face him. "You look dead, but I will make sure!" Reaching beneath the green scrubs he had grabbed from the laundry room, he pulled out his sharp, curved knife. He then pulled back Jamil's head, exposing his throat. "Now I will make sure you never speak again until the day of judgment!"

The Teacher used the bedsheet to wipe Jamil's blood from the blade of his knife. He slipped the knife back beneath the scrubs and shuffled over to the door. Listening carefully for the sound of footsteps in the hallway and hearing none, he slipped down the hall, out of the hospital and into the night.

"I have many hours of driving in front of me, and the sun will be rising in the sky before I reach my new home," he mumbled to himself as he turned from the parking lot onto the main road. "But that will give the family time to settle in and set up our computer. And it will give me time to think through the changes that must be made to our plan. Jamil, that stupid fool."

* * * * * * * * * *

"More qahwah?" Nevi asked as she brought the pot toward Moshe's cup.

"Perhaps just one more cup. *Shukran!*" Moshe held out the small cup as she poured in the dark liquid. "I must admit that I'm completely mystified. Why did you contact us and then vanish? And who are these men?" Moshe gestured toward the two men standing against the far wall, still looking rather grim, though their hands were no longer inside their coat pockets.

"Oh, that's right! You've not been officially introduced. Mr. Ziyad Abu Ali—I assume that is not your real name, but it is the only name we need to know—this is Mr. Boutros Ghannoum and his younger brother Hamid. Boutros is an elder in my church. He is one of the spiritual leaders—like a priest or rabbi—of our church."

Moshe looked at Boutros, who remained impassive. But while still making eye contact, his hand reached back into his coat pocket—and pulled out a pen. Then Boutros could hold his dour expression no longer. He laughed out loud and said, "You see, my friend, this is what I used to keep you from running away. Truly the pen *is* mightier than the sword!"

And Boutros waved the pen over his head as a matador might wave his *estoque* before thrusting it down into the bull for a kill. Only the bull in this case was Boutros's own shirt pocket.

"Boutros, sometimes you are far too dramatic! Mr. Abu Ali, I am Hamid, and I offer my sincere apology for the way we treated you this evening. But that was the only way we could get you to come here without causing a struggle or drawing unnecessary attention to ourselves in Damascus."

"Why didn't you just tell me that Nevi had sent you and had asked you to bring me to her?"

"I think I'm best able to answer your question," said Nevi as she rested her coffee cup back on the saucer. "First, these men have never known me as Nevi. It was only a few days ago that I shared with them what God had placed on my heart to do for the Jewish people. And second, these men had never met you. I gave them a general description of what you would look like and where you would appear. But we didn't even know for certain when—or if—you would arrive. There was always the danger of them accidentally approaching the wrong person."

"So we decided to 'impersonate' the Mukhabarat," said Hamid, a smile breaking across his face. "We used intimidation to get you into the car, and then we drove around until it was dark. That way you had no idea where this house is located. Had we come to the door with the wrong individual, Radeyah would have simply said, 'This is not the one we seek,' and would have shut the door. We would then have told the poor man how lucky he was not to have been identified by the informant, how it very likely had spared his life. And then we would have driven him back into Damascus by another roundabout route and released him to go home—with, of course, a stern warning never to reveal his close encounter with the secret police unless he wanted to be arrested again."

"And, praise to our Lord, my description of you was sufficiently accurate—as was your sense of timing—that they found you on the very first evening. And that is how you came to be here." Nevi sat smiling and with a serene countenance that reminded Moshe of Esther.

Moshe rubbed his hands over his face, trying to sweep away the mental loose ends that littered his mind. He was back to reality, but there were still too many details he couldn't piece together.

"I think I understand most of what has happened, but some pieces still don't fit. One of the easiest pieces is your real name, Nevi. He just called you Radeyah, didn't he?"

"Yes, that is my real name," Nevi said. "It means contentment."

"Then that is what I will call you. Radeyah." Moshe liked its sound. "You saw or heard something that caused you to send an emergency message asking to meet with me. And then you vanished but sent these men to watch the location where you hoped I would come—with orders to bring me to you."

"Yes, Ziyad, that is correct."

"Then I have two questions. First, what is the information you have that is so important? And second, did you go into hiding because you sensed you are in personal danger?"

"Let me answer the second question first. I don't believe I am in personal danger, but I didn't know if I could conceal my emotions in front of my employer, General Habib. You see, the other night he held a special dinner, and I heard frightening plans being shared. That's the information I want to share with you. When the gathering ended, I asked my employer if I could take time off to visit with a friend. He was in such a good mood that he told me I could take off for a week—once I had returned to clean up from the dinner. The event took place a week ago, and I have now been away from my job for six days. So your coming is just in time. I wasn't sure what to do, so I called Boutros and asked him to help. He allowed me to come and stay here with his family. And after hearing what I had been doing for God's chosen people—and what was about to happen—he and Hamid agreed to help bring you to me."

"So what is the information that was so frightening to you?"

"My employer, General Habib, called me exactly eight days ago and told me to prepare a lavish dinner for up to twenty guests for the next day. Late that next afternoon a large bus pulled up in front of the house, and sixteen men got off. Each was carrying a small black case—like a duffel bag but with wheels—and they seemed to be very excited, though also a little weary."

"What was it about these men that caused you such fear?" Moshe asked, his mind now struggling to fit everything together.

"It was what they talked about once they were in the house. As a housekeeper and servant, I was invisible. They talked openly of their plan to travel to America and attack innocent people with missiles."

"But what can sixteen men with missiles do to such a large country?" he asked, though he thought he might already know the answer.

"I don't know all the details, but they talked about shooting down many airplanes all at once. They said the missiles had already been sent ahead to the U.S. I think my employer had helped arrange for that shipment. They also said they were flying into Mexico and would be smuggled into the United States. I think they were being sent to different places, but they didn't mention specifics."

"And when did this meeting take place?" Moshe asked.

"The meeting itself was a week ago tonight. When I came back early the next morning to clean up, the men had already departed. It took me the whole day to clean the house because I had to do all the laundry and the dishes in addition to my normal cleaning chores. It was late that afternoon when I met with Boutros and Hamid, prepared the message, placed the Hand of Fatima in my window, and drove out here to be with Boutros and his family."

"Radeyah, this information is important. I must ask you some additional questions about these men. Any scrap of information, no matter how insignificant it might seem, could be a vital clue in identifying and stopping them."

"I understand." Radeyah lifted her hands and turned her face heavenward. "Dear Father, please bring to my mind everything I saw and heard that night that might help prevent their attack from succeeding. I pray as King David did that you will put the wicked to shame. And I ask this in the name of your Son. Amen."

Nevi opened her eyes to see Moshe staring at her. "I hope I didn't offend you, but I wanted to ask God to provide me with His ability to remember everything of importance."

Moshe had heard Esther offer similar prayers to God, though never so openly. He brushed away the memories and turned to the matter at hand. "Radeyah, what did these men look like?"

"They all arrived with beards, like Muslim fundamentalists. But I remember my employer telling them that they needed to shave off their beards that evening. I assume they no longer have beards because there was hair in the rubbish bin and around the bathroom sink. Also, they all looked about the same height. Dark hair and young—maybe in their twenties and thirties—except for one who appeared a little older. His beard was silver, more thinned out."

"Any other personal characteristics that you remember? Specific names? Unusual accents? Anything that could help us spot them?" He had pulled from his pocket a small notepad and was scribbling everything down. He knew how critical these details could become.

"I remember one specific name. He was the older man of whom I just spoke—the one with the gray beard. His name was Ibrahim al-Samarri. I remembered it because he had an Iraqi accent, and I remembered that Samarra was north of Baghdad. Three men had no accent, which I guess means they were from around here—from Syria. The rest had slightly different accents. By that I mean that they seemed to come from a number of different Arab countries. They spoke fluent Arabic, so it was their native language, but they must be from several different countries."

Moshe never looked up as he wrote. He continued to write as he asked more questions. "You said they were traveling into the United States through Mexico. Do you remember who said this? Did you hear or see what type of passports they were traveling on? Did you hear what airline they were traveling on?"

"Ziyad, please slow down a bit. I'm trying hard to recall such details. But I'm better processing one question at a time," Nevi said, smiling, but also understanding his urgency.

"Go ahead; I'm sorry. Of course, take your time."

Radeyah took a deep breath and stood to take a walk around the room. "It was General Habib who did most of the talking on these subjects. He mentioned they would be traveling to Mexico and then on into the United States. I can't remember exactly what he said, but it seemed clear they would be splitting up into separate groups. He said they would be traveling on new passports, but I don't remember from what country they were issued. I do remember him stressing that they would be valid passports, though . . . whatever that meant."

Moshe looked up at Radeyah, his dark eyes willing her to remember more. "Anything else?"

"One last thing. Two of the men are left-handed."

"What? How do you know this?" he asked, looking up from his notepad.

"I was scurrying back and forth during the banquet when I overheard two of the men talking. They were pointing to two of the other men on the far side of the table. As I walked past I heard one say to the other, 'Look at them, they are both eating with their left hand! Uneducated

Pakistanis.' Oh, that's right! He said they were both Pakistanis!"

"That's amazing! But why did you remember that?"

"Ah, that is why *you* must be careful. No matter how much you try to speak flawless Arabic, there are still things you need to learn if you want to pass as an Arab. The left hand is the *unclean* hand. You are expected to eat with your right hand even if you are left-handed. These two men drew attention to their unsophisticated manners when they failed to follow this basic custom. More of the guests may have been left-handed, but these two Pakistanis stood out."

"Nevi, that's genius. Anything else?" Moshe paused and remembered the prayer she had offered before they began talking. Had it been answered before him in that moment?

"No, that's really all I can remember for now. The Lord will help me if there is more. I hope this will assist you." Nevi had answered with all the sincerity she could muster. She knew how passionately he felt about bringing justice to his country.

"Thank you all. You've done a great service to my people . . . and to me personally. I am deeply grateful," Moshe said as he stood. "I do need to get back to my hotel so I can reconfirm my flight from Damascus. Time is very short, my friends."

Boutros and Hamid rose from their chairs. It was their job to provide the transportation back into Damascus. Moshe turned to them. "Will you be able to take me back to my hotel? Or at least back to within a few blocks of the hotel?"

"We'll be most happy to do that," replied Boutros. "We too serve the God of heaven. You and your people are in our hearts."

"All I need now is a good cover to explain where I've been for the evening," said Moshe. "I know that some of the desk clerks work for the government. It is their job to keep an eye on Syria's visitors. I suppose I can say I went out to eat dinner, but they might check on that. Do you have any suggestions on what I could plausibly say I was doing this evening?"

This time it was Hamid's turn to smile. "Why not tell them you were negotiating to buy the finest pottery in all Damascus?"

Moshe looked at Hamid with a quizzical expression. "I'm not sure if I follow. What store is that?"

"You are standing in it, my friend!" And with that Boutros began bounding down the stairs, waving for Moshe to follow.

Turning on the lights in the first floor, Boutros turned to Moshe and said, "Welcome to Ghannoum's Fine Pottery. We make some of the most beautiful, and durable, pottery in all Damascus. Surely your organization would like to consider exporting our excellent wares!"

Grabbing several sample pieces, Moshe turned toward the Ghannoum brothers and announced with a flourish, "Gentlemen, I believe we have just formed a very fulfilling business arrangement. I shall take these samples to show my partners. And who knows, perhaps a few of the pieces will find their way onto the dining room table of the front desk manager of my Damascus hotel!" They laughed and patted him hard on the back.

Moshe turned to face Nevi, who had followed the three men down the stairs. "Radeyah, thank you once again for risking your life to save others. You are truly a remarkable woman, though you must remain Nevi to all those not here. I say that for your own safety. And once again I must remind you, if you ever sense danger, please let me know. We are ready to carry you to safety at a moment's notice."

"I know that, and I deeply appreciate your care. But as I said to you once before, my life extends beyond my time on earth. Should I ever be required to lay down my life here, I know it means I will instantly be transported into God's presence in heaven. So you see, I already have a plan in place that is the best available."

Her smile captivated Moshe for a few seconds. It seemed she was already in her heaven as she spoke. *What wonder!* Moshe thought as he followed his new friends to the car.

Twelve hours later Moshe stood at the British Airways ticket counter, receiving his boarding pass for the next flight to London. Only when he reached London could he sound the alarm of an impending attack. *I just hope Radeyah's God is truly on our side.*

CHAPTER 12

THE ARRIVAL

The cell phone rang loudly, jarring him awake. The Teacher had only gotten to sleep four hours earlier after his long trip from Islamabad. His hands groped along the top of the wooden box beside his bed, searching for the offending phone. "Allo."

"Your package arrived this morning. We have already repackaged it and forwarded it on to your friends. They should expect delivery in two or three days," a voice spoke in muffled tones on the other end of the signal.

"Thank you for such good news." The Teacher clicked the phone closed, ending a conversation that took less than thirty seconds. Such calls were kept intentionally short to evade satellite detection. He didn't understand the science behind it, but he knew enough to realize that the United States had the capability of listening in on virtually any phone conversation in the world—cell or landline—and no precautions were too extreme. But with billions of calls being made every day, they didn't have the physical ability to listen to every single call. So they used sophisticated computer programs to monitor key numbers and listen for certain words or phrases. The Teacher purchased cell phones with pre-paid units of time. Rather than renewing the time, he purchased a new phone when the time on the current one was used up. He also avoided using an individual's name, and he kept all phone conversations as brief as possible. He hoped these techniques would allow him to remain unnoticed by America's spy computers.

The call, though short, energized the Teacher. He walked to a basin of water sitting on a small stand near the door and scooped some of the cold water into his cupped hands, which he then splashed onto his face. The icy sting of the water helped wash away any remaining vestiges of sleep. He put on a robe and then pulled back the blanket hanging across the doorway and walked into the outer room. The room was completely dark and there were no windows since it was an inner room in the compound. He sat in the small computer chair, reached below the desk, and managed to strike the On button of the computer. The small machine whirred to life, giving an eerie green glow to the Teacher's travel-worn face.

It was nearly noon in Pakistan, but everyone in the compound had been padding about quietly so the Teacher could rest. They had worked hard the previous day making their new living quarters habitable. Extra care had been taken in preparing the Teacher's two private rooms. They set up his computer and organized the other files in the outer room. They chose to make the inner room his bedroom because its lack of windows made it ideal for sleeping. The light glow of the computer screen bleeding under the doorway signaled to everyone that the Teacher was awake and already at work.

His assistant knocked quietly on the outer door. "Yes, enter," said the Teacher, as he continued to focus on the different start-up screens appearing on his monitor in rapid succession.

"Sir, I thought you might like qahwah and a little food."

The Teacher looked up to see his assistant placing a small tray on a nearby table. An old metal pot with a long wooden handle sat on one side. Beside it rested an almost miniature porcelain cup and saucer. On the other side of the tray sat an old wicker basket holding five round loaves of flat bread. The steam rose high from the basket, and the darkened edges of the bread offered evidence of its being fresh pulled from the oven. Yogurt and a date palm paste garnished the plate.

The assistant poured the dark, frothy liquid from the pot. The rich, distinctive scent of the cardamom mixed with the aroma of the coffee smelled heavy and strong.

"Here you are. I hope you like it."

The Teacher, still staring intently at the computer screen, responded absently. "Yes, I'm sure I will; thank you."

"Would you care to tell me how your return trip to Islamabad went?" asked the assistant. "Did you find Jamil?"

"I found him, and he is no longer a threat to us," said the Teacher. "Unfortunately, Jamil had said enough to the authorities to force us to accelerate our plans. The missiles have arrived in the United States and are being delivered to each of the teams. They should receive them in two days. Our attack must happen soon. Any additional delay merely gives the infidels more time to uncover our plans. We cannot allow that—we simply cannot. Additional time tips the balance in favor of the Americans."

The young assistant was visibly grieved by the report. His reaction bothered the Teacher. Was he upset over Jamil's death, over the fact that Jamil had talked, or over the possibility that the plan might be threatened? He trusted his assistant, but he needed to know why he was upset. These days one couldn't even trust his closest confidant.

"What is it that upsets you so?" the Teacher asked, watching his reaction closely.

"I'm sorry if my reaction concerns you. I'm not upset about Jamil.

He received what he deserved. No, he deserved even greater punishment than he has received. I'm upset that such a wild jackal of a man clumsily compromised your plan. What can I do to make certain you succeed?"

The young man's response relieved the Teacher. "Don't be too worried, my son. I've thought through the changes we need to make to the plan. They are not major. They can be made quite easily. The one piece of information we still needed was the exact time for the arrival of the missiles—Allah seems to have smiled favorably on us in that regard. Today's phone call was the best possible news I could have received."

The assistant nodded and smiled, then retreated from the room.

Only the Teacher and a few deeply placed operatives in Syria, Canada, and the United States—mostly relatives on his father's side—knew about the missiles and the route they had taken from Pakistan. The Teacher had taken pains to alter the outside of all the containers to remove any labels, serial numbers, or other visible markings. He added additional padding inside each box to further secure the missiles. They were completely protected. He also had each box wrapped in plastic and packed into a sturdy wooden container similar to a soldier's footlocker.

The Teacher sent the boxes to a contact in Syria, an army general who also served in the government there. He shipped the boxes inside a large container labeled "Pakistani knives." The general then repacked the boxes in a shipping container, identifying the contents as pistachios. In fact, the rest of the container was indeed packed full of boxes of Syrian pistachios. The container was shipped to another relative who ran an import business in Toronto, Canada.

The relative in Toronto removed the sixteen boxes from the shipping container and then arranged, through another cousin, to load all sixteen boxes into a secret compartment in a semitractor-trailer bound for the United States. The compartment was really nothing more than a false wall inside the trailer, built across the front end. The wall, when bolted into place, provided a two-foot-deep gap between the front of the trailer and what appeared to be the front wall inside the trailer. The driver, a Pakistani native who had immigrated to Canada fifteen years earlier, drove for a trucking company that hauled brake parts for automobiles, trucks, and SUVs. The parts, manufactured in Canada, were shipped to Michigan to be used in a variety of auto assembly plants. The driver had discovered that by building the special wall he could also haul "privately contracted" items across the border, greatly increasing his personal income.

He had been smuggling items for nearly ten years—mostly cigarettes to Canada and Cuban cigars to the United States. He could make more money smuggling drugs in his secret compartment, but he had wisely avoided that cargo. False walls could fool inspectors, but drug-sniffing dogs could always detect the scent of marijuana or cocaine. Because he had refused to smuggle drugs, he had never been caught, and that—along with his close ties to the larger Pakistani community—made him the perfect individual to transport the missiles.

Because of the importance of trade between Canada and the United States, both governments had developed the FAST program—an acronym standing for Free and Secure Trade. The auto supply companies—whose parts he was carrying—as well as the transportation company for which he drove had signed up for this program, and they had encouraged all their drivers to complete a FAST Commercial Driver Application. He had done so, and was certified as a FAST participant. This made it much easier for him to get through customs at the border.

The missiles were loaded into his truck and sealed behind the false wall just before he drove to the manufacturing plant early the next morning to pick up a scheduled load of brake assembly kits for a new crop of Ford F150s scheduled to roll off the assembly line a few weeks later. The drive from Toronto to Windsor took several hours. He waited in line a few more hours at the Ambassador Bridge in Windsor for his turn to pass through customs. But his paperwork was in order, and a cursory look in the back of the trailer confirmed that it was indeed filled with brake parts destined for the Ford Rouge Plant in Dearborn. He passed through the primary security checkpoint into the United States with ease.

By the end of the day the brake lines and parts were safely unloaded at the Ford plant. The next day he would stop at two other plants to pick up some defective parts that needed to be returned to Canada. But he had one more stop to make before he could pull into the Metro Truck Plaza in Dearborn Heights for fuel, a hot meal, and a little shut-eye.

A few miles down the road, in an alley behind a Pakistani restaurant, the driver and the restaurant owner pulled the sixteen missile boxes out of the trailer and stacked them in the back of the owner's van. Tomorrow morning the owner would take the sixteen boxes to a nearby UPS Store to have them shipped Second-Day Air to eight different destinations across the United States—two boxes to each destination. The owner was the only link in the chain who had been given the names of the individuals to whom each missile was to be sent.

Twelve hours later the restaurant owner arrived at the UPS Store to send his packages. The shipping labels identified the shipper (fraudulently) as *Bombay Limited*, and the contents of the boxes were described as "gift box of Indian household gods." The shipper assumed (rightly) that most Americans couldn't distinguish between Indians and Pakistanis; nor would they appreciate the difference between Islam and Hinduism. After mailing the boxes, the restaurant owner placed a short second call to the Teacher in Pakistan. And then he slid back into anonymity to wait on Allah.

And now, as the Teacher sat in front of his computer monitor he felt a rush of adrenaline. The missiles were safely in the United States, and they had been shipped out to the individual teams. He laughed aloud at the thought of America's blind efficiency. In many parts of the Middle East, the idea of having sixteen packages travel through the mail and arrive intact without being opened was itself a minor miracle, never mind the idea of actually having packages arrive at a specific location within a specified time. America's arrogant obsession with both privacy and efficiency would soon be its own undoing.

They play with a viper and don't even realize the danger in its fangs, he thought, kicking off his shoes.

The Teacher spread a little date honey on a piece of bread and took a small bite. He washed it down with a sip of coffee and then turned back to his computer. It was time to inform the teams of the change in plans. He had spent several hours the night before during the long drive thinking through the operational details, and he felt comfortable with the changes. But comfortable or not, the plans needed to be changed and—*inch' Allah*—would be successful.

He opened Photoshop and selected a picture of the Dome of the Rock—one of several he had on his computer—and entered the message at the appropriate spot. In the Caption box he typed, "Dad thought you should pay particular attention to this photo." He then selected the Instructions line and typed the following:

"Change in plans. Packages to arrive in 2–3 days. Prepare to use within 14 days. Await final instructions before using."

The Teacher felt a smug satisfaction in his choice of pictures. He could have chosen from thousands of different photographs to put on his Web site, but he felt compelled to make every part of the operation, even the pictures he used, something to inspire his followers. Though less than twenty people would view the site, he wanted it to make a statement to them, to remind them of the greatness of the task to which they had been called. And so, while he chose several random pictures of Palestine to upload to the site, he had decided always to include his instructions within a picture of Haram es-Sharif—the "noble sanctuary"—as the bearer of information for a noble cause.

He then logged on to the Flickr Web site and signed into his "Smith Family Vacation" account. In just a few minutes he had uploaded the new picture onto the site, ready to be retrieved by his mujahideen.

Now it would be a waiting game.

* * * * * * * * * *

Moshe was glad he had booked his return flight from Damascus to London in business class. He couldn't afford to arouse suspicion, and leaving on coach two days after arriving on business class was just the kind of change that could raise eyebrows. Though only British Air would know, of course, one never knew who Syria's Mukhabarat had on its payroll looking for such anomalies.

Once through customs, he boarded the Heathrow Express to London's Paddington Station. As the train pulled away from the platform, he fished out his cell phone. Part of his cover kit included a prepaid cell phone with MobiNil, Egypt's largest cell phone company. The phone wouldn't work in Syria, but MobiNil had a roaming agreement with Vodaphone that covered most of Europe, including the United Kingdom. Moshe dialed a private cell phone number in London—a number he had committed to memory.

"Allo?"

"Hello, Charles? It's Ziyad . . . Ziyad Abu Ali! I just arrived in London! Where can we meet?"

"Ziyad, do you have a place to stay?" asked Mossad's bureau chief in London.

"No, I don't. Can you recommend a good hotel?" Moshe answered, trying to speak over the noise from the traveling train and the intermittent safety announcements over the intercom.

"Yes, I can. Where are you right now?"

"I'm on the Heathrow Express just leaving the airport."

"Very good. At Paddington Station go to the taxi rank and have the driver take you to the Hilton Hotel at Hyde Park. He should know where it is—it's on Bayswater Road. I'll phone ahead to make a reservation for you, and I'll be waiting for you in the lobby when you arrive. I assume we have much to discuss. See you then." The man hung up and didn't wait for Moshe to respond.

Less than forty-five minutes later Moshe walked into the hotel lobby. "Moshe, over here! So good to see you." Moshe turned to his right to see his contact, Ronnie Yadin, hurrying toward him.

"Everything is set for our meeting. Show the front desk clerk your passport and a credit card, and she will hand you your room card. You can put your suitcase in the room, and then we can go to our meeting. Oh, and I brought the jacket you left here last time. You really must be more careful!"

Moshe understood. Ronnie had placed his Israeli passport—and wallet—inside the jacket. Moshe had been required to leave all these items with Yitzhak before traveling into Syria. It would never be wise for an "Egyptian businessman" to be caught possessing an Israeli passport. Yitzhak had left Moshe's belongings at the Israeli embassy, and Ronnie had just arranged a clever way to return them.

"Thank you! I know it could have been embarrassing had you not brought this for me!" He was sure Ronnie would get the meaning. He carefully reached into the jacket pocket and found his documents. He then picked up his suitcase and hand luggage and walked over to the check-in desk. As he bent down to place his luggage on the floor, he went through the motions of opening his briefcase. He presented his Israeli passport to the clerk and opened his wallet to pull out his company credit card.

"Let's take your luggage to the room and then go out for a bite to eat.

It's a nice day for a walk."

It was only a short walk from the hotel to the Israeli embassy. The security guards knew Ronnie on sight, and he had alerted them to the fact that he would be returning with a guest. The guards gave them immediate entry. Once inside the compound, Ronnie called the ambassador to let him know they had arrived.

"Moshe, this will be a fairly high-powered luncheon," Ronnie said. "The ambassador himself asked to be present, and for at least part of the meeting we will be on a secure phone to Jerusalem."

"Who will be on the other end of the line?"

"They didn't say, but I suspect it could involve some fairly high-level people. Because this involves a threatened terrorist attack against our biggest ally, it is a major operation."

* * * * * * * * * *

Moshe finished his tasteless lunch and sat, his face clouded, wondering how best to share the information he had received. The ambassador could not help but notice his guest's change in countenance. As a battle-hardened former IDF officer who had served in the 1973 Yom Kippur War as well as the 1982 Peace for Galilee incursion into Lebanon, he knew the stress of anticipation was often greater than the actual stress of combat. Sitting, waiting, and wondering what would soon happen were the times when he worried most about the morale of his men. Once the battle started, they could *do* something to affect the outcome. Action overcomes anxiety. Combat personnel could rely on their training and skill to give them focus. But the sitting and waiting prior to battle could be torturous for even the most seasoned soldier.

"Moshe, I think you are as anxious to share what you have uncovered as we are to hear it. Do we have a secure connection to Jerusalem?" He glanced over to his administrative assistant, who nodded her head to let him know that they were on the line, though temporarily on hold.

"Good. Then let's get started. Bring our friends from Jerusalem into the conversation." The phone chimed, then echoed somewhat as the assistant completed the connection. The ambassador turned toward the speakerphone in the center of the table and said, "*Erev tov*, gentlemen. This is Ambassador Katzav with Ronnie Yadin and Moshe Zachar. I presume they need no introduction to you! To whom are we speaking?"

After a few seconds a disembodied voice floated from the speaker. "This is the director. Suffice it to say that there are a few others gathered here, but I would prefer not to share their names over the phone. I'm sure you understand."

"Quite understandable. Well, then, shall we get right to the heart of the matter. We are here to listen to a report from Moshe Zachar about newly gathered intelligence from our sources in Damascus. Mr. Zachar, please, go ahead."

Moshe looked around the table, and as he did his nervousness melted away. He knew exactly what he needed to say. "Thank you for giving me this time. I will try to be concise and clear, but I believe the information I have is critically important. I will be very open with you, but much of what I'm about to share is based on our most valuable human assets in Syria and cannot be repeated without jeopardizing those assets." Moshe moved slightly in his chair and drew himself closer to the table in order to speak more directly into the phone.

"Just over a week ago sixteen terrorists stayed overnight in Damascus at the home of a Baath Party official. They were traveling from a base in Pakistan to Mexico. From there they were to be smuggled into the United States, forming eight two-man teams.

"Approximately one or two months ago—we can't determine the exact date—a shipment of SA-7 handheld missiles was also sent from Pakistan to the United States. We do not know the route of the shipment or port of entry, but we can assume those missiles have made it to their destination—or will arrive soon. We do not know the total number of missiles sent, but we can probably assume that there were enough to equip all eight teams.

"The information received leads us to believe that this group is planning a mass attack in the not-too-distant future. We believe this is the case for two reasons. First, the terrorists appear to be trained in a way that prepared them to launch an attack, not to survive in America for any length of time. Unlike the September 11 attackers, these individuals are not coming to study and learn. They have already been trained, and they are coming to carry out the mission. Second, the missiles were shipped to have the time of their arrival coincide with the arrival of the terrorists. This timing could also imply that the length of time between arrival and attack could be very short.

"It appears that the attacks will be directed against multiple targets, but we don't know if that will involve multiple airports or just multiple airplanes at a single airport. The most frightening unknown is the final destination for each group of terrorists. We know that all the terrorists speak Arabic, but they appear to be from several different countries, including Pakistan and Syria."

Moshe paused to let his audience absorb the information. Some murmured to one another; others sat silent, pondering what they had heard. "That, in summary, is the information I was provided by our contact in Damascus. I believe we need to share this with the Americans as soon as possible, and I would like to suggest that I be allowed to go back to Chicago to do so." Moshe leaned back in his chair and cleared his throat to wait for a response.

"Why Chicago?" asked a new voice on the speakerphone.

"I was in Chicago just a few days ago when I got called back to this emergency meeting in Damascus. One of the leaders of the American FBI counterterrorism effort on gathering and interpreting information is currently based in Chicago. Also, there is a civilian in Chicago who has uncovered a possible secret method being used by an overseas terrorist group to communicate with its cell groups in America. They have no way yet of knowing whether or not this is the same group we have uncovered, but it's at least possible. I think this group is best positioned to make use of our information. Certainly I would expect them to brief Washington. But I'm afraid if we pass it on to Washington first through regular channels, it might take too long to reach the very group that can make the best use of the information."

The ambassador spoke up. "I realize this is not my field of expertise, but just how certain are you of the quality of this information? Are your sources trustworthy? For example, could the information about the number of terrorists be accurate but the information on their intended targets be wrong? How can we be sure that some of the groups will not target London, or Paris, or Mexico City?"

"Mr. Ambassador, I've met with the people in Damascus twice," Moshe responded. "I believe the information is accurate. I'm afraid I really can't go into detail because these sources are too important to Israel to risk compromising their identity. But I do believe the validity—and reliability—of the information I was given."

Another voice came from the speakerphone. "Mr. Zachar is right. We have had experience with these sources for some time, and the information has been gold. Not since Elie Cohen have we had individuals so highly placed in official Syrian circles."

Moshe wasn't sure who had just spoken, but he was thankful that the individual had continued his ruse, implying that there were multiple sources for this information—and that these sources were part of the government infrastructure. Moshe had vowed never to say or do anything that would compromise Nevi's identity.

Now it was Ronnie's turn to speak. "This information is indeed significant. But can you get the Americans to believe that an attack is imminent, especially since you can't reveal the identities of your sources? What if they simply choose not to believe you?"

The ambassador answered. "If, God forbid, the Americans should choose to disregard this information, then Moshe will understand how the prophet Ezekiel must have felt."

A voice from the speakerphone said, "I'm sorry, but I don't understand."

"When God called the prophet Ezekiel to deliver His warning to the people of Jerusalem, He told him, 'Son of man, I have made you a watchman. . . . Give them warning from me.' Ezekiel's task was to deliver the message, whether they listened or not. Let's hope America does a better job of listening to Moshe's words of warning than our people did in listening to the words of Ezekiel!"

"Amen," Moshe muttered so only he could hear.

* * * * * * * * * *

CHICAGO Ibrahim stared at the light beginning to shine through the thin curtain covering the one window in his room.

The flights from Islamabad to Abu Dhabi, from Abu Dhabi to Damascus, and from Damascus to London had been relatively short. But the flight from London to Mexico City was interminable. Ibrahim had never flown until this journey began, and he discovered that he had a deep fear of flying. For the entire flight his body ached for a cigarette, and the withdrawal made for an enormous headache. Not being allowed to carry his worry beads didn't help.

Because the men were all traveling on South African passports, they had to appear less Middle Eastern. They had shaved their beards and changed their style of clothes while in the home of the Syrian official in Damascus. That official had also told them the next morning that they needed to pack their *misbaha* and not carry the beads with them on the plane.

The misbaha had always served as Ibrahim's natural painkiller. The rhythmic click of the beads passing through his fingers and onto the pile below had a soothing, calming effect. He didn't know the history of the misbaha, so he didn't realize that they were the precursor of the Roman Catholic rosary—its fifty-bead cousin that the Crusaders brought back to Europe some four centuries after it had first entered Muslim culture. Ibrahim had tried to pretend that he held his misbaha, but it had not helped. By the time the plane landed in Mexico City, he was ready to claw his way through the side just to escape the confining space that seemed to squeeze all sanity from his soul.

The entry into the United States had been far less eventful than he had imagined. The passports they had received already contained a visitor's visa for the United States. They had been driven by bus to Matamoros where they spent a full day in their hotel rooms while the smuggler made the necessary arrangements. The following day they boarded the bus and drove to the border. The smuggler presented documents stating that they were a group of South African businessmen touring the *maquiladoras*— the duty-free factories along the U.S. border. They were also studying the impact of these factories and NAFTA on trade in an attempt to revive the economy of South Africa. They were on their way to a symposium in San Antonio to meet with key NAFTA officials.

The references to South Africa and NAFTA were sufficient to explain why a group of non-Hispanic foreigners were entering the United States at Brownsville. And since they had valid visas, were entering the U.S. as part of an organized tour, and had return tickets to South Africa—sched-uled date of return in thirty-two days—they were allowed to enter. If they failed to leave at the scheduled time, they would be considered illegal aliens. But the likelihood of being discovered and arrested before accom-plishing their mission was virtually nonexistent.

From San Antonio each of the terrorists used his passport and credit card to purchase airline tickets to their final destinations. Most flew on Southwest because of its reliability, but some had to fly on American, which required them to brave the confusion of DFW International Airport, located between Dallas and Fort Worth. Eventually all eight teams made their way to their assigned destinations where they were met by local operatives.

Ibrahim and Suleiman found themselves in a new—and for them very frightening—world. They had seen cities before, but never one as crowded as Chicago. They shared a small room in a three-bedroom apartment on North Oakley near Devon in the Little India section of Chicago. An older Jordanian couple lived in the apartment, but the contact had rented the front bedroom for both men. The room had a double bed, a dresser, and a small closet. It also had a single window that looked down on the street below. They also had to share access to the one bathroom in the apartment with the couple. Neither Ibrahim nor Suleiman complained about the accommodations. Neither man would have been comfortable living alone. The customs in the United States were just too different from what they were used to. Living with the couple gave them a sense of security that came from the familiarity of the surroundings.

On their first day in Chicago they had followed instructions and ordered a computer. They paid extra to have it delivered within two business days. It now sat on their dresser, looking completely out of place in their sparsely furnished bedroom. Twice a day the men checked online for any sign of a message from the Teacher. Finding the first message heightened their sense of anticipation. They had less time to prepare than they had thought.

On their second day in Chicago their contact drove them to the Illinois Department of Motor Vehicles to obtain drivers' licenses. Technically, they were not eligible to get a driver's license since they were foreign nationals without valid U.S. social security numbers. But with the aid of a "friend" in the DMV, they were able to obtain commercial drivers' licenses that day.

Every day since, they had spent the late morning and early afternoon learning how to drive in the city using a borrowed taxi—another family connection arranged by the Teacher. They had learned how to drive a car while in Pakistan, but there was a vast difference between driving in the desolate expanse of Pakistan—where the greatest danger was losing a wheel in a deep rut on a dirt road—and driving in Chicago where the cars and pedestrians made any attempt at forward motion challenging. They ventured out only in midday to avoid the crush of traffic during the morning and evening hours—"rush hour" as it was called here—though it seemed to the two men as if the people were *always* rushing.

Neither Ibrahim nor Suleiman felt entirely comfortable in their new surroundings, but progress would be made slowly and deliberately. "The training would prove helpful," Ibrahim admitted as they drove. "We must be prepared for the signal from the Teacher. Drink plenty of coffee and run!" They laughed together nervously, as if reading each other's mind.

CHAPTER 13

THE DISCOVERY

Greg glanced at the clock and saw that he had finished lecturing with just under two minutes remaining. Pointing to the clock, he smiled. "And don't say I never end early!" Nobody laughed. Greg looked at his stack of scattered papers and saw the note he had written before coming to class. "Oh, yeah, and don't forget that the first major paper is due in two weeks.

"For those who have never submitted a major paper to me before, let me answer two questions—and I base these on last year's papers. First, I don't physically count all the words to check your required length. Second, I do read *every sentence*. So don't try to pad the report. I grade by content, pure and simple. Have fun writing!"

The floor shook as students charged for the door and disappeared in seconds after his last word. It was crunch time—that time in the semester when every class seemed to have exams or papers coming due—and the students were starting to feel the pressure.

Greg gathered up his notebook and disconnected his portable computer from the data projector. Packing everything into his khaki Lands' End bag, he quickly left campus and headed home. It was time to see whether the Smith family had posted any new photos online.

He turned the key and pushed against the apartment door. Without even thinking, he groped for the light switch. Three banks of fluorescent lights hummed and then blinked on. The room, piled with books, had a slightly musty smell. Some individuals prided themselves on having all their books neatly arranged and cataloged. Greg was not one of those people. By his own admission, he had more of a piling system than a filing system. Every conceivable space on his shelves seemed to be filled with books. Some were stacked on the shelves while others were jammed into the space between the row of books and the next shelf.

Scattered around the office were other items—memorabilia—that were as eclectic as his own personality. Pictures of Greg at archaeological digs. A hand-carved, olive wood shepherd carrying a sheep on his shoulders. A stuffed "Pirate Larry" doll from the VeggieTales movie *Jonah*. A stone from the Elah brook where David fought Goliath. A Michigan J. Frog music box that played "Hello My Baby" while the frog in the box danced. And two "widow's mites"—ancient small coins like those tossed into the Temple treasury by the widow who was commended by Jesus. Each item came with its own story, and Greg would share that story with any student who asked.

He set his bag on the desk and started to reach inside for the stack of homework he needed to grade. But as he did he noticed the red light on his phone was illuminated—telling him he had a phone message. "You have—one—message," the machine intoned. "Message—one."

"Greg, this is Jillian. I assume you're in class. Listen, I just received a call from Moshe. He is in London, but he needs to come back and talk with us. He missed the last flight today, but he is scheduled to fly out on the first flight from London tomorrow. He will be arriving in Chicago at one tomorrow afternoon. We have a task force meeting scheduled for two. I wondered if you would want to go out to the airport with me to meet him and then be part of the meeting. Anyway, give me a call. There is more to this message, but I'd prefer to share it directly with you rather than to leave it on an answering machine. Call when you get the chance. You have my number. Bye."

Greg nearly deleted the message but then decided against it. He liked hearing Jillian's voice. Instead, he punched in her office number. Two rings and the phone picked up. "Agent Foster. Yes?"

"Jillian, it's Greg. I just got out of class and found your voice mail. What's going on, do you think? What are the other details?" He felt strangely anxious suddenly, and it bothered him. He hated uncertainty.

"Something significant may be going down in the U.S. There is no confirmed link as of yet, but my gut tells me the Internet link you uncovered may hold the key." Jillian paused to think about just how much she should share with Greg. After all, he was a civilian and had not been given any top-secret clearance.

Greg looked around his cluttered apartment and felt a sudden sense of unreality. "Wow... Did Moshe share any details on the phone, or do we have to wait until tomorrow to hear them? Um, by the way," he added, "I can go to the airport with you if you'd like. I've got two classes Friday morning, but they are done by ten. I also have a class in the late afternoon, so I need to be back on campus by quarter to four." He felt he was talking too much, but he was enjoying the thought of another extended car ride with Jillian.

"Thanks, Greg. I'll pick you up at eleven. And it's no problem to have you back in time for your afternoon class. The meeting ought to be done before then. Do you want me to swing by your apartment, or is there some other place I should meet you?"

"Let's rendezvous at the Starbucks where we first met. We can grab something to drink and then head to the airport."

"Sounds great. Have you found anything else?" she asked.

"I've not been able to do much searching for the past few days, but I was hoping to do so tonight. Now I'll be sure to check. Have your people discovered anything?"

"No, unfortunately, they have not. Looking for information from a single picture on the Internet is nearly impossible."

"Maybe I'll have better luck. See you tomorrow at eleven!"

"See you then!" As Jillian hung up she had a frightening thought. *We're in a race with time. If we don't get into these guys' heads, will thousands more families go through what my family did?*

* * * * * * * * * *

Greg sat in his easy chair with his computer perched on his lap. Installing a Wi-Fi hub in his apartment allowed him to sit in comfort while still having high-speed Internet access. And he needed to be as comfortable as possible because he wanted to channel all his energy to the problem at hand. *I need to think like a terrorist. No, that's not correct. I need to think like someone who is smart, but not necessarily an Internet guru.*

He found typing his thoughts helped him think through problems. So he opened Word and stared at the blank screen. He then started to type thoughts and observations in no particular order.

- Knowledge of EXIF files makes the person who developed the plan at least a high-end, nontechnical user. (Could he/they be computer professionals?)
- They don't seem to be computer professionals because the actual communication system is unsophisticated and open to discovery. The message is clearly visible within the EXIF data. (Wouldn't professionals know how to hide information to make it harder to retrieve?)

- Could the system be so simple because not all the individuals are sophisticated? (Communication involves two parties. Both sides must be able to use the system. Whoever set it up must make it simple enough for someone not computer literate to be able to use it.)
- If the messages are connected to Islamic fundamentalists, could that explain the use of the Haram es-Sharif picture and the term "Palestine." (But why say the picture was from the "Smith Family Vacation"?)
- A group could be trained to use a system while they are all together, but once they are scattered it would be very difficult to make changes to the system and explain the changes to those in the field. (Can we assume the system used before is "frozen" and will remain so?)
- The users couldn't predict how many messages would be sent or when they would be sent. Some plans could take days, weeks, or even months to unfold. (Assuming the terrorists needed to "check in" for instructions, how would they know where to look?)

He leaned back from his computer and stared at the thoughts on the screen. Were these good assumptions? And even if they were, what practical insight could he draw from them to help discover the next message? *If I were in charge of this group, how would I set up the system to help my people find my messages?*

He saw two possible solutions, both based on the same principle. *If I want to send a message to someone, I need to make sure that person has the ability to check in the same location—or in a very limited number of locations—for my message.* If a spy knows to look under the same park bench, for example, he could do so every day until he discovers a message. But if the spy was told the message would be left "in the park," there could be an almost unlimited number of places to look. And since he didn't know *when* the message was to be delivered or *where* it would be delivered, the odds of discovering it were slim.

So what was the "park bench" that could remain constant? One possibility was to search for "family vacation pictures" on multiple Web sites. Greg had been doing that, though, without success. This was the most obvious constant, and yet it posed problems. There were many family Web sites with vacation pictures, so the number of possibilities could be incredibly large.

But what if the family name was the constant? If it was, then how would the users know when a new message had been sent? Greg stared at his list for several minutes, letting his mind flow in many directions. And then the words seemed to jump off the page. *Of course!* He didn't need to know the specific site if he knew *where* in the site to look. *I can't look everyplace in a park for a message, but if I know the message is under a bench, I can check all the benches since that is a limited number—even in a large park.* So what was the photographic "park bench" under which he could look?

The original Smith Family Vacation message was discovered in the Haram es-Sharif picture—a spot venerated by Muslims, though now in a city controlled by an enemy of Islam. The only picture later removed from the site was that one. What if the terrorists are to keep looking for that picture to reappear? It could be the "bench."

Now to test out his theory. Greg went to the Flickr Web site, typed in "Haram es-Sharif," and hit Enter.

Bingo!

Flickr presented Greg with thirty-five possible pictures. The seventh was posted by "Smith Family Vacation," and it had been uploaded just two days ago.

It took him less than five minutes to locate the information he was seeking. He viewed the EXIF data, printed the information, and then backed out of the site. Tomorrow's meeting was going to be interesting.

* * * * * * * * * *

The other members of the antiterrorism task force were already gathered in the conference room when Jillian entered, followed by Moshe and Greg. Everyone stopped talking and started to find their way to their seats. Jillian stepped up to the podium to begin the meeting. Greg watched her from his seat next to Moshe along the wall. The drive to the airport had been relaxing. They had stayed away from terrorist plots but had talked of their families, Texas, and a bit about his church. He noticed how Jillian assumed a no-nonsense "FBI look" when she was on duty. Now she called the meeting to order.

"Thank you for coming on this short notice. We actually have two presenters, and I would ask you to listen and take notes—but not ask questions—while they are talking. There will be time afterward for questions. Mr. Zachar, would you go first; and Dr. Hanson, would you follow him?"

Moshe walked to the podium and turned to face his audience. The task force included representatives from local, state, and national government bodies. When Jillian had learned that Moshe was coming with important news, she placed a call to Frank O'Banion. Within an hour of that call, every federal agency had informed Chicago's FBI office, letting them know that they would have a representative at the meeting. The CIA, ATF, INS, and Homeland Security were the major players; but dozens of smaller agencies were also represented. The audience Moshe was about to address represented over forty different agencies or services.

"Agent Foster, thank you for hosting me again. I wish I were here to bring good news, but I am not. In the past few days I have again been in close contact with some very reliable sources in Syria. They have informed me that sixteen terrorists passed through Syria sometime during the last two weeks on their way to Mexico. From there they were to have infiltrated into the United States using valid passports fraudulently obtained from another country. Unfortunately, specific information on the country of issue was not available. It is the belief of these contacts that the terrorists have already succeeded in entering your country.

"Our sources were able to determine that the sixteen terrorists were to divide into eight two-man teams. Some time ago—between one and two months ago, to be precise—a shipment of SA-7 antiaircraft missiles was shipped to the United States, with the shipment's arrival timed to coincide with the arrival of the terrorists. Again, our assumption is that these missiles have already arrived somewhere in this country.

"That is the information we know with a very high degree of reliability. There are some other things we suspect, but which we cannot verify. For example, we suspect that these teams have been completely trained while outside the country. They are not entering the U.S. with the intent of blending into society only to act at some point in the future. We believe they have been prepared to strike within a relatively short period of time—days or weeks, not months or years. We also suspect that the teams are scattering across the United States, perhaps to attack multiple targets simultaneously. And with the type of weapons being smuggled in, we suspect that they plan on targeting commercial airliners.

"That, in essence, is the information we have gathered. I cannot, of course, compromise the sources of our information. But I am open to answering any questions you might have."

The representative from the INS asked the first question. "Mr. Zachar, how can you be sure that these terrorists have indeed made it into our country? Isn't it possible that they will be caught trying to come in?"

"That is, of course, our hope. However, we know the precise day when they flew from Damascus. The information we have indicates that they probably tried to enter the U.S. just about a week ago. There have been no signals back to our sources to indicate they delayed their plans or that they were turned away or detained at the border. Do you know of any instances of a group of foreign nationals trying to enter the U.S. from Mexico being detained?"

"No, sir, I don't. But I will check on it." The INS agent pulled out his cell phone as he walked from the room.

The representative from the CIA was the next to ask a question. "Mr. Zachar, I have two questions. First, playing the devil's advocate, I know your country has had an ongoing struggle with Syria, and it is in your country's best interests to have the U.S. continue to side with you against them. How can we be sure that your ongoing conflicts haven't affected your analysis of the data in a way that would help bring the U.S. into any conflict on your side? Second, to what extent do you believe this is an event sponsored by the Syrian government?"

Moshe flushed in anger at the veiled accusation. "I can start by assuring you that our purpose is not to secure America's help in Israel's ongoing struggle with Syria. Israel can defend itself. And right now we are engaged in quiet discussions with the Syrians to see if we can bring an end to these decades of conflict. I came not as a representative of Israel to seek your help but to help you. I'm risking the exposure of key assets within Syria, who have been of great assistance to Israel in the past. And the only reason I'm doing so is to help a key ally.

"Second, while it might be to Israel's advantage to tell you that this plot is sponsored by the government of Syria, I'm here to tell you that we do not believe that to be the case. Our sources indicate that this is a rogue operation that is unknown to the Syrian government. It does involve a minor government figure, but he is acting on his own to assist a terrorist group originally based in Pakistan. Bottom line: This is not a ruse to get the U.S. to pressure Syria, because we don't believe the Syrian government is involved in the plot. But we obtained the information from within Syria when that country was used as a transit point for the terrorists.

"There are a few other details that may or may not be significant. But they were provided, so I am passing them along to you. At least two of the men are left-handed. The group is made up of a mix of nationalities, based on the different Arab accents that were heard. And some of the individuals do not appear to be very sophisticated. It is likely that they grew up in rural areas or lived in more primitive conditions. That is everything we know."

No one else raised their hands to ask questions. "Thank you, Mr. Zachar," Jillian said. "This information is indeed helpful, though most disturbing. You were all invited here to interact with Mr. Zachar. However, just this morning I learned that there is another piece of information that you need to hear." She introduced Greg and recounted the details of his discovery.

The representative from the CIA again spoke up. "Are you talking about steganography, hiding a secret message in a picture? We've been working on several methods to uncover embedded messages within a visual image. And with all due respect, Dr. Hanson is not a trained observer. How do we—?"

Jillian broke in. "Let's hear from Dr. Hanson."

Greg stood before the group. He had quickly breathed a prayer. Aside from wearing an unaccustomed suit, he felt somewhat out of place in this law enforcement gathering of mostly grim-looking men. "No, sir," he said, turning toward the CIA man. "That's not what I discovered, though I know that is a technique that could be used. What I found is far more 'low tech' than that. In fact, it's the equivalent of hiding in plain sight— like the fugitive who rents a room next to the police station to hide out. It's so potentially obvious that it really doesn't require any effort to find the message, as long as someone knows where to look.

"Most people know about digital photography. But few people with digital cameras know that their camera takes more than just the picture.

Digital pictures also include information like the date and time the picture was taken, the type of camera, the specific lens setting, and other technical data. The format in which this data is collected is called EXIF, Exchangeable Image File format. A good software program that allows you to modify digital pictures, like Photoshop, for example, gives you access to this information.

"A few weeks ago I was searching for a specific picture on the Internet. I found the picture I needed, but I wanted to check to make sure it wasn't copyrighted, so I checked its EXIF data—and came across what appeared to be an embedded message. I shared this information with the FBI, and that's how I became involved in this current series of events.

"When I heard about today's meeting, I went back online to see if I could find any new messages. I discovered another message. And in the process I found what I believe to be the basic protocol being used by this terrorist organization to transmit messages to the individual teams."

The room was absolutely silent. Greg reached into his briefcase and pulled out several sheets of paper. "Here are the pages I came across last evening. I'll give copies to the FBI, and they can distribute them to the groups here that might need access. But I would also add that I believe this information should be given some type of security restriction. If the group ever discovers that we know the procedure they're using, it would be a fairly simple matter for them to change it. And if they did, our chances of discovering any new protocol would be extremely slim.

"I discovered that this group is using a photo-sharing Web site to set up what looks like a simple posting of family photos. And they are using a photograph of the same building in which to embed their messages. The photos are available to anyone online, but the odds of someone viewing this picture are very remote. And the site does allow the owner of the photograph to track the number of people viewing the picture. If too many others would happen to stumble on the site, the person sending the messages would know there has been excess traffic. When I realized this, I printed out a hard copy of the information. Again, I would urge you to restrict knowledge about this site, and limit those who are permitted to access it. If you don't, you could accidentally alert the group to our interest in them."

Greg felt his confidence growing. "Why do I think these messages are connected to the group that Moshe just told you about? Listen to their most recent message—the one that I found posted last night. 'Change in plans. Packages to arrive in 2–3 days. Prepare to use within 14 days. Await final instructions before using.' We just learned that the terrorists have arrived in this country and that the missiles were scheduled to be delivered at about the same time. Suppose the missiles were packaged together and sent to one location. Once there, someone repackaged them and sent them out to the individual cells. It appears that this message was sent to let the individual cell members know they will be receiving the missiles in two days and that the anticipated attack will probably be scheduled within two weeks. A final message will probably go out just before the attack, possibly with any last-minute instructions. Oh, one other thing. The photo was posted two days ago."

Greg finished and looked around the room. No one spoke. Jillian walked back to the podium.

"I agree with Greg that the specific information on the Web site needs to be restricted. Since Greg is the one who discovered it, I would like him to keep monitoring the site on a daily basis. We are asking the FBI's tech people to see if they can find any information about the person or persons who set up the site as well as the identities of those who are accessing the site. We may be seeking the help of other agencies on this, and if you have any individuals in your agencies who have particular expertise in these matters, please let us know as quickly as possible."

There were more questions and more discussion. After the morning session of the meeting broke up, Jillian invited both Greg and Moshe to be her guests for dinner. "I think we're all going to need a break once this day is over," she said.

* * * * * * * * * *

"Jillian, this place serves fantastic Italian food! How did you know about it?" Greg asked, breaking a chunk of garlic bread apart.

She smiled. "Well, I knew about Maggiano's from my time in Texas. It was a great place to go to celebrate birthdays, passing major exams, or any other excuse we could think of. About my first or second week in Chicago, I had to interview someone on the Near North Side. I was heading west on Grand when the light turned red. I was mumbling to myself about missing the light when I looked over to my left and *voilà*; there it was! I knew I would be coming back here for some type of celebration. I just didn't know what it would be!"

Moshe lifted his glass of wine. "I propose a toast to you for sharing this celebration with us!"

"Thank you, Moshe; you both are so kind. I have enjoyed this assignment, and much of the reason has been the opportunity to get to know both of you. I—" she paused as if trying to decide whether or not to continue.

"What is it? What else were you going to say?" asked Greg.

"It's actually on a completely different subject, and I'm not sure if this is the proper time to bring it up."

"What—you forgot your wallet and now we must all wash dishes!" Moshe said in a mocking tone.

"No, it's actually the one missing puzzle piece I've been carrying around inside me since my brother died in the World Trade Center attack."

Moshe grimaced. "I'm sorry for my inappropriate comment. Please share with us what is on your mind."

"Well, it's actually one of the fundamentals of building a good criminal case. Did the suspect have the *means* to commit the crime, did he have a *motive* for committing it, and did he have an *opportunity* to commit it? When it comes to Islamic fundamentalism I can understand the means and the opportunity, but I still can't fully comprehend their motive. And that's why they seem so unpredictable to me. What motivates them?"

Moshe responded first. "As an Israeli citizen, and one who himself was a victim of terrorism, I can offer a little insight. Most of the problem centers around the Israel/Palestinian crisis. In 1947 the United Nations voted to partition the land of Palestine into two separate countries. One part would go to the Jewish people living in the land, and the other part would go to the Arabs living there. This was a compromise solution to a very difficult problem. The Jews, somewhat reluctantly, agreed to the deal, but the Arabs did not. The State of Israel was born in 1948, but the State of Palestine was stillborn on that day. Instead, the land promised to the Palestinians by the United Nations was gobbled up by Egypt and Jordan.

"Another major war was fought in 1967. Egypt, Jordan, and Syria united together to 'drive the Jews into the sea.' Our people expected a great bloodbath. We didn't choose war; but we decided that if they did, we would at least choose how it started. We launched a surprise attack against the Egyptian air force and destroyed most of their planes while they were still on the ground. In six days we captured the Golan Heights from Syria, the West Bank from Jordan, and the Gaza Strip and Sinai Peninsula from Egypt. We offered to return the land in exchange for peace, but the Arabs responded three months later with their three no's: no peace with Israel, no recognition of Israel, no negotiations with Israel."

"But didn't Egypt and Jordan later make peace?" asked Jillian.

"Yes, they did, but it came at a price. Egypt was the first to make peace with Israel, and it cost Anwar Sadat his life. Jordan made peace with Israel between the end of the first Gulf War, and the start of peace negotiations between Israel and the Palestinians. Unfortunately, those negotiations bogged down because Yasser Arafat never had the strength of character to lead his people to peace."

Jillian nodded her head. "So the real motive for terrorism today is this ongoing conflict between Israel and the Palestinians over Palestinian land controlled by Israel. But if that's the case, why are they attacking the United States and other Western countries?"

Greg decided to enter the conversation. "The ultimate issue, I think, is this: Whose God is *really* God? Part of the reason Islamic fundamentalists have attacked the U.S. is because we have supported Israel's right to exist in their own land as a nation. But here is the deeper issue, the one that is lost on most Americans. When the United Nations voted to establish the nation of Israel in 1947, this was seen as an affront to Islam—or at least to those whom we would probably call Islamic fundamentalists. Islam teaches a form of what is called replacement theology."

"What's that?" asked Jillian.

"It's a belief that the Jews were once God's chosen people, but that because of their disobedience God set them aside and selected a new 'chosen people' in their place. Some Christians believe the church replaced the Jews as God's chosen people. I don't believe that is what the Bible teaches at all, but that's a discussion that would take all night. Anyway, replacement theology believes that God 'replaced' the Jews with the Christians.

"Islam takes that theology one step further. They would say that the Christians did indeed replace the Jews as God's chosen people, but that God has since replaced *them* with His *true* followers—those who recognize that there is no god but Allah alone and that Muhammad is his final prophet. So Islam is the true, ultimate, and final representation of God's people here on earth.

"Now, imagine what the formation of the State of Israel does to your theology if, as an Islamic fundamentalist, you believe this. You have been taught that you have replaced the Jews and the Christians and that your religion will take over the world. But the past eight hundred years have seen Islamic countries slip into poverty and misery even as the 'Christian' West advanced on all fronts. And then the group you considered twice cursed by God—the Jews—take control of land that you have conquered for—and consecrated to—Allah. And not only that; in 1967 they gained control of the third holiest site in all Islam—the Haram es-Sharif. How do you reconcile that present reality with the foundational beliefs of your religion?"

Moshe sipped his wine and looked thoughtful. Jillian seemed genuinely confused. "I don't know. How *do* you reconcile them?"

"One option is to question the fundamental beliefs on which Islam is based—to ask the hard question as to whether the things they have been taught might indeed be untrue. But for most true followers of Islam that's not even a remote option. A second possibility is to frame the problem as one that arises not from God but from His followers. 'Our religion teaches that we have replaced the Jews and Christians, but right now they are prospering while we suffer. Since this is not what God has willed, it must have come to pass because of our infidelity to him. Allah wants to bless his people, but we have been lax in following his commands. Only when we turn back and follow God completely will he give us the victory he has promised.'"

"So you're saying that the rise in terrorism is related to this turning back to God?"

"Indirectly, yes. It's no accident that the rise of Islamic fundamentalism parallels the rise of the State of Israel, especially the events of the Six-Day War in 1967. That is when these religious zealots started making major inroads into their Islamic communities. They really have a two-fold call. It's a call to religious purification on the part of Muslims. And

it's a call to reignite the struggle against non-Muslims who are opposing Allah's plan to bring all the world under his control. The two leading opponents are the Christians—in their eyes that's Western Europe
and the United States—and the Jews in Israel. And that's why the primary focus of Islamic fundamentalism has been directed against these
two groups."

Jillian looked genuinely troubled. "So where is the room for compromise? It sounds as if you are saying that the only possible resolution is for
one side to win and the other to lose?"

Greg pondered her question for a moment. "I'm not sure if I can
provide you with an answer. Certainly, the United States has been committed to the principle of religious tolerance. Our Constitution guaran-
tees the free exercise of religious liberty to all. But frankly, I don't know
if Islamic fundamentalism can ever acknowledge such religious tolerance.
In countries where Islam is the dominant religion, other faiths—including Christianity—are suppressed. For example, a Christian can convert
to Islam, but a Muslim is not permitted to convert to Christianity. And if
they are not willing to tolerate the free practice of other faiths, then we are
probably looking at a conflict that can only end when one side has van-
quished the other."

Moshe, shaking his head sadly, turned to face Greg. "You have just
described the entire history of Israel since 1948. And, at least so far, there
has been no end in sight to our conflict. But I sincerely hope you are
wrong."

"So do I," said Greg.

CHAPTER 14

THE DELIVERY

Suleiman pulled back the flimsy yellow curtain to look yet again down on the street. "This must be the day," he muttered as he strained to see the deserted avenue. "The message said two or three days, and this is the third day. It must arrive today."

"Patience. Your anxiety only makes the time seem longer." Ibrahim was the older of the two men, though only by about ten years. But the loss and struggle he had endured had aged him. His beard, before he shaved it off, had become mostly gray; and now the hair on his head was mostly white. Suleiman's strength and agility complemented Ibrahim's wisdom and experience.

"Ibrahim, don't you believe that—?" Ibrahim raised his hand to silence Suleiman. While continuing to hold up his right hand like a policeman signaling for a driver to stop, he cupped his left hand behind his ear. Suleiman understood, and cocked his head toward the window to see if he could hear what it was that had caught Ibrahim's attention.

A distant siren whined. The elevated train clacked by. It took him several seconds to isolate the low rumble of a truck. The pitch of the sound increased, signaling its approach. Neither Ibrahim nor Suleiman had ever studied physics or heard of the Doppler effect—which explained why the sound of something moving seems to increase in pitch as it approaches and decrease in pitch as it moves away.

Suleiman pulled back the curtains and strained to look down the street. Several buildings down was a brown UPS delivery van moving slowly toward their location. Just as it approached the house, the van slowed down and pulled to the curb. The driver stepped back into the storage compartment and emerged carrying a large box. He set the box on the ground by the truck and went back inside, emerging with a second box, identical to the first. He pulled his handcart from the truck, loaded both boxes onto it, and started pushing the cart up the front sidewalk. Suleiman and Ibrahim ran through the apartment, out into the hall, and down the stairs. They reached the front door at the same time as the UPS driver.

Ibrahim opened the door and said, "Do I need to sign anything?"

The UPS driver barely glanced up. "I just need one of your signatures here indicating you received both packages." Ibrahim put a scratched signature on the portable screen and smiled back at the nameless deliveryman.

Ibrahim realized in his rush he had written his name in Arabic. But he figured the scratch was basically unintelligible anyway. "Thank you," said Ibrahim, handing the monitor back to the driver.

The driver tipped the handcart forward and wriggled it from side to side to slide the base out from under the boxes. He then turned and walked back to his truck. He had too many Saturday delivery packages still on the truck, and he didn't have time to chat. Besides, a GPS device was monitoring his progress—another way to help ensure his "productivity."

As the driver hurried toward his truck, Ibrahim and Suleiman hoisted the packages onto their shoulders and walked back into the building. The climb up the stairs to the apartment was hard, but they wouldn't stop until the packages were safely in their own room. Ibrahim gently sat his package on the bed. He motioned for Suleiman to do the same while he walked back to close and lock the bedroom door.

"What is the matter, Ibrahim? Don't you even trust the family with whom we are staying?"

"Of course I do," replied Ibrahim. "But remember this. After the attack, the government will track down every possible lead. It is not too much to assume they will be able to discover the contents of these packages and track their delivery back to this house. For the sake of the family, I want them to be able to say that they saw the packages being delivered but that they never saw what was inside."

"But couldn't the family say this anyway?"

"They could. But what if the United States has some drug that forces a person to speak only the truth? Then they would be caught in this lie. They are a good Muslim family, and they really don't know who we are or what we will be doing. I want to spare them from becoming victims. I know what it is like to be caught in the middle of such a struggle, and I wish that fate on no one." Ibrahim paused and then took a deep breath. Everything whirled together in a flash in his mind. His own family's tragic death, the stress of the timing of this operation, the eventual devastation he would bring. It all converged in a single thought and made his heart skip. He sat down for a moment to calm his mind.

Ibrahim, like many others, didn't understand how the United States was able to gather all the information that it did. It was the great unknown piece of this puzzle that nagged away at his mind. The Americans. *What if they find out? What if they follow a tiny lead that leads them to a critical detail?* The rumor of such a truth serum gained validity because it helped explain how the U.S. government could obtain such highly accurate information. It made more sense to these men than some detailed explanation of the science of forensics.

Ibrahim and Suleiman looked in awe at the boxes on their beds. Opening the outer box, they found the package inside completely covered in plastic and packing tape. It reminded Ibrahim of an ancient Egyptian mummy. He sat on the corner of the bed while Suleiman stood on the other side. Taking a knife he had purchased in a local hobby shop, Ibrahim carefully sliced through all the tape and plastic midway along the sides of each package. The knife blade found its way into the cracks where the two sides of the inner box joined together. At three places on one side of each box, the knife was forced from the crack. These were the three clasps that held the inner box closed.

Ibrahim carefully pulled the plastic partially off the inner box and then cut the tape from around each clasp. He held the bottom of the first box while Suleiman reached across the bed and grasped the top. Pulling from opposite directions, they forced the tape-encrusted box open. Then they repeated the operation on the second container. Gazing inside, they discovered that everything had been wrapped in newspaper to provide extra padding and to keep the parts from being bumped around in shipment. They unwrapped the rocket tubes, grip stocks, and thermal batteries. The missiles themselves were packed inside the launch tubes, each of the tubes sealed with bubble wrap to keep the missile from being jostled.

Suleiman stood at the edge of the bed, seemingly transfixed by the collection of parts lying before him. "To think, Ibrahim, that such a small collection of weapons will soon be used to unleash such great destruction on this evil country!"

"*Inch' Allah*, Suleiman, that day will soon be here. But can I ask you something? What is it that started you along the path to becoming one of the mujahideen? You have heard my story, but I don't recall ever hearing yours. You are a Palestinian Arab, are you not?"

"Indeed I am. And perhaps that explains, at least in part, how I came to join this noble cause. I'm originally from the Balata refugee camp, just outside Nablus, in occupied Palestine. I was the next to the youngest of eleven children. Several years ago one of my older brothers was brutally murdered by the Zionist settlers. He was totally unarmed, and they gunned him down. He had been without work for two years while trying to support a wife and three young children. Out of desperation he tried to slip into a settlement compound at night. He hoped to steal one of their cars and take it back to Nablus to sell for spare parts. He did not want to steal, but he couldn't let his children go hungry. He was spotted crawling into the settlement, and they opened fire without giving him any opportunity to surrender.

"After that incident my mother urged me to go find work in Saudi Arabia. Jobs were available there for Palestinians, even though there were still hard feelings over our support for Saddam Hussein when he invaded Kuwait. My mother hoped that I would be safe and that I could earn enough to help support my brother's children.

"I went to Saudi Arabia, but it was a hard life. Many Saudis looked down on Palestinians and treated us much as the Israelis did. The jobs open to us were the ones the Saudis thought beneath themselves. I worked in a restaurant waiting on tables and cleaning dishes. I earned enough money to meet my needs—with some left over at the end of each month to send home—but I still felt imprisoned.

"Then, just over two years ago, I received news that my sister had become a martyr, leaving a young son to be raised by my mother."

"How did she become a martyr?"

"It started when her husband, Yousef, was recruited by the al-Aqsa Martyrs' Brigades. He died in an operation against an Israeli patrol in Nablus. My sister was left with her baby, but with little else. The leader of the cell let it be known that he would like to take my sister as his second wife. She did not want to marry him but to refuse was to bring dishonor—and even danger—on our family. She felt trapped, and the only way to preserve her honor, and to protect her son, was to become a martyr. She attacked a wedding party in a large Israeli settlement. I heard that the bride and groom were both killed, along with several members of the wedding party."

"And then what happened?"

"As they always do, the Israelis retaliated. I don't know who told them where our family lived—though I would like to find out so I could cut out his tongue—but the Israelis came to blow up our house in Balata. This is the house that my grandfather and father built when they were forced to leave our family home in Haifa during the first war with the Jews.

"The cell tried to ambush the Israelis when they came to demolish our house. There was a gun battle, and one Israeli was wounded. I never heard whether he lived or died. But two members of the resistance were killed in the operation. One was a cousin and the second was still another of my brothers. In the end, the Israelis did blow up the house, leaving my mother with nothing except a grandchild to raise—and another son to mourn."

"And this is when you decided to become a mujahideen warrior?"

"When I heard the news I was numb with grief and loss, but inside I was also churning with anger—anger at the Israelis, and anger at the ineffective Palestinian resistance. And did any of the Saudis come to express their sorrow at my loss? No. But one day in the mosque an older man walked over and sat down beside me—placing his hand on my shoulder. He was a Pakistani, Yousef, the assistant to the Teacher. Someone evidently told him what had happened, and he came to see me. He sat with me, prayed with me, wept with me. And he told me how Allah could use even these difficult circumstances to prepare me to serve him. He offered me the opportunity to help Allah gain a measure of revenge on those who helped support the evil Zionist enemy. A few weeks later he arranged for my transport to Pakistan, and that's where I met the Teacher—and you."

Ibrahim was taken aback by the similarity in their life stories. True, they were from different cultural and social backgrounds. But they had both faced unbearable hardship and tragedy. And during that time of intense struggle, both had been visited by a representative of the Teacher, who spoke of a way to heal their heartache and loss by channeling their pain into a plan to exact revenge. Ibrahim saw it as a clear example of Allah demonstrating his mercy by providing someone to offer comfort and hope. "Suleiman, let's repack the missiles and then drive out toward O'Hare Airport to search for possible launch locations. Now that the missiles have arrived, the day to use them cannot be far away."

"An excellent plan. But should we not send an e-mail to the Teacher letting him know that the missiles have arrived?"

"Yes, we should! I'll send the message while you repack the missiles."

Suleiman packed each SA-7 back into its box. Once he was finished he closed the boxes and placed them under the beds. He then gathered up the plastic and tape and carried it down to the Dumpster beside the back steps.

While Suleiman was doing this, Ibrahim turned on the computer. Once it was finished booting up, he opened Eudora and typed in the address of a Hotmail account—Qadissiyah15@hotmail.com—an otherwise nondescript address named for an early battle in which the Muslims defeated the Persians. The battle took place in AD 636, which was year 15 in the Islamic calendar, hence the number added after the name. Ibrahim thought this was a nice addition.

After typing in the address, he added a simple one-sentence message: "The packages arrived. I and S." And then he hit Send.

"Suleiman, it is your turn to drive. I will be the passenger. Do you have our city map that we can use to mark the best spots to launch the missiles?"

"I do!"

"Good! Let's drive out toward this place called Elk Grove Village and see what it is like on the western side of the airport. The prevailing winds are from the west, so it is most likely that we will be searching for an airplane that will be taking off in that direction. I also want to look at a park on the map called the Metro-Majewski Athletic Complex. It's right off Interstate 90 at the northwest end of the airport, and the information on the Internet said it was a remote location. Let's see if it will give us the view we seek!"

As they pulled away from the curb, Ibrahim felt a great sense of excitement. With the missiles in hand, the time for action was growing ever closer. And he was ready.

* * * * * * * * * *

The assistant was concentrating so intently on the computer screen that he never heard the soft slap of the Teacher's sandals brushing across the cement floor. "How is your search coming for identifying our likely targets?"

Turning so rapidly that he nearly fell out of his seat, the assistant put his hand to his chest. "Oh, I'm sorry, but you startled me! I'm afraid I was concentrating so much on the work at hand that I didn't hear you come in."

"Do not worry. I was just checking my e-mail, and I have received word from all the teams that the missiles have been delivered. It appears that one might have been damaged in shipment, but all the others seem to have arrived safely."

"Which team has the problem?"

"It is the team in Los Angeles—Walid and Muhammad. Now that we know all the missiles have arrived, I wanted to check to see how you were coming on identifying the likely targets."

"Very well. I have already developed a list of potential targets for Wednesday, and I will also develop a list for Thursday. I'm assuming the flights will be virtually identical for both days, but I want to check just to be sure. And with the possibility of only having one missile in Los Angeles, I will want to recheck the target I have selected to make sure it is one that can be brought down by a single missile. I should have all of this completed within the next two or three hours."

"Good. As soon as you are finished, bring the information to me. I want to send it out to the teams as quickly as possible. The coming week should, *inch' Allah*, turn out to be a wonderful week."

CHAPTER 15

THE DECODING

"Suleiman, you are becoming a good driver. You only tried to kill us three times today!" Ibrahim sighed heavily and wiped his forehead with his sleeve. "If you get any better, people may think perhaps you are *not* a taxi driver!" Ibrahim wrapped his arms around Suleiman's shoulders. "You drove me all around the airport; now could you at least carry me up the stairs!"

Ibrahim genuinely cared for Suleiman. He was like a younger brother. He made the same mistakes most young men make. Confusing bravery with recklessness, blind to the consequences of his actions, and living as if he were invincible. But he was willing to take instruction, and that set him apart from many his age. He had listened to the Teacher, and he was listening to Ibrahim.

"Ibrahim, let's reward ourselves this evening by going to a restaurant. I was told there is a great Lebanese restaurant downtown where we can eat shawarma and shish taouk," Suleiman blurted with the enthusiasm of an adolescent thinking with his stomach.

"Good, but first I need to check if a message has arrived in our absence."

Once the computer had fully booted, Ibrahim launched Internet Explorer, went to his bookmark for Flickr, and searched for the "Smith Family Vacation" pictures. In just a few seconds he saw the posted pictures, including a new one of Haram es-Sharif.

"Allah u Akbar!" he shouted when he saw the message. And he reached over to turn on the printer.

"What have you found? Is there a message?"

"There is, my young friend. And it could be the very message we have been waiting to receive. It's coded, so let me print it out and then we can decipher it, perhaps over dinner. We may indeed have something to celebrate!"

* * * * * * * * * *

Greg finally finished all his grading, but it was almost six thirty Saturday night. He had hoped to finish about five, but it had taken longer to read the papers than he had anticipated. Now he munched on a sandwich from Subway while he waited for his Mac to boot up. He wanted to check once again to see if there were any new pictures posted online for the "Smith" family. Fifteen minutes later he reached for his phone and punched in Jillian's number on the speed dial. He wondered if she'd be out on a Saturday night.

She answered after two rings. "Greg. What's up?" She propped herself up in her bed. After a hectic week she had gone home, microwaved a pizza, thrown on her nightclothes, and climbed into bed to watch a movie.

"There's another message, but this time it's in some type of code. I think you need to see it."

She climbed off the bed. "Where can we meet?"

"It might be best to meet at your office. Is Moshe still in town?"

"He is. The Israeli government has seconded him to us—at least for a week or so—to help us locate these guys. You want me to contact him and bring him to the office?"

"I think that would be good. Can we meet in an hour?"

"See you then." Jillian nearly dropped the phone trying to reattach it to the base. She ran to the closet, grabbed her jeans and sweater, and quickly got dressed. She hoped this was significant enough to disturb Moshe and make the trip to the office worthwhile.

* * * * * * * * * *

Jillian and Moshe were already at the office when Greg arrived. He passed quickly now through the security system, thanks to Jillian's arranging for him to receive special clearance and a temporary ID for automatic access. Once in the office wing, Greg didn't waste any time getting to the information.

"Thanks for agreeing to meet on such short notice," he said, slightly out of breath from the dash from the parking garage to the elevator cavern.

"No thanks needed," she answered, motioning toward Moshe, who was seated in a small chair in the center of the room. "Still nothing of real consequence on this end, unfortunately. What do you have?"

Greg shrugged his shoulders. "Actually, I'm not quite sure what I have. First, let me show you the message, and then let me tell you what I've been able to figure out in the limited time that I've had to think about it."

Moshe rose from his chair and moved across the room to be closer to him. Jillian motioned Greg to proceed.

He pulled two sheets of white printer paper from a folder. The two pages represented a complete printout of a Web page, including the message. The message itself was on the second sheet, near the top of the page. It said:

Headline: third or fourth day; have both locations prepared
Instructions: QUP ZZO 02 0011; ZGO WZO 427 0010; NRZ FHZ 363 0011; LIW ZZO 926 0116; OZC WZO 801 1311; WUD ZZO 046 0101; WVM FZO 477 1210; KWC MDZ 5836 1311

"This is some type of code," Moshe said. "Is there some way to decipher this, Jillian?"

"Greg, you've seen it the longest," said Jillian. "What do you make of it?"

Greg ran his hands through his hair and then grabbed a blank sheet of paper. "Let me start by saying that the code—or whatever it is—in that second part of the note is still basically gibberish to me. I think you need to send it off to whomever you have at the FBI, CIA, NSA, or even Mossad, and see if they can crack it, because I don't think we have a lot of time. But here are my thoughts on the message, which are still fairly random." He was quickly jotting his main points on the blank sheet of paper.

"First, the 'third or fourth day' seems to be some type of deadline. But we don't know what the starting point is for the message. Is it the third or fourth day from the time when it was posted, or is it the third or fourth day from a predetermined starting point? I have some trouble with the first possibility because these teams might not necessarily look for the message at the same time. What if one found it today but another found it tomorrow? It just seems to me like there needs to be some fixed starting point, but we don't know what that starting point is."

Moshe and Jillian both nodded that they were following him so far.

"Second, at first glance the code looks baffling, but it does have some sense of order. Look carefully at it. It has eight different segments, each separated by a semicolon. We are fairly certain that there are eight teams of terrorists. Therefore, it's possible that each segment is directed to a specific group. Also, each segment is fairly regular. Each has two groups of letters followed by two groups of numbers. Both sets of letters are always in groups of three, and the last set of numbers is always a set of four. But the middle set of numbers has two, three, or four digits. The pattern seems to be very regular, but I haven't been able to crack the code, at least not yet.

"The part I was thinking about while driving up here were the groups of letters. What comes in groups of three letters? Many people's names, if you list their first, middle, and last initials. But not all individuals have three letters in their initials—and some have more than three—so I'm not sure if the initials could refer to people. Airports have three-letter designations, but I couldn't match any of these letters up with specific airport codes that I know—and I know most of the major ones. I would assume the terrorists would be attacking major airports because that's where the larger airplanes are going to be, but that might be a false assumption. It's even possible that the division of the letters into groups of three was designed simply to throw us off track—to get us running down a false trail."

Jillian picked up the piece of paper on which Greg had been writing, as well as the two sheets he had pulled from his computer. "I agree with you that it's extremely significant, but we're still a long way from understanding what it all points to. It's Saturday night, and that is probably the worst possible time to send this out for analysis. But we'll work with what we've got. I'm going to fax this to our specialist team in Washington. They can start circulating it among the other agencies in our antiterrorism task force. We just might get lucky. Someone just might nail this at first glance." Jillian maintained an unusual confidence in the government's abilities to decipher these types of encryptions. She knew her optimism was not shared by many of her colleagues at the Agency, especially since the 9/11 investigations revealed such glaring inefficiencies in the system.

Still, her hope for finding some closure to her brother's death compelled her to trust her team.

"Moshe, you may want to fax this information to Mossad, as well. Who knows, hopefully someone will be able to put the rest of the puzzle together for us."

Moshe instantly sprang into action, understanding the press of time. Mossad also had some extremely resourceful people capable of cracking the thorniest of codes.

Within thirty minutes both faxes had been sent. Unfortunately, they could not have arrived at a more inconvenient time. Most of the FBI staff worked a nine-to-five, Monday-to-Friday schedule. The fax arrived at the FBI headquarters at nine thirty Friday evening. It was logged, filed, and placed in a folder for the analyst—who would return at nine on Monday morning.

The fax sent to Mossad didn't fare much better. It arrived in Tel Aviv at four thirty Sunday morning, the first day of the Jewish workweek. Unfortunately, the skeleton crew on duty was already focused on an operation being undertaken in Syria. A top leader of Hamas who lived in Damascus had ordered his followers in Gaza to launch rockets against Jewish settlements. On Thursday a small child was killed by one of the explosions. Mossad, working with agents from Jordan, were planting a bomb inside the terrorist's car that very evening. The next morning, when the suspect got into his car to drive to his office, he would learn a hard lesson about Israeli justice. Moshe's fax was placed in a bin to await the arrival of the full staff later in the day.

* * * * * * * * * *

"Suleiman, wonderful choice! The food was perfect." Ibrahim had been longing for a good Middle Eastern meal. This was a little bland— probably to make it more palatable to Westerners. But it was still good enough to satisfy Ibrahim's yearning for a reminder of home. "Let's go back to the apartment. I think there are some things we need to do."

Less than thirty minutes later Suleiman closed the door to their cramped apartment and dropped the car keys on the small table beside the bed. Ibrahim had already walked over to the computer and turned it on. He opened Internet Explorer and selected Arabic Broadcasting Services. In a few seconds their computer's speakers were broadcasting live Arabic music from Australia. Every so often the music would stop to re-buffer because of their slow connection. But it was still the music they both enjoyed, and the sound helped guard their conversation from anyone who might seek to listen in.

"Ibrahim, you have been very quiet this evening. Have you been thinking about the assignment?" Suleiman kicked off his shoes and walked over to where Ibrahim sat staring at the glowing laptop.

"Yes, I have, and I must assure you, my friend, that I was not quiet because I am worried. I believe Allah has been very gracious to us. We all made it into the United States, and the missiles have also arrived. You and I have adequate housing, and we have made good progress in finding a place to launch the missiles. I believe several of the locations we visited today are suitable." Ibrahim spoke softly, almost as if in a trance. He never moved his gaze from the computer.

"We must settle on one location at the northwestern end of the airport, but we must also find a location on the eastern side. And from what the last message said, we only have a few days. And we have not yet mastered the scanner."

"Ah, yes, the scanner!"

After ordering their Dell computer, Ibrahim had also purchased a Bearcat BC-92XLT portable radio scanner. The scanner would give them the ability to monitor police, fire, weather, and airport broadcast frequencies. "We have our scanner, but we are still not proficient at using it. We don't know the exact frequencies used by the control tower for departures. Nor do we know the frequencies for all the local, state, and federal law enforcement agencies. All this information is available on the Internet, but we need to obtain it and then enter it into the scanner. I want to get this information tonight, and then, beginning tomorrow, we need to listen to these frequencies. This will be vitally important to us." Ibrahim paused, took a deep breath, and finally turned his head slightly to look up at Suleiman, now watching closely over his shoulder.

"And we must plan our escape." Ibrahim's tone became more serious and ominous. It was the first hint of fear or maybe doubt Suleiman had detected in the man who possessed almost an ice-like calm and focus.

The feeling made Suleiman agitated. "I know this is part of the plan, but I do not like the way the Teacher kept stressing the importance of an escape plan. My brother, my sister, her husband, and my cousin all died as martyrs in the struggle with the infidels. Isn't it noble to die for such a cause? Why must we slink away like the jackal, only to be shot or captured? Why not die gloriously and roar like lions in our deaths?"

Ibrahim assumed the role of the father/teacher. "My friend, there is nothing wrong with dying for Allah in our struggle against the infidels. Indeed, that is a very real possibility. And should that happen, Allah himself will reward us for our faithfulness and welcome us into paradise. But the danger in your thinking is that you are only focusing on yourself. To die as a martyr might indeed be best for you, but is it best for the jihad? Think about this. If we shoot down a plane and then die, the plane is lost but so are we. Within a few weeks people will again venture into the sky. But if we shoot down the plane and then escape, the authorities will spend weeks—months—and many millions of dollars trying to find us. And people will stay far away from their airports out of fear that we might once again strike. By staying alive the force of our action is multiplied.

"We must go into this conflict prepared to die. But if we can attack—and live—the impact on the minds and hearts of those in America will be even greater. Now I must ask you one final question."

"What is that, Ibrahim?" Suleiman now felt even more uneasy than before.

"Have you purchased a knife? Remember, we don't have the time to obtain a rifle or pistol, but that doesn't mean we should enter the battle unarmed. A good knife, skillfully used, is indeed a potent weapon. And you *have* been trained how to use a knife in such a way."

"I have not purchased one, but I will make sure that I do tomorrow!" Suleiman sat down on the bed across the room from where Ibrahim sat at the computer. His heart had started to beat rapidly and made him dizzy and weak in the legs.

CHAPTER 16

FOUND

On Saturday night a cold front blew into Chicago. Icy rain pelted the windows of Greg's car as he drove back to his apartment. The dark clouds matched his mood. He had shared the coded message with Jillian and Moshe, but their efforts to decipher it proved to be fruitless. The message remained an incomprehensible mass of letters and numbers.

He had spent most of the day preparing for classes and grading papers. But he had one final item on his to-do list before he could give his body the rest it so desperately craved. He was still teaching a Sunday school class at his church, and he needed to prepare Sunday's lesson. "This is what got me involved in the whole mess in the first place!" he muttered to himself as he pulled out his Bible and the other books he would need. "Me and my curiosity. Should have stuck with Bible teaching."

Each week he was focusing on a key city in the Bible and then using history and archaeology to help make that city come alive for his class. This week he was focusing on the city of Babylon, which is now in modern-day Iraq.

The preparation went far more smoothly than he had expected. *Thank You, Lord, for Your kindness!* He found a number of Web sites with pictures of the ruins of ancient Babylon. It didn't hurt that American and Polish troops had been stationed at Camp Babylon after the fall of Saddam Hussein's regime. A number of Americans with digital cameras had taken pictures of the buildings inside Babylon that Saddam Hussein had rebuilt, lavishing them with gold while depriving the Iraqi people of the wealth that belonged to them. Several sets of these photos had been posted on the Internet.

He had great pictures and solid historical information. Now all he needed to do was to wrap that information around the key passages in the Bible. Using his Bible study software, Greg make a quick note of the major passages that focused on Babylon: Genesis 10–11; Isaiah 13–14; 39; Jeremiah 50–51; and Revelation 17–18. *That's way too many passages for a Sunday school lesson. I need to read through them and pare them down to the one or two key ones.* Greg had never been accused of underpreparing, even if he was exhausted.

He was just over halfway through his reading when he stopped, threw down his pen, and started muttering to himself. "Could it be that simple? Lord, if this works out, You will have made my day!" And then he moved his Bible to the side and opened his word processing program. Twenty minutes later he placed another call to Jillian—this time rousing her from a fitful sleep. He told her to get Moshe and drive down to his apartment. He had a little work to do, and since he was doing the discovering, they could do the driving.

* * * * * * * * * *

"Okay, Greg, what's the great news that was so important we had to climb out of bed and drive down here to see you?" Jillian's nerves were beginning to wear thin.

Moshe walked in silently and set his hat and umbrella inside the front door. He never said a word, but nodded at Greg to acknowledge his presence.

"Well, when you hear what I found you might be glad you skipped whatever you had planned in your dreams—even if it was dinner with the president!" He was joking, but Jillian's little fit bothered him and pushed him to sarcasm.

"Moshe, I don't suppose you've heard anything back from Mossad?" Greg asked, wanting to draw him into the conversation.

"No. I've heard nothing," Moshe answered before sitting down at Greg's small kitchen table.

"Well, I think I may have figured out the code. But I need to share *how* I came across the key to unlocking it first. It will make more sense that way, and it will give testimony to how powerfully the Lord works." He had remained discreet about expressing his faith—mainly, out of respect for Moshe and for fear of annoying Jillian. But this was an occasion where praise seemed appropriate and he offered it gladly to the Lord.

Greg asked Jillian to sit down. He offered his guests some coffee, which they declined. He took that as his cue to get to the point sooner than later.

"Moshe, I'm not sure if I really shared with you how I got involved in all this in the first place, but it really began with a Sunday school class I had agreed to teach. I'm teaching it again tomorrow, and I was staying up late tonight preparing. Each week I've been choosing a city from the Bible and taking my students there on a visit, so to speak. Tomorrow the city we are to visit is the ancient city of Babylon. It would be now in modern-day Iraq."

"I know Babylon, Greg," Moshe said respectfully. "My wife's family came from Iraq. Babylon is a city rich in biblical history and legend."

"Precisely. And I found some great pictures on the Web, and then I spent some time reading through the major Bible passages on Babylon.

My goal was to search for those clues that could help me make the city come alive to the students."

"What kind of things were you looking for?" asked Jillian.

"Things that would appeal to high school students. For example, the story of the Tower of Babel in the Bible is related to Babylon. I'm planning on asking them if they have ever struggled with a foreign language, and then I'll relate their struggles to that event. I try to find common points of interest that make the Bible more relevant to an audience who often view it as a dusty old book."

Jillian looked puzzled but tried to remain engaged. All this talk of the Bible left her feeling in the dark. She knew it was her own fault.

"Anyway, as I was preparing the lesson, I came to a very long passage on Babylon's destruction that was written by Jeremiah the prophet. He devoted two chapters of his prophecy to a detailed explanation of how God would destroy this powerhouse city named Babylon—which at the time he was writing was the greatest city in the Middle East. And then, right in the middle of chapter 51, I came across what I believe to be the key to unlock our Internet messages from the terrorists."

Moshe looked incredulous. "The terrorists are using the Bible to communicate? I can't imagine this could be possible."

"No, I don't think so! But they used a technique as old as the Bible to encode their messages. In Jeremiah 51:41 the prophet announced that 'Sheshach will be captured.'"

"What is 'Sheshach'?" Jillian asked, feeling silly for not pronouncing it correctly.

"Babylon," Moshe said. "Sheshach is Babylon."

Greg looked over at Moshe, who now stood looking out the terrace window, staring through the rain as if lost in a distant memory.

"You know the prophecies, Moshe?" Greg asked him quietly.

"I do. It's been years since I've read Jeremiah or any of the ancient writings. My grandmother used to have me read them to her at night to help her fall asleep. She was blind from childhood but believed the reading of the Hebrew prophets held special healing, calming powers. I remember the story of Jeremiah's Sheshach. Yes, Sheshach is another name for Babylon. The name Sheshach is what scholars refer to as an *atbash*, a code formed by reversing the order of the Hebrew letters. In Hebrew the name Babylon is really three letters—*bet, bet,* and *lamed*—together they are pronounced *Babel.*"

While Moshe spoke, almost musing, Greg wrote the Hebrew letters out on a sheet of paper for Jillian to see. He handed her the paper, and she looked at the letters. Her face twisted a bit in confusion, but she realized this was a moment she would not forget.

Greg interrupted Moshe to fill in some of the details. "Jillian, as Moshe knows, the Hebrew language is written from right to left, so the two letters on the right are the "b" sound in Hebrew. They are also the second letter in the Hebrew alphabet. In fact, the English alphabet, as well as the Hebrew and Greek alphabets, have common roots."

Greg sketched a simple chart on the paper in front of him.

English	ABCD	aye	bee	cee	dee
Hebrew	אבגד	aleph	bet	gimmel	dalet
Greek	αβγδ	alpha	beta	gamma	delta

"Okay, I think I'm following you. Go ahead," Jillian said, rubbing her fingers against her temples as though she were trying to force the information into her brain.

"Moshe, may I continue?" Greg asked the older man, now turned with his back to the rain-soaked window.

"Of course. Please proceed."

"Okay, the word *Babel* or *Babylon* in Hebrew is made up of three letters. Jeremiah the prophet used an atbash, an early form of a cryptogram, to write the name of the city in code. In place of the second letter of the alphabet, he used the second letter from the *end* of the alphabet. And for the last letter of the word, which was the twelfth letter of the Hebrew alphabet, he used the twelfth letter from the *end* of the alphabet. Sort of like one of the simple codes most kids make up when they first learn how to send 'secret messages' to one another on the playground."

"So you are saying that the messages we are trying to unlock are nothing more than simple cryptograms?" asked Moshe.

"Right. And it's so simple it almost worked. They started with a solid premise: The lower your profile, the less sophisticated your disguise needs to be. Most people would never think to look at the EXIF data of online pictures, especially pictures posted on what appears to be a family vacation Web site. Any messages hidden in the EXIF data would also escape the attention of the NSA cybersleuths who are focusing on phone calls, e-mail messages, and information posted on known Islamic Web sites. The terrorists knew that the odds of someone even finding their message were virtually nil. So they employed a simple cryptogram to add one additional level of security. And it had to be simple because the recipients are not highly educated individuals. They probably wondered if it was even necessary, but they decided to use it just in case. Show the code to the average person and they wouldn't even begin to know how to decipher it. In fact, even if they stumbled on the correct code, it's likely they *still* wouldn't know they got it right." Greg sat down in the recliner and tried to analyze Jillian's reaction. In the back of her mind was the known fact that most impossible cases were cracked when the most obvious and less sophisticated scenario was taken seriously. The FBI had seen this a thousand times in past situations. Most times, the answer was right in front of their noses.

Greg smiled, almost reading her thoughts. "You have to admire how simple they made this, Jillian. This was so simple that it was elegant—and it really could have worked."

"But obviously it had some major flaws because you discovered it, don't you agree, Dr. Hanson?" Moshe asked politely, not wanting to concede any credit to the thug terrorists.

"Actually, I think it's safe to say that God should get the credit for unmasking the plot. From a human perspective, the odds of it being me who stumbled on the site originally—someone who knew about EXIF and who was actually concerned enough about copyright issues to bother to check—must be astronomical. Like Mordecai in the book of Esther, I think God just had me in the right place at the right time. And I think He did so for a purpose."

Moshe smiled back at Greg and affirmed, "For such a time as this, Dr. Hanson. For such a time as this."

Jillian finally chimed in with no small degree of impatience. "Greg, all this is impressive, but you still haven't told us what the code actually said when you deciphered it. How about a little help for the biblically illiterate over here!"

"Okay. Back to the code. The code itself is quite simple. I just wrote out the English alphabet from A to Z and all numbers from 0 to 9, and then on the line below I wrote them out in reverse. Like this:

He took another sheet of blank paper and scrawled out a rough grid to make his point.

```
ABCDEFGHIJKLMNOPQRSTUVWXYZ   1234567890
ZYXWVUTSRQPONMLKJIHGFEDCBA   0987654321
```

"How did you know that the numbers went from 1 to 0 and not from 0 to 9?" Jillian asked Greg without looking up from the paper.

"I didn't at first, and I thought I might have to try it both ways. But

I started by assuming that the terrorists might use the numbers in the order that they appeared on the computer keyboard, and that's from one through zero. And then afterward I was able to verify that this is the correct order."

"You verified it? How?" Jillian asked again, this time looking directly at Greg.

"I'll get there, but let me finish. I used the code, the atbash, just like Jeremiah used it when naming Babylon. I reproduced the message that we found on the Website. It now reads as follows:"

Headline: third or fourth day; have both locations prepared
Instructions: JFK AAL 19 1100; ATL DAL 794 1101; MIA USA 858 1100; ORD AAL 295 1005; LAX DAL 310 0800; DFW AAL 175 1010; DEN UAL 744 0901; PDX NWA 6385 0800

"As I looked at the list—remembering that there are eight segments—I was struck by one clear pattern. The first three digits are airport designations. JFK is Kennedy International in New York City, ATL is Atlanta, MIA is Miami, ORD is O'Hare here in Chicago, LAX is Los Angeles International, DFW is Dallas, and DEN is Denver. I didn't know PDX, but I looked it up online and it's Portland."

Jillian clapped her hands together as if killing a mosquito. "No way!" she shouted. "Eight airports covering most of the United States. Got to hand it to these freaks. They are thorough, aren't they?"

Greg nodded in agreement. "And that was the clue to help me understand the last set of numbers. These airports are scattered across four different time zones. If terrorists are going to attack across the United States, they will need to do so simultaneously. They figured that out on September 11. Once the plot was discovered, we grounded all other flights. If the terrorists began by attacking planes on the East Coast, it's a safe bet that

FOUND

we would ground all flights within an hour. That means the attacks on the other airports would have failed."

"So how do you launch a simultaneous attack nationwide?" Moshe asked. "You would need to find flights that are taking off from each airport at approximately the same time."

"Yes, and you also would need to adjust for time zones," Greg said. "So look at the list, only this time insert a colon right in the middle of the last four numbers. You have an attack in New York at 11:00, an attack in Atlanta at 11:01, and an attack in Miami at 11:00. But in the central time zone, you have an attack in Chicago at 10:05 and in Dallas at 10:10. These are matched in the mountain time zone with an attack in Denver at 9:01. And, finally, there are two attacks in the pacific time zone—at 8:00 in both Los Angeles and Portland. Before someone could even sound the warning to close all the airports, the simultaneous attacks would be over."

Jillian now looked carefully at the rest of the information. "If we know where and when, then is this final information the specific airlines and flights to be attacked?"

"It is. That's the last part of the puzzle. Well, it's not actually the last part, but I'll come to that shortly. The second three letters are the code for the different airlines. This confused me for a few minutes because I know some of the airlines by their two-letter designation—AA for American Airlines, for example. But once again I went to the Internet and found a site that listed all the official three-letter designations for the airlines. And they match. Once I realized that the second set of letters referred to airlines, it became quite easy to identify them with just a little help from the Internet. AAL is American Airlines, DAL is Delta, USA is USAirways, UAL is United Airlines, and NWA is Northwest Airlines.

"The final part of the puzzle was identifying the first set of numbers. By now it became pretty obvious that this must refer to specific flight numbers. The fact that the numbers in the code were two, three, or four digits long now made sense. But just to be on the safe side I went to each airline's Web site and checked—these are real flights leaving at those times from those airports."

"Unbelievable!" said Jillian. "They could kill thousands!"

Moshe was visibly angry, his mind moving quickly back to Ariel. He felt the heat of the explosion all over again and heard distinctly the sirens and screaming victims lying in pools of blood. Esther . . . Aloud he said, "And as they do, they could also halt all air travel in the United States. The economic consequences of such a comprehensive attack could devastate the U.S." Moshe had enough experience with the economic consequences of terrorism to look beyond the immediate loss of life—as tragic as that was in and of itself.

"We must do something with this information," said Jillian.

"What do you have in mind?" asked Moshe.

"Well, possibly warn the airlines, engage Central Intelligence, who will determine the depth of the communication; perhaps even the White House would need to be notified. At the very least, Homeland Security needs to be alerted to the information. And sooner rather than later. They may consider raising the terror alert to red."

Moshe tried to speak calmly. "Miss Foster, with all due respect, if you choose to move too quickly with this information, you will have accomplished nothing. We don't know where the terrorists are. If they catch wind of this discovery, they will simply go into hiding temporarily. How long can you keep the airlines grounded? A day? A week? A month? And once you start flying again, what is to stop them from choosing new targets? I recommend proceeding . . . but cautiously—we must do nothing to alert them that we may know about their plans."

Jillian bit down on her bottom lip and tapped the table with the fingers of her right hand. "I don't know if I could live with myself if I heard on the noon news tomorrow that eight airplanes were shot down—and I knew about the plan and did nothing to stop it. That's unconscionable!"

Greg interrupted. "You both are making good points, but can I add two additional pieces of information? First, we do know the time of the attacks, and I think we might be able to pinpoint the specific day. Remember the first part of the message—the part about the 'third or fourth day'? It seemed too vague to me, especially if these terrorists are trying to pull off simultaneous attacks. And then I wondered if the apparent lack of clarity was on my part, not theirs. Do you know the Muslim names for the days of the week?"

Jillian shook her head no, but Moshe raised his finger, signifying he understood. "Of course. Their names come from the Hebrew calendar. Sunday is the first day of the week, and their name for it is, simply 'first day.' Sunday through Thursday are all named the same way. Only Friday and Saturday receive different names. Friday is 'gathering day'—the day they assemble at the mosque. And Saturday is the 'sabbath day'—which comes from the Jewish *Shabbat*."

Greg smiled broadly. "You are exactly right! And assuming they were told that the attack would take place on the 'third or fourth day,' that would identify the attack as taking place on Tuesday or Wednesday—this coming Tuesday or Wednesday! Jillian, you have two or three days to work out a strategy for finding these individuals."

"Well, that's some consolation," she said. "But didn't you say that you had two pieces of information? What's the second?"

"Remember the other part of that first statement—where they are told to 'have both locations prepared'?" Greg asked, looking first at Jillian then over to Moshe. "Well, I've done some thinking about that, and I think we can infer two things from that statement. The leaders of the terrorist organization know enough to realize that it's not always easy to pick specific targets, especially if they are airplanes. For example, here at O'Hare there are three major runways that an airplane could use to land or take off. Two are parallel, but the third runs off in a different direction. What's worse for the terrorists is that the direction for landing or taking off is based on the prevailing winds. I think the head honchos are telling the terrorists to develop contingency plans just in case the weather changes. Imagine the damage inflicted on the terrorist's ego to be waiting at one end of the airport with a missile only to have the target plane take off at the other end of the airport . . . heading in the opposite direction!"

"So you are saying that we should be watching for people driving around at these airports, scouting out possible launch sites?" Jillian asked, already thinking about a possible stakeout plan for the airports.

"Well, yes and no. I think that is part of the equation. But this also tells me that the terrorists must realize that they need to know both the direction and the time their intended target is taking off. Knowing that there are always delays at airports, how would you know precisely when the plane you are to target is actually taking off?"

Jillian answered. "Well, I suppose the best way would be to listen in on the airport departure control frequency to hear when the tower gives the pilot final clearance. That would tell me what runway he was on, and would give me about a thirty-second warning that he was about to fly over. And if I'm constantly monitoring for, say, an hour or so before the flight I'm targeting, I'll know with a high degree of certainty whether or not I'm at the correct location. I'll be able to coordinate the control tower's clearances with the actual planes going overhead."

Greg gave Jillian a thumbs-up and said, "And that serves as a warning and as a hope. It's a warning to be very careful what you broadcast over the normal police frequencies. These terrorists could already be monitoring them. At the first sign of a manhunt, they will break camp and run. But here's the hope. We could consider using these signals as a last-minute ruse to smoke the terrorists out. They will likely take up their position sometime before the targeted flight, so we can have patrols out looking for them. And when they hear the plane is about to roll down the runway, that's when they need to have their missiles out and pointed toward the sky. If we can trick them into revealing their position, it might make it easier for us to catch them."

Jillian laughed. "Greg, I'm not sure if I should admire you for thinking like a law enforcement officer or be wary of you for thinking like a terrorist!"

Moshe laughed too, though he sounded more nervous than relaxed. He more than anyone knew how critical details and timing were to the terrorist mind.

Jillian spoke up for both her and Moshe. "Greg, you definitely made it worth our while to come down here tonight. Thanks for all you have been doing for us. And you are right about not sharing any of this with your Sunday school class—or, for that matter, with anyone else right now. In fact, maybe I should come to your class tomorrow just to make sure you don't accidentally reveal classified information!"

Greg smiled back at her. "I would love to have you sit in on my class. Who knows, having a real live FBI agent in class might be just the thing I need to keep them under control! If you are serious, then just show up at the front doors at 9:30. I'll be around to escort you to the room!"

* * * * * * * * * *

Jillian and Moshe drove back on Lake Shore Drive toward downtown Chicago. Moshe said, grinning, "So you're going to Sunday school tomorrow, yes?"

"I just might," Jillian answered, laughing. "I still can't put my finger on it, but Greg has something that I feel like I've been seeking for some time. I can't explain it—really, I can't. It's the same sense of peace and purpose my mother possesses. I don't know what it is, but God knows I need it."

"I know of this peace. Esther had it too," Moshe responded, his voice choking on the words. "She had it too."

The moment came and left with silence. Moshe realized he and Jillian had a strange connection in this longing. But matters at hand still seemed more pressing than religion.

"Jillian, like you, I think Greg has unlocked this terrorist code, and I think the information could be incredibly useful to us. I also think this warrants calling an emergency meeting of everyone involved with the task force. If I were you, I would contact them tonight, and set the meeting for tomorrow afternoon. Every day could be critical in bringing this to a successful conclusion. While we were at Greg's apartment, I received a text message from Mossad. It's important, Jillian, but I did not want to share it in Greg's presence . . . for security purposes, you understand."

"What is it, Moshe?" Jillian asked, knowing it must be important.

"Other sources in Damascus told Mossad that a container of pistachios had been shipped from Syria to Canada just over two months ago. What makes it so critical is that the packers were asked to place another box inside the shipping container. That box was large enough to contain multiple SA-7 missiles."

Jillian groaned and turned to look out the driver's window. "We're running out of time," she murmered, fogging the window with her breath.

CHAPTER 17

"LIFT UP THE TAIL"

Ibrahim rubbed his hands while reading the message. This was it—the message they had been waiting for! He reached over and hit the printer's On button, tapping his fingers nervously as the machine blinked and buzzed its way to ready green. He selected the Print command from the menu—he had not learned the different keyboard shortcuts—and then stood up to wait for the printer to spit out the coded information.

He started to walk toward the door to go downstairs and summon Suleiman, but he stopped and shook his head, mumbling to himself, "You have spent too much time with Suleiman; you are becoming as excitable as he is!" He forced himself to take a deep breath and relax. The hum of the printer motor and rollers broke his thoughts. He looked over to see the sheet of paper sliding from the bottom of the printer. Ibrahim walked across the room at a measured pace. But while he could control his external movements, he could not control the tidal wave of emotions surging through his body.

"Suleiman! Where are you?" The Teacher had instructed Ibrahim and

Suleiman not to use their real names—even when talking just to them-selves—but old habits were hard to break. *These are the names given to us by our parents, and they are the names by which we are known to Allah,* Ibra-him reasoned in defiance of his Teacher's command.

"Ibrahim, I am here! What do you want?" Suleiman took one final sip of coffee and then carefully placed the cup back on the saucer. He looked up to see Ibrahim bounding down the hall and into the kitchen holding a sheet of paper in his right hand. The way he held the paper—clutched tightly against his body—told Suleiman it must be important. "What do you have in your hand, my friend? Is that a message for us?"

"Are we alone?" Ibrahim asked to be sure.

"Yes, we are. They went out for groceries only twenty minutes ago."

"Good! Read this, and you will understand my excitement. I went to the Web site, and I printed this information from the new picture of Haram es-Sharif."

Headline: It will be the fourth day. Have both locations prepared.

Instructions: Lift up the tail! Look for outgoing objects previously identi-fied.

Suleiman smiled as he read the terse message identifying both the day and objective of the attack. "So, my friend, we will strike our blow for Allah in just three days! Do you think we are ready?"

"I'm afraid there is still much to do," Ibrahim said sternly but with a reserved excitement. "We have selected our primary site on the west, but we do not yet have a good site on the east. And we must see if we can track airplanes from each direction to make sure we will have sufficient time to fire the missiles. I believe we must find answers to all our questions today. We should leave here very soon."

* * * * * * * * * *

Greg paid for his coffee and blueberry muffin and got them both to go, even though he'd stay for a while. He liked having the to-go bag for the muffin—which he rarely finished—so he could take it with him for a late-day snack. Stopping at Starbucks for breakfast on his way to church had become part of his normal Sunday routine.

Balancing the muffin on the lid of his coffee, he grabbed his bag and wove his way through the tables to the far corner of the room. He opened his laptop to look over his Sunday school lesson one last time. But first he would check to see if there was a new message for the terrorists.

The new Haram es-Sharif picture appeared almost instantly in response to his search. *I wonder if Jillian will really come to Sunday school.* He smiled at the thought, then reached for a piece of paper and a pen to copy the message.

* * * * * * * * * *

Jillian had made her way to the office earlier than normal. A dozen phone calls later she had arranged for an emergency meeting of the task force for two o'clock Sunday afternoon. She glanced at her watch and saw it was still only 8:30. If she hurried she could make it to Sunday school. She wondered what Greg would think if she really showed up for church. She didn't want to be obvious. *That's it,* she thought. *I'm going.* She reached into her purse, pulled out a small cosmetics bag to freshen up, then dashed down to the street to grab a cab.

Fifteen minutes later her cab skidded to a stop at the entrance to Greg's church. Nicely dressed people were filing up the stairs to the wide entrance to the church welcome center. As she went up the steps, suddenly a feeling of awkwardness came over her. She had gone to church as a kid, but not even once since leaving home for college—apart from some Christmas and Easter services she had gone to grudgingly when visiting her mother. The only church service that had ever meant anything to her was the memorial service held for her brother. Maybe she would say a prayer for him today. Maybe he would notice her from wherever he was.

The moment she stepped inside the building, she felt as if everyone there would know she was a total pagan. Somehow it didn't matter. Something inside made her keep going. Her conversation with Moshe about Esther told her this was right—it was something she was supposed to do.

Jillian hadn't taken two steps inside the church doorway before a nice couple who appeared to be in their midforties greeted her immediately. "Good morning, and welcome to the Evangelical Community Church. I'm Monique and this is Chris, my husband." She pointed to a tall man with a broad smile wearing a sweater and khaki pants. "Welcome to ECC!" he said, reaching to shake Jillian's hand.

"Are you here for Sunday school?" Monique asked, taking Jillian's arm and patting her on the elbow.

"Yes, I'm Jillian Foster, a friend of Greg Hanson's. He invited me to sit in on his Sunday school class. I think he teaches high school." Jillian felt her face flush and her lips quiver. It felt as if her whole body was shaking for everyone to see.

Lord, if You are real, how about sending a little of that peace You apparently give to people more deserving than me. Amen (I think).

Jillian knew she had just uttered her first prayer in maybe twenty years—she only hoped it made it past the foyer ceiling. Monique beamed as she put her arm around her. Suddenly she felt perfectly at ease, and a warm calm came over her.

"Jillian, we are so glad you're here!" Monique chirped, almost singing with a central Texas drawl that made Jillian feel right at home. Monique told her that she and Chris had moved to Chicago only a few months before from San Antonio and made Evangelical Community Church their home away from home.

"Greg Hanson is a *wonderful* Bible teacher and the perfect gentleman. You will be so blessed. Our son, Adam, is in that class. He absolutely loves it. I'll take you."

The gracious woman reminded her of her mother—modest and unassuming but sparkling with grace and a wide, Texas smile. Perhaps there was something to all this faith stuff after all.

* * * * * * * * * *

Sunday is a normal workday in Pakistan, and U.S. Ambassador Mark Ryan had already spent most of the morning attending to the paperwork that had piled up in his absence. He had traveled to Karachi to visit with the staff at the U.S. Consulate—a trip that had been more symbolic than substantive. And for whatever reason, those few days away seemed to coincide with a rash of incidents and events that had become of pressing interest to the United States government. So he was now reading through the newspaper summaries and reports from the embassy staff, deciding which should be sent through normal channels and which—if any—demanded a higher priority.

He looked down at the folder he had just opened. It contained a summary of different newspaper accounts of an attempted missile attack on a Gulf Air flight from Abu Dhabi to Islamabad. He had seen a report on the attack while in Karachi and knew that the attempt had failed. The would-be attacker was paralyzed when his truck flipped over. He was taken to the hospital, but he died when his throat was slit during the night. The authorities had not discovered who killed him, and it was likely they never would. Some papers had speculated that the attack might be connected to the ongoing tensions between the Sunnis and Shiites, but no firm connection had yet been made.

Ambassador Ryan was just about to toss the file into the stack reserved for unimportant/normal /routine communiqués when he noticed a one-page sheet that must have slipped from the folder. It was a note from his new personal assistant, Christian Johnson.

Ambassador Ryan:

General Abdul Akhtar from Pakistani military called with information about the man who tried to shoot down the Gulf Air flight. A policeman was able to interview him before he was killed. He had been trained in Pakistan as part of a team to be sent to the United States to shoot down airliners. When he was not selected for the mission, he became upset and stole the SA-7 missile and truck. He hoped to shoot down an airplane to vindicate his name, but failed.

Police traced the license plate to a farm in the Federally Administered Tribal Areas, but it had already been deserted. In their search, the military also uncovered a cache of SA-7 missiles, similar to the one used by the man. The military advised that the missiles and the terrorists might be in transit to the United States, or might already have arrived there.

Respectfully,

C. J.

Ryan immediately picked up his phone and buzzed for his assistant. "Chris, I just finished reading the report on the Pakistani man who tried to shoot down the airplane, including your attached note. Have you already forwarded the information from General Akhtar on to Washington?"

"No, Mr. Ambassador, I have not. It looked important, but I thought you should read it first."

Ryan closed his eyes and exhaled slowly. *Doesn't she realize how important this is?* But he pushed those thoughts to the side and said very calmly, "Thank you, Chris. Please buzz Bill Martin and have him come to my office immediately."

Bill Martin was the official CIA agent posted to the U.S. Embassy in Pakistan. The embassy also had other CIA personnel posted in nonofficial cover, but Bill was exactly who he claimed to be.

The buzzing of the intercom interrupted Ryan's thoughts. "Yes?"

"Mr. Martin is here, sir."

"Please send him in, Chris. And thank you."

Bill Martin was not the stereotypical CIA agent found in spy novels or Hollywood movies. He was neither burly nor sinister. He didn't even own a trench coat or fedora. Rather, he looked more like some nerdy junior high science teacher late for class. He wore a rumpled white shirt, a dark red tie, and thick black-framed glasses to aid his tired eyes. "You called, Mr. Ambassador?" he said.

"Yes, Bill. Thanks for coming on such short notice. I just found a note attached to the report on the attempted downing of that Gulf Air plane about ten days ago. I thought you might find the note rather interesting." The ambassador reached for the memo and handed it to the waiting agent.

Bill drew the document close to his face and began reading. At one point he paused and adjusted his glasses. "This could be significant. Has it already been sent to Washington?"

"No, unfortunately, it has not. That's why I called for you. This has more significance for national security than it does for diplomacy. It should have been sent several days ago. I want you to send it on to your people as quickly as possible and ask them to pass it along to whoever else might need to see it. I'll then send it to the State Department with a memo explaining what happened. And, Bill, please make sure that Washington realizes how important it is to get this information out to those who need to know about it. It's already been sitting on a desk for too long!"

"Consider it done."

Within an hour the dispatch was sent.

CHAPTER 18

CASTING THE NET

Jillian watched and listened to Greg teach his Sunday school class. She really was impressed. He was animated and funny, and demonstrated a genuine care for the teenagers. He respected them, and Jillian could see that they knew it. He had a clear gift of bringing the stories of the Bible to life. Jillian felt as if she had personally visited the ancient city of Babylon, touched the walls of King Nebuchadnezzar's palace, and listened to the gentle, rhythmic flow of Euphrates River lapping against its outer defenses. This was not the Sunday school experience she remembered as a kid.

Greg's final picture was of an Army Humvee parked next to the modern-day Ishtar Gate in Babylon. In the photo several soldiers wearing sunglasses and desert fatigues stood next to the vehicle, looking up at the gate. One young man blurted out, "What's behind that gate?"

"It's actually an entrance to the present-day Nebuchadnezzar Museum in Babylon, and the gate is only half the size of the one King Nebuchadnezzar built there 2,500 years ago. Perhaps someday some of you will visit this place and see it for yourselves."

"Doubt that could ever happen," piped up a teenage boy in the back of the room.

Greg smiled at the honest response. "Well, right now it's not too safe," Greg acknowledged. "But who knows? By the time you are in college you might be able to take a trip to Iraq. But even if you can't, every time you come across the mention of Babylon in the Bible, you now have a picture in your mind of what it might have looked like."

Jillian looked down at her watch. It was exactly 10:30 when the Sunday school bell rang—forty-five minutes after Greg began teaching—but it seemed the class had only taken a few minutes. Some of the kids bolted for the door, but several went up to talk with Greg or to look at the props he had brought in for the class. He had an adobe brick, a book from the Museum of the Ancient Near East in Berlin with color photographs of the Ishtar Gate, and a jar of tar that he had used in class to cement together two small pieces of brick.

"Jillian, thanks for coming. I hope you weren't bored to tears." She looked up to see Greg calling to her from the front of the room.

"Bored? Not on your life! That's the first time I actually paid attention to a Bible lesson. I really learned something today. Thank you. Where were the teachers like you when I was going to church?" Jillian stepped forward and put her arms around Greg and hugged him gently. "Thank you. It was very nice being here."

"Thanks, Jillian," he answered, blushing slightly. He stepped back to let a few more teenagers pass by. "You're very generous with your words. But I thank the Lord every time He gives me the opportunity to teach the Scriptures. I pray something sticks, if you know what I mean."

"I think your prayers have been answered," Jillian responded as she walked toward the door. "Those kids were mesmerized by you. It was fun to watch."

They walked together toward the worship center, where crowds of people were beginning to stream in off the street. "Will you be able to stay for the worship, Jillian?" Greg asked, hoping she would agree.

"I'd love to, but I really have to go make preparations for a major meeting of the task force this afternoon. And, by the way, you are invited. The meeting will take place in our offices at two." Jillian was putting on her coat and watching to see his reaction.

"A meeting this afternoon—well, let's see; I think I can do that. Wait; that reminds me. I found another message this morning. I need to share it with you privately and before the meeting, if at all possible."

Jillian realized she had let down her professional guard somewhat to accommodate Greg's invitation to church. She still had a job to do that for now took precedence even over the Almighty.

"Greg, I don't want to force you to skip church, but is there any way we could meet now? It will take me some time to get everything ready for the meeting, and I think it's important for me to hear what you found."

"Of course," he responded. "I think the Lord would understand my missing church today to give attention to a matter of national security. Besides, church isn't what my faith is all about." Greg sensed an opportunity to go deeper. "The Lord is more concerned with our hearts and our willingness to come to Him on His terms—not on our terms—somehow trying to satisfy Him by attending church or paying our tithes on time."

"Greg, I only meant to say how much I appreciate your making an exception to your normal Sunday activities in order to stay in the loop on all this. Who knows, maybe I'll return the favor and come to church with you in the future." She tried to say those last words in a flippant way, but in reality she thought attending church—especially with Greg—was probably a really good idea.

"Good," Greg said, sounding relieved that he had not offended her. He liked the fact that Jillian was not a shrinking violet. She owned her spirit and her beliefs—or lack of them. He respected that in her, and for him it made her all the more attractive.

A longtime church member and family friend popped Greg on the shoulder as he passed and snapped Greg back from his thoughts. "Jillian, of course I'll join you. Let me unplug my computer and gather up all my stuff, and then we can walk to my car. How about lunch . . . ah, on me this time!"

* * * * * * * * * *

The meeting started precisely at 2:00. After hearing Greg's report on the latest message, Jillian had him drive her back to the office. He dropped her off at the corner of Jackson and Dearborn and went in search of somewhere to park. By the time he got back to the Dirksen Federal Office Building, the guard on duty had instructions to let him in. He arrived at the office in time to watch Jillian direct all the last-minute preparations for the meeting. The information from Greg caused her to reconsider her initial plan. Events were moving rapidly, and she was responding to those changes.

"Jillian, you impress me!" he finally said.

"Why? what have I done that's so special?" she asked, feeling her face redden.

"Your ability to organize is phenomenal. I can't even get my office organized, and here you are developing a plan in cooperation with several major organizations—across multiple cities—to wage war against an unknown terrorist organization in the United States."

"Thanks, I think. I enjoy the challenge, really. I just hope all the effort pays off. Things could still go very badly."

"I agree. Is there anything I can do to help you get prepared?" he asked, not wanting to be presumptuous.

"As a matter of fact, there is. Could you make sure that we have thirty chairs in the conference room? And then could you check to make sure the speaker system for the telephone is hooked up? We will have a large number of individuals joining us via audio hookup, and I want everyone feeling relaxed and cared for."

When all was ready, Jillian began by thanking the participants for giving up part of their weekend. She introduced Greg, who stood to face both those in the room and those watching a simulcast of the meeting from remote locations.

"Thank you all for your patience with me. Let me begin by explaining why I've been asked to speak to you. A few weeks ago I stumbled across a system developed by what appeared to be a terrorist organization to communicate with individuals here in the United States. It involves using the Internet in a way that allows messages to hide out in the open."

A voice from the speakerphone chimed in abruptly. "This is Carl with the FBI in Spokane. Can you elaborate on how these messages were hidden?"

Greg was about to answer when Jillian interrupted. "Carl, Jillian here. That's a great question, but I would prefer that Greg not answer it for two reasons. First, it is complicated. It would take some time to explain the process, and time is too precious a commodity right now to waste. Second, it is irrelevant to our meeting, at least for now. You just need to know that the FBI has checked it out, and both the method and the messages are legitimate. Greg, please proceed."

There was silence on the other end of the conference phone, signaling Jillian's redirect had been heard and affirmed.

"Thanks, Jillian. Uh, the key point is that I stumbled onto their system and shared that information with Special Agent Foster and with others here in Chicago. We have uncovered an apparent plot to have eight two-man teams infiltrate the United States with the intent of shooting down eight airplanes simultaneously. We know the specific airlines targeted, the specific cities, and the specific date and time of the attack."

Jillian put up her hand to interrupt Greg. "This is Jillian again. Everyone asked to be part of this meeting—those in the room as well as those listening on speakerphone—needs to know that you are included because your city is one of the eight target cities if our theory is correct. For everyone's benefit, let me list the cities: Atlanta, Chicago, Dallas, Denver, Los Angeles, Miami, New York, and Portland." Jillian paused between each name so the participants could write them all down. "Please continue, Greg."

Greg cleared his throat and took a sip of water from the glass placed in front of him on the conference table. "If what we have pieced together is correct, the attack will launch this Wednesday, a little less than three days from right now. The terrorists have targeted airliners that are scheduled to depart from these cities within approximately a fifteen-minute window. And they have selected five separate U.S.-based carriers. The exact ground location for each attack is extremely difficult to predict because the terrain and layout of the areas for each major airport are vastly diverse. Does anyone have any questions?"

Greg had not been given official permission to prompt the group for questions. Jillian knew that that was something not normally done and was usually reserved for higher-ranking intelligence officials or representatives of the National Security Council or Senate Foreign Intelligence Committee. Greg served as little more than a civilian analyst with a really good hunch. And Jillian had not fully apprised him of proper protocol.

She stepped to the podium before anyone could respond. "Thank you, Dr. Hanson. Let's wait for questions until after the briefing is complete. Next to speak is Mr. Moshe Zachar, representing the Government of Israel. Moshe is on special assignment to us from Mossad. Mr. Zachar, please share your information with the group."

Moshe walked toward the podium. "Thank you, Agent Foster. And good afternoon to all of you distinguished colleagues. A few weeks ago Mossad received hard information that a previously unknown group based in Pakistan was training terrorists to send to America to try to shoot down airplanes. Unfortunately, we only received the information after those terrorists had traveled through the country to which our agents are assigned. Our agents also learned that a shipment of SA-7s had been sent through the same country a month or two earlier. Their destination was also said to be the United States."

Moshe paused to clear his throat. Someone handed him a glass of water, and he took a sip. "Thank you. Allow me to continue. The sixteen terrorists are all of Middle Eastern descent, but from various countries. They were described as Muslim fundamentalists, but they have sought to disguise that fact. We know, for example, that they shaved off their beards prior to entering your country. They are all about one-and-three-quarters to two meters in height—I'm afraid that piece of information is not too helpful because it ranges from five-and-a-half feet to six feet—but it's the information we received. They all have dark hair and are in their twenties and thirties. That is, with one exception. One man—and he is the only one whose name we know right now—appeared to be somewhat older because he was graying. His name is Ibrahim al-Samarri, which identifies him as having come from the Iraqi town of Samarra, north of Baghdad."

A voice from the speakerphone interrupted again. "Have we been able to trace this individual—what did you call him? Ibrahim, or something like that?"

"So far, we have not," Jillian responded. "He is certainly not one of the known terrorists we battled in Iraq following the toppling of Saddam Hussein's government. But we are continuing to try to track down that potential lead. Moshe, please continue."

"Thank you. For lack of a better explanation, we suspect that most of these individuals are relatively unsophisticated. That is, they have never had a great deal of experience living in a Western, technologically oriented society."

"But they have had some exposure to technology," Greg interrupted. "The system for communicating with them involves their looking for messages on the Internet, then decoding the information to find their instructions."

"Yes, thank you. I don't mean to imply that you will find them riding donkeys to the airports. But—and this is very important—we do believe they have received sufficient training to complete their mission, as long as their mission takes place sooner rather than later. They have not been sufficiently trained in a way that would allow them to remain underground for any extended length of time without an extensive support system. And we don't believe they have that level of sophisticated support either. They were trained primarily to do one job, and to be successful they need to do it soon. The longer they are in the United States, the more likely they are to make a mistake and be caught."

Moshe and Greg scanned the room and watched the heads nodding in approval. Some of the individuals leaned toward one another and traded comments. It was an encouraging sign that perhaps some of this information was sinking in.

Moshe continued with his remarks. "Finally, and this might not be that helpful, we were told that at least two of the men are left-handed. It is probably a worthless piece of information, but it was observed so it was reported."

Jillian thanked Moshe and looked down at her sheaf of papers. "That's almost everything, but I do want to add just a few additional details. Just before the start of today's meeting, I received a fax from bureau headquarters. You may or may not have seen a small news item a week or so ago about a failed attempt to shoot down an airplane in Pakistan. At the time it was thought to be connected to the ongoing struggle between the Sunni and Shiite factions in that country." Several heads nodded. Jillian held up the fax and continued. "We have just learned from Pakistani sources that this is not the case. Evidently the young man responsible was a terrorist-in-training for the operation in our country who washed out of the program. In his anger and zeal he stole a missile launcher with the intent of shooting down a plane to prove that he was worthy of being selected for the task. Obviously, we now know why he wasn't chosen. When first questioned in the hospital, he said the group had been trained to attack planes as they were taking off.

"The Pakistani government traced the license plates on the truck he used back to a farm in the Federally Administered Tribal Areas. It had already been abandoned, obviously in haste, because the army discovered a stash of SA-7 missiles that had been left behind. Someone slipped into the would-be terrorist's unguarded hospital room at night and slit his throat. Most likely it was an individual from the terrorist group showing their displeasure at his actions. It adds no new information to what you have heard, but it is a grim reminder that the group we are seeking plays for keeps. Now, what questions do we have?"

"Rodriguez here, from Dallas—the Texas Rangers. Thanks for inviting us to the meeting. I have one obvious question. What are we expected to *do* with this information? We have an attack coming. We know when— but we don't know by whom. We know the cities they plan to attack, but we don't know the exact spot where the attack will happen. Do we close down DFW Airport, put out public announcements to be on the lookout, or what? If we cause people to panic, we could have more people killed by would-be vigilantes, or in traffic accidents, than would be killed in any plane crash."

Jillian responded. "We've all been thrown into the difficult position of making up the rules as we go along, Mr. Rodriguez. And I understand your concerns. My first thought was to do whatever was needed to protect the lives of the people on those planes. And I still believe we must do that. But if we go about this in the wrong way, we could create an even greater problem. Moshe, you had some thoughts on this based on your experience in Israel. Could you share those thoughts with us?"

Moshe looked somewhat surprised at Jillian's request, but he stood and walked toward the podium. "Obviously Israel and the United States are not exact parallels. Israel is small, and your country is very large. Israel has had to deal with terrorism as a day-to-day threat for over sixty years, while it has only occasionally been a threat within the United States. These are fundamental differences, and so some of the things we do in Israel would not work here in the United States. For example, if we suspect an impending terrorist attack, we do announce that fact. Our people continue about their daily lives, but they are extra vigilant. We increase police and army presence, set up roadblocks, and watch for suspicious people or packages. But I do not believe this would work in the United States—at least not right now. I believe such a warning would only spread panic. People would refuse to fly, and you would suffer the exact economic blow intended by the terrorists. Even more important, such an announcement would allow the terrorists to postpone their plans. They would still have their missiles, and they could attack at another time, or even at another airport."

"So are you saying that we should do nothing—just sit back and wait to be attacked?" Rodriguez blurted back through the phone.

"No, not at all. But I am saying that you have two days until the planned attack, and you need to use that time very wisely. I would suggest a three-phase plan. Phase One is to see if you can find any of the terrorist groups before the day of the attack. This must be done in a way that doesn't arouse suspicion. You must not let the news media catch wind of what you are doing, or the terrorists will go underground. I would assume the FBI will provide you with secure information about any links or leads they are already tracking in your city. That should get you started. Phase Two must take place on the morning of the attack. You must think like a terrorist and try to determine where they would position themselves to attack an airplane as it takes off. Flood the area with police, but don't use your normal radios for communication. Assume all regular security frequencies are being monitored. Phase Three must be reserved for the final moments before the attack. If necessary, close down the airports just before the attacks are to take place. Halt all flights on the runway, and put all arriving flights into a holding pattern or divert them to other airports. You cannot let the attacks happen, but you must not tip your hand to the terrorists until the very last moment."

Jillian waited for comments from the silent group. When there were none, she said, "I know that we all sense the gravity of the situation. It's now three o'clock here in Chicago. I would propose that we temporarily discontinue the meeting to allow each city to discuss these matters among themselves. Each of you has an emergency response plan or a crisis plan, and I would suggest that you gather whatever additional personnel you might need. Let's convene again in exactly four hours to continue our discussion and to see if we can develop a coherent response to present to Washington. One final word of caution: Please do not let one word of this get out into the public. I believe Moshe is correct. It would cause panic among the general population, and it would also allow the terrorists to go underground. And neither prospect is very pleasant."

* * * * * * * * * *

After most of the groups from the different cities had hung up, Jillian spoke to those gathered around the conference table and to those still listening on the phone. "Well, how do you think it went?"

A voice from the speakerphone responded. "Jillian, I think it went as well as could be expected. Right now I suspect there are a number of people in seven other cities who are still sitting shell-shocked. But you shared enough information to help them begin to prepare a defense."

"Thanks, Frank. Could you and the others in DC stay on the line a little longer? I would like to let those who are here in the room from Chicago get on their way. They have things to do just like all the other cities. We will divide up those in our office into two groups. One will work with the agencies from Chicago on our own threat while the others will work with me to help coordinate the overall response. Bill, I would like you to be our liaison to the Chicago task force. Work with our bureau chief on any specific manpower needs you might have."

Bill Johnson smiled at Jillian and then turned to the others seated in the room. "Okay, our first order of business is finding a command center we can use. Mr. Mayor, do you think we could use the city's Emergency Operations Center in a way that won't draw attention to ourselves?"

The mayor sat straight up in his seat. "Of course we can. I'll have our press people announce a routine training exercise focusing on . . . on the upcoming severe weather season. We'll make it so boring that the press won't want to cover it. We have space in the center where our group can meet privately. Once the press gets their story they will leave, and no one will question why we are still using the facility."

Bill and the mayor led the rest of the group from the room, leaving Jillian, Greg, Moshe, and a few other staff. Frank O'Banion's voice finally came from the speakerphone. "Are they all gone?"

"They are, Frank."

"Good job, Jillian. We're not home free yet, but the element of surprise has passed from the terrorists to us. Now, what do you suggest that we do next?"

"First, I think we need to get some information to the different groups. Frank, did you have anyone there taking notes? It's important that these people receive whatever leads or information your people at the bureau have been tracking for however long. Be as specific as possible.

This is no time to get territorial on these guys! And I think we need someone higher up the food chain to contact the president."

"Agreed," Frank said.

"Nice job, Agent Foster. Thanks for the meeting and for the excellent work in Chicago," spoke up a voice Jillian had not heard before—a voice she didn't recognized.

"Excuse me—sir?"

Frank laughed and answered, "Well, let's just say that from where I'm sitting—in the Oval Office—I think most of the individuals and agencies you are concerned about have indeed been appropriately informed. And from the expressions on their faces, they have already agreed to move forward with the plan you have proposed. Now, Jillian, I'm really going to put you on the spot. What do you suggest we do next?"

Those sitting in the room with Jillian could see the red blush that had crept into her cheeks. But those listening on the phone could only hear her clear, steady voice. She glanced briefly at Greg, who nodded confidently back at her.

"I think we need to pour all available resources into this, and we need to start at both ends of the equation. On the one side, we need to start from the point where the terrorists entered our country and try to work forward. On the other side, we need to start at the point of their final destination—the sites they are actually planning to attack—and work backward."

"What, specifically, do you have in mind?" Frank asked again.

"First, we know that both the missiles and the sixteen terrorists came into the United States from Pakistan through Syria. We also know that they crossed into our country through Mexico. We need to do everything possible to start tracking down how they came in. Let's have some people start at that end and see if they can track these teams from their point of entry.

"Second, at the same time, we need to step up police patrols outside the airports. The terrorists were told to prepare two possible sites for attack, and we can assume this is due to uncertainty over weather and wind direction. This means they are probably driving around the airports looking for fields, parks, or other open spaces where they can track the flight paths of departing planes. It can't be in a highly populated area, because they would be more likely to be spotted there. We have two days to watch for them. And if we do spot them, we can tail them back to their hideouts—and hopefully nab them and the missiles."

"What can we do to stop unauthorized leaks? I agree that if the terrorists get wind of the operation they will go underground. But I must also respect the Constitution—which includes freedom of the press."

Jillian now had a context in which to place that voice, and she did recognize it. "Mr. President, I would never suggest that we try to restrict the press. But I also believe that we have the right to try to keep what we are doing as secret as possible for the sake of the many thousands in our country who could be placed in danger if these terrorists learn that we know about their plot. If any reporters get wind of this, I think we should bring them in and explain the seriousness of the situation, perhaps offer them an exclusive inside look at the operation in exchange for their willingness to sit on the story until it breaks. It's a risk, but it's a risk we must take."

"Any other thoughts before we hang up?" This time it was Frank's voice.

"Yes, Frank, we need to develop a way for the different task forces to communicate. There are too many scanners available that track police, fire, and even airport communications. I think we must assume that these terrorists would have such equipment. Is there any way we could outfit the different groups with some high-tech equipment, something that can't be monitored?"

"I'll check on that with the different groups here, but I think something might be possible. It would likely be a temporary loan of some very top-secret stuff, but I think we can make that happen. We will develop some type of plan here and then inform you and the other groups how it will work. And, Jillian, thanks again for the work you've been doing. Pass along our thanks to the others with you. We are in their debt!"

"Will do, thanks!" And with that the phone went silent.

CHAPTER 19

PULLING IN THE FISH

Police work—whether local or national—is slow, methodical, and, at times, tedious. Much of it is done behind the scenes, outside the glare of publicity, gathering evidence and tracking down those who have committed a crime. The word "gumshoe" originally described shoes with gum rubber soles that allowed an individual to walk around quietly. By the early twentieth century, the word was used to describe detectives who would do their work quietly, stealthily, as they searched for criminals. And in that sense FBI Special Agent Raoul Hernandez was a gumshoe of the finest sort.

Hernandez, attached to the San Antonio Field Office, received a call at home Sunday afternoon. By early evening he boarded Mexicana flight 837 to Mexico City. As he walked down the Jetway, he spotted a swarthy man with dark, curly hair and deep brown eyes holding a sign that read "Señor Hernandez." The man was short; he appeared to be only about five-and-a-half-feet tall, and was dressed in a white linen suit and a bright red tie. A thick, dark moustache hid the upper part of his lip, and he reminded Raoul, in a vague sort of way, of a television film critic in the United States. Raoul waved at him, and the man immediately walked forward to shake Raoul's hand. *"¡Buenos noches, Señor Hernandez! ¿Cómo está usted? Me llamo Ernesto Lozano. ¿Habla usted español?"*

"Si. Señor Lozano. ¿Cómo esta usted? ¿Hablas ingles?"

"Yes, I do. As I said, my name is Lieutenant Ernesto Lozano of the Federal Judicial Police. I have a number of relatives from my mother's side who live in the Brownsville area, and I spent several summers with them when I was young. I then took English in high school and in college. So what brings you to Mexico? The information I received was very incomplete. In fact, I was only told your name, the flight number and arrival time, and that I was to meet you and offer whatever assistance I can to you."

"I'm here on a very urgent matter," Raoul explained. The men found a place to talk where they wouldn't be overheard, and Raoul continued. "We received a tip that sixteen suspected terrorists arrived in Mexico about two weeks ago. They then traveled from here to the United States. We are very anxious to find those men. I've been asked to see if we can track their route from here. Our assumption is that they remained together as a group and that they were all using forged or stolen passports from the same country. Unfortunately, we do not know what country."

"Do you know how they traveled into the United States?"

"We checked the passenger manifests provided to us by all the airlines, and we did not find any group that seemed to match their description. For now we are assuming they didn't fly into the United States because of the measures put into place after September 11."

"Do you think they crossed the border on foot?"

"That's possible, but we don't think it's too likely. Sixteen non-Hispanic individuals trying to cross the border at the same time would be very risky. Their speech and mannerisms would stand out, and they would not be familiar with the terrain."

"Then what other options would they have? There is limited train service, but the only connections are through San Diego, El Paso, and Del Rio."

"That remains a possibility, but I was also wondering about bus service. I assume there are regular bus routes from Mexico City to the various border crossings. But I would also like to check on charter buses. If I were in charge of this group, I would want to keep them as far away from the locals as possible to avoid arousing suspicion."

"Well, I can see we will have a busy evening tonight. Follow me; my car is parked just outside. We can go to the hotel to drop off your suitcase and then stop for some dinner on the way to my office. We will narrow the list of possible options tonight, and then tomorrow we can start making phone calls!"

Monday morning was pure gumshoe detective work. As Special Agent Hernandez tracked down ticket agents and conductors on the different rail lines to see if they remembered a group of foreign men traveling together, Lieutenant Lozano called all the tourist bus companies in Mexico City to ask for the same information. The first break in the case came just before noon. Hernandez saw Lieutenant Lozano begin scribbling furiously in his white tablet. *"Sí! Sí! ¿Diez y seis o diez y siete? Ah! Bueno! ¿Cuándo? Ah! Bueno! ¿Dónde? Muchas gracias. Adiós!"*

"What was that all about?"

Lieutenant Lozano turned to Hernandez, and a toothy grin expanded along the bottom of his moustache. "I think we found your men! I just spoke with a representative from ADO GL, one of our bus companies that runs charters for tourists. They had a contract to pick up a group of sixteen South Africans—and their local host—in Mexico City exactly fifteen days ago. The group chartered the bus for a trip to Matamoros, continuing on the next day to San Antonio. The group stayed at the Holiday Inn Select Airport Hotel that next evening, and the bus returned to Mexico the following day. But only the tour host returned with the bus to Mexico; the sixteen passengers remained in San Antonio."

"What else did he say?"

"Evidently the men were somewhat unusual. When the driver returned home, he shared two unique things about the trip with his dispatcher—that's the fellow I talked with on the phone. First, according to the driver the passengers said almost nothing during the entire trip. 'It was like driving a bus full of corpses to a funeral!' is what he told the dispatcher. And second, the host who had arranged the charter spoke fluent Spanish, but with an accent. That's why it stood out."

"Amigo, I owe you a big steak dinner. But first let me place a call to my office in San Antonio. They can begin tracking these men from there."

* * * * * * * * * *

Since Mexico City is in the same time zone as San Antonio, Texas, Agent Hernandez's call arrived at the FBI's regional office at 12:17. By 1:30 a team of agents were at the hotel. A check of the registry showed eight double-occupancy rooms for one night paid for with a single credit card that, as would be discovered later, was registered under a fictitious name using a mailing service for an address. But the clerk on duty did remember the men because they spoke with thick accents, and they all requested shuttle transportation to the airport the next morning.

"Johnson, copy down the names on these registration cards," Hernandez barked. "We might have the break we need! Then call headquarters and give them the names, date, and checkout time. If these guys flew from San Antonio International Airport that morning, we should be able to track them down with this information. Especially since we know the eight cities that were to be their final destinations."

Since the events of September 11, the government requires that the names for all ticketed passengers must correspond to the names on photo

IDs presented by the passenger at the time of check-in and boarding. This helps guarantee that only ticketed passengers are able to board. The government actively checks the manifests of all incoming international flights against a watch list of potential terrorists, but they can also check other manifests should the need arise. And this was one of those times. Within an hour the identities, flights, and destination cities for all sixteen men were compiled.

"Jackpot!" Hernandez shouted, slamming his hand on the table. "Sixteen subjects traveling to the eight target cities, all in pairs." The analyst handed the information to the director of the San Antonio office.

"Yeah, but it's not as helpful as we would want. We have names, but we don't have pictures. And we have cities, but we still don't know where they are living in those cities."

"Is there any way to look at video from the airport surveillance cameras, like they did in London after those bombings? You know, see if we can find some pictures of these guys."

"We can try to do that, but I'm not too optimistic. First, we don't have nearly as many surveillance cameras as the Brits. Second, it's been two weeks since these guys went through airport security. Do we even keep camera data that long? And third, even if we have a picture, do we have anyone who can positively ID the picture as being one of the bad guys? If we show the hotel clerk or the worker at the airport check-in counter a group of fifty photos, will they be able to pick out the correct ones? We can try, but I think time is working against us. But check on it anyway!"

* * * * * * * * * *

Jillian was just walking out of her office to head toward the ladies' room when the phone rang. She was tempted to let it roll over to voice mail but decided instead to pick it up. "Special Agent Foster here."

"Jillian, it's Frank. I just wanted you to know that we tracked down the place where the terrorists entered the U.S. They traveled by charter bus from Mexico City to San Antonio using South African passports. They had valid visas, and they told the border guard they were here to study the NAFTA trade agreement and its possible application in South Africa."

"Frank, don't our people know the difference between a South African accent and a Middle Eastern accent?" Jillian rose in annoyance.

"Don't get too bent out of shape, Jillian. The border is extremely crowded, and everything looked legit with these guys. They had return tickets to South Africa, and this particular threat was totally unknown at the time. Besides, with globalization, an accent and a passport no longer have to match. Think about our country. The guard wasn't suspicious about the discrepancy in accent, but who's to say we would have done any better?" Frank knew Jillian needed calming at this point. Still, he could see her point—it did seem like some pretty sloppy checking.

"I know. So what information do we have?" She sat back down, wishing she had continued to the bathroom.

"We know the names as they appear on their forged passports, and we know which pair of men was assigned to each city by tracing their domestic flights from San Antonio. But I'm afraid we don't have any solid physical descriptions."

"I've been thinking about that," Jillian said almost to herself. "Remember several years ago when they had the licenses-for-bribes scandal here in Illinois?"

"Yeah, it eventually brought down the governor didn't it? What about it?"

"Well, these guys are new to America, and they need to travel around to scope out the airports. They can't use public transportation to do that because the public transportation system is too spotty. And they can't carry missile launchers on a bus or in a taxi. So they only have three choices. They can have someone else drive them around all day, they can drive themselves without a license, or they can apply for a driver's license."

"Well, the third option is unavailable since they need permanent residence status and proper documentation to obtain a license. So that only leaves the first two, right?"

Jillian paused, then answered. "Actually, I would argue in reverse. If this is a tightly controlled operation, I don't believe they have undercover operatives who could serve as their drivers. Remember, someone outside the U.S. designed this whole operation. If he had that many people already here, why not use them? The odds for success would be far greater. And this group has been so careful up to this point to fly under the radar of U.S. law. Why would they jeopardize their whole operation by having novice drivers out on some of our most congested highways without a valid license? They are the drivers most likely to make a simple mistake and violate some traffic law or get into a minor traffic accident. And if they are stopped by the police without a valid license, the whole plot is in jeopardy. So I think their only real option is to work out a way to get a license."

"But how likely is that?" Frank asked, knowing Jillian was not easily taken off her point.

"Again, I go back to the incident here in Illinois several years ago. What if this terrorist group has family connections to individuals working in the various state departments of motor vehicles? Or, more realistically, what if they have contacts with other groups that have people working there? For the right price there are many individuals willing to look the other way when issuing such documents."

"So what are you suggesting?"

"Find someone you can trust in each state, and have them run these names through their list of registered drivers. In some cases, the data is so recent it might not even be in the state's computer system. They might have to hand-check them. But have them look for drivers' licenses for these men. And if they find the licenses, they will find pictures to go with them. It sure would be nice to have faces to go with these names!"

"We'll get right on it, Jillian. Let's hope you're right about this." With that, Frank hung up the phone and Jillian dashed for the hallway.

* * * * * * * * * *

ATLANTA "Good afternoon, this is the 9-1-1 center. How may I help you?"

"Hello, my name is Betty Fulsome, and I live in the Morning Glory apartment complex just west of Roosevelt Highway and north of Riverdale Road. It's just on the west side of Hartsfield-Jackson Airport." Betty Fulsome had lived in Morning Glory apartments since her divorce from her husband of twenty-nine years. Their marriage was ended by a sordid affair—he said he didn't love her anymore and never looked back. She'd made the apartment a home and for the most part felt safe, but didn't take any chances with things or people that gave her a funny feeling.

"Yes, ma'am, I see your address on my screen. What it is you want to report?" the operator responded.

"Well, I'm not sure exactly, but I'm wondering if some people might not be burying a body out here."

"Excuse me, did you say you want to report someone disposing of a body?" the operator asked with a bit more interest.

"Well, I'm not sure, but that's what it looks like. Just north of where I live are some woods and a street called Horton Drive. Much of the area is still woods, but part has been cleared off, you know, like for development. Anyway, the other day I saw a taxicab parked out in the area with two men standing outside looking around. Well, today they're back, and it looks like they're digging a hole. It just looks suspicious, so I thought I'd better report it."

"Thank you, ma'am. We will have someone check it out. But I would suggest that you stay away from the window so no one spots you, just in case."

Turning to the supervisor on duty, the 9-1-1 operator reported on the incident. "Robby, I have a report of two suspicious individuals in a field just to the west of Hartsfield. They're driving a cab, and they appear to be digging a hole. The caller thought they might be burying something in an open field. It could be entirely harmless, or it might be nothing more than someone engaged in illegal dumping. Do you want me to dispatch a patrol car, or is this related to that special bulletin we received this morning?"

"Well, it doesn't sound like much, but we'd better check it out. Pass this information on to the Airport Precinct Police, but use the telephone rather than the radio. Tell them that the caller specifically mentioned two individuals in a taxicab. And give the exact location."

In less than five minutes, the information was passed along to the crisis response team that had assembled at the airport. FBI Special Agent Carol Welliver was the agent in charge.

"Okay, thanks for the information. If you receive any additional calls, please let us know immediately." Slamming the phone onto the receiver, Agent Welliver turned to the group. "We've got our first contact. This might be the real thing, or it might be a case of two guys being in the wrong place at the wrong time. Let's not have a repeat of the incident in the London subway with the Brazilian national. We don't need to take down an innocent noncombatant. But at the same time, don't let your guard down. If these are the bad guys, they are highly trained. If you are forced into a life-or-death situation, shoot to kill."

A sergeant from the Atlanta Police Department raised his hand. "Agent Welliver, our chopper is already airborne. Do you want us to direct him over the area so he can keep an eye on the car? It's carrying some of the new communication gear, so we can contact him without using our normal frequencies."

"Fine. But make sure the chopper stands off far enough so as not to spook the suspects. Have him serve as our eye in the sky to help direct the other units into place so they hit the target at the same time. Let's send the SWAT team across Roosevelt and then out to the end of Horton Drive. And then I'd like one patrol car to go into the housing complex south of Horton with another going out Riverdale Road and then up the Global Gateway Connection. That should block every conceivable entrance and exit. Now let's get going! And remember, no radio traffic. Use only the new communication gear. And no sirens!"

It actually took the different units fifteen minutes to reach their assigned locations. The first to arrive was the police helicopter, which tried to fly over the intersection of Riverdale Road and Roosevelt Highway as if it was checking on a traffic accident. "I have taxicab in sight. The trunk is open and it looks like the two men are throwing shovels or something similar into it. Now they are closing the trunk. I think they are getting ready to leave. The car is parked just off the end of Horton Road, on the south side. I see the SWAT team van pulling into the east end of Horton Road. I would advise that you drive up the road about three hundred yards and then block the road with the van. Position the SWAT team on both sides of the road to intercept the car. It will be there in a minute or two.

"I see the patrol car that is making its way through the apartment buildings. About thirty yards past the last building on your right, there appears to be a dirt road that leads off to your right. If you can, drive down that road for about a hundred yards. There's a paved road there, and you should see the suspects drive past from your left to your right. Once they are past, drive forward to block any possible escape. Be advised that the SWAT team will be about four hundred yards in front of you. Take cover beside the road in case there is any shooting.

"Okay, I see the last patrol car just turning onto Global. Once you pass the apartment complexes on your right, continue on for another hundred and fifty yards or so. Then you should see a clearing on your right. I'm not sure from here whether or not you can drive into the clearing, but if you can, do so until you come to a street. The other squad car will be about two hundred yards in front of you, so you will be serving as the back door for this operation.

"Okay, the suspects are in their car and have started moving. Get ready; here they come!"

* * * * * * * * * *

The taxi driver turned to his friend, a smile of satisfaction breaking out over his face. "Musa, I think we are ready. The spot we have chosen is perfect!"

"I agree! I was worried about those apartments being so close, but the trench and mound we have prepared will shield us from any prying eyes while we are waiting. And once the missile is fired, it will be too late! By the time someone calls the police, if they have even seen the spot from which we fired, we will already be on our way out to the highway!"

The two friends were so busy talking that they almost drove into the black step van before they saw it. "Mohammad, watch out!" The taxi slid to a halt, dirt and dust rising up in a cloud around the car. The two men had their windows down, and the dust swirled in like a sandstorm off the desert.

From somewhere off to the side of the panel truck, a voice boomed through a loudspeaker. "This is the police. Come out of the car with your hands up!"

"What! What is this? Who is there?" Musa screamed out loud, cursing and beating the cracked dashboard of the car.

Eight men dressed in black bulletproof vests and matching Kevlar helmets stepped from the woods on either side of the road, their M16 rifles pointed directly at the taxi. "Get out of the car, *now*! Put your hands in the air or you will be fired upon."

In a panic, Mohammad slammed the car from Drive to Reverse and mashed down on the accelerator. The rear tires began spitting dust and stones as the tires clawed into the ground, trying to gain traction. Immediately, the SWAT team opened fire, riddling the cab with bullets and breaking the glass completely out.

By now the car was about ten yards away from the SWAT team, and backing away rapidly. It was also weaving from side to side. Mohammad felt a sharp stab of pain in his left arm as a bullet ripped into—and through—the humerus. Instinctively he used his right arm to turn the steering wheel clockwise. To the SWAT team it looked as if the driver was trying to turn the car around to head in the other direction. A stand of trees momentarily blocked the car from their view, but they knew the driver had to move forward if he hoped to escape.

Mohammad pulled down on the gear shift with his good arm and then pushed as hard as he could on the accelerator. As soon as the car shot out of the trees the SWAT team opened fire again. Mohammad was temporarily shielded by Musa, but Musa had no protection. He looked to his right as the car bounced back onto the road. The last thing he ever saw in this life was a rifle flash. A spray of blood covered the inside of the car and temporarily blinded Mohammad. Instinctively, he wiped the blood from his glasses. He turned to see Musa slumped over against the side window, lifeless, his neck and torso soaked in blood.

Mohammad then saw the police car parked in the road directly in front of him. Holding his good arm on the inside of the steering wheel to gain leverage, he whipped the wheel to the left, hoping to force his car past the other. But the space was too narrow, and the ground too rugged. The left front wheel hit a rutted tire track and forced the front tires sharply to the right. Mohammad cried out in pain as the steering wheel turned violently to the right, snapping his wrist. The back of the car skidded to the left and came to rest against a tree. Mohammad, not wearing his seat belt, was thrown against the doorframe, shards of glass from the shattered window lacerated his forehead. He pushed against the door handle and tumbled out onto the ground.

Patrolwoman Deshanda Green ran toward the driver's side of the car, her service revolver drawn and ready. She and her partner had taken defensive positions on either side of the road when the shooting had started. The taxi had swerved toward her when it tried to pass the police car and might have hit her had the deep rut beside the road not forced the back of the car against a tree. But the thought of having someone driving like a madman directly at her got her heart racing—and made her very angry.

"Okay, freak, get on the ground, facedown, and don't make any stupid moves! You hear me? I said, get down on the ground and don't move!"

Mohammad didn't really hear what she had said, but his mind did register the presence of someone else behind him. He turned around, and saw this, this *woman* in a police uniform. No woman could stop him. If this is all that stood between him and freedom, then Allah was indeed smiling on him. *I will show her how foolish it is to oppose the plans of God!* And he stumbled toward her, unsteadily, trying to make his two useless arms look as threatening as possible.

"Okay, stop now! You hear me, I'm ordering you to stop! One last time, stop now!" But Mohammad kept coming, and when he got to within five feet compassion, ended and training kicked in. Deshanda fired three rounds from her Glock 9mm handgun, hitting Mohammad three times square in the chest. Two of the rounds pierced his heart, and he crumpled to the ground, instantly dead.

Deshanda stood with her gun trained on the suspect until she was certain he would not rise again. And then she lowered her gun and allowed her humanity to come to the surface. "Oh no, I killed him! I ordered him to stop, but he kept coming and I killed him. Why didn't he listen!"

Her partner was now standing beside her. "Deshanda, it's not your fault. You did what you had to do. You did what you had to do."

* * * * * * * * * *

"Helen, this is Betty. Betty Fulsome! You've got to watch the Evening News tonight. What channel? Honey, it don't matter what channel 'cause this will be the lead story on them all. I just saw the wildest shootout since the killing of Bonnie and Clyde. Two men were shot to pieces by the police, and it happened right here in the woods behind my apartment. No, I've not been drinking! Just watch the news tonight." Betty hung up, only to pick up her phone again to call another friend.

* * * * * * * * * *

"Jillian, this is Frank. We got our first two suspects. Unfortunately, we didn't get them alive. They tried to run, and they died in a shootout in Atlanta."

"That's okay, Frank; at least we got one of the teams. Two questions. First, did they find the missiles? Second, have they been able to keep the operation under wraps?"

"The missiles were not in the taxi they were using. We have recovered their drivers' licenses, and right now we are assuming that they used valid addresses for those licenses. We have the home staked out, and we are waiting to see if they were living alone or with someone. And we have a plan to keep the operation under wraps. It's a shoestring-and-bailing-wire plan, but it only needs to hold together for another thirty-six hours."

"Frank, did you say they were caught in a taxi?"

"Yes, I did. It was a Yellow Cab Company hack. Atlanta is working now to see how they got hold of it. So far, we have no reports of any cabbies turning up missing."

"What if this is part of the plan? Tell the police to be very careful in what they share as they talk to the cab company. If I were looking for a way to case an airport as inconspicuously as possible, I couldn't think of a better disguise than a cab. People almost never pay attention to cabs because they are *supposed* to be around airports!"

"Good thoughts—I'll pass them on to Atlanta. And I'll let you know if anything else shows up. Oh, one other thing. The taxi also had a police scanner. We initially assumed it belonged to the legitimate driver, but it could mean that the terrorists are listening in on the emergency radio frequencies."

* * * * * * * * * *

"WAGA, Fox 5, Atlanta. How may I help you?"

"Hello, my name is Betty Fulsome, and I want to know why you didn't cover the major shooting out by the airport this afternoon."

"I'm sorry, ma'am; let me put you on hold and direct your call to the news desk."

"News desk, Chip here."

"Hi, it's Tricia on the switchboard. I've got a caller who wants to know why we didn't cover the major shooting out by the airport this afternoon."

"Probably because there was no major shooting. Nothing came over the police scanner, and there wasn't anything on the other networks. But put her through, and I'll talk with her."

"Hi, this is Chip Sloan from Fox 5 News. How may I help you?"

"Chip, my name is Betty Fulsome, and I want to know why you didn't cover this afternoon's major shooting out by the airport."

"Ma'am, we received no report of a shooting, and we monitor the police emergency frequency all the time. We also watch our competitors, and they didn't report it either."

"I know, and that's why I'm so upset. Earlier today I called 9-1-1 to report a suspicious car behind my apartment complex. About twenty-five minutes later everything went crazy out there. The 9-1-1 operator told me to stay away from the window, but I just had to look. I saw the SWAT team firing automatic weapons like they were at a turkey shoot. Then this suspicious car—it was a taxi—roared out into the open away from them. But just when it looked like it might get away, I heard a crash, like they ran into something. And then I heard three more shots. After that, a couple ambulances raced in and then drove away. But they never used their sirens. Now, you tell me what was going on?"

"I don't know, but this sounds interesting. Again, could you give me your name and the specific address where this happened?"

Ten minutes later, the reporter was on the phone to Jim Carter, the media relations officer for the Atlanta Police Force. "Jim, Chip Sloan here from Channel 5 News. We're checking on the multiple shooting that took place this afternoon over on the west side of the airport. What can you tell me about it?"

"Chip, I'm sorry, but I have no information on a shooting."

"Come on, Jim. I have a witness who says she saw the SWAT team and heard automatic rifle fire coming from the woods just to the west of Roosevelt Highway. Now what gives?"

"Wait a minute; let me check. Oh, here you go. An independent film crew had filed a permit to film in and around Atlanta this week. One of the locations listed was the woods bounded by Roosevelt, Riverdale, and Global Gateway. They're filming some type of futuristic drama called *Police State 2025*. I'll bet that's what your source heard."

"Yeah, you're probably right. Thanks for checking. I'll call the lady back and let her know what she saw. She'll probably be on pins and needles waiting for the movie to come to her local Cineplex!"

Both men laughed and hung up the phones.

CHAPTER 20

FINDING THE NEEDLES

By Tuesday morning, more of the puzzle pieces fell into place. The police raided the Atlanta home where the two terrorists had been hiding. The family who owned the house was originally from Pakistan. A cousin had asked them if they would rent out a room to two men for a few weeks while the men looked for a place of their own. But the family knew nothing about the men's background or their purpose for being in the United States.

With only two days remaining until the planned attack, the police decided to hold the family and charge them with aiding illegal immigrants. The family was held without access to a lawyer, clear grounds for dismissal of charges that the police had no intention of filing. But they had to keep the family from contacting any friends or relatives who might be able to get word back to the head of the operation. The SA-7 missiles were stacked on shelves inside the garage. They, along with a new computer found in the two men's room, were taken away by the FBI for careful analysis. Any scrap of information could become a valuable clue.

The case was progressing, but time was running out. And the strain was showing on Jillian. She was sleeping on a cot in her office and living off Starbucks coffee.

"Morning, Jillian!"

She snapped her head to the right, her eyes ready to burn fiery holes into the face of anyone who could be so cheerful this early in the morning. And there stood Greg.

"Oh, good morning." Jillian self-consciously began using her fingers like a comb to smooth out the tangles in her hair. "Sorry I'm such a mess. I spent the night here, and I was working on the case most of the evening."

"I think you look great, a little overworked, maybe. And that's why I brought you a little something to help you get started this morning. Here's a breakfast box for you from Corner Bakery. You have a choice: bagel and cream cheese or the muffin box?"

"Thank you so much! I'll take the bagel, if that's okay with you."

"The choice is yours. I like 'em both. I really can't stay 'cause I've got a class at nine. But I just wanted to drop by and let you know that you're in my thoughts and prayers. This is a tense time, and I'm asking God to give you great peace and wisdom."

"Thanks, Greg. Knowing you are praying for me *is* important right now!" she replied with all the sincerity she could muster.

"Well, time to head back to class. I'll come by later this afternoon to see how things are going." Greg left as quickly as he had appeared, but as usual, brought a lift to Jillian's day.

* * * * * * * * * *

Jillian was almost finished with the bagel when the phone rang. "Hello, this is Agent Foster."

"Jillian, it's Frank, and I got some good news. Each of our South African passport friends can now be identified by his driver's license photograph. You were right. Evidently this terrorist organization, or some other group with whom they are working, has planted someone in the license bureau in each of these states. We have the different authorities working on that angle. But we now have mug-shot-quality photos of all sixteen men. And the two killed yesterday do match up with their mug shots."

"That is great news. How soon can we get those pictures out to the crisis management teams in the remaining cities?"

"They are being sent right now. You should have copies in just a few minutes. Oh, I also come bringing two other pieces of good news."

"You have the home address for each of the other teams!"

"Well, yes, as a matter of fact, I do—at least for most of them. Five of the remaining seven teams also used the address of the house or apartment where they are staying as their home address. Each of those locations is under surveillance right now. And guess what? We found taxis parked at those houses. They *are* using cabs to case the airports."

"Fabulous news," Jillian exclaimed, taking her last bite of bagel. "I'm assuming you will pick a specific time to gather up all our chicks. Which two groups are still AWOL?"

"Unfortunately, it's the ones in Chicago and Dallas. So it looks like you have a little more work to do there. Jillian, I think we have reached a point where we can direct the collection of the chicks from here. I would like you to put all your energy into finding the two bad guys at your location."

"That makes good sense. We will officially hand off the other groups to you and focus on our own two suspects. You said you had two other pieces of good news. What's the second one?"

"We found the first set of SA-7 missiles. They were hidden in the garage of the people with whom the suspects were staying. The people seem to be innocent participants in this drama, but we are still holding them in custody—incognito. We assume we will find the missiles with the other groups as we roll them up."

"Well, we're not at the end, but hopefully the end is in sight. Once you gather up the five teams you have identified, we can put all our resources into finding the final two groups. Two groups still missing—and just over twenty-four hours to find them, I wish we weren't cutting it so close."

"I'm with you. But keep pressing on!"

* * * * * * * * * *

"Well, Suleiman, do you still believe this is a good location?" And as if to punctuate his question, Ibrahim kicked the football—*soccer ball*, he reminded himself—toward his younger comrade.

Ibrahim had already decided the park would be a very suitable place for their attack, but he felt it was his role as the older, wiser man to help train the younger warrior. *Inch' Allah*, the attack tomorrow would not be their last. And lessons successfully learned in one battle only made the warrior more skillful, more cunning for the next.

"Yes, I think this would be a good location," answered Suleiman, though the hesitancy in his voice betrayed his lack of confidence.

"And why do you think so?"

"Well, it is open, and we have a clear view of all the airplanes taking off," he said, phrasing it more like a question than an answer.

"But if that were the case, then wouldn't a better spot be right over there?" And Ibrahim pointed just beyond where they were standing toward the Northwest Tollway. The outbound lanes were moving freely, but the inbound lanes were still snarled in bumper-to-bumper traffic.

"No, that would not be better because we could be seen down there. A policeman or someone else with a gun might see us and try to stop us."

A broad smile swept across Ibrahim's face. "So your head is not filled with dust from the desert after all! You are correct; this is a good site for an attack. And let me share with you why it is so. First, it is a good site for all the reasons you have said. We have an excellent view of the airplanes as they take off. And though it is an open park, we are still secluded. We can see the cars below, but they cannot see us. But let me tell you the other reasons this is a good spot. First, tomorrow is a school day and this athletic field will be empty. Second, the area behind us is a sanitation facility. It is not a site many people want to come and visit. Finally, we have an excellent escape route. Within five minutes after firing our missiles, we can be on either of two major highways going in all directions of the compass. And that will make it very difficult for someone to catch us! Now, let's see exactly where we will park our car and fire our missiles."

For the next thirty minutes the two men walked the entire length and breadth of the Majewski Athletic Fields—a small facility with three baseball diamonds and three soccer fields. Returning to the small parking lot that divided the two soccer fields on the west from the one secluded field to the north, Ibrahim stopped and looked over the landscape one last time. "Yes, this is still the best spot. Here is where we will park, and from here we will fire the missiles. Now, we must go one last time to look for a site to the east."

"But is that really necessary? We have been here four different times, and the airplanes are always taking off to the northwest, right over our heads."

"That is true, my friend, and that is what I expect will happen tomorrow. But we have our orders, and we must carry them out. The best location on the east is in Dam Number 4 Forest Preserve. Let's see how quickly we can find Devon Avenue."

* * * * * * * * * *

Frank O'Banion was pleased with the way Jillian Foster had handled the terrorism task force. Had he known at the beginning what he knew now, it is almost certain he would not have selected her for the assignment. It was simply too strategic to be run by a rookie. *But that's the way the game gets played,* he reminded himself. She was young and at times temperamental, but she was also doing a first-rate job—and he was not about to change quarterbacks after the play had been called in the huddle. Still, he wanted to make sure she didn't make a "rookie mistake." In this contest the stakes were just too high. So he decided to stay in phone contact as often as possible—to be the coach on the sidelines offering advice, encouragement, and words of caution to the talented but green quarterback running the offense. At least that's what he told himself as he reached for the phone.

"Jillian, it's Frank. Anything new to report?"

"Hi, Frank. No, nothing new on our end. We have patrols out scouring every possible place a terrorist might use to fire a missile, but the possibilities are almost endless. How are the other teams doing? Have you started rounding up the bad guys?"

"No, but that should start within the hour. The plan right now is to take them when they are away from the houses, if at all possible. We'll stop them for a traffic violation, and then have some backup swoop in and whisk them away. Then we'll go to each house with a search warrant and arrest the occupants for harboring illegal aliens. The idea is to handle those arrests as quietly as possible."

"Sounds like a good plan," Jillian said, feeling at ease just hearing the calm in her voice. "Anything new on the pair in Dallas?"

"No, they are having the same problems as you. Lookin' for a needle in a haystack, you know."

"Well, thanks for checking in on me, Frank. If I need you I'll give you a call."

As she hung up the phone, Jillian chuckled to herself at Frank's fatherly phone calls to "check in."

* * * * * * * * * *

The arrests of the five known teams were almost anticlimactic in their efficiency—and every law enforcement officer involved said a silent prayer of thanksgiving that they went so smoothly. In each case the police waited for the suspects to leave the house. At an appropriate spot down the road—one with few bystanders—a police car slipped behind the taxi and turned on its emergency lights. When the taxi pulled to the side of the road, the officer came forward and casually mentioned some minor traffic infraction. "Sir, your driver's side brake light is out," or, "Sir, you failed to use your turn signal when you turned left at that last intersection."

The officer asked the driver if he could step out of the car and show him his driver's license and proof of insurance. Though this was not normal police procedure—usually individuals are asked to remain in their car—the drivers all complied. The officer then looked at the license to verify that it was indeed one of the individuals they were seeking. After that he said, "That you sir, this will just take a few seconds," and he walked back toward the squad car.

At that moment two unmarked cars came roaring down the street. The first car pulled in front of the taxi to block its escape, and the second pulled up even with the driver's side door. Four heavily armed members of the SWAT team, each with their service weapons drawn, poured from the vehicles shouting, "Hands up! Don't move! Put your hands up where we can see them!" The suspects, surrounded and outnumbered, gave up without a struggle.

Within two minutes the suspects were inside the squad car and on their way to a holding cell in the nearest federal building. The taxi, driven by one of the SWAT team members was driven to the forensics lab for careful analysis. Five minutes after the traffic stop there was no visible evidence that anything had taken place. Pedestrians and local shop owners were left wondering what had happened.

Thirty minutes after the arrest, a single, unmarked police car pulled up to each of the houses or apartments where the men had been staying. Other unmarked units were in the area but kept a discreet distance away. Whoever answered the door was handed a search warrant, informed of his or her rights, and arrested. The team then searched for several very specific items: boxes that held the SA-7 missiles, a computer, and any clothing or other objects left by the terrorists. The materials and the occupants were taken to the car and driven to the police station. Most neighbors didn't even realize a major police operation had taken place.

* * * * * * * * * *

Greg was on his way to the dining hall in the Student Union when he spotted his favorite weatherman on television. Greg was a news junkie, and he especially enjoyed WGN's chief meteorologist. He usually watched him during their 9:00 p.m. newscast, but today the meteorologist was doing the noon news as well.

"As you know, this has been a remarkable spring thus far. Since 1871, when Chicago began tracking precipitation data, this is the fifteenth driest spring on record. And last week's storm, as powerful as it was, barely made a dent in that deficit. But as I've been telling you for the past few days, the different models are suggesting that this current pattern might be about to change. This buckle in the northern jet stream that is forming out in western Canada will soon bring colder air roaring through our area where it will collide with warm, Gulf moisture streaming up from Louisiana and Mississippi. We could see several dramatic swings in temperature over the next four or five days. The real question is where the frontal boundary will form. If it sets up to the south and east of the city, lining up somewhere here between Detroit and St. Louis—as some of the models predict—then we could experience rain overnight followed by a warm, sunny day on Wednesday, with the winds blowing briskly from the southeast. But if this low over Colorado begins moving eastward, the frontal boundary might only extend from the Wisconsin/Illinois border back down toward the Quad Cities area. And if that happens, we will have a sunny start to the day with showers moving in later in the afternoon. We'll keep a close watch on this, so tune in tonight for further updates. But right now you might want to carry an umbrella with you tomorrow—just in case!"

Greg smiled as he turned and walked into the dining room. *I'm not sure if he is any more accurate than some of the other meteorologists, but he certainly packs more information into his forecast than anyone else.* He made a mental note to put an umbrella in his car anyway, just in case. He also decided to go by the dean's office to let him know he was canceling his Wednesday classes and taking the day off as a "personal day."

* * * * * * * * * *

The briefing at the Emergency Response Center was just breaking up when Jillian sensed her cell phone vibrating. She fished it out and clicked it open. "Hello? Special Agent Foster here."

"Jillian, it's Greg. Are you interested in getting a quick bite to eat?"

"Sure, as long as it's quick. I'm down by city hall; where are you?"

"I'm northbound on Lake Shore Drive. How 'bout I swing by and pick you up."

"Okay, I'll see you outside in, say, fifteen minutes."

* * * * * * * * * *

After picking up their order, Greg walked Jillian over to a booth near the back of the restaurant. "How familiar are you with Google Earth?"

"I'm not really that familiar with it. Why?" She answered but stayed busy opening her sandwich, which she couldn't wait to devour.

"Well, I think it might help you narrow your search for the terrorists. You know Mapquest. Well, think of Google Earth as Mapquest on steroids. Google lets you find a number of things, including driving directions. But more important, it weds map data to satellite data so you can see more than you can on a simple map. A map can show you a blank space, but Google Earth can let you see if it's woods, a playground, or a quarry. It's like taking a virtual helicopter tour of an area, but with all the street names painted on the roads below. Here, let me show you."

In just a few minutes Greg had pulled up the satellite image of O'Hare Airport. "Okay, here's the airport. On a typical map of Chicago, you would see streets all around it, but the map wouldn't tell you what's on those streets. Are they empty lots or packed row houses? Using a map alone, you're forced to drive up and down most of those streets checking to see if it could be a spot that the terrorists might use. But this program allows the map to come to life."

"That's incredible! Can you zoom in closer?" Jillian asked before taking another bite.

"You mean, can I increase the level of detail? Easy. Watch!" Greg slid two fingers across his computer's track pad, and the image zoomed in closer. It was as if Jillian was looking out the window of an airplane coming in for a landing. Houses, eventually even cars, appeared on the screen. But it was even better than being in an airplane because all the streets and parks were labeled.

"Look! I can even see airplanes on the runway!" He continued to "fly" around different parts of the airport and surrounding area.

"Now, let me zoom out slightly and tell you why I think this might be helpful. We know the terrorists need to position themselves within a fairly narrow range outside the airport. If they are too close, airplanes taking off will go past their line of sight so rapidly they won't have time to lock on to the heat signature from the engines. But if they are too far away, the airplanes might have climbed too high or begun turning in a way that takes them out of the missile's effective range. So using what we know about the missiles, we can draw two imaginary circles around the airport—one representing the minimum distance and the other the maximum distance from which we can reasonably expect them to operate."

"That makes sense, and your circles are fairly close to the ones we came up with ourselves."

"Okay, now look at the map." He moved the screen slightly so her view was less distorted. "How many open spaces do you see that would serve as launching sites for missiles? Obviously, they could theoretically stop alongside the highway and fire, but that seems unlikely. They would be seen, and it also means that someone could try to disrupt their plan. No, they would probably look for a place that is isolated yet open, a place where they could watch the different flights go over and then pick out the specific flight they have been assigned to destroy. A place . . . like these two right here." Greg moved the cursor and pointed to two open spaces on the northwest side of the airport.

"This first one looks like an open field just off Higgins Road. It's in a warehouse and transportation area, so there would likely not be many people nearby. The second area is a small park just off the tollway and Wil- lie Road. That spot intrigues me because the park will probably be empty on a school day."

Greg then repositioned the map until it showed the eastern end of O'Hare Airport. "And if I were looking for a spot on the eastern side of the airport for my attack, it would probably be here, somewhere in these forest preserves."

"An excellent piece of deduction, Mr. Holmes!" Jillian giggled and finished off her sandwich. She was starting to get a real kick out of Greg's zeal for detective work. "But that's still a lot of ground to cover. And that happens to be the very spot we have been searching."

"I knew you would be three steps ahead of me. One last thing." He paused for a moment, as if reflecting on whether or not he should continue.

"What's that?"

"Well, I don't want to sound melodramatic, but it's just that I know how much you really want to catch these guys. I want to make sure you keep yourself safe tomorrow!"

Greg was smiling as he said these last words, but Jillian sensed a deep concern on his part. Rather than brush those concerns off, she wanted him to know that she appreciated the fact that he cared.

"That's sweet, but I'll be fine. We know what we're doing, really," she put her hand on his and smiled. "You have become very special to me, and knowing that you care is important. But don't worry about me. I'll be functioning as the mobile command center for this operation. That sounds rather fancy, but it really means I'll be in my car and on the radio with all the different units in the field. Moshe has agreed to ride with me as a liaison from Mossad to observe how we handle the operation."

"Any chance that I could also ride along as a civilian observer? After all, I do have a personal interest in this since I helped find their messages!" Greg grinned with hope.

"I'll check with my boss, but right now I don't see that as a problem. You've been in on the operation from the beginning, and it seems right to have you there at the end."

CHAPTER 21

TIME

The economic engine called Dallas–Fort Worth International Airport powers much of the economy of northern Texas. When the airport opened in 1974, few could envision the impact it would have on the region. Part of its success came from its sheer size. The entire airport covers nearly thirty square miles and has seven major runways. As airline travel increased because of deregulation, DFW shouldered an ever-increasing share of those travelers.

The airport also brought expansion to the neighboring communities. When it first opened, much of the surrounding countryside was nothing more than empty prairie and farmland. But that open space quickly disappeared as people—and businesses—moved toward the new airport.

The cities of Arlington and Irving lay just to the south of DFW. Each had experienced some growth prior to the opening of the airport because they straddled the main highways connecting Dallas and Fort Worth. For years Irving boasted Texas Stadium, the football field with a hole in the roof so, it was said, God could watch His beloved Cowboys play.

Arlington focused on entertainment and education—Six Flags over Texas, the Texas Rangers baseball team, and the University of Texas at Arlington. But when DFW opened, both cities profited from the infusion of businesses and people.

But if the impact south of the airport was significant, the impact to the north was monumental. Prior to the opening of DFW, most of that area was a smattering of farms and small towns. Coppell, Flower Mound, and Grapevine were nothing more than dots on a map to most people. But all that changed. The entire northern edge of Dallas began a rapid, relentless march toward the Oklahoma border.

The terrorists didn't know the history of the area, but they did know it had taken many days to find suitable locations to fire their missiles. On the north side of the airport, the best place seemed to be one of the few remaining fields between the airport and Grapevine Mills Mall, west of the intersection of LBJ Freeway and International Parkway. But getting into—and out of—the area was difficult. A taxi driving across open pasture would clearly be visible from the air. And if it had rained recently, the car could become stuck in clay soil that kept water from draining off the fields.

"Most merciful Allah," prayed Anwar, the leader of the team, "please keep your winds blowing from the south. Having the plane take off toward the south will make our task so much easier!"

"Anwar, I couldn't help but hear what you have prayed. Why does a south wind make our work so much easier?"

"Ah, my younger cousin, you finally ask a question I can answer! I would like the wind to blow from the south because it will help us succeed in our mission. If the wind blows from the north, then the airplanes must take off to the north—into the wind. And if that happens, then we must drive our car out into an open field and trust Allah that no one sees us and that the car will not get stuck. But if the wind blows from the south, then the planes will take off to the south, and we can use the place we have discovered down there. It is easier to reach, it is more secluded, and it gives us a better opportunity to escape."

"But when will we know which location to use?"

"We will know as soon as we wake up in the morning and look outside. So pray now, my cousin, and then go to sleep. Tomorrow we will find out whether Allah has seen fit to smile on our prayers."

Anwar turned off the light and padded across the room toward the bed. He felt good about tomorrow. Yes, he had prayed, and that was comforting. But he had also watched the evening news. There was no mention of the police searching for or finding any terrorists, so their plan was still a well-guarded secret. And the weatherman with the bowtie predicted the wind would continue to blow from the south. In less than twelve hours America would be on its knees! And with that pleasant thought to comfort him, Anwar fell asleep.

* * * * * * * * * *

Billy Ray Wilson loved his job. "Where else can I play golf and get paid for it?" As a sales representative for SignalTech Industries, he had spent the last twenty years managing his firm's account for the GM plant in Arlington. The plant produced SUVs, but with ever-rising fuel prices, the market for gas-guzzlers had started to slip. So Billy Ray was courting other industries that might need the computer modules manufactured by his company.

Today looked to be a good day. Months of intense negotiations with Caterpillar seemed to be paying off. His many trips to Peoria in the dead of winter produced a verbal understanding for a rather substantial order. Last night the purchasing agent flew down to tour the plant and, if everything appeared satisfactory, sign the deal. In one of their earlier meetings the agent mentioned he loved to golf—and that was all the hint Billy Ray needed. The schedule for today began with a 7:32 tee time on the West

Course of the Hyatt Bear Creek Golf Resort. They would be done by noon, grab a bite at a nice restaurant, start their tour of the plant at one thirty, and—hopefully—sign the contract by four!

The course was in ideal condition. Several spells of rain earlier in the month had helped North Texas slip into its spring shade of green, and the bluebonnets were in blossom. In another week or two they would hit their peak, but they still blanketed the hillsides in their unmistakable shade of blue. And scattered through the fields were patches of Indian paintbrush, their orange-red blush complementing the green grass and the azure bluebonnets.

Billy Ray was a native Texan, and he loved his state. He enjoyed its people, with their sense of optimism and their can-do spirit. He also liked the land itself and its many scenes of beauty—from the stark grandeur of the Davis Mountains to the long stretches of prairie dotted with cattle ranches—sporting names like the Lazy Z and the Crooked W. But to his way of thinking, the most beautiful sight of all was a Texas hillside covered in bluebonnets in the spring. "Tom, isn't that beautiful! It reminds me of that song by Tanya Tucker." And Billy Ray belted out his baritone rendition. "When I die I may not go to heaven; I don't know if they let cowboys in. If they don't just let me go to Texas, boy! Texas is as close as I've been."

"Billy Ray, you are unbelievable! Is everyone down here like you, or do you just get paid by the Texas tourism board to talk up your home state?"

"Well, Tom, as they say down here, 'When it's true, it ain't braggin'.' Let me quote a sign hangin' in a restaurant over in Dallas. 'Never ask a man where he's from. If he's from Texas, he'll tell you. And if he's not, you'll just embarrass him.'"

Tom snorted in laughter. "You are one proud Texan! But I do have to admit that this is about as pretty as it can get on a golf course. Now, tee off, partner, before I change my mind about signing that contract!"

* * * * * * * * * *

Anwar and his cousin, Hamid, awakened to a gentle breeze coming from the south. "Just as you requested from Allah," said Hamid.

And just as predicted by the weatherman, thought Anwar.

They left the small apartment that had been rented for them in Grand Prairie and drove west on Route 30. Even after two weeks of driving, the traffic still bothered Anwar, causing a pain that started in his shoulders and crept up his neck into his head.

Turning north on Highway 360, they drove for six or seven miles—Anwar kept forgetting to check the odometer—until they reached Mid Cities Boulevard. They turned right and drove several hundred feet until they passed over a small bridge. It appeared to be nothing more than a culvert through which a small stream—or perhaps excess rainfall—would flow. About fifty feet past the culvert, Anwar stopped the car in the middle of the road and then turned the steering wheel to the left to begin his Y-turn. He drove back over the culvert in the opposite direction and then gently pulled the car to the side of the road. Switching off the ignition, he pocketed the keys, opened the door, and stepped out. Once Hamid got out and closed his door, Anwar pushed the Lock button on his door and pushed it closed. The car would be safely locked while they were gone.

He opened the trunk and looked inside, his eyes widening as he stared at the two boxes. He looked around to make sure no one was coming and then reached in to grab the first box. "Quick, Hamid, now is our chance. Grab your box and head toward the ditch."

The boxes were heavy, but each man was able to hoist one onto his shoulder and carry it. Hamid nearly fell going down the side of the bank into the culvert, but he managed to regain his footing. "Be careful! Both missiles are essential for our success. We do not want to be the only group who fails to carry out our mission!"

Bending low, the two men carried the boxes through the culvert.

Though they were both short by Western standards, the culvert still required them nearly to double over and carry the boxes on their backs. On the other side they paused to rest.

"Look, Hamid, there is our destination!" said Anwar, pointing over to the right toward a small mound surrounded on three sides by trees and brush. "That is where we will prepare our weapons and hide until it is time!"

Anwar lifted his head and then crouched down rapidly, signaling with his free hand for Hamid to do the same. A few seconds later Hamid understood the meaning of the command as he heard the rising pitch of an approaching car. The car continued on down the road, and Hamid let out a long breath of air. "Come; up the hill. Hurry!"

* * * * * * * * * *

Ibrahim and Suleiman quickly loaded the boxes into the trunk of their taxi and slammed down the lid. Glancing around, they looked for the telltale movement of a curtain that might signal a watching neighbor. But everything was quiet, except for the barking of a dog many streets over. They got into the car and started the engine.

Ibrahim was nervous, but it wasn't because of the mission. Rather, it was the weather. The sky was dark, with steel gray clouds racing across the horizon. The tall buildings downtown, usually visible as small silhouettes off in the distance, seemed to have vanished in the mist.

"What is troubling you, Ibrahim?"

"It is the weather, my young friend. If the clouds remain as they are, then we might not succeed in our mission. The airplanes will be invisible to us, hidden from view. And if the clouds bring rain, then the flight we are to target might be delayed. If the other teams are able to fire their missiles, the Americans will close down all their airports, and our opportunity will have passed. I am not troubled by the prospect of failure, but I am troubled by the thought that we may never have the opportunity to succeed."

"Do not worry, my friend and mentor! If any of our group is close to Allah, it is you. I am confident he would not bring us this far only to let us fail. The skies will clear you will see!"

"Yes, my friend, you are right. You are the teacher this morning!" he said more cheerfully than he really felt. *The young man is correct,* he admitted to himself. *Why worry about those things I cannot change? I should be focusing on those things that I can control.*

As he inserted the key to start the car, Ibrahim turned toward young Suleiman and smiled broadly. "Come, young warrior! Today, *inch' Allah,* we bring this city and this country to its knees!"

"Which of our locations should we choose?"

"The wind has always blown from the west. Let us trust in Allah to do the same for us today." And they headed toward the Northwest Tollway and the Majewski Athletic Fields—a decision that would prove to have enormous consequences for them, and for Chicago.

* * * * * * * * * *

"Jillian, this is Greg. I'm coming up Lake Shore, but I'm not even close to Soldier Field yet. Traffic was a little heavier than I expected, and the traffic reports are saying that there's an accident at Lake Shore and Jackson. Yeah, I know that's a problem. Listen, why don't you and Moshe just head out, and I'll try to catch up with you out near O'Hare. Look, I gotta go. There's a police car coming up from behind, and I don't want to get pulled over for talking on my cell phone while driving. Talk to you later!"

Greg sat the phone on the passenger seat and made a split-second decision to hop on the Stevenson and then jump onto the Kennedy. Traffic would be heavy going into the Circle Interchange, but once he reached Ohio Street it should open up again. Thirty minutes later he passed the Ohio Street exit and started to accelerate. He looked to his left at the traffic crawling along on the inbound lanes and breathed a silent prayer of thanksgiving. "Thank You, Lord, for letting me drive in the opposite direction! Just thirty minutes to O'Hare." As Greg focused on the coming mission, his foot pushed harder against the gas pedal.

The strains of *Für Elise* brought him back from his musings, and he looked down to see the needle of his speedometer hovering at about seventy. He quickly pulled his foot off the gas and glanced around to make sure no police cars were nearby. His cell rang and he reached over and he flipped it open. "Hello?"

"Greg, it's Jillian. Where are you?"

"I'm almost to the 90/94 split. How about you?"

"We're a little ahead of you. You must have gotten stuck in traffic downtown. Anyway, I'm just about to exit at Cumberland Road. We're setting up a temporary command post right at the corner of Higgins and Cumberland. The winds are really starting to shift, and the National Weather Service says that by 9:30 a front will have moved through. They are predicting a steady wind blowing in from the southeast with clearing skies and a rising temperature. We are assuming our terrorists will try to attack from somewhere along the eastern side since the planes will be taking off in that direction."

"I've been thinking about that. I heard the same forecast last night, but what if the terrorists aren't news junkies? They've been in town for a week or two, and the wind has consistently been blowing from the west. If they haven't listened to a weather forecast, they might still go to their primary launch site. And once they get set up, they won't have enough time to change."

"Good thought, but we can't take that chance. I'll divert a few patrols over to the west, but right now we have to concentrate all our forces here on the east. Until we know where they are, we have to assume they are on the side where the planes will be taking off."

"I understand, but I'm still concerned. I think I'll just drive out west and look for a taxi parked in those places I showed you last night."

"Okay, but be careful. We don't know if these guys have any weapons in addition to the missiles, and we certainly don't want to spook them and have them running loose with SA-7s."

"I know, and I won't do anything foolish. But it wouldn't hurt to have another pair of eyes on that side of the airport, would it?"

"No, I guess it wouldn't. Just make sure you call if you see anything that looks suspicious!"

"I promise. Good hunting!" And Greg threw the phone back on the seat.

* * * * * * * * * *

"Fantastic drive, Tom! This is a short par 4, and you are in great position!"

The front nine had gone well. Billy Ray and Tom were evenly matched. That's not to say they were good golfers. Tom was fourteen over par through the first eleven holes, and Billy Ray was fifteen over. But they were enjoying the golf—and getting to know each other.

Tom's drive off the tee went thirty yards farther than Billy Ray's, but Billy Ray was in the center of the fairway while Tom was off to the left in the first cut of rough. Billy Ray was 130 yards from the green, and he got to hit first. Taking his nine iron, he swung easy and made excellent contact with the ball. It sailed crisply into the air, its long arc appearing to take it right toward the hole. Billy Ray started shouting to the ball, "In the hole! Go in the hole!"

The ball missed the hole, but only by three feet. It bounced once and then checked up and came to rest about ten feet from the pin. "Yes! All right, Mr. Caterpillar man, beat that!"

"Good shot, Billy Ray! But watch this one!"

Tom enjoyed golfing with Billy Ray, but that didn't mean winning wasn't important. He was one stroke ahead at the start of the hole, and he intended to be at least one stroke ahead at the end of the hole. He was only a hundred yards from the pin, the perfect distance for his pitching wedge. But the ball had settled down in the first cut of grass. Tom knew he had to make good contact, or else the grass would grab his clubface, forcing it closed. If that happened his ball would hook to the left and land short of the green in some high weeds. To compensate, he opened his clubface slightly and swung just a little harder than normal, and he was rewarded with the *swish* and *click* of the club sliding through the grass and striking the ball. He turned his head to watch the ball's flight, and that's when he realized he had overcooked the shot. The ball appeared to be headed to the back of the green or even off the green. "Sit, ball! Sit!"

The ball landed just off the back edge of the green, but it immediately took a high bounce—disappearing into the trees and brush behind. "Nuts! It must have hit a sprinkler head!" Tom saw his one-shot lead evaporating—assuming he could find the ball and get it up and down in three for a bogie.

Just then the ball came flying back out of the woods, landing on the green. "What the—?" shouted Billy Ray. "You got some kinda homing device on that ball?"

"No, I don't, but that sure was unusual. Let's go see what it hit."

"Hamid, why did you do that?"

"I threw the ball back out so they would not come here to look for it."

"Don't you think they will wonder how it jumped out? Quick—try to hide behind that tree. And don't make a sound! Hopefully they will not see us and will just go on their way."

Tom and Billy Ray drove their cart around the back side of the green, careful not to get too near the putting surface or the left side bunker. They drove through a gap in the trees and up on the mound. "I don't see what the ball hit to make it bounce back on the green like that. Maybe it was— hold it, what's that?" Billy Ray followed Tom's finger toward a clump of trees on the far side of the mound. There he saw two men crouching down. One was holding a knife in his hand, and the other seemed to be holding some type of weapon like a machine gun, or a bazooka, or a, a—

Billy Ray filled in the blank. "Let's hightail it out of here! That guy's got a missile launcher!" Billy Ray had spent four years in the army, and he knew what an SA-7 looked like—and what it was used for. He mashed his foot on the gas pedal and whipped the steering wheel hard to the left, almost throwing Tom from the cart. The two men jumped from behind the trees and started running across the top of the mound, trying to catch the cart before it built up speed and got away.

"Step on it, Billy Ray! They're gaining on us!"

"Anwar! Come on; we must catch them!" Hamid, the younger and faster of the two men, had been the first to jump up once they had been spotted. But he froze, like a deer in a car's headlights, until Anwar had said, almost in a hissing whisper, "Get them!" That one lost second made the difference. Though Hamid almost caught up to the cart as it wheeled around, it rapidly gained speed as it drove down off the hill. Hamid was almost able to grab hold of one of the bags fastened on the back of the cart, but the driver yanked the wheel to the left, and Hamid slipped and fell on the smooth grassy surface. He jumped up and continued running after the cart for another hundred feet, but then even he gave up.

Then Billy Ray broke through the trees and drove the cart across the green, making one zig in his route just as the younger of the two men lunged for the cart. He left the man sprawled across the green, and the cart bounded down the fairway toward the tee box. "As soon as we get past the drainage ditch on our left, I'll turn and head straight back toward the clubhouse. Here, take my phone and call 9-1-1. Tell them we just ran into a man holding what appeared to be an SA-7 missile launcher just behind the twelfth green on the Hyatt Bear Creek Golf, West Course. Tell them it's right outside the southern entrance of DFW Airport. They'll understand."

Hamid ran back to his partner. "Anwar, what should we do?"

"There is nothing to do; it is in Allah's hands. There are only twenty minutes left until the plane is scheduled to depart. Let's listen to the police scanner. Perhaps the men will be so frightened that they will forget to report what just happened. Perhaps they will not be able to remember where we were. Or perhaps the police will come, and we will not be successful. That is all in Allah's hands. So let's just listen to the scanner and prepare our weapons."

Tom's call was received by Arlington's Dispatch Services center. Over the past two days all the cities bordering DFW, along with the cities of Dallas and Fort Worth, had been contacted by the FBI and told of the impending threat. The information that had been passed to all emergency response centers had, amazingly, not been leaked to the media. Still, the emergency response dispatcher was surprised when she actually received a call related to the terrorist threat.

"Hello, Arlington Dispatch Services. How may I help you?"

"Listen, we just ran into a guy outside DFW airport who's getting ready to fire a missile!"

"Okay, sir, calm down. Please tell me where you are and what you saw."

"It's hard to calm down! I thought we were going to be killed. We were playing golf on the—what's the name of the course again Billy Ray?—oh yeah, the Hyatt Bear Creek Golf Resort, West Course, the twelfth hole, and we came across two men hiding in the woods behind the green. One man had a knife, and the other had a—what was it again?—an SA-7 missile launcher. They chased us, but we managed to outrun them in our cart. That was about two minutes ago. As far as we know they are still there."

"Thank you, sir. Can you stay on the line while I transfer that information?" But before Tom could answer he was put on hold.

Calling her supervisor, the dispatcher relayed the information. Within thirty seconds, it was going out on special communication equipment to the task force assembled at both the north and south exits to DFW. "We just received a report of two men with an SA-7 launcher on the south side of DFW. Subjects were reported on the Hyatt Bear Creek West Golf Resort hiding in the woods behind the twelfth green. One man reported with launcher and second subject reported with a knife."

The dispatcher returned to the phone to talk to the men. "Sorry to make you wait. Help is on the way. Tell me; where are you right now?"

"Billy Ray, where are we right now? Okay. Ma'am, we are bouncing our way across the fourteenth hole on our way back to the tenth. We plan on heading up the tenth hole back to the clubhouse."

"That's excellent. Please stay at the clubhouse once you arrive. We have help on the way. You should be safe there." And the line went dead.

* * * * * * * * * *

Sergeant Phil Runyon finished writing down the information and then turned to the pilot. "Rick, get us to the Hyatt Bear Creek West Golf Resort as quickly as possible!"

"So what's the news?" Lieutenant Rick Smith hadn't been issued one of the special tactical radios, and the normal police frequencies he had been monitoring while they were flying up and down the Trinity River on the west side of Dallas only had sporadic reports of a three-car accident on LBJ and a bank robbery in progress down in South Oak Cliff.

"We have a confirmed report of two men with an SA-7 at the south end of DFW. They are at—" and Phil reached down for the pad where he had written the information, "Hyatt Bear Creek Golf Resort, West

Course, behind the twelfth green, hidden in some trees."

"I've played that course! And I know that hole. It's a pretty par 4 with a mound and some trees behind it. And it's right on the corner of 360 and Mid Cities Boulevard. Let's make tracks!" The Bell Jet Ranger III shot forward and quickly covered the ground between the Trinity River and DFW. Along the way, Lieutenant Smith kept in contact with air traffic control while Sergeant Runyon was coordinating their position with the ground units converging on the scene.

"Rick, that missile does worry me a little. If they see us, we could be sitting ducks."

"Don't worry! I learned a few tricks flying in Iraq. I don't intend to let them see us until it's too late for them to do anything about it. I'll swoop in, drop you off, and take off. Just make sure you don't stand up till I'm gone. I don't want you getting a free GI haircut from my rotor blades!"

"I understand. The squad cars will be converging on their position from 360 on the west and from Mid Cities Boulevard on the east. That leaves the golf course as their only escape route. And that's the direction we'll come in."

Phil shared the plan with those on the ground. He then turned to Rick. "How soon till we are there?"

"Not long at all. Look, there's the course straight ahead."

Phil could make out a golf course in the distance. He didn't know the layout of the course, but he was glad to know Rick did. He could pick out Route 360, and he assumed the road running along the back of the course was Mid Cities Boulevard. And if that was the case, then the hole in the upper left must be number twelve. "Is that the spot over there?" he said, pointing to the far corner.

"Sure is! Hey, look just beyond the hole. There's a car parked along-side the road. I think it might be a taxi."

"You're right, Rick. Let me pass that on to the others. We need to make sure we block their escape!" Rick relayed the information and then picked up his assault rifle. "We're getting close. Can you get down real low and come up the length of the fairway to drop me off just before the green?"

"I was thinking the same thing. The low approach and those trees at the end might just keep them from getting a good look at us—or a good shot at us—before I have a chance to drop you off. Once you're out I'll scoot on back down the fairway and then gain some altitude just in case the bad guys try to sneak away in some other direction. I'll be your eyes in the sky—except we won't be able to communicate because they didn't issue me one of those special radios!"

One more glitch in the plan! Now it feels like a real operation, Phil thought.

Phil watched in amazement as Rick brought the copter down to within ten feet of the ground and roared down the fairway. *Just the way it looks when they show the holes on television,* he thought in amazement. Before reaching the green, Rick froze the helicopter in flight and spun it a quarter turn to the right. The chopper was now parallel to the clump of trees, shielding Phil.

"It's time! Jump!"

Phil pushed open the door and jumped out onto the fairway. Rick turned the helicopter back to the left to keep the tail rotor pointing away from Phil. He nudged the helicopter backward as if he were going to back into the trees, then raised the collective and the helicopter rose and shot over Phil's head back down the fairway. Phil realized his precarious position and dived into the sand trap just to the left of the green. *No shots; that's good.*

Working his way to the back side of the trap nearest to the mound, he peered over the edge. He scanned the woods looking for movement, shapes, outlines, something to indicate a person was there looking back.

Nothing. He climbed from the bunker, pulling his rifle into firing position. The sprint from the bunker to the edge of the woods was the longest fifteen yards of his life.

Pausing at the edge of the woods, Phil listened for any sound or movement. At first he heard nothing, but then he thought he heard faint voices. He took a few steps forward and then paused to listen again. He heard a man say,

"I tell you; that helicopter knows we are here. Did you see how close he came to us! He must know we are here!"

Another answered, "But he did not stop. He was only checking on the report made by two very upset men. He saw nothing out of the ordinary, and he went away. Listen to the scanner. Do you not think they would be summoning more help if they knew we were hiding here waiting to attack? Just grab your missile. It is almost time."

Phil had to make a decision. He could wait until help arrived, but that might be too late. These men were preparing to fire their missiles at any time. As still another plane roared overhead on its way out of DFW, Phil decided the best course of action was to act rather than react. Stepping through the trees into the clearing, he pointed his rifle toward the men and shouted, "Police! Put your hands up!"

Anwar glanced up, his face almost passive—as if he had been expecting the man to appear all along. In contrast, Hamid had the look of a cornered lion—wild, angry, frightened. The events of the next few seconds took on an almost surreal quality for Phil.

Hamid reached into his back pocket for his knife and started toward Phil. But he was only able to take two steps before Phil fired a three-round burst into his torso. The knife flew from Hamid's hand and his body twitched briefly, like a broken marionette, before crumpling to the ground.

Phil had focused so intently on the man he had shot that he momentarily took his eyes off the other. But when he looked back, he saw the man had his SA-7 launcher on his shoulder, and it was aimed in Phil's direction. Phil instinctively dived to his left just as Anwar pulled the trigger. The rocket roared past Phil and through the trees, hitting the ground about fifty yards away in an explosion of dirt and dust.

Phil hit the ground so hard that he momentarily had the wind knocked out of him. He jumped to his feet, but the other man had already disappeared. Phil looked around to see where he had gone. *There!* Phil caught a brief glimpse of the man just as he slid down an embankment into a ditch.

Phil started sprinting after the man. He paused briefly, realizing he had dropped his rifle when he hit the ground. But he patted his hip and felt the reassuring bulge of his service revolver still in its case. He pulled it from the pouch and resumed his chase. He reached the embankment before realizing it led into a culvert under the road. The man was making a dash for his car! He reached down for his special walkie-talkie, but it was gone! It must have fallen off when he hit the dirt. The man was getting away, and he wasn't sure he could catch him in time.

Just then he heard the familiar sound of a helicopter. There! It was Rick. He must have seen the missile explode and gone high to see what was happening. Phil waved his arms frantically at Rick. The copter wiggled in reply. Phil pointed to the car to signal that the terrorist was heading toward it. He wasn't sure whether or not Rick understood. The suspect popped from the other side of the culvert and dashed toward his car.

Phil took his revolver and fired across the road at the man. His rounds hit the car, but the man was making his way along the far side of the car, using it as cover. The suspect opened the door and slipped into the passenger side. Phil heard the engine turn over, and he knew the man was getting away.

Then Phil heard the shrill scream of sirens. An Arlington police car skidded to a halt in front of the suspect's car, and a voice from the police loudspeaker ordered the man to surrender. But instead of following orders, the man threw his car into reverse and began to make a Y-turn in the road. The officer must have been told about the nature of the suspect, because as soon as the car started to back up, he emptied his service revolver into the driver's side window. The driver slumped over as his car shot backward, finally coming to rest against the fence of the golf course, just fifteen feet from where Phil was standing.

Phil ran back into the woods to find his tactical radio. "This is Sergeant Phil Runyon. Both bad guys are down. I repeat. Both bad guys are down. Please send two ambulances to the corner of Highway 360 and Mid Cities Road. Also send some more people to help secure the site and to search for the second missile. One was fired, but it was not aimed at an airplane."

Not at an airplane—just at me!

CHAPTER 22

THE FINAL OPPORTUNITY

"Ibrahim, we are here. And look, the sky is clearing!"

Ibrahim craned his neck to look up through the front windshield. The dark gray clouds that seemed so threatening less than an hour earlier were giving way to puffy while cumulus clouds—with patches of blue showing between. "Yes, Suleiman, it does appear that Allah is with us this morning."

He eased the taxi onto the Elmhurst Road exit ramp. At the top of the ramp he slowed to make the hard right turn onto Willie Road. The driver behind was watching the oncoming traffic on Elmhurst and starting to accelerate when he glanced up and saw the taxi slowing to a stop. He swerved sharply to his left, narrowly missing the back edge of the taxi.

"Stupid cabbie! Use your turn signal!" he shouted. But the windows in both cars were closed, so Ibrahim did not hear what he said. But even if he had, he would not have cared. He was focused on the mission.

The taxi bounced down Willie Road to a spot where the road made a sweeping bend to the left. That's where Ibrahim made a sharp right-hand turn onto the dirt road leading to the parking lot. But instead of parking in the lot, Ibrahim turned to the right and drove onto a grassy field that paralleled Willie Road. He crept along the edge of the field looking for just the right spot. When he found it, he backed the car to some trees that stood guard between the soccer field and the road.

"There, we are secure. If anyone drives into the parking lot, he should not see our car. It is the perfect place to prepare for our attack!"

* * * * * * * * * *

"Jillian, it's Greg. I'm just leaving the tollway and turning onto Elmhurst Road. I should be at the park in less than five minutes."

"Greg, remember what I said before, and be careful. If you see anything, call me and then stand back. Let us handle everything."

"Trust me; that's what I intend to do. I'll just park my car and walk around. Hopefully, nothing will be amiss. But if I see anything, I'll call you immediately."

* * * * * * * * * *

For the crew of American Airlines flight 99, the flight from London to Chicago had been routine. They left Heathrow twenty minutes late, but they were back on schedule for a 10:15 a.m. landing in Chicago. Captain Steve Johnson and First Officer Victor Sanchez were in the cockpit while Frank Murchison, the extra Flight Officer—FO–B, usually shortened to FB—was seated in the jump seat directly aft of the center control console.

Captain Johnson had settled back in the left seat after his rest break and was handling communication with Chicago Center while Sanchez had the controls, though the Boeing 777 felt as if it could fly itself. As he descended to twenty-four-thousand feet, Sanchez looked off to his left at Grand Rapids. He knew Lake Michigan stretched out in front of him though it wasn't visible through the low cloud cover.

A chime sounded and "CABIN INTERPHONE" appeared on the upper engine instrument screen. Captain Johnson lifted the phone out of its cradle. "Joe here."

"Captain, we have a medical emergency in coach." Years of training and experience allowed flight attendant Betty Adams to speak in a calm, steady voice even as her pulse was racing.

"What seems to be the problem, Betty?"

"We've got a passenger—white male, appears to be about sixty—complaining of severe chest pains. He's perspiring heavily and he seems very pale and clammy. It might be a heart attack."

"Okay, I'll call Chicago and declare an emergency, get us a straight shot in. I think we can be on the ground in about thirty minutes or so. We'll have the EMTs waiting at the gate when we arrive. I assume you've already unpacked the oxygen. Do you want me to ask if a doctor is on board?"

"I think that would be a good idea. In the meantime, we are moving him to one of the empty seats in business class."

"Sounds like you have everything under control. Let me know if his condition changes." Switching the panel from Comm1 to PA, Captain Johnson tried to use his most reassuring voice. "Ah, ladies and gentlemen, I've just learned that one of our passengers is experiencing physical difficulties. If there is a medical doctor, nurse, or EMT on board who would be able to assist the flight crew, I would appreciate it if you would click on your overhead call button at this time. Thank you for your assistance."

Switching back to Comm1, Johnson contacted Air Traffic Control. "Chicago, American 99, flight level two-four-zero. We have a medical emergency on board and would like to request as expeditious an approach as possible."

"Roger, American 99. We show your position to be just west of Grand Rapids bearing two-zero-zero. What's the nature of your emergency?"

"American 99. We have a passenger who is displaying symptoms of a possible heart attack. We would like to get him on the ground as soon as possible and would request an EMT meet us at the gate."

"Roger, American 99. Be advised that a front is moving through the airport right now. We anticipate winds will be out of the southeast at about fifteen knots within the next half hour. Come right to two-four-zero and begin descent to one-four-zero."

"American 99. Right to two-four-zero and descending to one-four-zero."

* * * * * * * * * *

Greg parked in a small lot between two soccer fields. He stepped from the car and pushed the door almost shut, stopping just before it latched. *No sense making any unnecessary noise. If someone is here, I don't want to announce my presence.*

He decided the best approach would be to make a quick walk around the exterior of the park—just to look for people or a car, most likely a taxi. He walked east along Willie Road, stopping first at the three baseball fields. He saw nothing suspicious. He continued east until he reached the large parking lot for the remaining soccer fields. From here he could look all the way across the fields to some type of warehouse or shipping facility in the distance. Nothing.

He walked south until he came to a fence marking the edge of the park. Beyond the fence the ground sloped down into a drainage culvert. Beyond the culvert was the Northwest Tollway. He decided to walk west along the fence line, which brought him back to the lot where his car was parked. Still nothing.

The culvert turned north and crossed under Willie Road. Greg's car was parked very near the spot where the culvert went underground, so he walked west from his car to explore what appeared to be the last soccer field. At the far end of the field was an empty parking lot, and he walked toward it. He was just about to turn around but decided he might as well go all the way to the end.

As he reached the parking lot, Greg was surprised to see another field just to the north. He hadn't seen it before because a line of trees had hidden it. He started to walk toward the field, but something inside made him pause. *Now that looks promising.*

He walked in the grass bordering the parking lot until he had reached the access road. Stepping carefully so as not to make any sound, he walked across the road to the line of trees and shrubs on the far side. He stopped to listen and thought he heard voices, but he couldn't see anything. If someone was on the other side, he was well hidden and very quiet.

Carefully pulling back on the lowest branches, Greg tried to peer through the undergrowth. A rush of wind from the southeast startled him, and he froze in his tracks, hardly daring to breathe. Just as the meteorologist had predicted, the front was coming through and the wind was starting to pick up from the southeast. The sound of the wind gave him courage, and he pulled back the remaining branches. About fifty feet away he could see the front of a burgundy car that had been backed into the trees and shrubs lining Willie Road. The car, which looked like an older model Chevrolet Caprice, was barely visible, but he could clearly see the sign lamp on the roof. A cab.

He was just about to step backward when he heard voices coming from beyond the car. He leaned to the left to see if he could find the source, but the bushes obscured his view. "Yes, the wind *has* shifted directions. It is now coming from the other way. Ibrahim, what should we do?"

"What *can* we do, my friend? It is too late to change locations. Either Allah will turn the wind around or he will not."

Greg backed out of the bushes as quietly as possible and crossed the roadway to the parking lot. He had to put some distance between himself and these men—and then he needed to call Jillian. He ran the length of the soccer field back to his car. Climbing inside, he flipped open his phone and hit the speed dial for Jillian's number.

"This is Jillian. Greg, is that you?"

"Yeah, it's me . . . and I've found them! I walked around the entire park, and I found one field tucked away from the rest. I almost missed it. To the side of that field, backed into the trees, was a burgundy taxicab. I heard two men talking, and they were arguing about what to do now that the wind had shifted to the southeast. The one man called the other 'Ibrahim.'"

"Greg, exactly where are you right now?"

"I'm at Metro-Majewski Athletic Fields near where Elmhurst intersects the Northwest Tollway. But don't drive down Willie Road from Elmhurst. The men are hidden in a field right there, and they will hear you coming. Exit from the tollway at Elmhurst, and don't use your sirens. Go beyond Willie and make a right on Oakton. Make another right on Mount Prospect, and then turn right onto Willie. I'll walk down to the far end of the park and meet you there. How soon can you be here?"

"Our units are scattered all around the east side of the airport," she answered, "but I'll tell them to get to you as quickly as possible. Moshe and I should be able to get to you in about ten minutes. We'll also have someone contact the airport to stop all flights."

"I'll be watching for you—and praying!" Greg hung up the phone and felt his chest go tight. He took a deep breath and prayed, "Lord, please be gracious and show Your favor. I really need You to intervene on behalf of these innocent people. Amen."

* * * * * * * * * *

"O'Hare approach, American 99, seven thousand feet. Be advised that the doctor attending to the passenger does believe the passenger is having a heart attack. We need to land ASAP," the captain radioed directly to the tower.

"Roger, American 99. Intercept the fourteen left approach course."

Captain Johnson turned to First Officer Sanchez. "Victor, it's yours to bring on in. If there is any silver lining to this cloud, it's that we'll arrive in Chicago early and won't have to sit and wait for a gate to come open."

Bing. "Flight attendants, please prepare the cabin for landing."

"Ladies and gentlemen, the captain has signaled that we are on final approach. Please stow any items that you may still have out under the seat in front of you. Return your seat back to its upright position, and place your tray table in its upright and locked position. I would also ask you to remain in your seats once the plane has taxied to the gate until the EMS personnel have attended to our passenger in distress."

* * * * * * * * * *

"Ibrahim, the wind is not about to change. Have we failed?"

"No, Suleiman, we have not. The wind is in Allah's hands, and he turns it as he wills. Perhaps he did not want us to attack the airplane that was selected. But airplanes are still flying overhead, only now they are landing. It might be that Allah wants us to bring down a plane that is landing—maybe to show the Americans that no part of their journey is safe. It is nearly ten o'clock, the time when the others will be attacking. Let's choose the next large airplane and see if we can bring it down!"

* * * * * * * * * *

Jillian and Moshe pulled to a stop in front of Greg. "Has anyone else arrived?"

"No, you're the first. And I think we're running out of time. It's almost ten, and these boys know they're at the wrong end of the airport. They could shoot at the next plane flying over and call it a day. We'd better hurry."

"It might not be that serious. The order was given to close down the airport. All flights in or out should have ceased. Let me just check to be sure that's happened." Jillian picked up the special walkie-talkie. "This is

Special Agent Foster. Can you verify that someone has contacted O'Hare to suspend all flights in and out?"

"Be advised that all flights were suspended except for American Airlines flight 99 inbound from London. They had declared a medical emergency and are on final approach, so we thought it best to let them land."

"That's not good! What runway are they using?"

"Runway fourteen left."

"Is that the one closest to the tollway?"

"Let me check. . . . Yes, it is."

"How far out are they? Can you contact the tower and have them waved off?"

"I'll try to contact the tower, but the plane might already be on the ground by the time I get through. We didn't have enough special communication gear to give the tower one."

"Well, when you do get through, tell them to have all their emergency equipment ready to roll. That plane is heading into a trap!"

Jillian handed Greg the walkie-talkie. "Greg, I need you to carry this. We *are* out of time, and we can't wait for reinforcements. Moshe, I assume you know how to use a gun?"

"Israel Defense Force—and Mossad—trained! What have you got?"

Jillian opened her trunk and pulled out an M16 from the special weapons' case. "You take the assault rifle; I'll use my Glock 9. Get in the car and let's roll!"

Jillian and Moshe jumped into the front seat, and Greg climbed in the back. She stomped on the gas pedal and pulled out onto Willie Road.

Greg leaned over the front seat to give directions. "See up ahead where the road bends to the right? That's where you will turn onto the dirt road that leads to the last parking lot. About fifty feet down the road, that row of trees comes to an end, and there will be a field to your right. Turn onto that field. Their car will be about fifty feet down to the right, and they were standing somewhere beyond the car."

"Thanks, Greg. When I hit the brakes, everyone bail from the car. Moshe, if they don't respond immediately to our commands, shoot to kill. We get one chance, and one chance only!"

* * * * * * * * *

"O'Hare Tower, American 99. Runway in sight."

"American 99, you're cleared to land. Runway fourteen left."

* * * * * * * * *

"Ibrahim, here comes a large airplane. Is this the one?"

"Yes, Suleiman, this is the one. It is landing, not taking off, so we must make sure that our missiles are locked on before we fire. Have patience and you will be rewarded!"

"What is that?" Suleiman turned to notice a car racing toward their position.

But Ibrahim was concentrating so much on the incoming plane he didn't hear Suleiman, or the car.

* * * * * * * * *

Jillian roared down the dirt road, pushing a cloud of dust and dirt out from the rear wheels. Inside, the three passengers were bouncing up and down in their seats. They had unfastened their seat belts so they could bound from the car as soon as it stopped. Turning the steering wheel sharply to the right, Jillian nearly put the car into a skid. But she quickly corrected, and the car lurched across the soccer field.

"There!" shouted Moshe, pointing to the car. "And there are the men!" Moshe's arm moved left, toward an open space about thirty feet beyond the car.

Jillian slammed on the brakes and the car skidded to a halt. Pushing open her door, she jumped out shouting, "Police! You are under arres—" But before she could finish her sentence, the missile raced from Ibrahim's launcher toward the inbound jetliner.

* * * * * * * * * *

First Officer Sanchez was at the controls. The automated voice in the cockpit called out "One thousand feet."

"Whoa, what was that?" Sanchez shouted, blinking at the sky around him.

* * * * * * * * * *

Jillian, Moshe, and Greg watched in horror as the missile slammed into one of the airplane's engines. Fire and smoke poured from the point of impact. For some reason, Suleiman also watched Ibrahim's missile rather than firing his own. *Indeed, it does look like a dragon's tail!* Ibrahim, dumbfounded, finally shouted, "Suleiman, fire the missile before it's too late!"

Suleiman raised his missile, but as he did Moshe and Jillian both opened fire, striking him in the chest just before he could pull the trigger. As his body recoiled, his arms instinctively lowered. The missile shot into the air, but at a far lower trajectory, sending it toward the Busse Woods Forest Preserve, where it exploded on impact.

* * * * * * * * * *

At almost the same instant as the first missile hit the Boeing 777, FB Murchison shouted "Engine fire left!" Captain Johnson reached behind the throttles and pulled the fire handle to stop the flow of jet fuel to the engine. He then twisted the handle to the right to release the first extinguisher bottle. The fire slowed but didn't stop. In order to have a backup generator operating, the FB reached up to the overhead panel and started the Auxiliary Power Unit. The cabin shook and groaned as passengers screamed and cried out in terror.

The intercom blinked on, and the FB picked it up. "Frank here."

"Frank, there's a fire in the left engine, and it's continuing to burn. A passenger said he believes a missile struck us. He is a former Navy pilot, so I thought you ought to know."

"Thanks, Betty. We're kinda busy here." And the phone clicked off.

"Fire's not out in the left engine. And a passenger who's a former pilot says it looked like we were hit by a missile."

Captain Johnson reached down and turned the fire suppression handle to the left, releasing the second bottle of carbon dioxide.

"The fire light is out. Fire extinguished."

First Office Sanchez heard the discussion and could tell from the yaw that something had happened to the left engine. He immediately increased power to the right engine and called for the flaps to be raised slightly. The 777's Thrust Asymmetry Computer worked as advertised, automatically adding right rudder, so Sanchez only needed to apply slightly more pressure to the right pedal.

"Five hundred feet."

Captain Johnson got on the radio. "Tower, American 99. We are declaring an emergency. We have lost our left engine. Please roll the emergency equipment."

"American 99. They're already rolling."

Switching the panel from Comm1 to PA, Captain Johnson prepared the passengers for a possible crash landing. "Ladies and gentlemen, we've had a left engine failure. Please follow *exactly* the instructions of our flight attendants. Do *not* use the left overwing exits or doors 2L or 3L."

Before Captain Johnson could finish giving all the instructions the rear wheels touched down. Because of the flap settings, the plane was traveling faster than normal and hit the ground a little harder than usual. But it eventually rolled to a stop on the runway. As it did, the emergency equipment raced up the runway behind it, surrounding the plane. One truck began pumping foam onto the left engine as a precaution.

The flight attendants quickly had the right side doors opened, and within two minutes all the passengers were standing safely on the runway—all, that is, except for the heart attack patient, who was lying on the ground beside one other passenger who broke her ankle sliding down the emergency chute.

* * * * * * * * * *

Moshe ran toward the wounded terrorist, who appeared to be trying to get to his feet. But just as he reached him, the man jumped up and pulled a knife from his waistband. Each stared at the other—and for a fleeting moment seemed to recognize the other's face. Then the man lunged at Moshe, who squeezed the trigger on the M16—sending the terrorist into an eternity very different from the one he had imagined.

In all the commotion with Suleiman, Ibrahim had slipped quietly to his left. The passenger-side door to the taxi had been left open so they could listen to the police scanner. Ibrahim crept along the side and slipped into the front seat. He watched the male policeman set his rifle down and kneel beside Suleiman. And now, not twenty feet in front of him, the policewoman was walking in front of his car toward her partner, her handgun still drawn and trained on his dead companion. This was Ibrahim's chance to escape, and, *inch' Allah*, perhaps he could kill this policewoman at the same time.

He turned the key in the ignition, and the taxi roared to life. He immediately pulled the shift lever to "D" and pushed on the gas pedal. Jillian was focusing so intently on covering Moshe that she didn't hear the car start up. But Greg did and started running to a point where he could intercept it. Then he realized what the driver intended to do, and he altered his course—running directly toward Jillian.

Just before the car reached her, Greg ran in front of it, diving at her and pushing her to the side with all his might. The car missed her, and nearly missed him. But the passenger's side door, still swinging wildly, caught Greg on the leg just above his knee. The impact spun him around, tossing him across the field.

Jillian didn't see the car hit Greg. But as she picked herself up from the ground, she looked back to see the car speeding around the trees—and Greg lying on his side, motionless. "Greg!" Jillian shouted as she ran toward him.

She gently rolled him onto his back. He was breathing but unconscious. And his right leg was twisted to the right at an unnatural angle. "His leg appears to be broken," said Moshe, who had rushed over and was now kneeling beside Jillian. "Does he still have the walkie-talkie? Call for an ambulance and put out a report on the terrorist who escaped."

* * * * * * * * * *

Ibrahim drove out onto the tollway, this time heading southeast. For the first time since he had been driving in Chicago, he appreciated all the traffic. It offered some measure of protection. The police had uncovered their plot. But how? Were they the only team to have been discovered, or had all the teams been compromised? And if the police knew about the plot, did they also know about his false identity?

That last thought made Ibrahim panic, though only briefly. He had carefully planned his escape, originally planning to fly from Midway Airport to Houston on Southwest Airlines, and from there to Mexico City on a Mexicana flight. The tickets were in his shirt pocket! But if they knew who he was, then going to the airport was lunacy. He might just as well go stand outside a police station and shout out his name. No, he needed another plan. But plans take time, and that was something he didn't have at the moment.

Ibrahim decided that the most important thing to do was to get away from the taxi. No doubt the type of taxi, the color, and even possibly the license plate was right now being broadcast to every policeman in Chicago. They would all be on the lookout for this car. But where to go? Why not the airport? That is the one place where a taxi could go unnoticed, at least a little while.

Ibrahim drove into the daily parking garage. *Perhaps it will take them longer to find it in here. And then they will assume I came to the airport and left on an airplane.* The more potential leads the police had to spend time tracking, the fewer resources they had for the one lead that might actually help them find him.

Ibrahim bought a ticket on the Blue Line train, and he rode it through downtown, exiting at the Clinton Street Station. Walking two blocks north to Union Station, he went inside and looked for a train schedule. He could not appear suspicious or give the impression he was on the run. And that meant he could not ask the ticket agent, "What is the first train leaving the station?"

Once again, fortune seemed to smile on him. The Texas Eagle was departing at 3:20, in less than three hours. He could book passage on that train all the way to San Antonio, Texas. It would not arrive there until after midnight the next evening, a trip of nearly thirty-three hours with seven additional stops. It was long and grueling, but he could bypass all the security found at an airport. And the additional time would allow him to work out the next phase of his plan. Walking up to the ticket agent, he did his best to appear friendly and casual. "Hello! I would like to purchase a round-trip ticket to San Antonio to visit my elderly mother!"

* * * * * * * * * *

A rhythmic *click* and *hum* were the first sounds to push their way into Greg's consciousness. They were followed by a squeezing sensation on his left arm, almost as if someone was trying to wrap his fingers around his forearm. Greg tried opening his eyes, but the brightness forced them closed. He tried sitting up, but a feeling of nausea overwhelmed him. "Where am I? What happened?"

He heard a voice that sounded vaguely familiar. He knew he should recognize it, but the face behind the voice also seemed lost in some foggy mist. Greg tried to will himself into consciousness, and gradually—much too gradually—the fog began to lift.

"Doctor, he seems to be coming around." Jillian had stepped out into the hall to summon the doctor. Then she quickly went back into the room and sat beside his bed. "Greg? Greg? It's Jillian. Can you hear me? How are you feeling?"

"Jillian? I feel awful—like I've been hit by a truck."

"Well, you're not too far off the mark!"

He forced open his eyes to see who had just spoken. "Moshe! What brings you to town?"

"Actually, I never left. Do you remember what happened yesterday?"

"No. Wait; let me think—if I can. We were chasing the terrorists, and they shot off a missile that hit a plane. Was the plane okay?"

Jillian answered. "Yes, Greg, it landed safely."

"And then Moshe shot one of the terrorists just as he tried to fire the second missile. And then the car started. And then, then—Jillian, are you okay?"

Jillian felt tears well up in her eyes. "Yes, Greg, I'm okay. But I'm not sure we're able to say the same about you—at least for a little while. You broke your leg when the car hit you, and you also had a concussion and some internal bleeding. But the doctors patched you up, and you are on the road to recovery."

"No wonder I feel so poorly. Did we get them all?" Greg moaned as he tried to focus his eyes.

"Almost. We nabbed the team in Dallas before they could launch their missiles. But the fellow who hit you is still on the loose. Early this morning the police found the taxi parked in the daily parking lot at O'Hare. They are trying to find out if he was able to get out on some other flight. We're scouring the country looking for him."

"Jillian, thanks for being here. And you too, Moshe. Thanks for watching out for me."

She reached out for Greg's hand. "It's the least I could do for you after you saved my life. Can I share something else with you that I think you will want to hear?"

"I'm always up for good news. Go ahead."

"After they took you away in the ambulance, I drove Moshe back to his hotel. Then I called the president of your school and told him what had happened—how you had helped stop a band of terrorists and also risked your life to save mine. I went home and changed and then came to the hospital. But by the time I got here they had already taken you into surgery.

"As I sat in the waiting room, trying to fight back tears, the president of the school and the academic dean came into the room. I think someone told the president who I was, because he came up to me and put his arm around my shoulder. He asked if I would like to join them in praying for you. I wasn't sure what to say, but I knew this was a time for prayer—so I agreed.

"After we prayed the president asked about me—and my spiritual journey. I wasn't sure what to say, so I told him what I had shared with you about my mom and my brother. I also told him about our talk over dinner at the Grande Lux. Then he looked at me and smiled—not in some fake or condescending way—but as if he was looking deep into my soul. And he said to me, 'Why do you find it so hard to trust what Jesus has done for you?'

"I tried to explain that it just didn't make sense. How could something that someone did two thousand years ago make a difference in my life today? And why would someone want to die for me? Those were my stumbling blocks.

"And then he looked at me and said, 'How do you feel about what Greg did for you today? He was willing to give his life to save yours. And he did it because he genuinely cares for you. That's just what Jesus did two thousand years ago. And it can make a difference in your life today because He didn't stay dead. He rose from the dead, He's alive right now, and He wants to have a personal relationship with you.'

"And suddenly it all made sense. Greg, late yesterday afternoon I put my trust in Jesus as my personal Lord and Savior. I now understand what you and Mom have been trying to tell me!" And with that, tears of joy began trickling down her cheeks.

Greg reached up and tried to put his right hand around her neck. "Jillian, I'm so happy right now. I have been praying for you since we first met. That's the greatest news you could have ever shared with me!"

Moshe felt uncomfortable with the turn in the conversation. It's not that he didn't accept Greg's or Jillian's faith. But he had always been taught that Jesus was not for the Jews. So he decided this would be a good time to make his exit. "Jillian, if you'll excuse me. I feel I need to go get some rest and report in. I'll see you both in a few days." And he slipped out the door.

* * * * * * * * * *

It was past midnight when Ibrahim arrived in San Antonio. As he stepped from the platform in the Southern Pacific Railroad depot near St. Paul's Square, he could see the Alamodome rising up in the distance. The city looked quiet and peaceful, and Ibrahim thought it might be nice to take a walk. *Yes, a walk would feel good after being trapped on the train for a day and a half.* Perhaps the ticket agent could help with directions. "Sir, what is the best way to get from here to the bus station?"

"If you don't want to be mugged, the best way is by taxi."

"So it is not a good idea to walk?"

"Not unless you don't value your life. The few dollars you will pay for a taxi will be money well invested."

"Then what is the address of the bus terminal?"

"It's over on North Saint Mary's Street, but you don't need to try to remember that. Just tell the taxi driver you want to go to the Greyhound and Kerrville bus Company terminal. He'll know how to get there."

Ibrahim arrived at the terminal and found that there was a Kerrville Bus leaving San Antonio at 8:00 a.m. that would arrive in El Paso at 9:00 that night. Nineteen stops—and fourteen hours—just enough time to plan the next leg of his escape. The South African passport would be a liability. He had to assume they had traced his entrance into the United States. He would use his driver's license to cross over into Juarez. *Inch' Allah*, the border guard would be too distracted to look closely at the name on the card. He would buy a camera, T-shirt, and ball cap in El Paso—to make him look like every other American tourist. If he made it across the border, he could take a bus to Mexico City and find the one individual whom he knew could help him return to Pakistan—and to the Teacher.

His side had lost the battle, but the war would continue until the Christians and Jews were defeated. And his thirst for revenge was great.

EPILOGUE

The elevator doors slid open, catching Greg in midyawn. He quickly closed his mouth, but not before being spotted by Moshe. "What's wrong? Are you bored with the view already?"

"You know very well what I'm doing! Don't tell me *your* ears didn't pop on the way up."

Greg started out of the elevator, but his left crutch caught on the entryway, nearly sending him sprawling forward onto the black marble floor. Moshe tried to reach out, but Jillian was already there—wrapping her arms around his waist to keep him from falling.

"Thanks Jillian; you saved me from still another embarrassing moment," was all he could think to say.

"Jillian, I think he's falling for you in more ways than one!" Moshe said, laughing out loud.

Jillian felt her cheeks turning warm, and she knew she was blushing. She hoped Greg was too preoccupied to notice.

"Moshe, if we wanted a comedian for the evening we would have hired a clown. Now, how about helping Greg to our table," she said, waving her finger like a schoolmaster.

"Yes, ma'am!" And Moshe gave a mock salute, then fell into line behind Greg, ready to grab him should he lose his balance. But Greg was careful to position each crutch before putting his weight on it. It took some time, but they eventually made their way to a table in the southeast corner, right next to the windows. Lake Michigan stretched off to the east. The blue sky was darkening as the sun dropped ever nearer to the horizon on the west. The silver glint of the sun sparkled off a lone plane that was rising majestically in the distance, the edges of its white contrail turning a golden hue.

"See that plane? Had just a few things turned out differently, I don't think it would be there right now." Moshe's voice dropped off, as if he were searching for just the right words. "We're here to celebrate justice, but I'm not sure if we can really take the credit."

"I think you're right." Jillian set down her glass of water and looked up at him. "I was sent to Chicago to find a way to help our government become more efficient in collecting, organizing, and reporting data on terrorist activities. And we foiled the largest plot against our country since September 11. But how did we do it? It wasn't really the result of any information we gathered, even though we are spending billions to do so. We succeeded because a college professor teaching a Sunday school class had enough scruples to check the copyright on a picture. And we succeeded because some secret sources in Damascus heard about a group of terrorists coming to the United States. Come to think of it, that second piece of information is about the only one that came through any kind of serious intelligence-gathering operation."

And you would be shocked if you knew the source of that information as well! thought Moshe. "So are you saying that the task is hopeless? That we should give up?"

"No, I'm not," she answered, folding her hands as if to pray. "But I think I've learned a crucial lesson these past few days. We can do everything in our power to stop terrorists from attacking—and we should—but ultimately our efforts alone won't make that much of a difference. I've come to realize that there is a God who is at work in our world. Things I once chalked up to chance or accident just happen too often to be mere coincidences. I think God must ultimately get the credit for what we did. We did our part, but our efforts alone were not enough to give us success. I don't know how else to say it, but that's the conclusion I've come to."

Greg rubbed his hands over his eyes, as if he were trying to concentrate.

"Greg, is something wrong?"

"No, but I'm trying to remember the verse that captures the very thought you just expressed. Let's see if I can get it right. 'The lot is cast into the lap, but its every decision is from the Lord.' It's in the Book of Proverbs."

Moshe seemed genuinely perplexed. "How does that fit with what Jillian was just saying?"

"Think about it. The casting of lots back in Bible times would be similar to, say, our rolling dice today. It was a selection process that seemed totally random. Any one of the possible choices had an equal chance of being selected."

"Assuming the dice weren't loaded!" Jillian added with a smile.

"Yeah, assuming the dice—or lots, in this case—were not somehow altered to affect the outcome. The writer is saying that there are times when life appears to us to be totally random; the outcome is up for grabs. But then he adds 'its every decision is from the Lord.'"

"So what does that mean?" Moshe asked, now solemn.

"It means that God is behind what is taking place, even when events appear to us to be random. In this case I think He would be saying that it's no accident I found that first picture, or that Jillian just happened to be in Chicago with the terrorism task force—or, for that matter, that Mossad just happened to have a contact who had access to information on this terrorist group. We could never have foreseen how these seemingly random events could connect, but God made it all happen."

Moshe thought a few seconds before responding. "I wish I could accept what you just said, but right now I can't. I struggle to find God's hand in Esther's brutal murder by another young woman claiming to act in God's name."

"Moshe, I understand. And I can't even begin to explain why something so horrible happened to you and to Esther. It's best left in the mystery of God's will. But I know that still doesn't take away the pain or bring back your sweet wife." Greg always knew that all the theology in the world can't calm the unbelieving soul. There must be at least a tiny seed of faith.

"Someday, perhaps God will help you see His purpose. Someday, I pray you find Him in your questions."

Moshe nodded and smiled. That was enough for now.

The server arrived to take their dinner orders, and the conversation moved in other directions. After dinner Jillian insisted that they have dessert and coffee. "You need to try their warm pear streusel cobbler. It's the perfect ending to a lovely meal."

The server took the order and ambled back toward the kitchen. Moshe looked out the window at the Chicago skyline, now silhouetted against the night sky in thousands of lights. "Jillian, your reputation must have preceded you! We certainly ended up at a nice table with a spectacular view."

"Well, in my humble opinion, the Signature Room in the Hancock Center has the nicest view of any restaurant in Chicago. And I said I wanted only the best for my friends! Okay, seriously, someone from the mayor's office called our office and arranged for this as a way to express their thanks for what we did."

As they finished the cobbler, Greg felt his leg beginning to ache. "I hate to cut short such a perfect night, but I'm not sure how much longer I'm going to be able to drag this leg around."

Jillian stood up, and Moshe reached back for Greg's crutches propped against the corner. "Greg, I think I should say my good-byes here. I fly back to Tel Aviv tomorrow."

"Moshe, the pleasure of meeting you has been all mine. I hope you have an opportunity to come back this way in the not-too-distant future."

"I, too, hope to return; but I'm not sure when that will be. As you probably know from the news, peace talks in the Middle East finally seem to be getting back on track. And this time, with both the United States and the European Union working together, perhaps we will find a way to bring genuine peace to the Middle East. Greg, you don't look pleased. Is something the matter?"

"Moshe, this is the wrong time and place, but I'm concerned about those talks. Yes, I want peace, but perhaps I just know too much."

"What? Do you know of another terrorist plot to stop the talks?"

"No, I just know the Bible. 'When people are saying, "Peace and safety"—' Look, there's not enough time to talk about it right now, but just be careful. Don't put too much trust in the promises of others to protect your country. I know that doesn't make much sense, but I hope someday it will. In the meantime, just don't let your government put too much trust in the promises of others. That's all I can say."

"I've learned to listen to what you have to say, and I will take your words to heart." Moshe could sense Greg was bothered, but why would prospects of peace in the Middle East trouble him so?

Jillian reached down to grab her water glass. "One final toast before we part. 'To better times in the future, and to friends. May our times together in the future be times of joy.'"

Greg looked into her beautiful face and smiled. *Indeed, may they be times of joy!*

* * * * * * * * * *

Ibrahim sat in brooding silence for most of the ride from Islamabad. For the first hour or so, the driver tried to start a conversation. "What was it like in America? Were you frightened? How did you escape?" But Ibrahim's terse answers eventually shamed him into silence.

I have failed! What can I say when the Teacher asks what went wrong? What can I say to gain his forgiveness? The churning in Ibrahim's stomach matched the heaving of the truck as it lurched over the rutted paths that passed for roads. Ibrahim felt himself becoming ill, and it took all of his willpower—and his worry beads—to fight off the nausea threatening to overwhelm him.

Finally, the truck pulled into the new compound. It looked different, yet remarkably similar, to the place Ibrahim had trained. That seemed like a lifetime ago—could it indeed have only been two months earlier? The truck skidded to a stop; the dust that had been following it down the road now caught up and enveloped the cab in its dry fog. Ibrahim opened the door and stepped out, feeling like a condemned man walking toward the gallows.

The Teacher appeared in the doorway of his home, his loose-fitting abaya fluttering softly in the afternoon breeze. He watched Ibrahim walk toward him—slowly, deliberately, eyes lowered so as not to make direct eye contact. In some societies that would be a sign of guilt or weakness, but he saw it for what it was—a sign of deference and respect bestowed on one deemed to be a superior.

"Ibrahim, my son, it is good to have you back." And the Teacher took the unusual step of reaching out to embrace him before he had said his customary greeting.

"*Dabir*, I am unworthy of your greeting. I failed in my assignment. Please forgive me for disappointing you so."

"Failed? My son, you—and you alone—succeeded. I do not yet know what went wrong, but according to the news reports most of the teams were caught before they even had a chance to reach the airport. Only two groups, including yours, were able to get into position. And you were the only one able to fire your missile and hit the airplane."

"But we were in the wrong position. The plane was landing, not taking off. The wind shifted, and we did not anticipate it in time to move."

"So now you are capable of predicting when the wind will change! Ibrahim, only Allah knows where the wind will blow. It was not his will for you to shoot down the aircraft we had chosen. In fact, the news today said that all flights in and out of the Chicago airport had been stopped. The only one allowed in at that time was the one you hit with your missile. So you see, that is exactly where you were meant to be!"

"But I so wanted to succeed. To give you pleasure for the trust you had placed in me."

The Teacher reached out and wrapped his arms around the now-sobbing warrior. "Ibrahim, I couldn't be more pleased with you were you my own son. You have proven yourself, above all the others, to be the wise, resourceful one. There will be other opportunities to exact our revenge—even greater opportunities than what we just attempted. You have skill, cunning, and now experience. Ibrahim, I want you to assist me in training the next group of mujahideen. Come inside and I will share with you what I am planning."

And Ibrahim the pupil moved one step closer to becoming fully like his master.

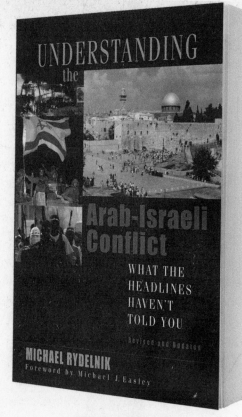

ISBN-10: 0-8024-2623-9
ISBN-13: 978-0-8024-2623-9

What the headlines haven't told you.

Michael Rydelnik, professor of Jewish Studies at the Moody Bible Institute, goes beyond media images for an in-depth, biblically-grounded look at the "crisis that never ends" – the conflict between the Israelis and the Arabs. This newly revised and updated edition highlights the most pressing issues facing this key part of the world today.

by Michael Rydelnik
Find it now at your favorite local or online bookstore.
www.MoodyPublishers.com